Dedication

This book is dedicated to the many headteachers, principals, and staff – teaching and non-teaching – governors, and LEA staff, with whom I had the privilege to work. In particular to those in the most challenging circumstances of urban and rural disadvantage who, against all the odds, fill their pupils' learning with excitement, enjoyment, and enlightenment, and their lives with opportunity, self belief, and hope for the future.

In the course of my career I worked with hundreds of Headteachers and Principals, many of them inspirational. A number of them rightly achieved the kind of national recognition and influence accorded to Roger Standing; countless others deserved to, but chose to work their magic out of the limelight. No occupation or profession is exempt from the worst excesses of human nature and unbridled ambition, but I'm pleased to say that not one of those with whom I worked evenly remotely approached the depths to which Roger Standing, Commander of The British Empire, sank.

So just in case you're wondering…I made him up.

1

The car was still there. He edged a little closer, hugging the side of the towering railway viaduct. He stopped for a moment and listened. Other than the sound of his breathing, and the rustling of the trees beyond the archway, there was silence.

He decided to wait for a while, to recover his breath, and take stock. This was not a place that people would come, approaching midnight, unless like him they had mischief in mind. The car, parked close to the kerb just short of the entrance, had been there for over five hours. At first he had thought it a Mercedes saloon, but the arrow head badging with the double M logo was one that he had never seen before. Whatever; it was large, and flash, and worth a mint. He still could not understand why it was parked here, rather than on the car park further down the street where the CCTV camera kept watch.

The first of the iron gates creaked noisily as he made the dog-leg exit between the railings. He paused, before stepping out from deep shadow into the pool of moonlight spilling over the cobbled street, glinting silver on the gaping radiator grill. He ducked instinctively, and cursed, as a bat swooped low above his head. His fingers closed reassuringly over the tool that lay deep in the zipped compartment of his bomber jacket. He pulled his baseball cap further down over his forehead and walked quickly towards the passenger door.

Crouching low, he peered inside

It was still there, in the front passenger foot well. He unzipped his pocket, withdrew the centre punch, and pressed it against the bottom right hand corner of the window. The sound, like a muted gun shot, echoed in the tunnel created by the archway walls, and hung for a moment above the parkland beyond the gates. A fraction later it was replaced by the wail of the car alarm. Golden flashes from the wrap-around headlights threw his silhouette into sharp relief. Straightening up, he placed the punch in the centre of the window, against the now crazed glass. A hole appeared the size of a golf ball. Two blows with his elbow were sufficient to allow his arm inside. The door refused to open. Cursing, he hammered the window with his elbow twice more until he was able to squeeze his right arm, head, and shoulders, into the car. With his body pivoted over the door panel he was able to grasp the handle of the briefcase. The shoulder strap caught momentarily on the rake adjustment lever before he was able to tug it free, and flee towards the park gates.

He jinked through the dog-leg like a rugby league winger, and sped onto the broad cobbled way his Nan still referred to as Fitzgeorge Street. He forked right uphill, not slowing until he reached the exit at the side of the Mayflower pub. Pausing only to stuff the briefcase up the front of his jacket, he stepped out onto the pavement on Rochdale Road.

The steel grey shutters were down on Mays' Pawnbrokers and Second Hand Jewellers, the bright red walls a muted glow in the glare of the street lights. Less than half a mile away, to the right, he could just make out the communication mast on Collyhurst Police Station. He hurried across the road, and jogged by the side of the Youth Centre, past the impressive mural that he had helped to create on the outside wall. He slowed crossing Teignmouth Street, and entered Ryder Street, briefly disturbing an ancient German shepherd and a mangy sheepdog in one of the back yards, before disappearing like a phantom into the maze of maisonettes and three storey flats.

The sound of the alarm ceased as suddenly as it had begun. The lights flashed despairingly for several seconds, and gave up. Only then was it possible to hear the feeble tapping inside the car boot. A long-eared owl, attracted by the sound, perched on the fence beside the car. With three dimensional hearing it was acutely, if indifferently, aware of the futility of the struggle within. The owl sat there for a full five minutes, its head rotating from time to time through three hundred and sixty degrees; listening as the sounds became weaker, and finally stopped.

Scanning the horizon one last time, it ruffled its feathers, spread its wings, and launched itself towards the moonlit sky.

2

Caton reached instinctively for the alarm, pressed the snooze button, and pulled a pillow over his head to shut out the unrelenting sound. It took several seconds to register that it was still there, and another to recognise it as his mobile phone. He pushed the pillow aside, levered himself up on one elbow, and picked up. It was Chester House. The words barely registered. At the back of his head there was a four point two on the Richter scale competing for attention.

'Can you repeat that?' he mumbled.

'I'm sorry Sir, Mr Hadfield was insistent. You're to meet him there as soon as possible.'

'Where is it again?'

'Collyhurst; the railway viaduct at the entrance to Sandhills, opposite the HMG Paints Factory.'

'That's the bottom end of Collyhurst Road; the Irk Valley?'

'That's it Sir.'

Devoid of sympathy, the alarm grinned back at him. Six twenty am.

'Tell the Chief Superintendent I'm on my way.'

Caton replaced the phone, and levered himself into a sitting position. The hammering in his head intensified. His mouth was dry, his eyelids glued together at the corners. The soaking wet pillow beneath his right hand confirmed that it had been another sweltering night. He threw back the sheet, instantly regretting the effort, and swivelled his legs to the side of the bed. He paused for moment or two, elbows on knees, head in hands. A line from T.S Elliot's Wasteland crawled to the front of his brain. The one about Sweeney rising ape-like from the sheets in steam.

It was just as well that Kate was away for a few days visiting her sick niece in Shillingford. It had been his first night out with his reading group for over a month. Never one to risk getting smashed, he had drunk steadily but cautiously at the Old Nags Head, always a drink or two behind the rest of The Alternatives. It was the lamb and cheese kebab afterwards, and dehydration, he blamed. He straightened up and reached for the phone. Time to ring Holmes.

Inevitably, it was Gordon's wife who answered.

'I'm sorry Marilyn,' he told her. 'It's Tom here.'

Her silence said it all. He heard Gordon mumbling incoherently as he struggled to come to terms with the rude awakening, and then Marilyn hissing in the background.

'Sunday! Why does it always have to be a bloody Sunday?'

When Gordon finally came to the phone he sounded marginally better than Caton felt.

'Morning Boss.' What have we got?'

'We won't know till we get there, but it doesn't sound good. Hadfield is already on his way, if that's any indication.'

'It must be special to get him out of bed of a weekend. Where is it?'

'Collyhurst Road. Under the arches by the entrance to that park that goes up to Rochdale Road.'

'Sandhills? I knew it when it was little better than a dumping ground.'

'Looks like it may still be.' Caton replied. 'I'll see you there. And there's no need to break the speed limits. There's a campaign on, and the last thing you need is three points and a disciplinary.'

'Me, speed? Wherever did you get that idea?'

Even down the phone he could tell that Holmes was smiling.

A quick shower, three paracetemol, and a fruit juice later, his headache was little more than an irritating pulse. Caton reached into the glove compartment, and took out a breathalyser. There was no point in taking chances, not with a pool car just a phone call away. Given that yesterday and today were rest days, no questions would be asked. The effort of taking a deep breath quickened the throbbing. The result was clear; below the legal limit, but not as low as he had expected. So much for the kebab theory. He started the engine, and pulled away.

There wasn't a cloud in the sky as he turned left onto an empty Liverpool Road. The light rain that had spread east during the night had passed them by. It was going to be another scorcher. The replica of Stephenson's Rocket sat patiently alongside the old station, waiting for the stream of children, parents and carers, filling the long summer holiday with a visit to the Museum of Science and Industry. As he turned into Quay Street he switched on the air-conditioning. By the time he reached the Ducie Bridge pub, and swung left into Corporation Street, the cool stream of air was having a soothing effect. He had some good memories of this patch from his time at Collyhurst. As

Head of the Specialist Detection Group he no longer worked a Division. But this was where he had learned the basics of policing a city.

He cruised past the red brick frontage of Joseph Holt's Crown and Cushion where he had met his very first informant. Past the Charter Street Ragged School on the corner of Corporation Street and Nelson Street, where he had learned something of the history of Manchester's pioneering philanthropic concern for the poor. He slowed to read the new signs on the side of the building. It now incorporated the King of Kings School, and the Jesus Army Centre. Plus ça change, plus c'est la même chose

At the Rosedale Joinery Works three small shrubs sprouted like a succession of green flags from the sides of the forty foot high brick chimney. On his right the Railway viaduct rose high above the valley; on his left a succession of ageing factories and workshops lined the River Irk; in centuries past a source of power, now channelled, and slow moving. Beyond St Catherine's bridge, where the road split at Dalton Street, he had to stop to show his ID to a motorbike patrolman, before taking the lower route onto Collyhurst Road, lined by railings through which wild white and purple buddleias sprawled. Between this point, and Vauxhall Street, a sea of red poppies bloomed on the embankment beneath the railway.

Up ahead he saw a line of cars parked on the right hand side. Beyond them, the tell tale tape stretched part way across the road, the only gap filled by two uniformed constables, and a community support officer.

As he showed his ID for a second time he became aware of a cluster of photographers snapping him from behind.

'How the hell did that lot get here so quickly?' he asked the constable in charge of the log.

'Search me Sir. Either they committed the crime, or they've been tapping into our communications.'

Caton shook his head. 'Neither would surprise me. Can we get them back from there?'

The officer shrugged an apology. 'Unfortunately, some of them were already here before we were able to set up this perimeter. They're over fifty metres from the scene, they don't have direct line of sight even with their zoom lenses, and they'd already contaminated this area, so the Chief Superintendent said to leave them.'

Typical of Hadfield. Keep the press sweet even if it made the investigation that much harder. 'Just make sure they don't get any closer,' Caton told him.

At the factory, a hundred metres further on, he was directed through the open gates into the yard, where he joined a line of official vehicles, vans and unmarked cars. He opened the boot, removed his incident bag, and locked the car. He paused at the factory gates and looked around. Diagonally opposite, at the entrance to a cobbled street leading to the railway arch, he could see a group consisting of Hadfield, the scene of crime team, and several uniformed officers, facing away from him towards the entrance to the park, hidden by the wall of the viaduct. To their right, a small empty car park with red and white entrance posts was presided over by a CCTV camera on a tall steel pole. Immediately beside him a sign told him that this was the HMG [H. Marcel Guest Limited] Paints Factory. He turned to look up at the square digital clock high up on the factory wall. It was 7.15am, and the temperature was already 23 degrees Centigrade.

Their attention was focused on a large black saloon car parked on the right hand side of the street, just shy of the entrance to the tunnel-like railway arch. They turned at the sound of his footsteps on the cobbles. Hadfield came forward, took him by the arm, and led him out of ear shot of the others. He was flushed, sweating, and tugged nervously at the collar of his shirt. Caton hadn't seen him this agitated in years. Certainly not since Hadfield had been promoted to Detective Chief Superintendent, and Head of the Force Major Incident Team.

'Before you say anything Tom,' Hadfield began. 'I know this is not strictly one for the SDG, but you were always expected to be a flexible team. And you and I both know that you're kicking your heels over the Chinatown Investigation while the National Crime Squad decides where they want to go with it. So you do have the capacity to respond.'

He paused, expecting some come back. Caton held his counsel. Secretly, he was becoming frustrated by the delay, and worried that his team was becoming stale. This might just be what they needed. Surprised and relieved, Hadfield ploughed on.

'In any case, there's no reason why this shouldn't be a quick one. Correction; it *has* to be. Quick and clean. And the Chief Constable is expecting daily updates so I expect you to keep me in the loop. Is that clear?'

Caton nodded thoughtfully. 'What I'm not clear about is what exactly we have here?'

Hadfield glanced furtively over his shoulder in the direction of the car, before fixing Caton with a troubled gaze.

'What we have here,' he said sombrely, 'Is a body in the boot of that car. To be precise…Roger Standing CBE.'

It took a moment for it to sink in. *'Standing?'* Was all Caton could think to say.

'Precisely. As you well know, he was a respected figure locally, nationally…even internationally. More than that, he was a personal friend of the Chief Constable. He wants the lid kept on this one. I want no surprise revelations, and any speculation squashed before it's begun.'

Caton shook his head. 'Revelations I can manage Sir, but with all due respect, speculation is way beyond our control.'

The colour rose on Hadfield's cheeks; when he spoke his voice was on the edge of shrill. 'Not this time. This time we *will* control it. Anything beyond non committal statements, and denials, you leave to the press office.'

Caton looked at the gaggle of press further down Collyhurst Road. He could just make out Larry Hymer, crime reporter with the Manchester Evening News, and what looked like one of the television news teams. *If you think that's going to stop the speculation you must be even more self deluding than I thought you were*, he was tempted to say.

'Here's the Detective Superintendent,' said Hadfield, spotting Helen Gates crossing the road from the factory. 'I'd better bring her up to speed. And don't bother to ask for extra hands. With the Labour

Party Conference coming up, all leave has been cancelled, and every available officer drafted in for training. It's going to tie up over a 1000 GMP officers.'

He hurried away, putting distance between himself and the dirty end of the work.

'Very good Sir.' Caton called after him. 'I'll crack on here then shall I?'

Without turning his head, or breaking his stride, Hadfield tossed his reply into a light breeze that would provide the only relief for those due to spend the remainder of the day baking out in the open.

'You do that Chief Inspector. You do that.'

Behind Hadfield and Gates, Caton spotted Gordon Holmes' silver Mondeo turning into the factory yard. He decided to kit himself up, and wait for his inspector before joining the rest of the Scenes of Crime team. He put his incident bag down on the curb, selected a white Tyvek all in one, and began to put it on over his blue vest, light sweat shirt, and lightweight walking trousers. He had noted Hadfield's disapproving look, but it was one thing to keep up appearances, another to self baste. He left the hood down for the time being, and slipped on a pair of white protective gloves. He was checking the battery in his voice recorder as Holmes rolled up.

'You look dreadful Boss.'

'And a very good morning to you Inspector.'

Holmes put his incident bag down, and began rooting through it. 'A case of, while the cat's away, was it?'

'Just a dodgy cheese and lamb kebab, and a hot night.' Caton replied unconvincingly.

'Very likely.'

Caton had forgotten how bad he felt, and now the throbbing had returned.

'Look, can we drop it?' he said testily.

Holmes pulled out a crumpled Tyvek.

'How long has that been in there?' Caton asked. 'Please tell me it's not the one you used last time?'

Holmes held it up to the light. 'It's not too bad.'

'Don't be daft Gordon, one way or another, it's contaminated. What's more, you're probably on camera right now. Can you imagine what a defence team will do with that? Caton reached down to his bag, took out another suit still in its sealed pack, and tossed it to his inspector. 'Get rid of it, and put this on. And get that bag sorted. It's a disgrace.' I'm beginning to sound like a headteacher, he reflected, and brought himself up short, realising just how inappropriate that was given the circumstances.

'So what have we got here Sir?' Holmes asked as he struggled to get his arms into the protective suit. 'And why us?'

'There's a body in the boot. They think it's Roger Standing.'

'Bloody Hell!' Holmes stood there, one arm half way in, the other out, like a demonic scarecrow. Instinctively he turned to look at the car. 'Bloody Hell.' He repeated. 'Why us?'

3

'The reason it's us,' Caton told him. 'Is that they think we've got some slack because the *Chinatown* investigation is in limbo.'

'And because Standing was a mate of the Chief Constable, and because Chester House thinks you can walk on water since we cleared up *Bojangles*,' said Holmes, forcing both arms into their sleeves.

Caton didn't bother to reply. There was no point; they both knew he was right. There had been rumours of a commendation. However much Caton might feel it like a millstone round his neck, he was just going to have to live with it. At least the team knew that he took pains to make sure they got the credit too. He suspected that they also respected the fact that he always took the flack, and never passed it on to the rest of them.

'Am I clear to get on with this Chief Inspector?'

Caton turned to find the portly figure of the duty pathologist advancing towards them. 'Mr Douglas,' he said. 'It's good to see you. Let's find out.' He led the way towards the huddle ahead of them.

Caton recognised the uniformed Inspector who came to meet them; Nadeem Saifi, newly appointed to the Collyhurst sub divisional station, and a prominent member of the GMP Black and Asian Police Association.

'Good Morning Mr Douglas, good morning Chief Inspector,' Saifi greeted them. 'SOCO have cleared a common approach path up to and around the car, and photographs have been taken of the body in situ. So you can go in as soon as you like. Mr Benson asks that you don't touch or move anything unless you absolutely have to.' He addressed himself to Caton.

'I assume that you are the senior investigating officer on this one Sir? So I am formally handing it over to you. I've set up an inner cordon of thirty metres, an intermediate one of a hundred metres, and because we have got all this open space and woods behind us, the outer cordon stretches right up to the Rochdale Road. If there's anything else you need us to do at this time please let me know.

Caton was genuinely impressed, this young man was going to go all the way; and on merit. 'Thank you Inspector,' he said. 'The Tactical Aid Unit are going to love you when they get here. I'll be sure to put in a good word for you with the Divisional Commander.' He glanced towards the car. 'Can you tell us who found the body?'

Saifi consulted his notebook. 'The overnight security for the factory – a Mr Sines - became suspicious when he saw the car was still here this morning. He drove up the street to take a look. When he saw that the window was broken, and there was blood in the car, he rang 999. While he was still on the phone his dog became agitated, ran round to the boot, and began barking. This was at 5.52am. A patrol car from Collyhurst arrived at 5.57am. A PNC check quickly established the owner, and licensed keeper of the vehicle, as Roger Standing. The officers opened the boot from inside the car, secured the scene, and immediately reported a suspicious death. I arrived ten minutes later.'

'And where are they now?'

He put his notebook back in his pocket and pointed towards the factory. 'All three of them are over there. We called up the key holder, and he's opened the canteen. I thought you might want to use it for briefings, interviews and breaks until everything has been set up.'

Caton hoped that Holmes was taking note; although he was beginning to think there was a limit to how many tricks an old dog could be taught. 'Well done Inspector,' he said. 'Detective Inspector Holmes will come across and take their statements as soon as we've finished here. Can you make sure they don't go until then?'

'Of course Sir.' Saifi threw a salute, turned smartly, and headed off towards the factory.

Holmes watched him go with an expression of open disapproval. Since when were officers in plain clothes saluted?

'Don't you dare say a word,' Caton told him. 'A little respect goes a long way.'

Holmes grimaced. 'A couple of months at Collyhurst is going to smooth the edges off him, you wait and see.'

Ahead of them, the pathologist was speaking with Jack Benson the Crime Scene Manager. Beyond them, the car sat incongruously in this landscape. It was a 2006 registration saloon; black with sliver trim. All the hall marks of a Mercedes Benz, but with a logo Caton didn't recognise. Whatever the marque, this was clearly the apogee of luxury, sophistication, and comfort.

'What is that Gordon?' he asked.

'Holmes' eyes lit up. 'It's a Maybach,' he said, with awe in his voice. 'Looks like the Maybach 62.'

Caton regarded him blankly.

'Mercedes top of the range, out of Daimler Chrysler: Five hundred and fifty hp biturbo engine, nought to a hundred k in five point four seconds. Set you back a minimum of a hundred and thirty thousand quid.'

Caton couldn't resist it. 'Puts yours into perspective.' he said as they reached the car.

The trunk was open. The three of them stood for a moment taking it in. The body of a man lay curled on his right side. He was dressed in an expensive looking three piece, black rope stripe, woollen worsted suit; with matching black socks, burgundy hand tooled leather shoes, and a blue tie spotted with white. Entirely appropriate for lunch at the Ritz Caton thought, but the last thing anyone would wear during the hottest summer on record. A broad strip of silver duct tape covered his mouth. The arms were bent behind the torso, and bound at the wrists with the same tape. The legs were similarly bound, at the ankles. His eyes were closed, and the colour had drained from his face. Blood had congealed across the front of the jacket and down across his hips, pooling on the carpet.

Caton and Holmes stepped back and moved to the side, careful to stay within the taped tramlines marking the sanitised area around the car. Mr Douglas set about his work. A video camera technician emerged from the group behind them and began recording his actions. The pathologist kept a running record going as he checked the pulse, took the body temperature, and examined the tear in the left hand side of the front of the jacket that appeared to be the source of the blood. At one point, he placed a finger over each of the corpse's eyelid and raised them in turn. Both eyes stared ahead, expressionless; the pupils blown.

Douglas lifted the head gently to the left, giving him the opportunity to seek, and find, purple and red patches running from the right ear across the neck, and out of sight beneath the classic city collar.

'Purple and red patches indicative of stage two hypostasis cover the right side posterior triangle. They are most strongly pooled at the omohyoid inferior belly.' The pathologist intoned.

He lowered the head, shook his own head dolefully, straightened up, and stepped back from the car. One by one he removed his gloves and dropped them into a self sealing plastic bag he took from his pocket. 'I suppose you want to know the impossible Chief Inspector?' he said.

'You know I never ask the impossible Mr Douglas.' Caton replied. 'We both know that it's going to get harder to tie down as time goes on. Your best estimate will do fine; I won't quote you.'

The pathologist looked back at the body, and across at the clock on the factory wall.

'Only that thermometer on the wall over there, and God, knows for sure what the temperature was here throughout the night, unless the digital sensors in this car cover the boot. If they do, and the data is retrievable, then I could give you a marginally better idea. As it is, from the degree of rigor, the stage of hypostasis, and the body temperature, I would say that death occurred certainly not less than six and probably not more than sixteen hours ago. As to the cause? At this stage it's looking likely that it was a combination of shock and blood loss, resulting from that wound on the left side of his abdomen.'

'Can you tell us anything about what might have caused that wound?' Caton asked.

'Until I get him back to the mortuary it's difficult to be precise. Judging from the size and nature of the tear in that suit, and the degree of blood loss, I would say that it was neither a blunt instrument nor a bullet. Beyond that it's impossible to tell.'

'So, most likely a sharp instrument. Would that be a blade?' Caton pressed him.

'Well, whatever it was certainly punctured the stomach. There is still swelling to the abdomen which, despite early rigor mortis, is palpable, suggesting extensive haematoma - the blood pooling in the stomach - and that's on top of the amount that you see on his clothes, and on the floor of the boot. The width of the tear suggests that it was probably a blade. Bigger than a pen knife. Possibly a kitchen knife. Unlikely to be less than five centimetres in length. Since there is no sign of an exit wound, if we assume - which we cannot - that it was thrust in all the way, it would have been less than eighteen centimetres long.'

'So, probably within the past eighteen hours, probably a blade, possibly a kitchen knife, possibly somewhere between five and eighteen centimetres,' Holmes said grudgingly.

The pathologist fixed him with an icy stare. 'You should listen to your Chief Inspector, *Mr* Holmes. I have already exceeded the limits of my remit in an attempt to support the early stages of your investigation. If you need any more than that, I suggest that you contact a psychic.' He turned abruptly, and spoke to Caton. 'I can fit him in first thing in the morning. Will you be there, or will it be the entrancing Inspector Weston?'

Caton smiled. Sarah Weston captivated everyone, even the ghouls that inhabited the mortuary. 'Given that she is still forensic liaison, it will probably be Inspector Weston.'

'In which case, I shall have the rare pleasure of actually looking forward to a Monday morning.' He closed his bag, and waddled off, holding the bag containing his gloves out to the left side, dropping it into the waiting hands of Jack Benson as he passed.

'Pompous ass.' Holmes muttered under his breath.

Sunday or no Sunday,' said Caton. 'The next time you arrive at a scene as SIO, and Mr Douglas turns up as the duty pathologist, you are going to have some bridge building to do, or you won't get past first base.'

He led the way around the car, noting the broken passenger windows, and the glass fragments on the street. The bulk of the glass was inside the car, in the floor well, and across both the passenger seat, and the driver's seat. The dark stain that he assumed was dried blood, was visible on the driver's seat, and smeared across the lower right hand quadrant of the beige leather steering wheel cover. A trail of blood on the pink, blue, and grey stone sets that made up the road, led from the driver's door, along the nearside of the car, to the boot, where the two of them stopped to compare observations.

'So, what are you thinking?' said Caton.

Holmes scratched the side of his chin. His brow furrowed with concentration. 'It looks like the window was broken from the outside, and after the body was moved. Otherwise there wouldn't have been any fragments on the driver's seat, and if there were, some of them would have been covered in blood. Which they're not. And whoever moved the body must have got blood all over the front of their clothes as they dragged the body out of the car, held it up, and lifted it into the boot.'

'I agree,' said Caton. 'So are we talking one event; two separate connected events; or two unconnected events?'

'God knows Boss. That's what SOCO's for.'

Caton nodded thoughtfully. 'You get across to the factory canteen,' he said. 'And get a statement from the security guy that rang 999, and the two patrol officers that were first on the scene. I'm going to get a feel for this, and then I'll come over and join you.' He waved to Jack Benson to let him know that it was now all theirs, and turned to watch as his inspector's muscular figure crossed Collyhurst Road. Gordon was not himself today, but then neither, he reflected, am I.

As soon as Benson's team were engaged, Caton followed the narrow strip of police tape under the tunnel-like railway arch up to the pair of iron gates designed to prevent off-road bikes from disturbing this pedestrian paradise.

High on the whitewashed bricks of the upper section of the arch walls, through the eyes of local children, a brightly coloured mural on a wooden panel recorded the history of the area. Fragments of broken glass lined the left hand curb of the street beneath a No Tipping sign that proclaimed: - *'Offenders will be prosecuted; Maximum Fine £2,500. Illegally dumped rubbish may be searched to identify ownership.* Caton found it ironically apt for the situation in which they found themselves, except for the maximum penalty, and the word *rubbish*.

A larger sign welcomed visitors to the Irk Valley Project. Way marked paths, beginning here at Sandhills, ran up from Collyhurst to Higher Broughton, and from Cheetham Hill to Moston. High on the walls of the railway arch, bay willow herb sprouted opportunistically. Beneath them, in the corner, crisp packets, polythene bags, and plastic bottles had been blown into a tidy pile.

Beyond the gates, despite the intense heat of the past few days, the fields of long grass were green, but the tips were beginning to whiten, and the golden rod fading before its time. The ground sloped upwards, gently at first, and then steeply. The path divided, one branch swinging north west, the other eastwards, both disappearing into the row of trees through which he glimpsed a red bus as it headed north up Rochdale Road.

The wind rustled the leaves in the trees on either side of the broad metalled street, cobbled with more of the huge stone sets. Beyond the furthest copse, the early morning sun caught the white wooden bell tower of St Malachy's RC Primary School. Roger

Standing CBE; respected headteacher; self-publicist; doyen of the right wing press; and friend of the Chief Constable. Caton wondered what had brought him here; to this place and this condition. In the final analysis he would be remembered, above all else, for a violent and ignominious end; stabbed, bound and dumped in the boot of his own car.

As he turned to go, a pair of crows - scavengers that would be hawks - idly circled high above the hill, riding on thermals rising from slopes warming in the early morning sun.

4

Caton arrived back in the Incident Room shortly after 10.00am. He was relieved to find Ged, the Incident Room Manager, back at her desk. They had all been shocked by her husband's sudden illness, and premature death, and amazed at how she had coped, mainly through throwing herself into her work with even more determination. It was over three years now, and she was still the first in when the balloon went up.

Detective Sergeant Carter had also come in. The two of them had already set up the white board and brought out some new display charts, having taken an executive decision to move the Chinatown display – for the second time in six months - to the office next to Caton's; the room that Division had still not been able to wrestle back.

'You've been busy.' Caton said, as he bent to help Ged move one of the tables.

'Good morning Sir,' she said, more brightly than the occasion warranted. 'This is a turn up for the books. Is it really him, or is it just his car they've used?

'I'm afraid it is Ged.' He said, putting the table down and stepping back to check its position.

Carter came over to join them. 'In which case, we won't be able to move for reporters, cameramen, TV crews, and top brass. Talk about being under the microscope.'

Caton nodded. 'Thank you both for coming in. I really appreciate it.'

'Wouldn't have missed it for the world Boss,' said Carter.

'Nor me Sir.' Ged added, opening up a box of marker pens and setting them out along the bottom of a flip chart. 'DI Weston is coming in as well. She should be with us in about ten minutes.'

Sarah Weston's husband, a property developer, frequently worked thirteen hour days, even at weekends. She was another who welcomed the excuse to come in on a rest day. As liaison for his team with SOCO, the Forensic Science Service, and the duty pathologist, her presence would be a real bonus.

'What about DS Stuart?' he asked.

'Joanne is up in the Lakes with Abbie,' Carter told him. 'Haystacks to Darling Dodd, I think she said. They'll be lucky if there's a signal up there.'

Caton knew he was right. His own mobile connection came and went all the way along those ridges. Even if they could contact her there was no way she'd get back before late afternoon. 'What about DC Woods?' he asked.

'Dave's got a game with Leigh Vets. Down at Macclesfield, I think he said.'

'He's playing Rugby Union... on a Sunday, in July?'

'It's a pre-season warm up apparently. They want to get off to a good start. Surely you remember? They came from behind to win the League this year. Promoted to North West Division 3, North.'

Caton had no idea what he was talking about.

'Don't tell me you missed out on that.' Carter said.

'He even went so far as to email everyone a copy of the Match report: *'The forwards worked tirelessly, Dave Woods tackling above his weight.'* The fun we had with that. He's only just started to live it down.'

Now he remembered. There was something on the canteen notice board about Woods *'Over performing, with a light weight tackle.'* He'd removed it before the Divisional Commander saw it. It was hard enough getting Woods motivated without having everyone taking the proverbial.

Benson was still out at the crime scene with his team. That just left the Allocator, who was on annual leave, and Duggie.

'Mr Wallace should be in shortly,' said Ged. 'I don't think his wife was too pleased.' she added conspiratorially.

'Don't worry,' he said. 'Once we've logged what we have, and set up a schedule for tomorrow, I'll let everyone go. Any calls from the press, just refer them to the Press Office at Chester House.'

'Just what I've been doing for the past hour and half Sir,' she said, shooing him gently to one side. 'There won't be anyone in the canteen, so I'll get the drinks sorted.'

'See if you can sneak another fan out of one of the other offices,' he said. 'It's going to be like a furnace in here.'

Thirty minutes later, the four of them were seated in front of the boards. DI Weston, and Duggie Wallace - the team's senior collator, crime intelligence analyst, and liaison with the Serious Crime Analysis Section at CENTREX – Caton and DS Carter. Gordon Holmes arrived, sweating, just as they were about to start. He flung his jacket onto one of the tables, and slumped down in a chair. His broad forehead might just well have had do not disturb written across it. Nobody did.

'Right then,' Caton began, 'First off, we can't expect too much help with this from any of the Divisions, and only limited support from the Tactical Aid teams. They've got their hands full training for the Labour Party conference until next week. Five of the other FMIT teams are tied up with their own investigations, and two are still in the Crown Court. You know how important the first forty eight hours are, so I'm going to make an exception on this one. Late nights, and early mornings, are the order of the day. If we get the breaks, then we can ease off a bit next week. Until then, let's give it everything we've got.' He looked around the group. Everyone was nodding; not surprising, given that in the early days of an investigation he always had to force them to go home before they fell asleep.

'Let's consider the facts,' he continued, pointing to the first of the display boards. We've got the body of Roger Standing CBE, a nationally famous headteacher, stabbed and bound in the boot of his own car. The car is locked. The keys are missing. On the basis of the pattern of the fragments on the driver's seat, and the fact that there were none on the deceased's clothing, SOCO are of the opinion that the front passenger window was smashed after the body was moved. His wallet was still in his breast coat pocket; apparently undisturbed. There was a Rolex Oyster on his left wrist. No sign of a mobile phone. The integrated car phone and satnav are still intact.

'Death occurred ...'

'Probably' Holmes muttered to himself.

'Death occurred,' he continued. 'Somewhere between 5.30pm yesterday evening, and 1.30am this morning. What we don't know is how long it actually took him to die.'

DI Weston raised her hand. 'But Mr Douglas should be able to give us a better idea tomorrow.'

There was a distinct snort from DI Holmes. As though trying to emulate his bullish physique.

'Thank you Sarah.' Said Caton, his patience beginning to fray. 'We've had no sightings reported as yet. And we are still waiting on the CCTV footage from the Marcel Guest car park, and from the traffic and public order cameras.' He turned to Holmes who, despite cradling the cup of coffee Ged had just brought him, was giving a fair impression of having nodded off.

'Gordon. Perhaps you could remind us how the body was discovered.'

His eyelids flickered; then opened reluctantly. He placed the mug on the floor beside him, and levered himself into a semi-upright position, then reached behind him for his jacket and retrieved his notebook from a pocket. Licking his fingers theatrically, he leafed through several pages. The others watched this performance in an uneasy silence.

'A Barry Sines, a security guard with DTU Security, first saw the car at 9pm on Saturday evening, shortly after he'd come on shift. Marcel Guest was fourth on his list of site visits. He didn't check it out, because it isn't unusual for people to use it as a rendezvous; a sort of a lover's lane. He became suspicious when it was still there at 5.52am this morning.

'He'd not driven past at all in the intervening nine hours?' Sarah Weston asked him. 'Doesn't sound like much of a security service.'

Holmes looked up from his notes; irritated by the interruption. 'He would normally have done another sweep at 1pm, but he had to respond to three alarm calls, one of which - near the new Fujitsu Building in West Gorton - was an attempted break in. By the time they'd sorted it, it was too late to fit that one in. Or so he says.'

He turned back to his notes, and pretended to consult them before picking up where he'd left off.

'He parked up behind it, and got out. He immediately became suspicious. Luxury model, broken window, no occupants, stain on the driver's seat. Didn't take a genius. He rang 999. His dog – an Alsatian called Sabre - started barking and straining at the leash. It led him straight to the boot. Police Constables Aaron Jones and Andrea Medila arrived from Collyhurst at 5.57am. They pinged the licence, and came up with Roger Standing. They had a discussion about whether or not to open the boot, or wait for their Inspector. In the event, they decided someone might be still be alive in there, but they couldn't get the door open. Medila, being the slimmest, leaned in through the passenger window – probably destroying a load of evidence in the process – and released the boot catch. They could see he was dead. After that, they did all the right things. Reported it as a suspicious death, got Sines to wait in the van, and took up positions at each end of the street; one at the corner of Collyhurst Street, the other under the railway arch.' He closed his notebook with an air of finality, and waited for the questions.

'Did they see, or find anything, that might have been connected with what happened?' Carter asked.

'Holmes shook his head.

'Was anything touched, or moved, that SOCO will need to know about?' Sarah Weston wanted to know.

'He shook his head again, then he thought better of it, and flipped his notebook open. 'Obviously there's going to be some trace of PC Medila's uniform on the shattered glass on the window rim. She was wearing gloves, so there'll be traces from those on the boot release, and she says she steadied herself by holding onto the roof with her left hand; so ditto there.'

'Which means she most likely wiped or smudged the perpetrator's prints on the boot release.' Weston reflected out loud.

'What would you have done in her position?' Caton asked her.

She took a deep breath, and thought about it. 'I don't know Sir. Given the car had been there all that time, I would probably have waited for SOCO. The chances that someone would still be alive, and then die in the next fifteen minutes, would be pretty remote. On the other hand…'

She didn't need to say what they were all thinking. Hobson's choice. It was as familiar to them these days as stab vests. Damned if you do, damned if you don't. Caton broke a silence that hung like a blanket.

'Thank you Gordon,' he said. 'Moving on. Mrs Standing has been informed. I had to get the Cheshire force to handle it. The press were already at her door. The family home is in Nantwich. Her husband was supposed to be staying over in town; a regular occurrence apparently. She says he would often go into the school at weekends. She had no idea what he had planned for this weekend, other than that he wouldn't be home until Tuesday evening at the earliest. She's coming in tomorrow morning to make the identification.'

Carter raised a hand. 'Did they ask where he stays when he's in the city, Sir?'

Caton nodded. 'Good question, and yes, they did. He has a penthouse apartment at Number 1 Piccadilly.'

Carter gave a low whistle. 'On a head teacher's salary?' he said. The others sat up in their seats. Even Holmes went so far as open one eye.

'Don't the Beckhams have one there?' Duggie Wallace asked.

'Used to.' Holmes muttered.

'How did she take it Sir?' Sarah Weston wanted to know. 'Mrs Standing?'

'Quite calmly,' he said. 'The officers couldn't decide whether she was in shock or genuinely unaffected.' He gave them a moment or two to mull over the possible implications, and decided to move on. He picked up a green marker and stood beside the first of the flip charts. 'O.K. That's as much as we know to date. Let's move on to the key questions.'

Carter kicked them off. 'What's the motive? Car jacking or street robbery gone wrong?' Their responses came in a rush, reflecting the practiced way their minds had been processing the data from the start.

'The car's still there,' said Weston. 'And his wallet and Rolex. But it looks like his mobile has gone. And we don't know what else there was in the car.'

'If it wasn't robbery… if it was instinctive, impetuous, unplanned… why hide the body?' the collator asked.

'What was the car doing there in the first place? Said Weston.

'Why is the passenger window smashed?' Asked Carter.

'Where are the car keys? Come to that, where are the rest of his keys?' Weston wondered.

Wallace joined in. 'Where's the weapon?'.

'What else is missing from the car?'

'Why was he not reported as missing?'

'Was he actually working on Saturday, and if so where and why, and who with?'

Caton used the pause in the flow to catch up. He stepped back and checked the list. 'Who, statistically, is the most likely person to have killed him?' he asked. As they began to chorus the well rehearsed reply he bent down, and added it to bottom of the list:

Who was the last person he was known to be with?

Fifteen minutes later, they had exhausted their review of the questions. Caton gave them a comfort break, mainly so they could get another drink of water, and splash their faces, and sent Ged in search of another fan. The air conditioning was either on the blink or stretched way beyond capacity. When everyone was back he began to pull it all together.

'I've got the head of the tactical aid unit, and the Allocator, coming in twenty minutes,' he told them. 'I want to go over the immediate actions with you. There is only so much we can do today, and we have to get it right. You know the theory. It's like the golden hour for major trauma. The longer we leave it to get answers to these questions, the harder it's going to get.'

They quickly agreed that they could leave the search for the weapon, the keys, any discarded contents taken from the car, and door to door enquiries, to the Tactical Aid Team, supplemented - through negotiations Caton would handle - with the North Manchester Division. Working with Traffic, Division would also maintain the road block at each end of Collyhurst Road, with statements taken from anyone using the route in the previous twenty four hours.

They also needed the footage from the CCTV and traffic cameras – starting with the one at Marcel Guest. Caton said he'd request Chief Superintendent Hadfield to set up an appeal for witnesses through the papers, television, and radio, from midday on Monday. Duggie Wallace and his team would begin to compile all of the data out there to do with Roger Standing, and pull together lists of all known and suspected car jackers, muggers, and drug users convicted of assault or violent crime. They also needed his mobile phone number so they could track it down and to get a log of his calls. Everyone was to use their informants and sources. Holmes was far from happy at the prospect of having to go crawling to his old adversary, Inspector Lounds from the Force Drugs Unit, but bit his lip and made a note. He perked up however when Caton handed him a task he could well have taken on himself.

'Gordon,' he said, wiping a trickle of sweat from his forehead. 'I want you and Nick to get over to Number One Piccadilly. Get the key to Standing's apartment from their security people. There's bound to be a twenty four hour desk in that place. Check when he was last there, and who with, and if anyone can have got in, with or without keys, in the intervening period. Have a brief look, but don't compromise the forensic search we'll arrange for tomorrow. Tape it off, and seal it up. And then find out the best way to track the comings and goings. Anyone tries to get in there, we bring them in.

'What if it's the wife?' Nick Carter asked, not unreasonably.

'Don't worry,' Caton replied. 'We'll deal with that when she arrives tomorrow. I'll arrange for DS Stuart to bring her to the mortuary.'

Holmes was the last to head for the door. Caton asked him to step into his office for a word.

'What's going on Gordon,' he said. 'You've been like a bear with a sore head all day. And we both know I'm the one with a real sore head. So what's your excuse?' He sat down on the edge of his desk, and gestured to his inspector to take a seat.

Holmes began to rub the stubble on his poorly shaven chin and shifted uncomfortably in his seat. 'It's beginning to get Marilyn down,' he said at last. 'She thought when I was transferred to this team it would be more office based, all the leg work having been done in the initial investigations. A bit like cold casing. That we'd have our nights and weekends at last. Trouble is we had all the pressure of Bojangles, then those two weeks in Shanghai, and now this is another one where we're in it from the start. It wasn't supposed to be like that.'

Caton wasn't buying it. Holmes loved being part of this team. 'Come on Gordon,' he said. 'You know as well as I do this has been like a picnic after all those years working shifts, and weekends. When was the last time you worked a weekend? March? You're talking four months. There's got to be more to it than this.'

Holmes sagged back in his chair. He was sweating heavily. Caton watched the pretence slip away.

'You're right,' Gordon admitted. 'Marilyn is pissed off, but it's not that. Jimmy's got in with a bad crowd. We found out last week he was wagging school. All those kids they caught in the truancy sweep last week? Jimmy was number one hundred and ninety two. Got picked up in the Arndale. He's not the slightest bit repentant. Next thing I know we'll be getting prosecuted for failing to make him attend.'

'It can't be that bad, we've all done it one time or another.'

'I bet *you* didn't'

'As a matter of fact I did; in the Lower Sixth. Three of us reported in sick and sloped off to Old Trafford for an England Test against Australia. Unfortunately, the High Master had the same idea. He spotted us through his binoculars, waited until the tea interval, and then pounced. I got a roasting from my aunt, and was gated for two weeks. To be honest, I think the old boy had a sneaking admiration for what we'd done.' Caton was surprised to hear himself slipping easily into the public school vernacular that he'd never really been comfortable with, and hadn't used in over twenty years.

'Come on Boss,' said Holmes, adding to his embarrassment. 'How can you compare a handful of seventeen year olds from Manchester Grammar School going to a Test Match, and a thirteen year old dossing round the Arndale with a load of adolescent shoplifters?'

'Is that what they were doing?'

'Well… it's only a matter of time.'

Caton got off the desk and pulled up a chair. 'How about you stop projecting,' he said. 'And find out what the problem is. Is it push or pull? Is the work too hard, or is he being bullied? Or is it because he's just desperate to be in with the in crowd? When you know that you can start to do something about it.'

'And what if he's just bored? What am I going to do then? Bribe him? Pay the teachers an incentive allowance? Kick him up the arse, and wait for him to do a runner?'

'If it was me,' said Caton. 'I'd start by listening to him, and then go in and see his teachers.'

'Have you ever tried listening to a monosyllabic thirteen year old boy with attitude?' Holmes scorned, mopping his face with the back of his hand.

'I thought that was a phase they all went through. I know I did.' Caton replied. He paused, and waited until he'd caught his DI's eye. 'And, most of today, you've been doing a pretty good imitation of it yourself.'

Holmes grunted in the way that only he could. Then a smile began to spread across his face. 'Must be rubbing off,' he said grudgingly.

'That's better.' Caton encouraged.

Holmes picked up his jacket and headed for the door. He turned and looked wearily at Caton. 'Well thanks for that Boss,' he said. 'I'll give it a try.'

Caton had been trying to phone Kate all afternoon, but her phone was off. He tried again, and had to leave a message. *See you Wednesday Kate. Miss You... Love You.* It was never enough. She'd promised to book something for them both when she got back. He had a feeling he was going to have to tell her to cancel it.

He'd just turned his attention back to his in tray when Ged popped her head around the door.

'Sorry to bother you Sir,' she said. 'But the assistant premises manager at Roger Standing's school has just rung to ask how long you're going to be.'

'Tell him I'm on my way,' he said getting to his feet,' and then get yourself of home. And thanks for today. You've been brilliant.'

She smiled, shrugged it off, and left. Caton reckoned he had every reason to be grateful. Ged had been like an anchor for him ever since the team had been set up. M's Moneypenny, to his Bond. He made a mental note to remind her of the leave she'd accumulated, that without his insistence, he knew she would never take.

As he let himself out, dusk was falling over the city. A deep red glow, from behind and below the West Pennine hills, lit the underside of puffy clouds shot with the most delicate purple and violet, topped with wisps of white. He was reminded of another definition of the golden hour. One that he had come across on Wikpedia. One that photographers use.

"The golden hour: the first hour after dawn, and the last hour before dusk."

He already knew where Roger Standing had been in the first hour after dawn. He would give anything to know what he was doing in that last hour before dusk.

5

It was 7.30. precisely on Monday morning. The day had started a touch cooler, and despite the fact that he was wearing a suit – albeit one in summer lightweight linen – Caton understood why Holmes had complained about the air-conditioning. He turned it up a couple of degrees. Gordon was in a much better mood than yesterday, and his own headache was a distant memory.

A mobile television news crew, and several paparazzi, were already parked up outside in the school bus bays. With mild interest, they watched the Skoda Octavia pass. No point in stirring themselves for one of the detective chief inspector's "*No comments.*" The real opportunities would come when the kids began to arrive.

Caton brought the car to a halt at the imposing entrance. The two ends of a soft sand coloured brick wall, eight feet high, terminated in thick pillars that supported two huge and ornate wrought iron gates. On the right hand side, the words "*Courage and wisdom embodied in one*" had been fashioned. High up, on the left pillar, the name of the school was proudly displayed. On the right, black lettering on a stainless steel plaque identified Roger Standing as the Chief Executive of the North Manchester Harmony Academy Trust, and Principal of the High School.

'I wonder how long before that comes down?' Holmes ruminated.

Caton was about to get out, and approach the intercom panel perched inexplicably on a post inside the grounds, just within arms' reach, when the gates began to swing silently and smoothly inwards.

'I always said you had an aura about you Boss.' Holmes quipped, as Caton gunned the engine.

'Nothing to do with the CCTV then?' Caton pointed out the tiny lenses embedded in the each of the plaques, an inch or so below the final line of text.

'Now that is clever. I wonder if there's someone on duty twenty four seven?' Said Holmes.

Caton had the same thought. At least they would then know if Standing had been and gone the evening before, and when. And, more importantly, with whom.

They pulled into one of the rows of bays marked *Visitors*. Caton turned off the engine, and checked that the batteries were good in his voice recorder.

'Is the SLO joining us Boss?' Holmes asked.

The School Police Liaison Officers worked closely with the schools on education, prevention and even detection issues. They had already proved valuable in past investigations.

'Apparently, this is the only high school in Manchester that doesn't have one.' Caton told him. 'The Head and Governors opted out of the scheme when the school was set up. I can't for the life of me imagine why.'

As they exited the car a tall man, of African Caribbean appearance, came through the automatic glass doors to meet them. He wore a loose denim suit, white shirt with a black tie, and a pair of brown shoes with a crepe sole, that Caton's aunt would have called brothel creepers. At six feet three or four he was only a few inches taller than Caton, but dwarfed Gordon Holmes. In his late forties, early fifties, Caton decided. Well built, yet moving with a smooth and confident poise. He could have been a basketball player in his youth. He smiled as he came towards them.

'Detective Chief Inspector Caton. Good to see you again. Detective Inspector Holmes, welcome to Harmony Academy High,' he said, his right hand held out in greeting. 'I'm Darren Howe, the assistant premises manager.' His smile broadened. 'That's caretaker, to you and me.'

Caton shook Howe's hand for the second time in as many days. The man's grip confirmed the impression of athletic strength.

'Good morning Mr Howe.' Caton said, 'We're here to see the Acting Head.'

The pupils in Howe's eyes contracted briefly. 'That will be Miss Given, the *Headteacher*,' he said. 'She's expecting you.'

'Headteacher?' said Holmes, 'We thought Roger Standing was the Headteacher. They can't have replaced him so soon?'

The assistant premises manager stepped courteously aside as the massive doors glided effortlessly apart. 'Everyone thinks that,' he said. 'In fact, Mr Standing is...was, Chief Executive of the North Manchester Harmony Trust, and *Principal* of the school. But Miss Given is the Headteacher.' He followed them into the vast foyer with its dome shaped roof flooding the entrance hall with light. 'Mr

43

Standing was a very important and very busy man. He was away as much as he was here. He left the day to day running of the school to Miss Given.' He paused at the reception desk. 'I have to ask you to wait here for a moment while I find out if Miss Given is ready for you.'

He rounded the long sweep of highly polished wood that served as the reception counter, swiped a card through a slot at the side of a door, and slipped inside. The door closed automatically behind him.

Caton studied the counter. It was made of hard wood, with a distinctive smell that reminded him for some reason of the house in Chorlton he had shared with his parents, right up until the accident. It had a colour somewhere between walnut and burnt caramel. Carved along the edges were panels depicting alternating scenes of some of Manchester's most historic buildings, and clouds and waves crashing upon rocks. Caton could make out Castlefield, the Town Hall, the Cathedral, the Chetham School of Music, Sinclair's Oyster Bar and the Wellington Inn, the Central Library and John Rylands Library. He found himself wondering if Urbis and the Beeston tower would figure centuries ahead in a similar display. Beside him, Holmes ran his fingers along the edge of the counter; already burnished deep ochre by the sweat of a thousand students and staff.

Above the desk a large sign welcomed visitors in over 50 languages. Ahead of them, the entrance hall opened up into a corridor twelve metres wide, along the walls of which hung framed pieces of exceptional student artwork. Paintings, fabrics and photo images, were interspersed with exhortations to succeed in life, work, and relationships. Some fifty metres away, the corridor opened up into a vast atrium dotted with small trees in steel containers, beyond which a broad steel and glass escalator headed up and out of sight.

'Are you sure we didn't take a wrong turning and end up in the Trafford Centre, Boss?' Holmes mused.

'You're right,' Caton agreed. 'This wouldn't be out of place as a shopping mall, or the headquarters of an international corporation.

'I see you've been admiring our reception desk gentlemen.'

They turned to find an elegant and attractive woman, of medium height, in her mid thirties, wearing a brown silk trouser suit and cream blouse, advancing towards them. She stopped in front of Caton, and extended her arm. Her hand was cool, and her touch as light as a feather, but Caton sensed for the first time the meaning of the expression an iron fist in a velvet glove. She examined him keenly with dark brown eyes the depths of which were accentuated by the arched sweep of her eyebrows.

'Detective Chief Inspector. 'She said. 'I am Juliette Postlethwaite; Associate Head Teacher, and Personal Assistant to Mr Underhill. This must be Detective Inspector Holmes.' She turned to Holmes, and shook him by the hand. 'Please, follow me.'

She led them around the counter, behind which they could now see an array of computers, a printer, several telephones and a bank of monitor screens. She swiped her magnetic card, and ushered them into a long narrow corridor with doors at intervals along its length.

'These are our interview, tutorial and senior management team offices,' she told them. 'You'll notice that there are no windows on this side. That's to preserve necessary privacy. All other rooms in the school are fully glazed, and open to the world. '

'You mentioned a joint venture of mutual benefit Miss Postlethwaite?' Caton prompted, conscious that it had been her only allusion to Roger Standing.

'That was the Trust. Mr Standing conceived of a way in which to use the opportunities presented by two of the Government's initiatives – City Academies and School Trusts – to create a family of schools with new technologies of learning at their core. To raise standards of education to a level of excellence, and prepare the students for careers and life styles as yet undreamt of. In effect, to mould their own futures. A quite brilliant concept.'

'And how does that work exactly?' Caton asked as they took a right turn.

'Mr Standing put together a trust involving this school, and eight partner primary schools from across the city. Barry Underhill Computer Systems not only matched, but far exceeded, the funding already provided by the Government. That enabled this new building to be created, and substantial improvements to all of the other schools. All of the schools have been equipped with state of the art information technology, and twenty first century teaching and learning software and techniques. Mr Underhill, is Chair of Governors of this school, and Deputy Director of the Trust.' She stopped in front of a door directly ahead of them. 'And here we are.' She knocked once, opened it, stepped aside, and ushered them in.

The room was essentially a large office, eight times the size of Caton's. The walls on three sides were lined with wooden book shelves holding an orderly assortment of box files and books, interspersed with miniature sculptures, and ceramic pots. The fourth wall consisted of a pane of glass from floor to ceiling that looked out onto a pebbled courtyard containing rhododendrons, and a carved wooden bench beside a circular pool. In front of the window, a desk with a computer keyboard, a flat screen monitor, and a single in-tray, faced inwards as though resisting distraction. Four leather easy chairs, to the right of the desk, surrounded a low wooden coffee table set out with table mats, and a small bowl of cut flowers. At the furthest end of the room a big man, and a woman with short blonde hair, were deep in discussion at a table surrounded by six seats. In front of them was a scattering of papers.

The couple looked up. The woman put down the piece of paper she had been holding, and came to meet them. A little shorter than Postlethwaite, perhaps five feet three, she was wearing an immaculate black two piece suit that flattered her. She had serious blue eyes, and a small tight mouth that brooked no nonsense. Her companion, a few steps behind, was tall, the same height as Caton but broader. He wore a navy blue blazer, white shirt, black tie, and dark grey trousers. In his late forties, he was already beginning to thicken around the waist. There was something about his face that Caton found familiar.

'Chief Inspector, I'm Sandra Given; Headteacher. I'm sorry to have kept you both waiting.' She waved towards the table behind her. 'We have been really busy…you can imagine.'

Caton noticed that she too had immediately known which of them he was, despite the fact that he and Holmes were standing side by side. She had also studiously ignored his inspector, and had failed to introduce her colleague.

'Miss Given,' he said. 'This is my colleague Detective Inspector Holmes.' She gave Holmes the curtest of nods. Caton continued. 'We would like to say how sorry we are about the loss you must all be feeling, and the need to intrude on you, and the school, at this time.'

'Thank you,' she said unconvincingly. 'Now perhaps we can get on? We still have a great deal to do, and staff and students will be arriving shortly. This is the final week of term. A *lot* to do.' she pointed to the chairs around the coffee table. 'Please take a seat.'

As they took their seats Holmes stuck out his hand towards the mystery man, who grabbed it and shook it vigorously.

'Sherlock!' he exclaimed. 'How are you?'

'Ronnie Payne,' Holmes declared. 'I'd heard you'd retired. What are you doing here?'

'I'm the Premises Manager,' Payne told him. 'Retrained when I got out. This is the perfect job. Security and buildings.'

Caton remembered. Payne had been a constable in Salford when he was there. They had never worked together. He still had the unmistakeable bearing of a police officer. They never seemed to lose it. Confident, alert, sceptical.

'Mr Payne,' From behind her desk the Head's voice cut through the conversation. 'Can we get on please.'

'This is a preliminary stage in the investigation,' Caton began. 'And I have just a few questions for you, which shouldn't take too long. Detective Inspector Holmes will be taking notes.' On cue, Holmes opened his notebook, and clicked his biro several times. It never failed to irritate Caton. 'Before I start,' he began.' Is there anything you'd like to ask me?'

Given leaned forward and placed her hands on the desk. 'We understand that you're treating Roger Standing's death as suspicious.'

'That's correct.' Caton replied.

'In what way suspicious?' she pressed.

'In the sense that he doesn't appear to have died of natural causes, and at this stage we can't account for his death.'

'And what precisely does that mean?' she asked with an air of exasperation.

The Premises Manager came to her aid. 'That it isn't clear whether it was an accident, suicide, manslaughter, or murder.'

'I *had* worked that out for myself,' she snapped.

'And until the post mortem has been completed I'm afraid I can't tell you any more than that.' Caton told her.

'So we have to find out from the papers, or the television?'

'The only thing that I can confirm, is that we're confident that Mr Standing didn't take his own life.'

'Well, that's a relief, anyway,' she said. The look on Caton's face persuaded her to qualify it. 'Only in the sense that that could have reflected badly on the school.

And no doubt questions would have been asked about whether it had anything to do with his work.'

'I am afraid those question will still have to be asked,' Caton said firmly. 'Which brings me neatly to my first question? We need to establish Mr Standing's movements on Saturday, and particularly during the afternoon, and early evening. Do any of you know if he happened to have been at the school during the day?'

Ronnie Payne uncrossed his legs, and sat up in his chair. 'That's an easy one to answer,' he said. 'Mr Standing arrived at the school at 4.33pm, and left at 8.16pm. He spent the entire time in his office.'

'And how have you been able to establish that?' said Caton.

'We have an electronic system of registration for pupils and staff alike.' He took from his breast pocket a card identical to the ones which Darren Howe and Juliette Postlethwaite had used. 'There's a magnetic strip on here which gives access to secure parts of the building; administrative offices, computer rooms, and the like. The really clever part is an electronic chip through which we are able to record the entry and exit of every student and staff member. Not unlike the ones that motorists can now use to open their car doors, and start their engines without a key. There's no need for attendance registers.' He spotted Sandra Given rolling her eyes and added hurriedly. 'Except, of course, we keep print out copies for the Ofsted school inspectors.'

'And what about visitors?' Holmes asked him.

'They have to sign in at the reception, where they're given a temporary coded name badge with an inbuilt chip. We made an exception for you this morning because it was so early, and let's face it, you do have identification of your own.'

'But Mr Standing would have insisted.' Juliette Postlethwaite reminded him.' No exceptions, he always said.'

I checked the CCTV monitors first thing.' Payne continued, ignoring her comment. 'They also show Mr Standing arriving, making his way to his room, and leaving.'

'Do those monitors cover his room?'

'No. Only the corridors, open spaces, classrooms, study areas, general offices, and staffrooms areas are covered. Mr Standing regarded anything other than that as an invasion of privacy.'

The detectives exchanged glances. Caton recalled a quotation from his fifth form excursions into the Roman satirist Juvenal. *Quis custodiet ipsos custodes?* Who shall guard the guards themselves?

'Is there an intercom link to these cameras?' Holmes asked.

'Only from Mr Standing's office, this office, and the senior administrator's office.' Sandra Given replied tetchily.

'So we know that Mr Standing went to his office,' said Caton getting them back on track. 'Did anyone else come into the school during the time he was here?'

Payne was adamant. 'Definitely not. There were contract workers in the sports hall resealing an area of floor where we'd had a leak. Mr Howe let them in at 9am, and saw them off the premises at 1.30pm, setting the alarm as he went.'

'And he didn't need to come back to let Mr Standing in?' Caton asked.

'No. He had the code. All of us in this room know the code too. With all of the security features, there is no need for either Mr Howe or me to be around to let people in.'

'So anyone can come and go as they please?'

'No. Just the leadership team, and the Chair of Governors. Staff have to arrange for one of us to let them in. Frankly, with all the web based links we've got, there isn't much call for that. They can do all their preparation online, and feed it straight into the whiteboard panels. It's only physical stuff, like displays and shifting furniture round, and they can get the classroom assistants and technicians to do that after school.'

Caton looked down at the list of questions he'd prepared. 'Do you know if Mr Standing had any appointments later that evening, or if he might have received any calls – from any of you for example?'

Sandra Given took over. 'Mrs Murphy, Mr Standing's Personal Assistant, will know of any work related appointments.' She lifted from her in-tray a sleek two-way radio – much neater than GMP's standard issue Caton noted - and spoke into it. 'Mrs Murphy. Would you come to my office please, and bring Mr Standing's diary with you?'

While they were waiting Ronnie Payne answered the second part of Caton's question.

'There were no in-coming calls to Mr Standing's phone during the time he was in school, and none immediately before or after. Just one from a London area code at 9.20am. Number withheld.'

Caton and Holmes looked at him in surprise. 'How would you know that Ronnie?' Holmes got in first.

'All calls are automatically logged at the switchboard, which has a last five calls service on every line. It's another of the security features. Not much use with pay-as-you-go mobiles though.'

There was a timid knock on the door, and a tall slim woman in her mid fifties walked in. She was wearing a dark grey jacket over a lilac cardigan, and a matching grey three quarter length skirt. Her platinum hair, lightly streaked, was layer cut, and fell just short of her shoulders. Her face was more homely than attractive Caton decided. She had been crying, and her effort to dry her eyes had smudged mascara around the edges, and onto her cheek bones. In her left hand she carried a black A2 diary, embossed with gold.

'Mrs Murphy.' Given said abruptly, 'Detective Chief Inspector Caton wishes to know if Mr Standing had any appointments on Saturday.'

The PA addressed herself to Caton

'No sir. He didn't. Not on Saturday. He did tell me that he would be coming in for a few hours in the afternoon, and I did put it in the diary to remind me, in case anyone wanted to contact him.' Her voice began to falter. She paused for a moment to collect herself. 'I always enter it into my computer, and I can access that from home.'

Caton held out his hand. 'May I have a look.'

She handed him the book. The entries were neatly made, in a cursive hand reminiscent of his mother's handwriting. There was a single entry for the Saturday. He turned to the front of the diary, and began to flick through the pages. Most of the entries were self-explanatory: Governing Body meetings,

Trust Board meetings, Parents Evenings, Open Days, DFES London – which Caton took to be the Department For Education and Skills. There were a smattering of references to Downing Street, and the PM, both of which were written in capital letters. He noticed a number of weeks blocked out for trips abroad. There were two references which appeared infrequently, and were also in bold, and accompanied by exclamation marks. One was RGI, the other, Overseas House.

'What are these.' He asked, pointing them out to her.

As she leaned over his shoulder he caught a scent of stephanotis. It triggered a memory. Laura, his former wife, walking down the aisle towards him, smiling nervously through the fine lace veil, the waxy five star blooms of the bouquet wafting their scent ahead of her.

'Overseas House,' she said.' That's the Local Authority Education offices. Unless it says otherwise the appointment would have been with the Chief Education Officer. The Reporting Inspector is the one who led the Ofsted inspection team. We had our first inspection in May.'

'And very positive it was too.' Sandra Given announced. '*An outstanding school with no weaknesses.* We shall not be receiving another inspection for at least six years. Although I have no doubt we will now have to endure even more visitors that than we had before.'

Caton couldn't decide whether Sandra Given was in denial over the death of her colleague, or simply devoid of empathy. In either case, there was a gulf between her demeanour, and that of Mrs Murphy. 'I'll need a copy of this.' He said, handing the diary to her.

'No, you keep it,' she replied, on the brink of tears. 'I have the one on the computer. Mr Standing kept a copy – plus his personal appointments - on his own BlackBerry phone. He would have had that in his briefcase'

'And he would have had his briefcase with him if he was working in school?' Caton asked, wondering if this could be their first breakthrough.

'Oh yes, and he did. You can see it quite clearly on the CCTV tape.' Payne added helpfully,

'I need a description of that briefcase, the phone number of his BlackBerry, and a copy of the tape.' Caton told them.

'No problem.' Said Payne. 'The briefcase is easy. We bought it for him when his CBE was announced. It's an Aspinal Chairman's Briefcase. Black English bridle leather, lined with suede, silk pockets, and a silver lock. You'll find a photo of it on their web site.' He took a business card from his wallet, wrote the phone number down, and passed it to Gordon Holmes. 'I'll get you the tape on your way out.'

As Caton placed the diary on the coffee table, the door opened. Payne, Given, and Postlethwaite rose to their feet as one, leaving the detectives flat-footed, a full second behind.

6

The new arrival was the same height and build as Gordon Holmes: five feet six and close to a hundred and eighty pounds. There the likeness ended. In fairness to Holmes, he decided, this man was a little thicker around the waist, but, unlike the inspector, the very model of sartorial elegance. He wore a light grey check suit in a wool and silk mix. The double buttoned cuffs of his classic white silk shirt protruded two centimetres from the sleeves of the jacket. The ensemble was completed by a dark grey abstract patterned silk tie, and a pair of soft brown leather shoes. Caton's money was on Savile Row. It was, however, his air of quiet authority that most impressed.

'This is Mr. Underhill, Chair of Governors of this school, and Chair of the Board of the Harmony Academy Trust.' Sandra Given announced as though royalty had entered the room.

Underhill walked towards Caton, and nodded with a barely perceptible inclination of his head, during which his eyes never left Caton's. He held out a podgy hand. His grip was damp but firm. 'Chief Inspector,' he said. 'I'm pleased to meet you. Please call me Barry.'

'Inspector Holmes and I are pleased to meet you Mr Underhill,' Caton replied, ignoring the invitation. 'I'm only sorry about the circumstances.'

Underhill inclined his head towards Gordon Holmes, and exchanged another handshake. 'Gentlemen,' he said, please, be seated.'

Sandra Given moved to relinquish her place behind the desk. He waved her back and sat down instead beside Caton, leaving his personal assistant hovering uncomfortably by the door. She closed the door and crossed to the conference table at the far end of the room, where she picked up a chair, and placed it at the outer edge of the magic circle.

'What are you able to tell us Chief Inspector?' Underhill inquired.

'There is very little we can tell you at this stage sir,' Caton replied. 'Mr Standing was found dead, in his car. We're awaiting the results of the post mortem to determine the cause of his death. I can confirm that it was not suicide. But beyond that, I'm afraid I can't comment.'

'Cannot, Chief Inspector? Or will not?' Underhill's eyes were penetrating.

'Both I'm afraid,' Caton said calmly, holding his gaze. 'I'm sure you understand.'

The businessman smiled thinly. 'Of course,' he said. 'You're a policeman after all. You're here to ask questions, not to answer them.'

'In which case,' Caton responded. 'Perhaps you can tell me if you were aware of any appointments which Mr Standing may have had planned for this weekend?'

He thought about it for a moment. 'No, I'm afraid not. Roger and I were due to meet tomorrow evening before our monthly meeting of the Board. He didn't mention any meetings before then, nor would I have expected him to.'

Caton looked around the whole group, leaning forward slightly to ensure that Miss Postlethwaite felt included. 'Were *any* of you aware of any recent threats to Mr Standing, or concerns he might have had for his own safety?'

He watched them closely. They shook their heads as much in apparent disbelief as certitude. Except for Underhill. His face remained impassive. Caton decided to press him.

'Mr Underhill?'

He was slow to reply, and in that hiatus Caton saw the Chairman's eyes narrow almost imperceptibly.

'No, Detective Chief Inspector, I was not.'

Their eyes locked, and Caton let the answer hang in the air. 'In that case,' Caton said. 'I'd like to thank you all for your co-operation.' He turned to face the headteacher. 'I'll be in touch shortly Miss Given, to arrange for Mr Standing's room to be searched, and to follow up on any enquiries that might arise from our investigation.'

'Will that really be necessary?' she retorted. 'It's not as though he was killed on the school premises.' It sounded cold and unfeeling, which was exactly how it was received in the room.

'I appreciate that, Miss Given, but we don't know why, or by whom, he was killed.'

'But you can't really imagine that it had anything to do with this school?' she blustered.

'Our job is to establish the facts; to do that I have to keep an open mind. I'm afraid experience has taught me that includes imagining the unimaginable.'

'Then you must have a very active, and a very uncomfortable, mind.' She said softly.

She was right about that Caton decided. He nodded to Holmes, who closed his notebook and put his biro away. They rose as one.

'We don't need to take up any more of your time,' Caton told them. 'You must have a lot to do.'

'As it happens, we do,' said Given. 'The children and staff will be arriving now. Some of then will have heard the news, others may not. There will be a lot of distress. Everyone will be offered counselling...'

'Through the Local Education Authority.' Ronnie Payne added, to Given's obvious annoyance.

'The pupils and students will be sent home,' she continued. 'And the school will be officially closed for two days as a mark of respect, and to give everyone time to recover so that when lessons do recommence it will be with the minimum distraction. Staff will be expected to come in.'

'Then we'll leave you to it,' said Caton. 'And thank you again.'

'I'll get you that tape.' The premises manager said leading them towards the door. Underhill remained seated, grasping the arms of his chair, staring out of the window at the Garden of Peace.

A sound like the twittering of birds in an aviary met them as Caton and Holmes descended the escalator. It swelled as they crossed the mall, and morphed into the chatter of the monkey house at Chester Zoo. At the end of the corridor closest to the reception several members of staff were trying to organise the melee of students that had formed in the entrance, and direct them towards the main hall. Small clusters of students, and of staff, in animated yet muted conversation, eyed them both with a mixture of curiosity and suspicion, parting to let them through, before closing up again into their tight circles. In the driveway, they passed a group of girls comforting one of their number in a flood of tears; the only evidence of raw emotion they had encountered since arriving an hour before.

As they reached the car they heard the first few bars of the Foden Richardson's Band rendition of *Slaidburn*. Caton pulled his mobile phone from his pocket. It was Ged.

'DS Stuart has been on Sir,' she said. 'She's just picked up Mrs Standing. They should be at the mortuary for 9.30am for the identification. The Post Mortem's due to start at 10am, so she's hoping the traffic isn't too bad on the M6 motorway.'

Caton looked at his watch. 'She's pushing it,' he said. 'But the universities aren't back yet, so they might just make it. Give Mr Douglas a ring and ask him if he can hold on for a few minutes if they get stuck in a jam. I'm sure he will, but he won't be best pleased.'

'DS Stuart wanted to know if you'll be joining them.'

'No, I'll leave it to her to gauge her reaction. Ask Joanne to bring Mrs Standing back to Longsight. We can interview her together. Tea, biscuits and tissues at the ready please.'

'DS Stuart also said that their son is flying in from Paris later this morning. He'll be accompanying his mother to Nantwich. She thought you ought to know.'

'Thanks for that Ged. We'll be with you in half an hour.'

He flipped the phone shut, put it back in his pocket, and tossed Gordon the car keys. 'You drive,' he said. 'I may need to use the phone. And take it easy.' He opened the door and climbed into the passenger seat. Holmes switched on the ignition, and set off, steering an uncharacteristically cautious path through the tide of students on the drive.

'What did you think Gordon?'

'How they reacted?'

'How they reacted.'

'One at a time, or altogether?'

'One at a time.'

Holmes eased out of the gates, indicated left, and was quickly into gear. As the road opened up in front of them he began to scratch his chin vigorously.

'If you keep doing that you're going to wear a hole.' Caton told him.

Gordon laughed, and rested his hand back on the steering wheel. 'Howe, the *caretaker*,' he said, using the emphasis to underline his antipathy to all things modern, including poncey job titles. 'He was what you'd expect. Respectful, guarded, polite. Ronnie Payne...well he behaved like a cross between he was still in the force, and also a private detective. Could be really helpful to us though.'

'If he doesn't get over enthusiastic, and start meddling.'

'The Headteacher, Given, she could do with discovering her female side. Might help if she got an empathy transplant. Given is totally self obsessed; Juliette Postlethwaite is obviously Underhill's mole; she didn't give a damn about Roger Standing. As for Underhill himself, you can see how he got where he is. Just the right sentiments, checked out where we are up to, and gave nothing away,' he started rubbing his chin again. 'And if you ask me, there was something to give. He knows something he's not telling.'

Pretty good assessment Caton decided. There *was* something about Given. And beneath Underhill's veneer of authority, superiority even, Caton had detected nervousness.

'What did you think about Standing's personal assistant, Mrs Murphy?' he said.

'Held a torch for Standing. Maybe she'd had an affair with him? Maybe she was *still* having an affair with him?'

'Or perhaps she was a loyal and devoted secretary?'

'Either way Boss, she was the only one of that lot that seemed to give a damn about him.'

'I can't put my finger on it,' Caton said. 'But don't you think there was something funny about the atmosphere. Hardly any hysteria from the pupils, and the staff seem to be in two camps – shocked and concerned, or conspiratorial.'

'I picked that up too. They're all so bloody calm about it. Headteacher found murdered within a mile of the school. Yet it's almost as though it wasn't really such a surprise!'

Gordon's put his finger on it again, Caton decided. With the possible exception of Mrs Murphy, nobody had seemed surprised.

'You know what they say,' Holmes said, as he drove past Fort Collyhurst and the police pound. 'The King is dead. Long live the King. Only this time, it's a lady. Only in the case of that Sandra Given I use the term *lady* loosely.'

DS Joanne Stuart was back from the mortuary within the hour. She found Caton in the major incident room watching the video of Roger Standing leaving the school on the Saturday evening. He saw her come in and pressed the pause button.

'How was she?' he asked.

'That's just it sir,' she said, throwing her jacket over the back of the chair beside her desk, and shaking her blouse loose. 'Icy cold, calm and collected. But not like she was in shock, if you know what I mean? She only agreed to have the family liaison officer in the house to help keep the press away, and on condition she leaves this evening. Refused to let her travel up to Manchester with us. Never said a word in the car, just stared out of the window until we were passing the airport. Then out of the blue she said; *My son is flying in this morning; from Paris. He is going to stay with me for a few days.* That will be a comfort for you, I said. She didn't reply. Then about two minutes later she said; *It's going to be another hot day by the look of it. Do you think you could turn the air conditioning up a little please?* Well, against my better judgement, because it was already giving me goose bumps, I did. Not another word until we got to the mortuary. When they showed her the body, she looked at it for a few seconds, then she turned to me and said; *Yes, it's him.* Just like that. Matter of fact. There was no emotion in her eyes, or her voice. Then she said; *'It's very cold in here. Can we go now?'*

'And now?' Caton asked.

'She's having a cup of tea in Division's victim support team room. Under the circumstances, I thought it would be more appropriate than leaving her in an interview room. It's not as though she's a suspect.' She caught the look on Caton's face and hurriedly corrected herself. 'Well, she is of course; until she's eliminated. But it's not as though we have good reason to suspect her at this stage...so I thought...'

'It's alright Jo,' he said. 'You did right. We shouldn't keep her long. Just the preliminary questions, then you drive to the airport with her to collect her son. You never know, she might loosen up a little on the way back home.'

Margaret Standing was not what he had expected. At about five three, and a little less than eight stone, she was slight, though not unattractive. She wore a dark lilac three quarter length jacket over a white camisole, and a dark grey skirt. Her hair was a lighter shade of grey, and expertly permed in soft curls. Her head bent slightly as she sipped her tea. He could see the slightest hint of mousey-brown at the roots on the crown of her head. She looked up at the sound of the door closing; more curious than startled. Her eyes were pale blue, watery like a shallow pool. Not tearful though. Eyebrows plucked and shaped, a touch of violet mascara; pale pink lipstick carefully applied. Elegant, but without the aura, the presence, he had expected. But then, he had to remind himself, this was the widow of a recently honoured commoner, not the product of generations of blue blood, intermingled, honed through finishing schools, to radiate the kind of smug humility, etiquette and manners that gave a veneer of superiority, and self assurance, that might have distanced her from the common herd. She put the cup down, sat back in her chair, and folded her hands on the table in front of her. Her nails were flawless; manicured and painted to match her lipstick. So perfect, he decided they must be artificial.

In his mind he ran through the brief biography DS Stuart had given him on the way down from the incident room. Margaret Standing, fifty seven years old. Former teacher. Married Roger Standing in 1974. One son. Add to that, widowed September twenty second 2006. Not a lot to go on. He eased back the chair, and sat down.

'Mrs Standing,' he began. 'My name is Detective Chief Inspector Caton. I'm leading the investigation into your husband's death. I'd like to offer my condolences. I can't begin to imagine how you must be feeling.'

He paused to see if she was going to respond. She merely dipped her head in acknowledgement, so he carried on.

'I promise I won't keep you long.'

Another nod.

'We really need to know if your husband was planning to meet with anybody on Saturday afternoon, or evening. Did he give you any indication that he might?'

She glanced down at her hands, and then looked directly at him. 'I really have no idea if my husband was intending to meet anybody last weekend.' No edge to it, simply a statement of fact.

'Did he tell you what he had planned for the weekend?'

'Only that he had some work to catch up on, and would be staying over; possibly until Tuesday evening.'

'Was that usual?'

'What you have to understand Mr Caton, is that my husband was a workaholic. In thirty years of marriage I never knew exactly when he would be home from school. When he *was* at home he would usually work past midnight. And once he had the apartment, it made it easier for him to stay there rather than travel home late at night. So yes, it was usual.'

Her eyes were steady, her tone daring him to draw conclusions; giving none away.

He changed tack. 'Were you aware of any threats against your husband, Mrs Standing?

She held his gaze. 'Why Mr Caton. Do you know of some?'

'No, but I wondered if you might.'

'I am afraid not.'

'And had there been anything about your husband's manner, or behaviour, that might have suggested that he had worries or concerns?'

She allowed herself a brief smile. 'My husband was never worried or concerned. He was busy, excited, intense, determined, driven, but never worried or concerned. You see Mr Caton, he was supremely confident. There was always an aura of certainty and invincibility about him.' She looked down at her hands again, her voice suddenly softening. 'It was, I think, what first attracted me to him.' Just as quickly the mask returned. She consulted her watch. 'My son will be arriving shortly. Can I go now?'

'Of course,' said Caton. 'Detective Sergeant Stuart will drive you to the Airport, and then take you and your son home. I would, however, like to come and see you both tomorrow; early afternoon if that's convenient?' Again he thought he detected a tightening in her face. One eyebrow lifted slightly.

'Is that necessary? I really don't know anything at all.'

'On the contrary Mrs Standing, something that seems of no relevance to you, may turn out to be really helpful to us. We will in any case need to check all of your husband's things. Would that be alright? I'd rather not have to trouble you with a search warrant.'

'No I quite understand Mr Caton,' she said. 'How many of you will there be? I could prepare some sandwiches, or a light lunch.'

'That's very kind of you,' he replied. 'But it really won't be necessary Mrs Standing. DS Stuart and I will be coming, with one of our technical support team.'

He pushed back his chair, and stood up. Joanne Stuart rose with him. They waited while Margaret Standing took her clutch bag from the chair next to hers, removed and checked her mobile phone for messages, and replaced it before rising to join them

Caton held the door open. 'Thank you again, Mrs Standing,' he said. 'I really wish you'd reconsider having someone from family liaison stay with you for the next few days.'

She looked up at him, coolly. 'No thank you Mr Caton. I'll have my son with me.' She pointed to the sign on the door. 'In any case, isn't this term more accurate; Victim Support? I really don't want to have to feel like a victim.' She paused for a moment as though intending to add something else. Whatever it was, she must have thought better of it. 'Goodbye.' Was all she said as she followed DS Stuart into the corridor, and through the fire doors towards the reception.

Caton watched the door close, and perched on the edge of the table for a moment. There was a dignity and composure about her that would not have been misplaced in Debrett's Guides to the British Aristocracy. He played back the interview in his head. There had been no slipping into the present tense. She knew that her husband was dead. Accepted it. Didn't seem at all curious about how he had died. No calls for revenge. Just a quiet acceptance that the police would do all they could. Or was it something else? His mobile rang briefly and stopped. He checked the last number and redialled. It was Ged.

'I'm sorry sir,' she said. 'I forgot you were in an interview. As soon as I realised…'

'Don't worry, Ged,' he said. 'We've finished. What is it?'

'There are two officers from Special Branch here to see you. A Chief Inspector Crispin, and an Inspector Warhurst,' he sensed her hesitating. 'I'm afraid they're waiting in your room sir.'

In his mind's eye, he could see her flinching, one hand over the ear piece, waiting for the onslaught. Special Branch. What the hell did they want? Somehow he managed not to explode. He counted to five. '*My* room?'

'I'm really sorry sir. At first they wanted to come into the incident room. I knew you wouldn't want that. I told them you wouldn't be long. I said I'd bring them a drink in reception, or they could wait in the canteen. They were that insistent. I just thought it was the lesser of two evils.

'Don't worry Ged,' he said more calmly than he felt. 'I'll come straight up.'

7

The two of them were seated in easy chairs either side of the coffee table. They rose to greet him. Both wore lightweight jackets over tee shirts and casual trousers. One was in his mid forties, the other his early fifties; both approaching six feet tall. The older and broader of the two held out his hand. It was large and strong. He had the look of a boxer. Possibly ex forces.

'Detective Chief Inspector Miles Crispin' he said. 'And this is Detective Inspector Warhurst.'

His lean companion smiled, and thrust out his hand. 'Mark.'

Caton shook their hands, gestured for them to sit back down, and took the remaining chair. 'Special Branch,' he said. 'You're not with GMP though?'

Crispin shook his head. 'No. we're not attached to your lot, at least not in the formal sense. We're from the Met.'

It stood out a mile. Not just the Home Counties accents, but the arrogance.

'SO12?' Caton said. 'I thought Special Branch had been disbanded. That you'd merged with the Anti Terrorist Branch to form a new Anti-Terrorism Command?'

They looked at each other as though sharing a joke.

'Your information regarding our demise is a little premature,' Crispin told him.

'Five weeks and four days premature to be precise.' Warhurst chipped in.

'September 2nd is the glorious day when SO15 will be dragged kicking and screaming into the world.'

'However,' Crispin continued, 'Mark and I will be transferring to SO1, in Protection Command.'

'Specialist protection?'

'Precisely. We get to keep the *Special* part. Only right and fitting.' They grinned at each other again. A regular double act. This was a routine he guessed they'd had plenty of practice with in recent days.

'So, what are you doing here?'

They put on their serious faces.

'This matter of Roger Standing.' Crispin said. 'We happened to be in Manchester – assisting with the preparations for the Labour Party Conference – and were asked to pay you a call.'

'Asked by whom?'

'By our chain of command. It seems that someone has taken a special interest. Hardly surprising, I would have thought, given Standing's connections to the Prime Minister, and the Department for Education and Skills.'

'Which are exactly?'

They exchanged glances. This was clearly going to be harder going than they'd anticipated.

Crispin leaned forward in his seat and began to spell it out, with a patronising air of exasperation.

'Given the remarkable success Standing has achieved at Harmony High, and the model which the Trust could provide for other partnerships of schools in deprived areas, don't you think it was inevitable that the Prime Minister, should have taken an interest?

Want to learn some of the lessons? You could say he was an unpaid professional voice; an occasional adviser. Someone who could be called upon as a sounding board.'

'I thought his leanings were more to the right?' Caton responded.

'If there are lessons to be learned from good practice – doesn't it behove whichever government is in power to take notice, regardless of the source?' Warhurst put to him.

'Behove? So that's why they call you the Special Branch,' said Caton.

Crispin ignored the comment, and delivered a barb of his own. 'Politics is the art of the possible,' he said. 'Pragmatism always wins over principle at the ballot box. Surely they taught you that when you were studying at the university here?'

He was putting down a marker. Letting him know how thoroughly they'd done their homework. *We know all about you Detective Chief Inspector Caton. You know bugger all about us. Fifteen Love.* The silence hung between them like an invisible net. Caton broke it first.

'It was good of you to come by. We need all the help we can get.' He took pleasure in the look of puzzlement on their faces. 'What can you tell me about Mr Standing that might assist with my investigation?' He said.

Crispin bristled visibly. 'I don't think you understand Tom.'

So it was Tom now was it? Must have touched a nerve.

'We're here to find out what happened to Roger Standing and, specifically, if you have any leads so far.'

'For whom?'

'We've just told you, our superiors.'

'Why exactly?'

Crispin was on the edge of his seat; the rising pitch and volume of his voice betraying his frustration. 'Are you really that naïve, or are you being deliberately bloody minded! One of the Government's high profile advisers gets topped in Manchester, just a month or so before the Party Conference pitches up here. And you want to know why the PM's Office wants to know what's going on?'

Caton saw the look on Warhurst's face, and the dawning realisation on Crispin's. Whoops, didn't mean to let that out did you? He gave them a couple of seconds to let it sink in, and then said:

'I've been ordered to keep a lid on this. Not to talk to the press. Not to fuel any rumours. Since when has any government in recent times been able to resist putting whatever spin it wants to on whatever information it gets? For all I know they may want to play this down, or even play it up. I can't be party to that. Not if there's a chance it might get in the way of this investigation.'

The veins in Crispin's neck began to stand out, blue cords tightening as his skin flushed red against the pale tee shirt. 'More than your job's worth is it?' he exploded. He turned to his colleague. 'No surprise that wonder boy here hasn't fulfilled all those early predictions – youngest Chief Constable ever? Don't make me laugh! He hasn't got the balls for it.'

Caton stood, walked over to his desk, and held down the reception button.

'Yes Sir?'

'Please Cancel those refreshments Ged. We won't be needing them after all. Then come down to my office and show Mr Crispin and Mr Warhurst out.' He released the button and turned to face them. 'This has nothing to do with protocol. My concern is that nothing jeopardises this investigation. You lecture me about naivety? You come to me with nothing, and you want me to give you everything I've got. Well my boss gets a daily report. He reports to the Chief Constable. If you want to know where we're up to, get your boss to ask mine.'

Crispin nodded to Warhurst, and they both stood up. 'Don't worry Tom,' he said. 'We will. And don't think they won't tell us.'

'That's up to them. Now, unless there's something you've remembered that might help me with this investigation, I have to get on.'

There was a knock on the door, and it opened. Ged hovered politely in the corridor.

As they reached the doorway Crispin turned, and stared at Caton hard and long.

'We'll see you around Tom,' he said. 'You can count on it.'

Caton had just cleared his head, when the phone rang. It was Larry Hymer, chief crime reporter at the Manchester Evening News. All he needed.

'Tom. It's Larry here. I've been trying to reach you since yesterday. Your gate keeper's got it double barred.' He consciously downshifted the irritation in his voice; replacing it with a gentle tone; almost wheedling. 'Roger Standing. They're pressing me for a front page piece. What can you give me?'

Caton sighed. 'I'm sorry Larry. Strict instructions, you'll have to go through the press office at Chester House.'

'I've tried them. Waste of space. I quote: *We can confirm that the body of a man has been discovered close to the Sandhills Urban Pathway in the Irk Valley. A formal identification has yet to be made. A post mortem is taking place this morning. We are treating the death as suspicious.* Suspicious for God's sake. We all know it's Roger Standing, and that he was bundled up in the boot of his car. You must be able to give me something?'

'I'm sorry Larry, but not this time. The post mortem should provide some additional information. Why don't you try them again this afternoon?'

'Thanks a bunch, Chief Inspector.' The irritation was back in spades. 'I'll remember this next time you want a special favour.'

'And there was me thinking your editor was only too happy to help the police in the pursuit of justice.'

'Quid pro quo, Tom, you know the rules, Quid quo pro.' The line went dead.

He had a point, Caton conceded. Hymer's paper was a regular vehicle for appeals for witnesses or missing persons. Larry had even been known to help plant the odd story to help winkle out a suspect. Come to that, his own intelligence network had occasionally proved particularly useful. On the other hand, they were often one step ahead of the national dailies when it came to hot news, courtesy of Larry's informal links that he suspected went all the way up to the top. Caton knew he wasn't really going to hold a grudge. There was too much at stake for him, and his paper. Rules were rules, and Hymer knew they cut both ways.

Caton went down to the canteen and bought a tuna sandwich, an apple, and a hundred percent fruit juice. Back in his office he was just about to start clearing the forty seven emails that had accumulated over the past twelve hours when Ged rang to tell him that DI Weston was back from the mortuary.

'Ask her to get herself a drink and join me,' he said. 'And tell her to bring Duggie with her.'

Sarah always brightened up a room. Today she wore her standard post mortem uniform: a short brown jacket that accentuated her tall lithe figure, over a white tee shirt, and black jeans that sat neatly on a pair of black and white Carrera suede lace-up training shoes. She put her folder on the table, settled into the seat facing Caton, and self-consciously flicked her blond bob.

'Duggie's right behind me,' she said, her blue eyes appraising Caton warmly. 'You look like you had a better night last night Tom. Is Kate still away?'

The friendship borne out of their mutual battle with the inspector's exams meant that they had few secrets from each other, and enjoyed a safe familiarity when alone. She had her husband, and he now had Kate. In the position Caton had reached it was good to have one colleague he could regard as an equal, and trust completely; not only good, exceptionally rare.

'Much better thanks,' he said. 'But I wish I could say the same for this morning.' He was about to tell her about his brush with Crispin and Warhurst when Duggie Wallace knocked, and came in. His short and chunky frame contrasted markedly with DI Weston's. The copious supply of Jaffa Cakes he kept at the side of his computer was just one example of his addiction to all things sweet. He dropped a large green file on the table, flopped down beside her, pulled a grubby handkerchief from the pocket of his jeans, and proceeded to mop his brow. Caton reached across, and turned up the fan another notch. Wallace was right; it was getting hot in there.

'What have you been doing with that Duggie?' Sarah enquired. 'Cleaning your shoes?'

He grinned, and stuffed it back in his jeans. 'Yes, as a matter of fact, and the computer screen.'

Caton was eager to get started. 'OK.' he said. 'DI Holmes, and DS Carter, will be joining us as soon as they've finished at the apartment. DS Stuart is on her way back from the wife's house. 'I suggest we crack on. Sarah, let's start with you.'

She opened the folder in front of her. 'It's pretty straight forward really. The cause of death is confirmed as ex-sanguination - loss of blood - due to a deep wound injury. The wound is consistent with stabbing. A single thrust with a thin bladed instrument; almost certainly a knife. The blade is estimated at fifteen point two four centimetres – or six inches to you and me – possibly with a saw toothed back, and a curved point. Mr Douglas says it's notoriously difficult to be precise because of the way the tissues sometimes respond, depending on how the knife is withdrawn. There are also two small rectangular bruises on the surface of the skin; indentations just broader than the width of the blade, and a few millimetres deep. He says that's consistent with the hilt or guard of a sheath knife, or a combat style knife. He estimates the time of death as being somewhere between 10pm and 2 am. He states that death will probably have occurred anything up to four hours after the attack,' she looked up. 'He can't be precise. It depends on the shock as much as the loss of blood. The knife punctured the spleen, which began to fill up like a great reservoir of blood that gradually leaked out into the stomach cavity. Hence the swelling to the abdomen Mr Douglas observed at the scene. Other than that, he was in perfect health for a man of his age. A bit of osteoarthritis in his right knee - probably from an old sporting injury – and some furring of the arteries; nothing that he would have noticed. According to Mr Douglas, had fate not intervened, he could have lived well into his eighties.

'With a bit of a limp,' the collator suggested. 'Either that or a plastic knee.'

'No defence wounds?' Caton asked her.

She shook her head, her hair swirling softly from side to side. 'No, his hands and his arms were completely fine, apart from some bruising where he must have struggled to loosen the tape.'

'So he wasn't expecting it.' Caton mused. 'Didn't have time to react.'

'Or he didn't see the knife at all,' she added.

'A sheath knife, or a combat knife. We don't see many of those these days do we Duggie?' Caton said.

'Not really. I can't remember the last time. It's normally a domestic knife; usually kitchen knives, or a pocket knife. We get more machete attacks these days than ones involving combat knives. They probably get more of those in the States, what with the hunting and survival culture. Drug addicts tend to use needles, broken glass, razor blades, even screw drivers. And as for sheath knives, I thought it was only boy scouts that still used those; and there's talk of banning them from carrying them.'

'Have we any more from forensics, on the car, and the crime scene?' Caton wanted to know.

'Only that there were some prints on the front passenger door handle.' DI Weston replied. 'But there should be something from Jack Benson's team by the end of today. Any DNA results are going to take longer than normal. With most of their staff on holiday, the Forensic Science Service lab in Euxton is estimating a minimum of three weeks.'

'What about the knife, the missing BlackBerry, his mobile phone, his briefcase?'

Again she shook her head. 'Nothing yet from the search teams. They've covered the whole of the park and the surrounding woodland, and the underwater team have covered an eight hundred yard stretch of the river Irk. With the limited rainfall we've had this summer it's only knee deep at the moment, and pretty clear.'

'What about footprints?'

'No joy there either I'm afraid. You've seen it for yourself. All hard surface, and there are that many people up and down in the course of a day, what's there is blurred.'

Caton had hoped for more than this. 'How about you, Duggie,' he said. 'What have you got for us?'

Wallace wiped the sweat from his hands on the sides of jeans, and opened the thick file in front of him. As the team's crime intelligence analyst, and senior collator, he was always expected to have a raft of information, and even this early in the investigation he didn't disappoint. The ring binder was already a quarter full.

'I thought we were working towards a paper free office?' Sarah Weston teased him gently.

'Unless you care to crowd round my PC, or have me clog up your email with thousands of attachments,' he began, rising to the bait.

'It's all right Duggie,' she said. 'I'm only pulling your leg.'

He was already lost in the file, leafing through table after table.

'You asked me to do three things,' he began. 'Put together a database of anyone with a previous for robbery in North Manchester; compile some background on the victim; and compile some information about the North Manchester Harmony Trust.' He bunched together the first six sheets of printout. 'Not as many as you might expect, but plenty to be going on with. Basically, we know that the majority of theft with intimidation or violence is carried out multiple times by the same group of perpetrators. So far we've separated these out into two categories; those which are generally premeditated and planned, and those which are opportunistic. The next step is to identify those which involve robbery from a car, either parked or stationary, at lights, or a junction. There is another parameter we are going to apply to all of these categories – namely, those which involve the use of a blade.'

He paused to see if there were any questions. Sarah Weston had one. 'Would you place the MO for this one as premeditated or opportunistic?'

Wallace looked up at her and smiled. 'Good question,' he said. 'The smashed window makes it look like it was on the spur of the moment, but unless our man has a habit of carrying a sizeable roll of duct tape around in his pocket, you'd have to say it was planned. Fortunately that's not a decision I have to make. But that's why we've got two categories,' he turned to Caton. 'Then you can choose sir.'

'Aside from the categories, have you come across any specific MO that fits?' Caton asked him.

'You mean car, knife, tape, concealment?'

Caton nodded.

'Not in North Manchester. I ran a general search on those to start with.' He flicked to the back of the sheaf of pages. 'There were just seventeen on the system in the past ten years, with all those features. Seven of those were clear intent to harm: five down as murder, two as kidnap and GBH. Two of the murders are still unsolved but, like the others, are assumed to have been hits of one kind or another. The taping and concealment was a prelude to torture in all but two of the cases. One of the murders was an honour killing. The rest were an assortment of rival gangs, accusations of grassing, and fall outs between villains.'

'And the other ten?' Weston asked.

'All sexually motivated. Seven were rape, three involved sexual abuse short of rape. All the victims were women. Four were committed by the same man, in the Southern Counties, now in custody.'

'Did any of those involve stabbing?' Caton prompted.

'No. Three involved cutting – superficial, ritual. No stabbing. Only in the murders.'

'So, no comparable modus operandi?'

'I wouldn't have said so.'

They considered it for a moment. Then Caton said, 'Tell us about Roger Standing.'

Wallace removed two sheets from a transparent envelope at the front of the file and passed them one each.

'This is his entry in *Who's Who.*'

Caton read it through twice.

STANDING, C.B.E; Roger Charles, Chief Executive, Harmony Business and Language Trust Manchester since 2002; *b* 4 September 1950; s of late Frederick Standing and the late Gwen Standing; *m* 1971; Margaret Withers; one son. *Edu:* Royal Masonic School Bushey; St John's College, Oxford; Headteacher: King Alfred's Grammar School Hastings, 1983; Headteacher: Nantwich College Grant Maintained School 1988; Awarded Commander of The British Empire for Services to Education 2005. *Publications:* The Schools In Question, 1986; Leadership for Schools in the New Millennium, 2001. *Address:* Beech Hall, 17 Middlewich Road, Nantwich CW5 5PD; *Clubs;* Alvaston Hall Golf Club.

'Think of the trouble it would save us if we had one of these every time we had a victim.' Observed Sarah Weston.

'It's what it doesn't tell us that I'm interested in.' Caton reflected. 'When was this entry made?'

'An entry first appeared in 2002. He was given the opportunity to update it annually.'

'So he became Chief Executive of the Harmony Trust before he got his CBE.'

'You don't have to have an honour to get in Who's Who.' Wallace told them. 'I checked. Frank Skinner, Jonathan Ross, Lenny Henry, Aled Jones, they're all in there. It tells you on the web site.' He read from his own sheet.

'Who's Who *seeks to recognise people whose prominence is inherited, or depending on office, or the result of ability which singles them out from their fellows'*. That's been their policy since it was founded in 1897.'

'So how did he get into it?' Caton asked. 'Propose himself? Send them a cheque?'

'Oh no.' The analyst looked genuinely shocked. 'You have to be invited. Then a selection panel meets to vet all of the nominations. They trawl the press and media for potential entrants, and I suppose people already in the book send them suggestions.'

'Not much chance for us then Sir?' Sarah joked.

'Not if we don't get on with it.' Caton said pointedly. 'What do you plan to do with this Duggie?'

'We're going to see what we can do to fill out the gaps, as you put it. There'll be a load of media coverage starting with his first appointment as a head in 1983. I've got one of the team starting there, and working forwards. I've got another starting with the coverage of his death, and working backwards. The two of them should meet up somewhere in the middle of next week.'

Caton checked to see if he was trying to make a joke of it. Head down, he was already consulting another sheet.

'The Harmony Trust was a response to two Government initiatives; City Academies, and Education Trusts. The clever thing about the way Standing approached this was that he put the two together in a proposal that far exceeded any of the original intentions. He persuaded Underhill to stump up far more of the matched funding than required, used the extra investment to persuade some of the primary schools to come in with him, and before anybody knew it, it was up and running; the first of its kind. State of the art building, bristling with new technology. The kids start learning foreign languages – including Mandarin – from the age of three would you believe? There's a strong student exchange programme with France, Italy, Germany, and China. And there's a large sixth form college that wasn't even in the original proposal.'

'How did he manage that?' Sarah Weston asked.

'Apparently he snuck it in just before the planning permission went through. BUCS came up with a wad of money, and by then he was the blue eyed boy of the Prime Minister; an irresistible force. The rest of the high school heads and college principals went spare; but the City Council - which got caught between them, Government pressure, and parents who wanted it - caved in.'

'BUCS is Barry Underhill Computer Systems?' Caton guessed.

'That's the acronym they use on their products, and brand marketing. It's a major conglomerate with its headquarters here in Manchester. Involved in an entirely web based sale and distribution network for a wide range of Computer and other IT based products worldwide.

'And the schools?'

He handed them another sheet. 'This is the latest Office For Standards in Education - Ofsted - Inspection Report Summary. As you can see it's in two parts. The first deals with the high school; the second, with the primary schools. The bottom line however, is in the first paragraph.'

"This is an excellent school with no weaknesses. Under the exceptional leadership of the Principal and his team there has been a significant improvement in the Standard Attainment Test results, at all key stages, and in every school in the Trust. Of particular note has been the improvement in the raw scores in the core subjects of English, mathematics, and science."

And so it continued. Standards of teaching, learning and behaviour, value for money, governance, everything was judged to be exemplary.

'I've put the web link at the bottom of the page. If you're feeling masochistic, or having trouble sleeping, you can download the entire report. You'll be asleep in no time. Mind you,' he added, confirming his status as the office nerd, 'The statistics at the back are interesting.'

Before either of them could comment there was a knock on the door and Gordon Holmes walked in followed closely by Nick Carter. Holmes had his jacket slung over his shoulder, his tie loosened, and the top two buttons of his shirt undone. He was sweating profusely.

'What do you want first, Boss?' he asked. 'The good news or the bad news?'

8

'Let's start with the bad,' said Caton. 'Then it can only get better.'

Holmes mopped his brow with a crumpled handkerchief. 'Nick and I have just come back from Standing's apartment. We did like you said. Put our shoe protectors and gloves on, gave it a basic sweep, didn't do anything to compromise a full forensic search. It's clean Boss.'

'Very clean,' DS Carter agreed.

'Too clean,' said Holmes, stuffing the handkerchief into his trouser pocket.

'In what way?' Caton asked him.

'It's not just that it was tidy. There wasn't any dust on anything. No smudges on the door handles or glass surfaces. The kitchen sink and the bathroom wash bowl, the bath, everything had been wiped clean. There were no towels on any of the hand rails. All of the litter bins had been emptied.'

'So the cleaner had been in?' Sarah Weston suggested.

Gordon Holmes shook his head. Small globules of sweat parted company with the tips of his hair, and settled on his shoulders where he made a vain attempt to brush them away.

'No, that was the first thing we checked with the concierge,' he said. 'He had a cleaner who came in by arrangement once a month; always when he was away. The concierge had to let her into the apartment. The last time she came was…'

Carter read from his notebook. 'Thursday 13th of July. Since then, he'd used the apartment on at least five occasions that the concierge knows of. The last of those was the evening before he died.'

'That the concierge knows of?' Said Caton.

'More often than not Standing let himself in through the entrance from the underground car park. There are no CCTV cameras there because the residents value their privacy almost as much as their security. There'll be a record on their system though, because they have to use an individual swipe card, and all of the entries are recorded electronically, by apartment key holder, time, and date.'

'We'll need a copy of that record.' Wallace remarked.

'It's in hand,' Holmes replied, picking up where he'd left off. 'We had a funny feeling about how clean and cold the place was, but the real clincher was his PC.' He paused for effect. 'The hard disc is missing. And this is the best bit. We asked the concierge if anyone had been into that flat before us. And guess what?' Another pause, pregnant with expectation. 'A couple of BT electricians turned up at 7.30am on Sunday morning. They showed him an emergency service request for Standing's apartment. His broadband link had allegedly packed in, and he needed it sorting for some work he was doing for the government that had to be emailed that afternoon. They said they needed to check the wiring and the modem. The concierge had no record of the request, and did all the right things. He tried Standing's mobile phone – no reply. He rang the BT contact number on the chitty, and spoke to their supervisor, who confirmed the request. So he got his assistant to take over, and accompanied them to the apartment, staying to keep an eye on them.'

'Don't tell me,' Sarah Weston said.

'Five minutes into the job, all looking pukka, his assistant called him to say she had a tricky situation at the desk. So he went down to deal with it. He reckons he was away no more than five minutes. When he got back, they'd finished, and were already packing up. Said it was just a matter of replacing the modem.'

'And the problem at the desk?' Caton said.

'Two guys who came and started giving her a bad time. They claimed they wanted details of the driver of a car that they said had pranged their car, and then driven at speed into the underground car park. Just as the concierge arrived, they did a runner.'

'And he didn't put two and two together?'

'She was bit upset. That probably disoriented him. He made sure she was alright, and then made his way back up to the apartment.'

'But all of this will be on their CCTV surely?'

'It was, and it is. He checked at the time to see if he recognised any of their faces. Thought they might be the same paparazzi that had started stalking some of their clients.'

'But?' Caton said.

'He wouldn't let us have a copy, He's so spooked by all of this he says he needs a warrant to cover his back. But he did let us have a look at it, which is why it's taken us so long.'

'And?' Sometimes, Caton reflected, it was just like drawing teeth. Gordon Holmes enjoyed the control that came with the drip, drip, disclosure. But then that's what made him such a good interviewer.'

'And the images are pretty good. We didn't recognise any of them, but wouldn't have any difficulty matching them up from mug shots, or in an identity parade.'

'So they are either stupid, or don't give a damn about being recognised.' Duggie Wallace suggested.

'And my money is on the latter.' Caton said. The implications were obvious, and worrying. The case was becoming more complicated by the hour. 'What about the phone number the BT technicians gave for their supervisor?' He asked.

'An automated response; *This number is not recognised.*' Holmes replied. 'The other reason we're late is that we rang BT, and when we did finally get through the maze of options, and find someone with the authority to respond, they confirmed what we already knew. It's not one of their numbers. And there's no record of any request or job reference relating to Standing's broadband line.'

'So what's the good news?'

'The briefcase has turned up. Empty. In a skip on Thornton Street; just before it runs into Collyhurst Street.'

'So, that's what; quarter of a mile from the crime scene?'

'A bit more,' Holmes told him. 'Six hundred yards, give or take.'

'So, assuming that was the direction of escape, we're looking at Collyhurst, Miles Platting, possibly

Newton Heath, or Moston?'

'*If*, the perpetrator was on foot.'

'But if he was in a car,' Caton reasoned. 'Why risk being seen dumping it in a skip that close to the crime scene? And let's face it, Thornton Street's not on an obvious escape route by car from the railway arches.'

Silence descended like a blanket while they mulled it over. Eventually Caton decided to move on. 'We need to see if we can get a match on those fingerprints as soon as possible.'

'Don't worry sir,' Sarah Weston assured him. 'Jack's team will be making that their number one priority, but I'll still double check.'

There was knock on the door. Ged had on her seriously apologetic look.

'I'm sorry Sir,' she said. 'Mr Benson's on your line. He'd like a word. He says it's urgent.'

Caton moved to his desk, and picked up.

'Hello Jack, we were just talking about you.'

'I'm afraid you're going to have something else to talk about now Boss.' The SOCO sounded sombre. 'I'm up at the school, in Standing's office. Someone's been here ahead of us.'

Caton cursed silently. He'd had a feeling that the premises manager wouldn't be able to resist having a snoop around. As an ex-copper he should have know better, but the lure would have been too strong. 'Payne?' He said, his brain in free fall, racing through homophones; *Payne of glass, Payne in the arse...*

'No Boss. They had a warrant.'

'Who had a warrant?' he asked, measuring each word carefully.

'Two officers from Special Branch.'

'Crispin and Warhurst.'

'How did you know that Boss?'

'Never mind that. When did they turn up?'

'At 1.37pm. They had two other men with them. Presented the warrant to the Headteacher. She got Payne to go with them. Payne and the Head both assumed they were part of our team, turning up like you'd said we would.'

Caton did the calculations. At that time of day it was about fifteen minutes drive from Longsight to the school, especially for someone who didn't know the rat runs. That gave them less than an hour and ten minutes from the time they'd left his office to apply for a warrant, collect it, and get up there. And who the hell had authorised the warrant? No magistrate would have signed it, he reasoned, without the investigating officer's signature. He had difficulty controlling the rage he felt welling up inside him.

'What did they take?'

'Payne says they were extremely professional. They'd obviously agreed beforehand who was going to do what. One of them went through all of the desk drawers. Another went through the box files and books on the shelves. A third checked the filing cabinets in his side room – there's a toilet, basin and wine rack in there by the way – and the fourth one checked the computer, downloaded some programmes, and then removed the hard drive, a portable back up storage unit, and a load of CDs and memory sticks. They also went on the PA's computer, and it looks like they've copied - contrary to the Data Protection Act - the computerised Staff and Pupil Records. Only she can't be sure about that.'

'What else did they take?'

'Not a lot. A couple of files, and a print out of Standing's work diary.'

Caton said nothing, contemplating the enormity of what this meant for his investigation, and for his position.'

'What do you want me to do now Boss?' Jack Benson asked tentatively.

Caton took a deep breath, and held it while he collected his thoughts. He breathed out slowly, and in again.

'Have a look round. See if there's anything they may have missed. Then get over to Standing's apartment and see if you can find any traces that might yield us fingerprints, or DNA. Because they've been there too.'

He replaced the phone and let it all out.

'The bastards!'

They stared at him in amazement. This was their Boss. Chief Inspector *politically correct* Tom Caton. The man who never swore – well not properly – didn't approve of others swearing, and never lost his temper; certainly not in front of his team. And here he was, incandescent. Later, in the safety of the canteen, Holmes would confide that he had fully expected the Boss to spontaneously combust.

'Are you alright Tom?' Sarah Weston ventured.

He looked up, aware of them for the first time since the phone had rung. The colour began to return to his face as his reptilian brain crawled back into its cave.

'I'm sorry,' he said. 'You'd better get on and leave me to deal with this.'

'With what Sir?' Holmes prodded.

Only then did it occur to him that they'd only heard his half of the conversation. He sat down in the swivel chair behind his desk, his fists clenched on the top of the arm rests.

'Special Branch paid me a visit at lunch time, hoping to get a complete update on our progress so far. They wouldn't tell me why, well not really why, nor did they have anything to trade. I sent them packing. Jack Benson has just rung to tell me that less than an hour and a half later they turned up at the school with a warrant, and searched Standing's office. They removed the computer hard disc, and a load of other evidence. I think we can assume they did the same thing at his apartment the morning that his body was found. Only without bothering to get a warrant.'

No one could think of anything to say. They were too busy trying to process it.

'So if you don't mind,' he continued. 'I'd like you to go back to the major incident room, record what you've just shared in here, and carry on with the investigation. I have some phone calls to make.'

The contrast between the icy manner in which he said this, and the explosion just moments before, spoke volumes. He had entered that zone where anything is possible. Including murder. In silence, they gathered up their things, and left.

Twenty minutes later Caton knew precisely where he stood. In the dark. His calls to Chief Superintendent Hadfield, Head of the Force Major Incident Team, had been fruitless. Hadfield was unavailable. Only when Caton became deliberately aggressive – in the full knowledge that all calls were recorded *for training purposes* – did Superintendent Helen Gates finally call him back. She claimed to be as surprised as Caton, and he believed her. She asked him to give her ten minutes, and when she did ring back it was worse than he'd imagined. The Chief Constable himself had authorised the warrant, and Hadfield had been told to prepare and take it personally to the magistrate. Apparently the Home Secretary had contacted the Chief Constable. All that Helen Gates had been able to discover was that it was a matter of national security, unrelated to Caton's investigation.

'Such as?'

'Come on Tom,' she said. 'You know as well as I do that Special Branch have a duty to support MI5 and MI6 on all matters relating to national security. There's no way you or I are going to find out what those are, unless they're prepared to tell us.'

'Just an indication of which areas would be a start.' Caton retorted: Public Order, Immigration, Nationalities, Witness Protection, Anti-Terrorism, Special Protection, Customs and Excise. What the hell are we talking about here? Why can't they just give us a clue?'

'There's no need to shout Detective Chief Inspector,' she said, retreating behind rank and formality.

'I think there is, Detective Superintendent,' he said, coming down a few decibels, determined to get this on the record. 'A Commander of The British Empire has been murdered. According to Chief Superintendent Hadfield, the Chief Constable is pressing for a speedy, and diplomatic solution. I now find that my investigation is being hampered, undermined and prejudiced, by the authorisation of warrants to a third party – or parties – enabling them to remove potentially crucial evidence without the knowledge of the senior investigating officer. I also have reason to believe that these same people have made a similar search and seizure of property from another address, without a warrant…'

'I think you should stop right there!' Helen Gates voice came through hard, and with just a trace of panic.

I bet you do. Caton thought to himself. 'And since neither the Chief Constable nor Mr Hadfield appear to have confidence in my ability to handle this investigation,' he said calmly. 'I would like to be relieved as SIO. I shall also have to consider resigning from the force.'

It was a hell of a risk. There was no way he really wanted to do either. The investigation had just become more intriguing, and his job was his life. Caton knew that had just come across as an arrogant chancer who believed they couldn't do without him. Well now he was about to find out, one way or the other. There was long pause on the other end of the line. When Gates did begin to speak, her tone had softened.

'Well if that is your position Tom, you know that I for one would be very sorry to see you go. Please don't do anything hasty. Just give me time to talk to a few people.'

'I'll be here,' he said, and put down the phone. There was nothing to do now, except wait.

Forty minutes later, the pile in the in-tray had gone down by two thirds. He took an A4 sheet of plain paper from the printer tray, and decided to tackle one of the questions about the crime scene that was

bugging him. At the top of the page he
question, *Why leave him in the trunk...still*
underlined it.

Beneath the title he listed the possibilit
occurred to him.

- The perpetrator didn't intend to kill him
- He thought he was dead
- He was repeating a specific scenario that
historical significance for him
- To make Standing suffer
- To extend the getaway period
- He wasn't afraid of being identified – didn't tape
the eyes. So was it a stranger he wouldn't recognise?
Or someone disguised?

He had begun to dissect each in turn when Helen
Gates rang back.

'Tom. I'm sorry it took so long. Firstly, Chief
Superintendent Hadfield sends his apologies for not
having been able to contact you personally before
signing the request for the warrant. His office did try,
but was unable to reach you.'

He could tell she didn't believe a word of it herself.
He let his silence speak volumes. It was, in any case,
as much of an apology as he'd ever get.

'As for the reason for the warrant, the Home
Secretary made it a direct request on grounds of
national security. All that I've been told is that there
were concerns that Mr Standing's death might have
had some connection with the security arrangements
for the forthcoming Labour Party conference.
Naturally that would be a concern for the security
services, and therefore for Special Branch, given

their role in sourcing intelligence for those services.'

Caton couldn't see it. What role was Standing supposed to have been playing? Was he carrying a copy of the security plan for the conference around in his briefcase? Not a chance. 'Even accepting that to be true,' he said. 'And I have my reservations, what prevented them telling me that, and suggesting a joint operation? We could have carried out the searches together, and shared the information.'

To her credit, Helen Gates didn't even attempt an answer.

'Chief Inspector Crispin will come to your office in the morning,' she said. 'And let you have all of the data that was removed from the school. In return, you are to give them every assistance in their investigation, and they'll reciprocate in yours.'

And pigs will fly Caton reflected.

'What about the hard disc from Standing's apartment, and anything else they found there?' he asked.

'I don't know anything about that.' she said.

Again, he believed her. 'Just tell them Ma'am, that's a precondition for my co-operation.'

It was sometime before she replied. When she did, it was clear from her tone that this was an exception; not to be repeated. Not ever. It betrayed her annoyance that he was using her as a messenger; and her frustration that it was Hadfield who had put her in that position in the first place.

'I'll tell them Chief Inspector.'

This time she hung up first.

It was approaching 10pm as Caton pulled into the car park inside the gated block, and climbed the steps to

the entrance of his apartment. He opened the door and entered the code in the key pad to switch off the alarm. The wall of warm air reminded him yet again what a mistake the developers had made not to have air conditioning installed. But then ten years ago they would never have heard of global warming.

The heat of the day seemed to have stored itself in the cavity walls, brick exterior, the stone flags, and the cobbled courtyard, only now to be released into the living space that was his one bed-roomed apartment. He picked up the remote for the Bosch ipod hifi player, clicked play, and walked through into the bedroom. Cold Play's *Trouble* filled the silence. Too near the truth. A spider's web, and him caught in the middle. He turned it down a notch, threw his jacket on the bed, and went into the wet room to splash his face with cold water. He dried his hands, and tried Kate's mobile. It was engaged. He sent her a text. Just thinking about their last dinner together reminded him that he hadn't eaten since lunch time. There was a solitary spaghetti bolognaise in the chiller. He lifted it out and put it in the microwave. The remains of a bottle of red wine sat on the work surface. He pulled out the vacuum stopper and sniffed. He poured a glass and took it over to the tiny desk that held his computer. There were 10 items in the Bulk folder. He sent them straight to the trash bin. The only one in his in-box was from Kate; a match for the three texts on his mobile.

Maesie's fine. I'm doing a load of reading. Where you up to? Can't wait till Wednesday. Luv U Kate. XXX

He moved it into his Kate folder just as the microwave pinged. The pasta had turned into a cloying mess. Undaunted, he grabbed a fork and some ketchup, and settled down on the sofa.

He had just finished eating when the phone rang. It was Nick Bateson, teacher of English, and the self-appointed secretary to the all male Alternatives reading group. Nick was on a high as usual.

'Tom. Glad I've caught you in. We've agreed on the book for next month. Right up your street. It's Ian Rankin's *Fleshmarket Close*. It was Craig who suggested it. He's got a great question too. Listen to this:

To what extent does this book represent a social commentary, as much as a novel of mystery, detection, and suspense?'

It sounded like one of Craig's. Caton thought it a bit close to home right now.

'I'm sorry, Nick,' he said. 'I don't think I can make it this week. I've just picked up a major investigation.'

'Don't tell me. Roger Standing?'

'It is, as a matter of fact.'

There was long low whistle at the other end of the phone. 'Bloody hell. That was a turn up wasn't it? The city's buzzing with it. Nobody's talking about anything else in the staff rooms.'

'How much do you know about him Nick?'

'Everybody in the profession knows about Roger Standing. Very good at promoting his school, the Trust, and himself. Too good, most people would say. Don't wish to speak ill of the dead Tom, but he wasn't well liked. Caused a lot of trouble when he moved up to Manchester.'

'In what way?'

'Put it this way. He wasn't a team player. We only

ever had one Grant Maintained School in Manchester, and that was a primary school. Sure, there's always been plenty of competition, but plenty of co-operation too. Standing didn't want to play. He put together that Trust without a second thought for the impact it would have on the rest of the city. As far as the rest of the world is concerned he's done a brilliant job. In reality, all he did was cream off some of the highest performing white middle class schools, in the least challenging areas of the city, and suck them into the Trust. Made the rest of us look pathetic.'

'But I heard he had a reputation for multi-culturalism?' Caton said.

Bateson snorted down the phone. 'He was a cunning beggar. He offset some of that imbalance by recruiting 60 pupils from the local community – predominantly Asian pupils from families with high aspirations, and the wherewithal to support them. All of those pupils would have been going to other schools – including mine – and pushing up *our* examination results. And he carefully weeded out any that were going to cause problems, or bring down the test scores. And that's not the half of it.'

'You seem to know a lot about it.'

'Everybody in the game does Tom. It's just the right wing press, and that lot down in London, who only sees what they want to.'

Caton was used to Nick's left wing principles, but it was long time since he could remember him getting this heated.

'Our Head of History used to teach at Disharmony High.' Bateson continued. 'He left because of

Standing. You could do with having a word with him. I could fix it up if you like?'

Caton considered it for a moment. 'Better not,' he said. 'It might look as though we haven't a clue, and we're fishing blind.'

It was only when he'd put down the phone that it occurred to him that that was precisely what they were doing.

Caton opened the window in the bedroom, and looked out at the lights dancing on the basin at Potato Wharf. The cool night air more than compensated for the hum of the city. He left the window ajar, pulled down the blind, turned back the cotton sheet, and plumped up the pillows to support his back. He checked the bedside alarm, and found the page marker in his latest read; *The Kite Runner*, by Khaled Hosseini. Much as he loved this city, there were times when it pulled him into scenarios that would not have been out of place in Amir's Kabul. He had found himself drawn into this novel, connecting strongly with the young protagonist. Partly, he realised, because like him he had lost his mother young – in his own case, his father too - but also because of the sense of guilt both he and Amir had carried into adulthood.

Twenty minutes later, the book slipped from his fingers, and his head sunk deep into the pillows. He dreamed that he was following close behind Amir and his friend Hassan as they chased a kite; bobbing and dipping across the slopes of Sandhills. Ahead of them, a group of Taliban with archetypal thick black beards, black cloaks and Pathan turbans, Kalashnikov rifles slung across their backs, whips in their hands, emerged from the tunnel in Sandhills to surround the car, and its unsuspecting occupant. Drawn by the screams from within the car, he crept up stealthily behind the shorter of the Taliban as the whip prepared to strike again. Beneath the arm, as it reached the zenith of its arc, he glimpsed a young woman shrinking into the furthest recesses of the car, hands raised to her face in self defence. She began to scream again. As she raised one hand to fend off the blow he caught sight of her face. Wide green eyes, a face that was deathly white. It was Kate.

He woke in a sweat. The light was still on. According to his alarm clock it was only 1.46am. He retrieved the book from the floor, put it back on the table, sorted the pillows, switched off the light, and lay on his right side facing the window. A slight breeze fluttered the hessian. Cheery youthful voices carried lightly across Castlefield from the twenty four hour party that was Manchester. An occasional car headed down Liverpool Street, its headlights blazing briefly against the blinds. In the fourteen years since his divorce, during which he had lived ostensibly as a single man, he had never felt this alone. It was only since he had taken up with Kate that he had come to appreciate the meaning of loneliness, and only then when they were apart. He tried to picture her fast asleep beside him in the bed. Her auburn hair like a bronze fan across the pillows forming a halo around her face.

The voices faded, and his eyes closed.

9

When the alarm woke him Caton felt more refreshed than he had for days. A glass of orange and cranberry juice, a banana, a quick shower and shave behind him, he climbed into his Skoda Octavia, and headed for Longsight.

As he waited at the lights at the bottom of Deansgate, he switched on the radio, and selected Radio Manchester. Just two months into it's re-incarnation it still came up on his screen as GMR. The cheerful North East accent of Deidre Oxenholme informed him that whilst the remnants of tropical storm Beryl were still plaguing parts of the South East and East Anglia, it would be another dry and hot day across the region, and very hot in Manchester, with temperatures expected to top thirty three degrees in the city centre. Long the butt of jokes by his friends in the south about Manchester the rainy city, he took a quiet delight in the fact this year at least the city enjoyed both sunshine and the absence of hosepipe bans. And if the predictions were to be believed, the balance could well be shifting on a permanent basis.

Caton was still smiling as he drove under the barrier and pulled in to the Metropolitan Division Headquarters car park. His mobile phone rang. It was Kate.

'Tom. I'm *so* sorry. It seemed like every time you rang I was talking to someone, and then when I rang back you'd switched off. I assumed you were in meetings. I didn't want to ring you last night because I remembered you said you were going to try to turn in early.' She sounded warm, and cosy and sexy. He guessed that she was still in bed.

'I was, and I did. I really missed you Kate.' It was the first time that he'd had the occasion to say those words. He could tell by the pause that she'd also the registered the fact, and was storing the memory.

'I missed you too Tom. Really missed you.'

'Where are you now?'

'In bed.' Her laugh was low, and provocative.

'Lucky you. I'm just at the office. About to find out who's running interference today.'

'As bad as that?'

'Worse.'

'Well you can tell me all about it tonight,' there was a slight pause and then she added. '*Afterwards.*' Charged with promise. Sexy as hell.

She hurried on before he could think of a suitable response. 'I'll be setting off when the rush hour dies down, but I promised Professor Stewart-Baker that I'd call in at the university. He's agreed to join a network trying to establish a common framework for offender profiling that could be used by both statistical and clinical profilers. He wants me to help him.'

'That sounds like a good idea. So long as it doesn't end up with you doing all the work, and him getting all the praise.'

'Oh Tom. You're turning into a real cynic.'

'If you'd had a day like I had yesterday, then so would you.'

'Well it sounds like you need cheering up, I know

I do. So how do you fancy the Comedy Store, followed by an Italian?'

He realised that it was exactly what he needed. 'Sounds good to me.'

'Leave it to me, Amore,' she said.

'Certo, e grazie bella Caterina.' He replied.

She laughed. 'Grazie mille. And Tom…' her voice suddenly deep and husky. 'Aspertami.' And with that parting shot she ended the call.

Aspertami. *Wait for me.* Caton knew that he had been busy marking time for the past 14 years, and that it was Kate that he had been waiting for.

They were all in the incident room. The progress chart on the whiteboard had been updated. One of the flipcharts had its pages turned to expose a fresh blank sheet. Nick Carter, Jack Benson, and Joanne Stuart had pulled up chairs, and were busy debating with Gordon Holmes, who was sitting on the edge of a table adjacent to the interactive white board. DCI Weston and Duggie Wallace, still at their desks, rose as he entered, and came across to join the others. Two of Duggie's team, and several detective constables, continued to beaver away at their terminals.

Most of the windows had been opened as far as the safety locks would allow, but it was still oppressive, and the day had hardly begun. Caton laid his jacket over the back of a chair, switched on one of the portable fans, and perched beside Gordon Holmes, his feet firmly on the floor, his hands gripping the table.

'Day Four,' he said briskly. 'We don't have any names, and we don't have any suspects. I'm getting grief from above and, as you probably all know by now, Special Branch, and God knows who else, is running interference. We need a breakthrough.' Sometimes stating the obvious helped to concentrate minds. Some of them murmured their assent, others nodded; the only feedback he needed. 'So Mr Benson,' he continued. 'Standing's apartment?'

Jack Benson had his notebook open on his lap. 'We've concluded our forensic examination. It wasn't difficult,' he added wryly. 'The flat had been wiped clean. There were just a couple of Standing's own prints on a light bulb. All in all, it looks like a really professional job; brand new bed linen; thoroughly hoovered; new razor, face cloths, towels, the lot.' He looked up. 'Sanitised, is the best way to describe it.'

'No DNA?'

He shook his head. 'We would have relied on hairs in the bed, bathroom, toilet, in hair brushes or combs, by the dressing table, on the floor under mirrors, on kitchen towels, saliva on guest toothbrushes, dirty cups and glasses. You know the routine. All of them were either absent or replaced.'

'Was there anything else missing?' Caton asked him.

'I'm sorry Sir. Since we don't know for certain what was there in the first place, I'm not really able to answer that. There was no hard disc, nor any floppies, so I think we can assume they'd been taken. The only CDs, DVDs and tapes, were commercially produced ones, and we would have expected there to have been some blanks, or ones which had been home taped, or amateur filmed. No sign of a diary, or letters. But, given this was just his town pad, all of that's pure guess work.'

Holmes stood to ease his backside for a moment. 'Assuming it was Special Branch, how the hell did they get there so quickly?' he asked, echoing Caton's thoughts. 'We'd only just found out ourselves that it was him, and that he was dead.'

'They had six hours from the time the body was found, and the licence plate traced.' Caton reflected. 'You'd be surprised what the intelligence services can put together in that time.'

'Intelligence services? So you *do* reckon MI5 was in on it Boss?' Nick Carter said.

'I don't know.' Caton replied. 'But it has to be an option. Either way, it affects how we take this investigation forward. Chester House insists that we have to co-operate with Special Branch. So be it. But I want to make it crystal clear that this remains *our* investigation. We keep our cards close to our chests. Every document, every file, is password protected from now on. There'll be no off the record briefings, with them or anyone else. If they want to know anything they'll have to come through me. And when they do, it's going to be minimum disclosure. Is that clear?'

There was a mixed chorus of agreement littered with 'Sir' and 'Boss', and much sage nodding of heads. He was about to continue when one of Benson's team slipped his team leader a thin file, and whispered in his ear. Caton could see from Benson's expression that it was significant.

'Mr Benson? Have you something for us?' He said.

'Yes Sir. We've got a match for fingerprints from the briefcase and the passenger door handle. They both belong to the same person.' There was a corporate murmur as he consulted the file. 'Danny Quinn – nineteen year old petty thief, with twelve previous: three for burglary, six for street robbery – mainly mobile phones and money from younger kids – three for shoplifting. He's had two periods of community service, and three spells inside: one of three months, two of six months. The usual story. In care since he was nine. Mother a crack head, father absent from day one. When he was fifteen he stopped attending school. Started shoplifting, and robbing from other kids. When he had to leave care at seventeen he had no qualifications, no job, so he stepped up to burglary just to make ends meet.'

'Does he have a drug habit?' DS Stuart wondered.

'Not to speak of. A few times when he was arrested he had small amounts of recreational substances for personal use. Could have been done for possession. Probably deemed not to be worth the hassle, what with the other offences on the charge sheet.'

'Tell your team well done Jack,' said Caton. He stood up and went over to the progress chart, to see if there was anything he'd missed.

Duggie,' he said. 'What about Standing's BlackBerry; have we got anything on that yet?'

Duggie Wallace shook his head. 'I'm afraid not Boss. Apparently, it hasn't been switched on, let alone used, since last Saturday afternoon. I'm still waiting for them to send me his phone records for the last three months.'

'Well tell them it's really urgent, and see what else you can get on Quinn. Gordon, Nick, I want you to work together on tracking him down and bringing him in. Sarah, see if you can speed up the DNA – even if they do a have a stack of people on holiday they should be able to deliver the seventy two hour fast track for a high profile case like this. Tell them it's the Chief Constable's directive. Joanne, I want you to fill out Standing's background. I'm going back up to the school to see if I can find out what he was working on, and then you and I are going to call on the widow and her son. Any questions?' There were plenty of his own he could think of, but none that they had for him right now.

The staff car park was full. All of the visitor spaces had been taken. Only the bays marked *Chair of Governors* and *Chief Executive* were free. Caton pulled into the one marked *Principal*. Standing wouldn't be needing it now.

Sandra Given insisted on giving him the guided tour. Whether she intended it as a distraction or not, it suited his purposes. The odds were that the murder would either be about Standing's private life, or his work, and he needed to know as much as possible about both. Not just know; understand. He had to get right inside them. He'd learned early on in his career that motives were either staring you in the face, or buried deep, under layer after layer.

This one had archaeology written all over it.

Two hours later, he wondered if he was any further on. His mind was a jumble of wood and steel, aluminium and glass. Of wide sweeping corridors, and classrooms equipped with ergonomically designed chairs and tables, and individual electronic student tablets linked by wireless to the interactive whiteboards. There were special preparation and study rooms for staff, and a university standard library and study centre for the students. Language laboratories were linked directly to the Languages Resource Centre at the University of Salford, and the Centre for Chinese Studies at Manchester University. He had been astounded by the quality of the science laboratories and technology workshops, and the three lecture theatres. Much as he had gained from the then impressive facilities at Manchester Grammar School he would have loved to have had the opportunities that Harmony High offered; the huge sports hall, with its climbing wall and an indoor 80 metre track, long jump and high jump pits and cages for the throws, and the acres of sports fields with hard courts for tennis and football and hockey and netball. In addition to all this, he knew that they still had access to Boggart Hall Clough for cross country and outdoor athletics. But none of this told him anything new.

Nor had the interviews with Given, her deputy and assistant heads, the premises manager, and Standing's personal assistant. He'd gained the impression that Given was damning her former boss with faint praise, still far more concerned with how she was going to take the school and the Trust forward. Her deputy and assistant heads had been almost sycophantic in their praise of Standing; a foretaste, he predicted, of the funeral eulogy. But each of them, in their own way, had been more circumspect, guarded, cautious, than he had expected. A sure sign that there were things they could have said, but didn't.

Ronnie Payne, the premises manager, was the last to be interviewed. Caton hoped he might be more forthcoming given that he'd been on the force, had only been working here for a relatively short time, and as a non teacher might see himself outside that clique

Payne began by insisting that they go for a stroll. 'Walls have ears.' He said cryptically.

'Really?' Said Caton, given all that technology it might just be true.

'No.' Said Payne with a grin. 'I just fancy a breath of fresh air. But then, you never know.' Paranoid or not, he waited until they were clear of the building before starting. 'He was a funny guy,' he said. 'Bit of a mystery if you ask me. An enigma. You could never tell what he was thinking. He was always rushing. To a meeting, from a meeting; he could never spare a moment for a brief conversation. Passing the time of day would have been a waste of precious time for him. I suppose that's why nobody really liked him, not really. He was alright with me though. He was forever civil, sometimes he even smiled. Always had a smile for the students too, especially the girls.'

'Had he seemed any different lately?'

'Not that I noticed. To tell the truth he never seemed any different. Always busy, always above it all, like his head was somewhere else; which it probably was.'

A waste of time, Caton decided as he climbed into his car. Except for the time he'd spent with Roisin Murphy, the PA. She'd wept buckets. Between sobs she'd said something that echoed Payne, and in its own way was quite revealing.

'None of them liked him you know. Only me. I was the only one who really knew him. Really understood him.'

Really loved him, more like, he decided as he

fastened his seat belt. It hadn't been the right moment
to push a bit further, but that time would come. First
there was a lot more he needed to discover about the
late Roger Standing.

Back at Longsight it was evident there had been
limited progress in the hunt for Danny Quinn.
Everywhere the search teams had been someone had
already been there asking about the missing youth.
There were various descriptions of these inquisitors.
Several people recalled them saying they were *'with
the police'* but no one remembered the names they
gave, or even if they'd offered them. Caton had an
overwhelming feeling that it was vital that his team
got to Quinn first.

He was still pondering that when Ged came over
to tell him that Warhurst, and a Special Branch
colleague she'd never seen before, had dropped off
two cardboard boxes containing hard discs, floppies,
data sticks, and documents.

'*These are for Caton.* They said.'

'Did they say anything else?'

'They did ask how the investigation was going on.
I could see that they were trying to sneak a look at the
progress board, but we'd thrown a cover over it as
soon as reception rang to say they'd arrived.'

That made him smile. 'Good for you. What did you
tell them?'

'I told them that they'd have to ask you. I said
you'd be back anytime if they wanted to wait in the
canteen, or downstairs.'

'And?'

'They looked at each other, shrugged, and left.'

'Ged, you're a marvel.'

Duggie Wallace came to join them. 'Can I have a word Sir?' He asked. 'It's the data that Special Branch brought in. We're still going through all the stuff from his office at the school but it looks pretty innocuous. The hard disc from his apartment is suspiciously empty. Just some files that look to have been sent as attachments from the school hard disc. And all the emails have been deleted up to the day on which he died. Worse than that, I can usually recover most of the deleted files but someone who knows what they're doing has permanently wiped them. I've also got a suspicion that the time and date clocks have been reset.'

'Standing, or Special Branch?'

'Impossible to tell sir. But if I had to put my money on it, I'd say this was a specialist job.'

Caton chewed it over as he headed back to his office to collect his jacket, and to let DS Stuart know he was ready for the drive to Nantwich.

"Thank you Madeline. And now, here is Amelia with the latest from the Met. Office."

"Thank you Josh. Heavy thunderstorms over the southern half of England have spread to much of East Anglia, as far north as Lincolnshire, where gusts of sixty knots have been recorded. The heavy rain has created hazardous driving conditions in Surrey, and flash floods in Milton Keynes. There has been a landslip on the London Underground towards Heathrow. The temperature in London today is expected to peak at around thirty four degrees centigrade. Elsewhere…"

Caton switched off the radio, and looked up at the

huge pair of wrought iron gates. At their centre was a coat of arms. On a silver shield a black chevron, like an inverted V, separated a trio of three leaved clovers. On top of the shield sat a buck deer, atop a silver knight's helmet. Below the shield ran a motto: *Vivite et Amate, Semper Suspicientos*.   Caton searched his memory banks.

'Live and Love, Always Look Upward,' he told her. 'Something like that. Not bad as mottos go.'

'Except, in his case,' DS Stuart reflected. '*Always* was hardly as long as he might have hoped,'

The camera on top of the wall moved slowly on its axis. A moment later the gates swung inwards. Caton drove slowly up the sweeping drive, towards a house that rose like a mirage above the shimmering haze on the tarmac surface. In the centre of a gravel circle, blue water gushed from the mouth of a dolphin fountain. Caton parked at ten o'clock, and switched off the engine.

Facing them was a large Victorian mock Tudor mansion; a dozen double bedrooms at least, and probably as many bathrooms.

'It's very impressive isn't it Sir?'

'It is Jo; not to my taste, but impressive.'

'You haven't been inside yet.' she said, unbuckling her seat belt and smoothing her trousers. 'Prepare yourself.'

10

John Standing opened the door. At five feet six inches tall, muscular with a tendency towards leanness, he looked older than his thirty two years. His dark brown hair, cut moderately short, was lightly gelled, to give a tousled appearance above intelligent eyes, a firm mouth, and strong chin. Caton decided that most women would find this young man attractive, despite the sombre expression on his face.

For her part, Joanne Stuart was reflecting on how like her boss he was. Four years younger, and getting on for six inches shorter than Caton, but in all other respects a dead ringer. She'd had the same thought when he'd walked confidently into the departures hall at the airport. Now that she could see them together, it was even more obvious.

John Standing took his time appraising them. 'Come in,' he said at last, standing to one side. 'My mother is in the drawing room. She's expecting you.'

They entered a large marble floored hallway with doors to either side. A broad marble staircase, with wrought iron rails and balustrade, branched to left and right on each of two floors. At the centre of the first landing a gilded bronze nude female dancer, almost certainly art deco, took pride of place on a marble plinth, supported on a simple stone stand.

Muscles taut, reaching up from the point of her right foot, left knee raised and bent, her arms stretched skywards. The arching back allowed her head to fall, expressionless, almost level with her waist. Caton thought it the most beautiful and poignant figure he had ever seen outside of a museum or gallery. Wood panelled walls were decorated with wall hangings, each approximately a metre high and a third of a metre wide; almost certainly copies of medieval tapestries. On one side of the front doors was a large wooden trunk with iron handles; on the other an ornate cabinet stood over a metre high. On either side of each of the interior doors were matched pairs of high curve-backed wooden chairs. Above the centre of the hall hung a large iron chandelier.

It was beyond Caton how anyone could live in such a place. It should have felt warm and inviting. Instead, it felt cold, alien, and pretentious.

'I told you so,' whispered Joanne Stuart as they followed John Standing through the first of the doors on the left. It opened into a large sitting room with wooden floors and a scattering of rugs; cream sofas with gold cushions, and matching gold curtains. Ceramic figures and porcelain pots occupied various cabinets, several of them glass fronted. Unopened on the carved wooden coffee table lay a scattering of magazines and newspapers.

Mrs Standing stood beside and to the left of the large stone fireplace, the wood burning grate partly hidden by an ornate lacquered screen. Beside the screen a metal gong and a felt headed mallet hung from a glossy black wooden stand. What Caton assumed to be cards of condolence lay on their sides on the mantle piece in seven neat piles, as though someone had been in the process of sorting them.

'Mrs Standing,' he said. 'Thank you for agreeing to see us.'

She waved them towards the largest of the sofas. 'I wasn't aware that I had a choice.

'I'm sorry…' he began.

She waved his apology aside. 'What would you like; tea or coffee?'

'Coffee for me please, milk no sugar,' said Joanne Stuart.

'Just hot water for me please.' Caton added.

She looked at him quizzically. It was a reaction he was getting used to.

'I decided to cut down on tea and coffee some years ago,' he told her. 'I was finding it difficult to sleep at night, and when the doctor found out what my caffeine consumption was it was the first suggestion he made. Now I rarely have either this side of lunchtime.'

She moved away from the fireplace and sat facing them on the edge of an armchair. 'Very wise. Although my husband always insisted that green tea has significant health giving benefits, including protection against heart disease and cancer.' She turned to her son who was still standing to the right of the fireplace. 'John could you bring the officers a drink. I shall have an Earl Grey, with lemon.'

Caton asked how long she had lived in the house. She responded by asked what he thought of it, and was quick to notice his hesitation.

'It's all right,' she said. 'It was my husband's creation. In fact, I'm putting it on the market next week.'

'Where will you move to?' Joanne Stuart asked.

She smiled thinly. 'Oh, I'll stay around here. John wanted me to move to France and live with him, but I have my friends, the church, the amateur dramatics society; I may even join the WI and the local Ramblers.'

'Nantwich won't hold too many memories for you then?'

She looked up sharply. 'Oh it *will* have memories, but only those I choose. My husband was rarely here you see, and to be honest, I have always found this house depressing.'

Her son returned with the drinks on a tray. She reached forward for hers, and took a sip. As she placed the cup back on its saucer he perched on the arm of her chair and placed a hand supportively on hers.

'This is upsetting for my mother Chief Inspector,' he said. 'And I'm sure that you didn't come here to talk about the housekeeper, the house, or how my mother is going to move on with her life.'

It seemed to Caton that Margaret Standing was more angry than upset. Not an uncommon response to murder in his experience, but it was somehow distracted; not directed towards the murderer, or even the act of murder. He would have liked to pursue this further, but the son had a point. It was time to be a little more direct.

'You're quite right,' he said, 'However, if you could indulge me a little longer, there are few background questions I need to ask. It'll save us all a lot of time later.'

'It's alright John,' she said calmly. 'Ask away Mr Caton.'

'Thank you Mrs Standing,' he said. 'When did you first meet your husband?'

She cradled the cup in her hands. 'At university. We were both up at Oxford together, although I started a year later than him. I was at St Hilda's, reading Mathematics, my husband, at St John's, reading Modern Languages. In his second year he switched to Oriental Studies, which meant him doing an extra year, and the two of us graduated at the same time. He proposed at the May Ball in our final year, and we married later that year. A Christmas wedding.' She paused and set her cup down on the table. It had all come out without a shred of emotion; as though she was reading from a newspaper obituary about complete strangers.

'Did you both begin working as soon as you left University?'

'Yes. I began teaching at a large mixed comprehensive, my husband at the neighbouring grammar school.'

Caton noticed a hint of wistfulness in her voice.

'She was promoted to Head of Department in less than two years,' her son told them. 'Long before *he* got his first promotion.' He turned back to his mother. 'You could have been a Headteacher too; a good one.'

'I gave that up when…' she paused as though checking herself, '…John was born, and, when he was old enough, I went back part time for a while.'

'He discouraged her.' John Standing said bitterly.

'My husband felt that it was no longer necessary for me to work. And there was a lot of entertaining. It was easier that way.'

'Easier for him!' Her son retorted.

'How about you, Mr Standing,' Caton asked. 'Did you go to university?'

The son got up and walked away over to the bay windows. He stared out over the manicured lawns. His face was in partial shadow, making it difficult to read.

'Yes I went to university,' he said. 'Loughborough, I came away with an International Business BSc. Because our father brought us up to be bilingual – trilingual if you include a smattering of Mandarin – I was already fluent in French, so I took the Spanish option. In my third year of four, I did six months in France, and six in Spain.

'Did you go into business, or follow your parents into teaching?'

'Both. I have my own business teaching English to businesses and corporations from Paris down to the Cote D'Azur.'

'That sounds like a lot of work for one person?'

'It would be. But I hire qualified teachers of English as a foreign language, and train them to my own standards and systems. I use a similar approach to that used to train the SAS; a mixture of IT based packages, and total immersion.'

'Do you live in France?'

He turned then and came towards them, emerging wraithlike from the shadows.

'I've lived in Avignon for the past ten years. There are fast links to most parts of France, by train or plane. I'm about to extend the business into Spain.'

'Your father must have been proud of you.' Caton said. It would have been a logical thing to say, but he was also looking for any reaction. It appeared to take

Standing by surprise. He stopped in his tracks, measuring his reply.

'To be honest,' he said, 'I wouldn't know.'

For a moment it seemed that his mother might be about say something; perhaps to reassure her son. But if she was, she thought better of it.

'I realise that you must have given this some thought,' Caton said. 'But it's now quite clear that somebody murdered your husband Mrs Standing. It may have been the result of a chance encounter. We do know that his briefcase was stolen. But it could also have been a deliberate and premeditated act, and until we can rule that out we have to pursue it as a possibility.'

'Wouldn't you be better off pursuing the thief Chief Inspector?' The son asked with barely masked contempt.

Caton refused to rise to the bait. 'We are doing that Mr Standing. In fact we have a promising line of enquiry. But in the meantime it would be very helpful if you could humour me, and tell us if you were aware of any threats, however wild and improbable, against your father. Or of anyone who may have harboured a grudge against him. However insignificant that may have seemed to you.'

DS Stuart sat with her notebook open, and her biro poised.

'John?' said Mrs Standing pointedly.

'I'm sorry,' Standing replied. 'But I can't help you. There may have been the odd disappointed job applicant, or member of staff who resented his high expectations. I suppose there was the odd parent who couldn't get his kid into the school, or one whose son he'd kicked out. There may even have been loonies who resented his political views. But I wouldn't have known if that was the case. And let's face it; none of them stack up as a good enough motive for murder. In any case I was in Avignon. How would I know?'

Caton turned to the mother. 'Mrs Standing?'

Her reply was slow and deliberate. 'John seems to have covered all of the possibilities that occurred to me, and a few more besides. My husband was not always an easy man to work with, or to like. But it's inconceivable that anyone would want to kill him for such trivial motives.'

The son moved to stand beside his mother, and placed one hand on the back of her chair. 'If that's all Chief Inspector, perhaps we could leave it there; my mother is very tired.

Weary, was the word Caton would have used. And not, he surmised, just from the events of this week. He checked with DS Stuart, who shook her head so slightly he almost missed it.

'I don't think we need to trouble you any further today,' he said pushing himself out of a sofa far too low for a man of his height. 'How long will you be staying with your mother Mr Standing?'

'At least until after the funeral. Perhaps you could give us some indication of how soon we can arrange that for?'

'That's really a matter for the Coroner,' Caton told him. 'But since the cause of death has been established, and the Coroner's verdict is almost certainly a foregone conclusion, I would have thought that in this case you should be free to arrange the funeral in something like a week to ten days from now. I'll make sure the coroner's office contacts you.'

'Thank you Mr Caton,' the widow said, her voice devoid of emotion.

'There is just one thing,' Caton hesitated. This was always a difficult question to broach. 'Will your husband be cremated or interred?'

A look passed between mother and son exchanging an secret thought that Caton would dearly have loved to unlock.

'Why Chief Inspector? Will that make a difference?' John Standing asked.

'I'm afraid it might. In certain circumstances it may subsequently become necessary to exhume a body. Particularly where the defence raises an objection to the forensic evidence, or where additional evidence becomes available. But I would think it highly unlikely in this case. It's just that with cremation that possibility would be ruled out, and justice might never be done. In which case, just to be on the safe side we might have to delay the funeral to carry out even more exhaustive, and probably unnecessary, tests.'

Margaret Caton stood, and folded her hands in front of her. 'Some years ago my husband made it clear that he wanted to be buried. Unfortunately, we never got to discuss exactly where, and his solicitor has confirmed that it was not a matter raised in his will, or any of his other papers. His first choice would probably have been the parish church in Nantwich, had that been possible,' she said.

'Westminster Cathedral, more like.' Her son suggested bitterly.

She reached behind her and placed her hand on his, squeezing tightly. 'There is a pleasant cemetery at

Coppenhall, between here and Nantwich,' she said. 'It has a church within the grounds, and is the oldest in the area. I'm sure that would be suitable.'

'If it's alright with you, I would like to attend the funeral Mrs Standing.' Caton said.

'I understand,' she said; and it was clear from her expression that she did. 'But I should tell you that it will be a quiet and private affair. My husband's parents are dead, and he had no siblings. I've decided against an open reception. It would only turn into a jamboree. I understand a memorial service is to be arranged. Those that wish to pay their respects can wait till then.'

'Nevertheless, I would like to come.'

She nodded her head. 'John will show you out.'

As they reached the door she called after them. 'You *will* let us know when you catch him?'

There was something in her voice. Caton turned back to look at her. Whereas before she had looked and sounded strong, now she seemed frail, and weary. Not like the widows with whom he had had such conversations in the past – angry, shocked, and remote - more like a lost soul clinging to a raft in an empty ocean.

Standing led them through the hallway to the front door, and watched in silence as they crunched across the gravel.

'Very impressive Mr Standing.' Caton called out as he and DS Stuart passed the fountain.

'He used to have carp in there, but they died.' Standing replied, one hand on the door jamb.

They heard the heavy door close, and the latch drop, and were alone on the drive.

'I said you'd be surprised, Sir. In more ways than one.'

'Let's wait till we get out of here, Jo,' he said, opening the driver's door. 'This place gives me the creeps.'

They were well on the road before she judged he was ready to talk. 'Did you notice he never referred to him as his father, or dad, – always *he, or him*?'

'Yes Jo, I did. And Mrs Standing never used his first name either. Always *my husband* or *he.*'

'And there wasn't a single family photograph to be seen,' she added. Caton nodded; his eyes on the road, his mind going back over the conversations.

'Is that right about releasing the body Sir?' she asked. 'What do you think they were thinking, you know, when you asked them the one about cremation or burial?

'God knows,' he replied. 'My instinct was they would both have loved to cremate him, and scatter his ashes somewhere unpleasant.'

'I had the very same thought,' she said, flicking back through her notes. 'We can't both be wrong can we?'

They were approaching a bend, and Caton was riding the crown of the road. A black BMW appeared suddenly on the opposite side, its front wheels over the centre line. Caton swerved to avoid it, cursing his lack of concentration. Joanne Stuart clutched the grab handle, and pressed her other hand against the dashboard. The other driver screamed by, pumping the horn, mouthing obscenity.

With the car back under control, and the adrenalin leaching away, Caton turned his attention to the road ahead.

11

Caton followed Kate as they stepped out from the heat of the Comedy Store into the relative cool of the late evening air. They stood for a while leaning on the walkway railings, looking down at the pink and blue reflections on the surface of the canal. The colours threw highlights over Kate's glossy auburn hair, white blouse and linen skirt.

'That was fun,' she said, her eyes the colour of green turquoise.

'It was, until he went into his stupid coppers routine,' he said miserably. 'How do they do that?'

'Know that you're a policeman? He probably never would have done if you hadn't winced, and put your glass up in front of your face, when he asked if there were any policemen in the house. Call yourself a detective?'

Her laugh was light, her presence reassuring. She linked her arm with his as they pushed their way through the throng heading for the bars beside The Locks, across the bridge, and down the steps to the pavement, where a gaggle of girls with mini skirt pelmets, bare bejewelled midriffs and skimpy tops, waited in a binge fuelled haze for taxis and limousines.

Ten minutes later they entered Cockatoo's, passed under the copy of the Sistine Chapel Roof painted on the plastered brick of the railway arch, and were seated at a corner table, sipping Tedeschi Recioto Classico, Monte Fontana 2003 as they waited for the garlic bread.

'What do you think?' Caton asked.

She tilted the glass slightly, swirling the deep, dark, almost purple wine, against the white table cloth. She held it to her nose, and breathed in deeply.

'Alluring to the eye, intense to the nose, like a bowl full of summer berries.'

She took a large sip and rolled it around her tongue before letting it slip slowly down her throat. 'Full on the palate, masses of fruit – a little young perhaps – piles of tannin and moderate acidity. You can almost feel the heat of the vintage. She put the glass down on the table. 'It's gorgeous.'

'Just like you.' He said.

She arched her eyebrows. 'Alluring, intense, gorgeous?'

'A little young, with moderate acidity.'

She kicked him under the table.

He rubbed his shin. 'That hurt.'

'You asked for it,' she said grinning at his discomfort.

'Well it served you right for fishing for compliments.'

'I didn't,' she said grinning. 'I was just reading the label.'

They collapsed in a fit of giggles. People on the neighbouring table turned to look at them, before returning to their conversation.

'That's better,' Kate said when they'd both recovered. 'It took you ages to loosen up in the Comedy Store.'

'I know,' he said. 'I'm sorry, It's this case. It's really bugging me.'

'Roger Standing?'

'Yes.'

The garlic bread arrived, closely followed by his squid risotto and her penne arabatica.

'I met him once,' she said, tearing off a piece of the bread.

'How was that?'

'It's a couple of years back; not long after the academy opened. One of my undergrad' students was mentoring two of his sixth form pupils.

Caton finished a mouthful, and took a sip of wine. 'How did you find him?'

'Really creepy. He had those come to bed eyes. I could feel him mentally undressing me. A woman can always tell. If I didn't know better, I would have put him down as a serial womaniser.'

An alarm went off, and the light came on in the room in Caton's head where he stored his case files. It chimed with something Payne had said.

'Always had a smile for the students too, especially the girls.' It had escaped him at the time, but now…

'Speaking of which,' Kate said, leaning forward, her pupils dilating; tiny flecks of brown floating around on deep green pools. 'Shall we skip dessert?'

Caton emerged from a dreamless sleep. The pillow was wet, his hair cool and sleek against his forehead. He tried to stretch, and found himself trapped between the warm curves of Kate's body, and her left arm thrown carelessly across his chest. Her breasts formed a soft damp cushion against his back. With both of their knees pulled up into a spoon, her thighs and stomach held him fast, one leg tucked between his.

He wanted to stay like this, to ignore the insistent buzz of the alarm on his mobile phone a couple of feet away; to recall the urgency with which they had fallen upon each other, the abandon that explained why he was here, on the wrong side of the bed. He knew from the stirring in his groin that he had to go now, or selfishly disturb her sleep and turn up late for only the second time since he'd taken over the team. He took her hand, and gently lifted her arm until it rested on her thigh. He lay still for a moment, listening to the steady rhythm of her breathing, feeling the warmth of her breath on his neck. It was a sensation, reassuring and affirming, he had forgotten, and only re-discovered when she'd entered his life less than a year ago. He rolled slowly to his left, and slid onto his stomach until he was able to put one foot on the floor, and lever himself gently from the bed. He picked his way through the tangle of sheets and hastily discarded clothes to the other side of the bed, picked up his mobile, and cancelled the alarm.

She lay naked where he'd left her. One arm cradled her head, half hidden beneath the tumble of shoulder length hair. Her skin was smooth and white in the half light of early morning; the light tan she had picked up during their week in Venice already beginning to fade. He picked up his clothes from the floor, quietly took a fresh pair of shorts and socks from a drawer, and went through to the wet room.

Showered, shaved, and dressed, he made enough toast for the two of them, poured two fruit juices, and waited for the coffee that kick-started Kate's day to percolate. Through the kitchen window, in the gap between the Y Club and the YMCA hostel, he could see a man giving his hand to a woman climbing out of their gaudily painted narrowboat down on the Wharf. He had a pang of guilt that it had been over a week since he'd managed a session at the club. He missed it all; the jogging machine, the weights, and the swim. But he was young enough to go a week or two without it. And let's face it he told himself, you had plenty of exercise last night.

He carried the tray through, and placed it on the cabinet beside the bed. Kate began to stir. Her eyes opened, and she smiled. He bent over and kissed her lightly, smelling the dampness of her hair, and the sweet pool of sweat in the cleft of her breasts.

'What time is it?' she asked dreamily.

'It's only five past six,' he said. 'I'm sorry, but it's going to be a long day and I've got a mountain of paper to shift before the briefing. I've brought you some breakfast. I know it's early, but I thought you might be hungry. You can always go back to sleep.'

She smiled, pulled her knees up, and wiggled her toes. 'Course I'm hungry. We burned our fair share of calories last night.'

He bent to kiss her again, but she pushed him away gently. 'Pass me the sheet Tom. I'm getting cold.'

She wrapped it around herself, leaving her arms and shoulders free. 'That's better,' she said. 'Now you can kiss me.'

Caton looked at the clock on the wall. It was ten to eight. They would be getting their coffees and preparing for the briefing. He put the last of the documents in his out tray, and slid the chair back. He was still basking in the knowledge that this was really love; proper, adult, grown up love. Way beyond the first flush of a new relationship. He'd been worried that the trauma of the Bojangles case might have affected such a fragile beginning. If anything it had strengthened their bond. And in some ways it was it was even better now that the two of them weren't working together. They could offload on each other without expecting a response. Just like a married couple. The phrase had popped up like an unwelcome guest. He pushed it aside and reached for the Standing file.

The Standing investigation. It sounded odd somehow. Probably better than Holmes' alternative – *The Head Case* – which Caton knew they were all using informally. After his visit with Jo to the baronial home in Nantwich, he was beginning to think they had a point. He flipped it open, picked up his pen, and began to make notes in the margins.

The briefing was as it should be; brief. There was little to report, and the hunt for Danny Quinn frustrating. Everywhere they went he had been, and gone. And the mystery seekers were always one step ahead of them. Their paths had never crossed, despite the fact that there were three of his own teams out there. Caton was telling them that he wanted all of the web references and press cuttings they could find on Roger Standing, plus a full biography, anything they could find out about his marriage, and especially his links to Barry Underhill, when Ged brought him a note.

'We've got a result!' he told them. 'Danny Quinn

has just walked into Collyhurst nick. I say walked, actually he seems to have raced in there. Scared witless apparently. Gordon, I want you to come with me on this one. The rest of you know what you're doing?' There was a chorus of agreement. Caton held up his hand. 'Let's not get carried away just yet.'

There are two reasons why they call it Fort Collyhurst. The first, because it looks like a great concrete fort sitting squarely on the southernmost edge of the wild north east frontier of this city; the second, because it was actually besieged, on at least one occasion, by an angry crowd. It occupies the centre of the long red sandstone hill that culminates in Red Bank, and gave Collyhurst its name; wooded hill. Cattle grazed here in the time of the Norman Conquest. During the Hundred Years War archers practised their skill on the Common. Plague victims were tossed into pits down in the Clough. The woods, with the exception of those in the Sandhills Park through which Danny Quinn had fled, had gone. The stone quarried from this hill could still be seen in remains of the roman fort at Castlefield, and the elegant Collegiate Church now known as Manchester Cathedral. It was a pity, Caton reflected as he and Holmes made their way up the unforgiving grey steps, that some of that stone had not been reserved for this building.

'He's in the cells.' The custody officer shook his head in disbelief. 'The first thing he did when he got to reception was plead for us to lock him up. Most of them can't wait to get out. This one couldn't wait to get in. He claims someone is out to kill him.'

'Has he asked for a solicitor?' asked Caton.

'No. Nor his statutory phone call.'

'What did he have on him?'

The sergeant reached under the counter, and checked the log. 'He was wearing a pair of blue washed out jeans with a brown belt, a dark blue cotton hoodie, a dirty white tee shirt, and grey boxer shorts,' he looked up and grimaced. 'Probably white when he bought them. Also, white socks and a pair of brown and white basketball boots. We bagged the lot for forensics.' He looked down at the list again. 'Two pound ninety five pence, all in change, a Twix wrapper, and a set of door keys.'

'No mobile phone?' Holmes asked.

'No, nor anything else.'

'OK,' said Caton. 'Have you got an interview room free?

'I'll get someone to take you down.' He picked up the phone and dialled. 'By the way, there's already someone down there. A Chief Inspector Crispin.'

'What the hell are you doing here? And how did you get here so quickly?' Caton demanded.

'Good morning Tom. Going to be another warm one I see.' Crispin stretched his arms insolently, leant back in his chair, and linked his hands behind his head. 'Heard about it on the grapevine, and seeing as how we are co-operating on this, I thought I'd save you having to call me.'

'Would that be the same grapevine you used to insinuate yourself into Standing's Office and apartment?'

Crispin smiled. '*Insinuate*; that's nearly up there

with *behove* on the Scrabble stakes. And, just for the record, your boss signed the search warrant for the school, and the apartment had nothing to do with me.'

'Then how come your sidekick Warhurst dropped off the stuff from the apartment at the same time as that from the school?'

'I said it had nothing to do with *me* – well to be more precise – with *us*. I didn't say I didn't know about it.'

Caton started across the room. Crispin put his hands out in front of him, palms outwards; part defensive, part conciliatory. 'OK. It was our Friends.'

'Our friends, or your friends?'

'Ours.'

'MI5.'

The man from Special Branch slow handclapped. 'Well done.'

DI Holmes could contain himself no longer. 'They're the ones who've been chasing Quinn around the city. Getting in our bloody way. Scaring the shit out of him. We could have lost him!'

'Well you haven't. Or should I say, *we* haven't.' Crispin told him. 'And I'm not even sure they have been looking for him. Not when you were already doing such a good job.'

Caton had had enough of this. 'You're not sitting in on this interview.'

Crispin got to his feet, straightened his jacket and folded his arms. 'As I understand it you've been told to co-operate with us.'

'I am. It just happens that there is only room in here for two of us; Inspector Holmes and myself, and the suspect and his solicitor. Fortunately, this one has a viewing room. You can watch and listen from there. If you have any particular questions, I'm sure I can find a place for them.'

Crispin was about to say something, then thought better of it. He turned, picked his mobile phone up from the table, brushed passed them, and left the room.

They could feel the tension leach away. 'You were right boss,' said Holmes. 'MI bloody Five. No wonder he thinks he can push his luck, he's got the Spooks onside.'

Caton pulled up the chair Crispin had vacated, and sat down. 'I don't care who he's got onside, if he keeps playing it like this he'll get a red card; co-operation or no co-operation.'

'The door opened, and a uniformed PC came in, accompanied by Danny Quinn. Five feet four, drooping shoulders, arms limp, still visibly distressed. He was a pitiful sight in his white one piece paper suit, his hair matted, a three day growth of stubble, and red raw eyes staring from dark sockets above sunken cheeks. They would never have put him at nineteen years of age.

Caton saw him flinch as he passed Holmes to make his way to the other side of the table. This was a petty thief. But someone capable of planning, and carrying out this murder, dragging the dead weight of Standing, and lifting him unaided into the boot? And to what purpose? He doubted it very much. He turned to the constable standing by the doorway.

'Is his solicitor here?'

'She's on her way Sir.'

'Thanks, I'll buzz when we need you.'

Holmes waited for the door to close, and took the seat next to his boss.

'Danny,' Caton began. 'I'm Detective Chief Inspector Caton, this is Detective Inspector Holmes. I'm not going to start the interview until your solicitor gets here. Then I'm going to caution you. You know how it goes.'

Quinn gripped the table, and leant forward, his eyes wild, darting to and fro between the two of them, desperately seeking a lifebelt. 'You've gotta tell 'em Mr Caton. I didn't do 'im! I didn't fuckin do 'im!'

Caton held up his right hand. 'That's what we're here to find out Danny. But I can't discuss any of this until your brief gets here, and you've been formally cautioned. What I can tell you is that whatever's troubling you, I'll make sure that you're protected.'

Holmes leaned across and whispered in Caton's ear. 'We can caution him right now. See what he has to say *before* his brief gets here.'

Caton shook his head, his eyes still on Quinn. Concerned that by this simple action his DI might have fuelled Quinn's paranoia.

'We are going to do this by the book Danny. No tricks, no funny business. You tell me exactly what happened, and I'll make sure you stay safe.'

As though on cue, the door opened and the solicitor walked in. The same height as her client, but a full stone heavier, she wore a smart grey and white long sleeved shirt with button down collars, grey flannels and a pair of sensible brown shoes. Her face, just this side of pretty, was set in a stern expression that would have turned Lot's wife to stone. Holmes heart sank. Jessica Murden. Left wing activist, bleeding heart liberal, champion of the poor and oppressed; which in her book meant everyone who *wasn't* legally employed, middle class, a bureaucrat or a businessman – with the emphasis on man. Caton was secretly pleased; if only because it was going to stir up a hornet's nest for Crispin and his Friends. She nodded curtly at the policemen.

'Jessica Murden,' she said for her client's sake, knowing that her mug shot, accompanied by a health warning, was on every GMP police canteen notice board. Her voice cut through the air like a laser. 'I'm here to represent Mr Daniel Quinn.' She put her grey crinkle finish nylon briefcase down on the table. 'I hope you haven't started the interview without me Mr Caton?'

'You should know me better than that, Ms Murden.' Caton replied, no hint of disappointment in his voice.

She studied him coolly. He thought he detected a glimmer in her eye; was she resisting the temptation to smile?

'Very well,' she said 'I'd like to consult with my client.' It was a statement, not a question.

Caton nodded his agreement.

'But not in here,' she said. 'In one of the *other* rooms.'

The reason lay between them, unspoken yet understood. Caton didn't doubt that Quinn, with all of his previous, would know the reason for her request; the watchers on the other side of the two way panel. He looked across at him now, the young man's desperate eyes on Jessica Murden, trying to decide if his brief could save him. Caton pressed the buzzer.

As soon as the door had closed behind them

Holmes gave one of his characteristic snorts. 'I told you we should have cautioned him Boss; got on with it. He never asked for a solicitor in the first place.'

Caton flicked a piece of white fibre from the sleeve of his jacket. 'He didn't kill Standing, Gordon. Murden will suss that out straight away. She'll let him cop to the rest of it; tell us everything we need to know in exchange for us dropping that charge, and going easy on him in court.'

'She'll also go ballistic when she finds out about the heavies out there looking for him. She'll want twenty four hour protection.' Holmes said, unconvinced.

'Good.' Caton looked up at the wall concealing the two way mirror, and smiled. 'That will save us from having to initiate it ourselves.'

And so it proved. Caton, Holmes and Crispin, sat listening to the tape for a second time. Murden had done a good job. Quinn had calmed down, and had a chance to rehearse his story. Even so, it had come out like a stream of consciousness. Anyone could tell it was the truth.

"I was using the park as a short cut up to Rochdale Road. About quarter to nine. Said I'd meet a mate at the Mayflower at nine, that's how I know. I saw this car, just by the arches. Never seen a car like it before. Couldn't understand why it wasn't parked on the car park. They got a camera there… up a pole. There wasn't no one in the car, so I had a decko. There was this briefcase…down by the passenger seat. I could see somfin' shining, silvery like. There was a light still on in the factory up the road. I knew it 'ud be a bugger to break into, wiv a classy alarm. So I cum back later…'bout midnight. I broke the window, grabbed

the case, an' done a runner. I took it back to the squat an' emptied it out. Fought it might 'ave a computa in it. Just a load of old papers, an' a notebook."

"What did you do with the papers Danny?" Caton's voice.

"I chucked 'em on the fire. We ain't got no central 'eatin. We burn whatever, in the grate."

"And the notebook?" Caton again, hoping against hope.

"That too. Were'nt no use to me. Could've got me nicked." There was a pause while he wiped his nose on his sleeve. "Anyone could see the case was wurf a bob or two"

"We searched your squat the day before yesterday Danny," Holmes said. 'I was there. There weren't any ashes in the grate."

"I put 'em in a plastic bag and dumped em'. I'm not stupid Mr Caton."

"No one said you were, Danny. Go on." Caton encouraged.

"It was late. I ad a kip, and then the next mornin I tried a few people I know… nobody wanted the briefcase. Seems the word 'ad already got out. So I dumped it in a skip. I was on my way back to the squat when I got a call from Baz – he's a mate, shares the squat wiv me. Told me a couple of heavies turned up looking for me. Started by offering money if he told them where to find me… then making threats. Then your lot turned up Mr Caton, an' he knew the others wasn't bizzies. He was really scared. Scared the shit out of me too. Then it got worse. I went to see if I could stay wiv an old girl friend, and they'd already been there. I got to ringing ahead, and it was the same ev'rywhere. So I started sleeping rough. I was under the Grimshaw Lane Bridge last night … down by the canal in Miles Plattin'. Couldn't *sleep. I heard some voices, quiet like, comin' from the woods on the uvva side, by the recreation ground. I nipped over the fence into the Fact'ry, and crouched down. Two big bastards were standin' on the uvverside of the bridge, just off to one side. Like they was waitin' for somefink. One of 'em was speakin' into 'is mobile. Like, quiet. I knew they was lookin' for me. I sat there, shittin' meself. Then I heard a car comin' up Grimshaw Lane, from Oldham road. The engine suddenly cut, but I could hear it coastin' towards the bridge. That was it. I turned and run for it. Fru the factories, out onto Ten Acres Lane, and straight onto Newton Heaf. Reckon I lost 'em there. I spent the rest of the night in the woods at the back of Broadhurst Prim'ry School. Didn't sleep."*

There was a pause on the tape while he collected his thoughts. They remembered him shivering at this point, and Jessica Murden placing a hand on his shoulder to steady him.

"Ow did they know how to find me? I 'adn't told no one. I figured it out in that factory yard. My mobile phone. They must 'ave got the number off of Baz, and tracked it. I flung it in the canal first chance I got. Let 'em fish for it!."

"And then?" Caton prompted.

"Then I legged here. Straight to Jail. Didn't pass Go."

Caton switched off the tape.

'Got his sense of humour back at least.' Said Gordon Holmes.

'It didn't stop his solicitor insisting on an immediate visit to court, remand in custody, round the clock surveillance, no visitors, and an investigation by the PCC.' The Special Branch man pointed out bitterly.

'That's OK, Miles,' said Caton trying hard not to

appear smug. 'I've no doubt your Friends will manage to block an investigation – or at the very least have the conclusions doctored. In the meantime, we know where he is. And he'll stay there until the forensics come through, and if they clear him of the murder, as I'm pretty sure they will, my guess is that by the time Jessica Murden has had her say, he'll either walk away Scot free, or end up with no more than another spot of community service.' He stood up, and gestured for Holmes to join him. 'We're going now Miles. And I want you take a little message to your Friends. There won't be any more co-operation with you, or them, until someone tells me what they thought was in that briefcase that was so important that they had to beat us to it.'

12

Caton walked into the Incident Room just as the nine o'clock news began. Holmes was a pace behind, clutching the evidence bag containing Quinn's clothes

'You'd better have a look at this Sir. Its Detective Chief Superintendent Hadfield.' Ged told him, turning up the volume on the TV. The news presenter was busy marking time.

'We are hoping to go live to Dave West at the Greater Manchester Police Headquarters at Chester House, where a press statement is expected regarding developments in the investigation into the brutal murder of Roger Standing, CBE.' She cocked her head as she waited for the cue from her producer, and stared intently at the lap top on the desk in front of her. 'Yes, I think we have Dave West now; Dave can your hear us?'

The fact that the BBC North West's chief reporter was covering this told Caton that it was going to be more than just the usual sop to the media. He watched as Martin Hadfield appeared at the top of the steps and made his way down to the cameras. West glanced over his shoulder, and turned to begin the interview.

'Yes Sally, and here is Chief Superintendent Martin Hadfield, Head of the Greater Manchester Police Force Major Incident Team. Chief Superintendent, what can you tell us about the investigation?'

Hadfield drew himself up to his full height, pulled his shoulders back, and crossed his hands in front of his flies. He was a parody of a casino doorman. Caton suddenly realised that underneath the show of confidence and authority Hadfield was actually nervous.

'I am pleased,' he said directly to the camera. 'To be able to tell you that an arrest has been made today in connection with the murder of Mr Roger Standing.'

'Can you tell us who you've arrested Chief Superintendent?'

Hadfield shook his head. 'At this stage all I can tell you that it is a white male, nineteen years of age, who lives locally and is already known to the police.'

'Can you tell us what you believe the motive to have been?' the reporter pressed.

'I bet you can't.' Holmes muttered.

Hadfield looked decidedly uncomfortable. His right hand came up and tugged briefly at the collar of his jacket.'

'Whoops. Time he went on another body language course.' Observed Holmes.

'The suspect is being questioned as we speak, and I am unable to tell you any more at this stage. But I shall let you know as soon as we are in a position to do so.'

'Don't hold your breath.' Holmes said, warming to his double act.

'Give it a rest Gordon.' Said Caton.

'I would just like to take the opportunity to thank all of those members of the public who have contacted us so far, and urge anyone who believes they have any information that might help us, to continue to do so.'

'Can you confirm then that it was as a direct result of information from members of the public that you've made this breakthrough?' The reporter asked him.

'That's all I have to say for now, except,' Hadfield paused, as though preparing himself. He touched his collar again, 'That we are confident that this is the breakthrough we have been looking for.'

Holmes was unable to contain himself. 'Are we buggery!' he said. Then he muttered an unconvincing apology. 'Sorry Boss.'

Caton was beyond caring.

Dave West looked directly into the camera; he was positively glowing. It was the major scoop of the day; possibly the week. 'So there you have it Sally. A man has been arrested in connection with the savage killing of Roger Standing, one of the country's most outstanding and respected headteachers and educationalists. A killing that has shocked the city and the nation. We will bring you further news as it breaks, here on BBC Television in the North West. For now, back to the studio.'

Caton switched it off.

'How could he do that Boss?' Holmes asked. You told him half an hour ago that we don't have anything on Quinn apart from the theft. What was he thinking?'

'I don't know what the Chief Superintendent had in mind,' said Caton, conscious of the need not undermine his superior officer even further in front of a hushed incident room. 'But I'm sure he'd discussed it with the Chief Constable, and there must be more to it. I'll find out. In the meantime, we've all got plenty to do. Let's get on with it.'

As he returned to his room he reflected that he was

getting too polished at hiding anger and frustration from his team; the only problem was that when it did erupt, it shocked them even more. Made him look unstable. Small wonder if I am, he told himself. He looked at the clock. Nick Bateson didn't have a tutor group, one of the perks of being Head of Faculty. He might just catch him before lessons started. He took out his mobile and dialled. He was in luck, because he answered straight away.

'Nick. It's Tom. That colleague of yours…used to work at Harmony High. I'd like to meet him; as soon as possible.'

'Today?'

'If that's possible.'

'No problem. Lunchtime would be best. What time can you get here?'

'Not at school Nick. I want to keep this off the record.'

Bateson chuckled. 'Very Rebus,' he said, 'Not a bit like you.'

'Will he do it?

'He'll jump at the excuse to get out. How about the Gardener's Arms, on Moston Lane? It's only a spit away. But you'll have to buy him lunch.'

'What time?'

'Twelve thirty. He'll be there by twenty five to. You can get in a pint of J W Lees Best Bitter; he'll appreciate that. Unless I text you otherwise, he'll be there. His name is Jack. Jack Millington '

'Thanks Nick.'

'No problem.'

Caton had ended the call before he realised they hadn't discussed how they would recognise each other. Easy, he decided, I'll be the one in the corner, with a pint of bitter and an orange juice. Only trouble with that is, they'll assume I'm a cop, an alcoholic, or both.

In the event, Caton risked a half of bitter. It was a good one too; a perfect partner for the steak sandwich. Opposite him, Jack Millington, teacher of history rising fifty, flecks of grey in his full mop of curly brown hair, wiped the traces of the creamy head of beer from his top lip, and started in on his fish and chips.

'Where do you want me to start?' he asked.

'How about why you left Harmony High?'

Millington chewed his way through a mouthful, and washed it down with some beer. 'Roger Bloody Standing,' he said with venom. 'That's why; pure and simple. He was a bastard.'

'In what way?'

Millington laughed. 'In every way. Do you know your Shakespeare Tom?'

Caton had insisted on first names, to protect them both. He nodded.

"Smiles and smiles, yet is a villain." said Millington. 'That was Standing. On the outside a saint, on the inside a devil.'

'You'll have to be a bit more precise,' Caton told him, conscious that lunchtime only meant three quarters of an hour. The teacher put down his fork, and looked at Caton sombrely.

'He was a control freak, a sexist, and bully. Anyone who crossed him was on borrowed time. He made that clear from the beginning. Staff meetings were a joke. He or his minions would come up with proposals, and objections were savaged to the point that people stopped bothering. It was a steamroller. The first thing that he did was to ban trade unions. That was the writing on the wall for me.'

'I thought the city council encouraged people to join unions.'

'They do. But they no longer have any control over Harmony High, or the Trust. People can be in unions, but the Trust plays by its own rules. It doesn't recognise them. So no representation, and no action. Not unless you want instant dismissal.' He shovelled in a forkful of battered fish

'And you were a strong union man?'

Millington nodded. 'I was a union rep.' he mumbled through a mouthful. 'The National Union of Teachers. Had been for ten years. Made me Standing's public enemy number one.'

'What did he do?'

He squeezed a dollop of ketchup onto the side of his plate. 'Two months into the job he introduced lesson plan monitoring. Don't get me wrong, we'd all been used to it in our previous schools; mainly preparing for, and during, the dreaded Ofsted inspections. But not all the time. Even then it was usually the Head of Department or Faculty who monitored them, except for the NQTS; they had a Deputy assigned to them.'

'NQTs?'

He dipped a couple of chips in the sauce, and added a drizzle of vinegar.

'Newly qualified teachers. You'd probably call them probationers.' He popped the chips into his mouth, and took his time savouring them.

'Actually we don't anymore,' Caton told him. 'Must be marching to the same tune.'

'That's the point,' said Millington. 'Everyone is, but not Standing. He was treating us all like we were wet behind the ears. He visited classrooms and sat in on lessons. At the end of the lesson, if he had it in for you, he'd savage your lesson plan, even subjects he knew bugger all about. Pretty soon, he was leaving it to his senior management team, reserving for himself the ones he either wanted to wean, or to get shut of.' He lifted his glass, drank a third of it in one go, and wiped his upper lip with the back of his hand. 'All the toadies and favourites got glowing comments, even when we knew they were rubbish teachers. Pretty soon he stopped visiting them except to tell them how wonderful they were. The rest of us, he turned the screws on. Began dropping into class unannounced. Always chose the most disruptive classes. Started picking up on small things in front of the kids. I was gone by Christmas.'

Caton could tell from the way he paused, and started moving the last piece of fish around the plate with his fork, that this had been a kind of defeat for him. More than he was prepared to acknowledge. He speared the fish, looked straight at Caton, defiance in his eyes and voice;

'I've been teaching in this City for thirty two years. Consistently good results. The Local Authority used to send teachers from other schools to come and observe my lessons; find out how I did it. When the Head of the school I'm at now heard I was looking to get out of Harmony High he snatched my hand off.'

He put the fish in his mouth.

'You mentioned favourites?' Caton said.

Millington finished eating, raised the glass, downed the beer in one, and wiped his mouth for the final time. 'That's easy,' he said. They came in all shapes, and sizes. But they had one thing in common. No…that's not true; two things. They were exclusively female, and good looking. And now I come to think about it, they were all vulnerable in one way or another. I told you, he was a right bastard.'

'What about the other people he wanted to get rid of?'

'That's easy too; anyone who challenged him in any way, or who he felt wasn't quite up to the mark. And it wasn't just lesson monitoring, or teachers for that matter. In the first two years he had a twenty five percent turnover in all staff – teaching and non-teaching. And bear in mind – he'd hand picked them all in the first place. Doesn't say much for his recruitment and selection skills does it?'

'So there were plenty of people who had a serious grudge against him?'

'Dozens. And that's just among the staff. There were plenty of kids who hated his guts.'

'Pupils?'

'You'd better believe it. Any of the kids who looked like they might get the school a bad name were on a fast track down the road. Hard core truants, disrespect to staff – not just violence or abuse, mind – refusal to follow the discipline policy. One strike and you're out,' he grinned. 'Bit like that Police Authority that tops the league tables. Same thing with Harmony High. Wasn't just the dead legs either. There were two really bright kids, sixteen year olds, just coming up to their final exams. Wanted to start a student council; somewhere to debate things like uniform, lunches, study facilities, a school environmental policy, student rights. He had them in, told them to back off. When they didn't, he stitched them up. Claimed they were abusive to him. Got his sidekick, Given, to back him up. Those kids are both with us now. The silver lining is they'll put another two percent on our exam results. Make up for some of his less gifted pupils we've had to pick up.' he added wryly.

'So he's expelled all of these pupils? How has he got away with it?'

'*Permanently excluded*, is the phrase. Supposed to sound better than kicked out, but it comes to the same thing. Nobody can touch the Trust. Parents appeal to the Local Authority but they're powerless; have to refer them back to the head, and then the Governing Body. The governors and Trustees back up the Head, then it's the Secretary of State for Education. A fat chance; given that he's the PM's blue eyed boy.

Caton was finding it hard to believe. 'Did anyone try to take it further?'

'Oh sure. The parents of those two boys have taken it to the European Court of Human Rights. With them being in their final exam year, it was a clear breach of their rights, and it went against all of the official guidelines. Standing didn't give a toss. By the time they get a result they'll be at University. He would have claimed that it didn't do their career prospects any harm, and even if the judgement did go against him, the settlement would have been minimal, and BUCS would have coughed up. It makes my blood boil.'

Caton swirled the beer around his glass. 'If that's how it makes you feel,' he said. 'I wonder what it must have done to some of those staff, pupils, and parents at the sharp end, with nowhere to go. Did you ever hear any threats against him?'

Millington threw his head back and laughed. 'Where do you want me to start?'

Caton decided it was one of his catch phrases. His pupils probably used it to take him off.

'Loads of people said they were going to kill him – including me. We say it about disruptive kids too, in the heat of the moment. But we never mean it. In Standing's case, people falsely accused, their careers blighted, partners suffering nervous breakdowns. I wouldn't have thought anyone would have gone that far…but you just never know do you?'

No you don't, Caton reflected as he opened the car door and lowered himself in. Although in his experience people who made threats like that – in public and not in front of the victim - rarely went ahead and carried them out.

Millington had left ten minutes ago, but not before he had furnished Caton with a list of staff that he could remember having been victimised in one way or another by Standing, and the names of pupils who had been permanently excluded. Those who had expressed real deep hatred for Standing, including promises of revenge, were asterisked. The list included several parents who had come up to the school and confronted either Standing or Given. In both cases they'd had injunctions taken out against them to stay away from both the school and its staff.

There were thirty five names in all; and these were just the ones he could remember.

Caton realised he had missed something. He went back over his notes. Standing's penchant for attractive and vulnerable women. Had that included girls as well? He couldn't find any reference to it, but that didn't mean it wasn't a possibility. So as well as revenge, he could be looking at jealousy; a woman scorned, God knows what. He was going to need an army to get through this lot. So much for keeping a low profile. As soon as the word got out that they were interviewing people on this list the balloon would go up.

He suddenly knew what else had left him uneasy about Hadfield's press statement. It was the fact that it had been left up to Hadfield, and that he hadn't used the press suite, or invited the national media. Here was a really high profile case, that for once the Chief wanted to distance himself from. And there had been nothing from the politicians either. Normally the PM or the Home Secretary would have leapt at the opportunity to justify an increasingly hard line policy on policing and sentencing. Only the Opposition had come out and used it to highlight the supposed failure of Government policies. It merely confirmed what he already suspected. There was something about Standing, possibly about this case, that they weren't sharing with the Senior Investigating Officer. He was stumbling around in the dark, and Crispin and his Friends were one step ahead, using night sights.

He switched on his phone, checked his messages, and dialled the Incident Room. It was time to put the cat among the pigeons.

'Ged, put Mr Wallace on please.' The wait was brief, and Wallace characteristically cheerful.

'Good afternoon Sir.'

'I hope so Duggie, I really hope so. I want you to check for any crime reports or incident logs relating to Harmony High, or Sandra Given. I want you to do the same for Roger Standing, but in his case, back as far as you like. I'd like that before the close of play today.'

'Not a problem, Sir. We'll get onto it straight away.'

That was one of things he liked about Duggie Wallace. 'Put me back on to Ged.' He said.

'Ged, I'm going up to Roger Standing's school.' He said. 'They're not expecting me, so don't let anyone know except the Allocator. I don't want them getting any calls or messages for me. I'll give you a call as soon as I'm on my way back. Anything comes up, page me.'

Caton was as cool as the air conditioning in her office. Sandra Given was hot, flustered, and far from co-operative.

'I am sorry, Chief Inspector,' she said. 'But you really should have let me know you were coming.'

'I'm sorry too,' he said. 'But when I'm investigating a murder I'm not required to ask for an appointment every time I need to follow a line of enquiry. Next you'll be asking me if I've been police checked.' His humour was completely lost on her. She fiddled impatiently with a file on her desk

'Well I don't have that information to hand.'

'I find that hard to believe, in a school that has state of the art technology that includes computers networked to the electronic registration system. It's quite simple. I'll say it again. I need a list of every pupil permanently excluded from this school since it opened, and the same for every member of staff who has left in that time. I also need the names of any pupils, parents or staff that have made threats against Mr Standing, or yourself. And before you tell me there haven't been any, I know for a fact that there have.' He tried to catch her eyes but she stared down at the desk, avoiding his gaze. 'Ms Given,' he continued. 'You're impeding this enquiry, and I'm perilously close to arresting you for obstructing the police.' He knew it sounded pompous, and that he was stretching the truth, but it had the desired effect. She sat down on her chair, and placed one hand on her phone.

'Very well. The bursar will let you have a print out of staff who have resigned...' Caton interrupted her.

'Not *just* resigned, Ms Given.'

She looked up at him for the first time; radiating contempt. 'Nobody has been sacked, if that is what you are inferring,' she said. 'They have *all* resigned.'

'Thank you for straightening that out.' He said. 'But I still need their names.'

'She will also give you the names of people we have had occasion to take out injunctions against,' she could see him about to interrupt again, and was quick to forestall him. 'And those who made threats that we did not take as seriously. Our Head of Inclusion will furnish you with a list of pupils whom we have reluctantly had to permanently exclude.' She picked up the phone, and made the calls. When she was finished she said, 'If you can make your way down to the reception area and take a seat, I'll see that the lists are with you as soon as possible.'

'Thank you,' he said, and made for the door. As he placed his hand on the handle she called after him.

'This is not unlike an Ofsted Inspection, only much less pleasant.'

He turned, and held her gaze. 'I don't suppose you see many Ofsted Inspections that end up with the Headteacher getting murdered?'

13

The lists took longer than he had hoped, but it gave Caton the opportunity to gauge the atmosphere in the school. It never failed to surprise him how quickly the young came to terms with sudden death – especially when it was an acquaintance rather than family or friend.

Here at Harmony High, the transformation had been next to miraculous. The school seemed remarkably orderly and calm. During the change over between lessons pupils moved around the main corridor, of which his seat gave him a perfect view, cheerfully, and without any vestiges of the initial shock. Nor did the staff exhibit any of the tell tale conspiratorial signs he had seen on his first visit. If anything, it looked as though a weight had been lifted from their shoulders. He wondered if that was just his imagination. What was evident was that however instrumental Roger Standing had been in creating this school, however famous in his lifetime, his own particular pebble had dropped to the bottom of the pool, and in a matter of days the ripples had disappeared without a trace.

It was a salutary lesson Caton had learned early on in his career, and one that helped to explain why advancement had never held the lure for him that it did for so many of his colleagues. But in this case he sensed there were other ripples left in Standing's wake that were still there; the circles growing ever wider.

Back at Longsight, Wallace's team had delivered. There were twenty seven occasions when police had either been called to the school, or logged a complaint. In most cases the incidents had been dealt with informally, reasoning with the parties concerned, making sure they left the premises. On four occasions, people had actually been escorted from the premises: one member of staff, two parents, and one ex pupil. Three people had been formally cautioned for making threats, and breach of the peace. Injunctions had been taken out against all three individuals, and one of them – a parent – had subsequently been arrested for breaching the injunction.

All of the incidents could be tracked back to decisions Standing had made, except for four of them, where Given was the complainant. Caton had no idea how that compared with other inner city schools, but hoped it was far from the norm. All but seven of the names were on the list Millington had given him. That meant forty two names to check out in total. He made himself a mug of hot water, turned up the fan, and got to work prioritising them as best he could.

A large fan on Caton's desk blew an intermittent wind across the seminar table at which they sat, threatening to scatter their papers. The brick and insulated cavity build might reduce energy costs and emissions, Caton reflected, but it also kept the heat inside. To such an extent that there was talk of installing air-conditioning; tripling emissions, and literally throwing the environmental savings out of the window. He turned the motor down, softening the background hum, and reducing the air flow to a light breeze. Caton told them about his conversations with Bateson and Given, and passed them each a copy of the list he had drawn up. Gordon Holmes gave a low theatrical whistle.

'How the hell did he get away with it?' Dave Woods wondered.

'Hubris.' Said Joanne Stuart. The others looked at her. 'You know… *hubris*,' she said again, as though the mere repetition would enlighten them. She turned to her boss for support.

'How are the mighty fallen?' Caton said. 'The higher you rise, the further you fall. Those whom the gods wish to destroy they first raise up. It's the basis for all Greek tragedy. Most of Shakespeare's too. *Caesar, Macbeth*, the best example is probably *Coriolanus*. It's when the famous begin to believe their own publicity. Get to believe they're untouchable. They lose all sense of perspective. Think they can do anything they want. They're above the rules that govern ordinary people. That's when they take a risk too far, and it brings them down. Like DS Stuart said; hubris.'

'Isn't it a bit more than that sir? The way they got to be famous in the first place, actually sows the seed for their own destruction?' she prompted.

'Exactly,' Caton said.

'So he got was coming to him?' Carter said, less as a question, almost a statement.

'That's never for us to judge, or to believe.' Caton reminded him. 'Nor is it what necessarily happened here. It's an interesting observation, but it has no bearing on the case.'

'Still, it's a great word. Didn't we have a boss like that?' DC Woods muttered to Carter sitting next to him.

'And I can name a few prime ministers too.' Carter replied.

'Let's move on.' Caton said. 'You'll see that I've put these names in order of importance. I think we should interview all of them. I don't want any defence counsel claming that we didn't pursue all possible leads, and that there might be someone else out there with an even stronger motive and opportunity than their client.'

Everybody nodded but he could see from their faces that inside they were groaning. Forty two interviews, all written up, and he wasn't proposing to entrust them to anyone outside this group.

'Gordon,' he said. 'I want you to stay on the Quinn case. Crawl all over his story, and check on all of his known associates. I know he always went down as a lone operator, but there must be people he got his drugs from, who fenced his pickings, or who shared his squat, who could have been with him that night. Two people could easily have trussed Standing up, and put him in the boot. I don't expect it to shake down like that, but it would be good to be able to eliminate it.'

Holmes nodded. 'OK Boss.'

It made sense. A good defence council would want to push that as an alternative theory to the one that had fingered their client.

Caton looked at the rest of them. He could see from their faces that they'd already done the maths. 'I'm going to start with the first three on the list,' he said. 'DS Carter, I'd like you to take numbers four to eight, and DS Stuart, numbers nine to thirteen. They're all much of a muchness in terms of the degree of grievance they might be harbouring. DC Woods, I'd like you to start with number fourteen, and work your way down the list. As soon as we've reviewed the first day's interviews we can agree on how to share the others between us. Any questions?'

Her scent seemed to fill the apartment. Traces of Kate were everywhere. The bed was unmade, and the breakfast pots were still on the side in the kitchen. For once he didn't hurry to tidy up; an impulse that his aunt had drummed into him and that more than once over the years fellow students and colleagues had labelled as borderline obsessive. Tonight he found comfort in the disarray; as though somehow she was still present, instead of back at her own place in Fallowfield.

An hour and half, a shepherd's pie and peas, and a glass of Budvar later, he switched off the repeat of The Royle Family that always left him with a bitter sweet feeling about the human condition, and took *The Kite Runner* to bed. Three chapters to go that would ease him into a decent night's sleep.

The Education Welfare Office for the district shared a couple of portakabin's in the heart of the estate with members of the Education Psychology service. It was Caton's first port of call in the morning.

The nondescript grey cabins huddled behind a high wire link fence. The few windows, just below the edge of the flat roof, were long, narrow, and horizontal. One of them was boarded up. It was a classic urban defence against vandalism and graffiti. These buildings were shabby, anonymous, and unattractive. At one time they would have blended into the surrounding landscape of maisonettes and high rise flats. But the flats had gone, the maisonettes had been topped, and new houses had sprung up all around. The irony was that this council outpost was now the least attractive building for miles. It stood out like a sore thumb; asking for it.

He pressed the buzzer, and waited for the voice to ask him to identify himself. It never came. Instead there was a buzz, followed by a click, and a voice that said;

'Just push the door.'

He looked around for a CCTV camera, and failed to find one. So much for security. He pushed the door, and went in. He was in a long, narrow, corridor. A door part way down its length opened. A woman in her mid forties, clutching a green file folder, beckoned.

'You must be Chief Inspector Caton. I was expecting you. You're very prompt.' She stepped into the room, and stood aside to let him in. 'I'm sorry about the mess, but it's very cramped in here. We do the best we can.'

The room was larger than he'd expected. Six desks crowded the far side of the room, seeking maximum light from the narrow windows. Three more desks occupied the centre of the room. Shared tables stood between them, supporting two printers, and covered with files, and trays full of papers, letters, and memos. Along the side of the room where Caton stood ugly metal racks bent under the weight of countless books and box files. Bare strip lights, their upper surfaces coated in dust, attempted to compensate for the lack of natural light, and failed dismally. It reminded him of the first detective office he had ever worked some years ago, but it had never been as bad as this. Nor, he felt sure, would GMP countenance anything approaching it today.

'I'm just down here,' she said, ushering him to the last of the desks. Through the window of the door ahead of them he could see a mirror image of the office in which they stood. He counted two persons in that room, and one other in this room, in addition to Sheila Naylor. She caught him working it out.

'It's why they call us field workers,' she said, smiling. 'It must be the same in your line of work? Trying to spend as many hours between nine and four thirty, out on the estates, on the streets, in the schools, doing the real work, and then slaving till God only knows when, trying to catch up with the paper work.' She took a pile of reports from the spare seat at the side of her desk, plonked them onto the nearest table, and invited him to sit down.

'Can I get you a drink? I've just had one.'

'Me too,' he said. 'I'd rather we just got down to it if that's alright with you?'

'Of course. So how can I help you?'

He took a sheet of paper from his briefcase, and passed it to her. 'What can you tell me about these three? I understand they were all pupils at Harmony High, and were subsequently excluded, permanently.'

As she read the names a grim smile formed. She looked up at him, curiosity written all over her face.

'You've picked the cream of the crop here. Why these three? Apart from the fact that they were all excluded, they don't have a lot in common.'

'They do actually,' he replied. 'But can we come to that later?'

Caton watched her as she looked down at the names, trying to work out what it was that they had in common. She looked pleasant, bright, and ordinary. Her light brown hair was curly, and a little unkempt. She wore a loose fitting yellow cotton jumper, over a three quarter length skirt in a lightweight green fabric. A matching box cut jacket in green hung over the back of her chair. She had sensible flat heeled brown shoes. Approaching a stone overweight, the overall impression was homely, like her face; just the right kind of balance between professional and familiar. Caton could see her blending as comfortably into some of the most challenging homes she would have to visit, as the schools whose work she was doing.

'Gemma Watts,' she said thoughtfully. 'Now there's as sad a case as I've come across in some time.' She looked up at him with tired eyes that spoke of countless causes pursued, and lost. 'And believe me, I've come across more than I care to remember. Gemma was a lovely girl, I say *was*, because she's a shadow of her former self. Her mother died when she was twelve, shortly after she started at Harmony High; a stroke, out of nowhere. Her father's bringing her up. An only child, she's everything to him, all he's got left. When she started there, she was bright and happy by all accounts. When her mother died she went through a difficult patch, understandably. Quiet, a bit depressed. The only trouble was that it made her vulnerable. And you know what girls can be like?'

Caton nodded. After sixteen years in the force he'd got a pretty good idea.

'They began freezing her out, sending her to Coventry. Then it was accompanied by name calling. Then they started pushing her around, and sending nasty text messages to her mobile. She started missing school, pretending to be unwell. When her father finally got out of her what was going on he went up to the school. He was told she was imagining most of it, and the rest she should just ignore. It was just kids messing around. They'd have a word with them. She should come back to school straight away.' She paused, collecting her thoughts. Caton guessed that she found it disturbing just thinking about it.

'Jack, her father, decided to drop her off at school and pick her up at the gate. That first day back, they'd obviously been told to back off by the school, but it only made matters worse. Apparently six of them had started in on her after school, punching, and kicking. Gemma was a mess. Sobbing, covered in bruises. He took to her to North Manchester General A&E. It wasn't as bad as it looked – mainly superficial bruising, but they were both badly shaken up.'

'He reported it to the police?'

She shook her head, and saw the surprise in his eyes. 'You don't understand. She didn't want them punished, she just wanted them to stop. She didn't want to have to go to another school. And some of those girls, their parents are even worse than they are. They would have made life hell for the pair of them.'

He didn't doubt it. But then there were always ASBOs, and injunctions; easy for him to say. 'So what did he do?'

'He did it by the book. Asked for an appointment and went up to the school. Roger Standing, the Principal and Sandra Given, the Head, were away on a marketing trip in China. He got to see the Associate Head, Miss Juliette Postlethwaite.'

Caton nodded. 'I've met her.'

'Well she promised to take it very seriously, and promised to have it investigated,' she paused long enough for him to become impatient.

'And?'

'And the following day Gemma was excluded.'

Caton stared at her in disbelief.

'I know,' she said. 'He couldn't believe it either. It turned out that Postlethwaite took the word of the other girls for it that Gemma had incited them, and had actually struck the first blow. It was their word against hers. She got a fixed term exclusion.

Caton thought about how he would have felt. His blood was already boiling at the sheer injustice of it all, not to mention the incompetence, and he wasn't even related to her. 'He must have been blazing,' he said.

'He was. He went up the school and laid into Juliette Postlethwaite – verbally. Got himself escorted from the school. The following day he went up again and this time Ms Given was back. He tried to reason with her, but she didn't want to know. He lost it. Started making threats about her, Postlethwaite, Standing, and the school in general. The police were called to eject him, and an injunction taken out preventing him from setting foot on the premises again.'

'What happened to his daughter?'

'He went to Citizens Advice, who told him that the exclusion had been illegal, because legally, only the headteacher can exclude. He appealed, and won. The following day the Governing Body met, together with the Head and Principal, and excluded her permanently, on account of her father's behaviour.'

Caton had become familiar with the way that small injustices could so dramatically become compounded. Nevertheless, this story had disturbed him. 'She's better off out of there,' he said.

The Education Welfare Officer sighed. 'Ordinarily, I would agree. The trouble is the damage had already been done. She had a nervous breakdown, and became bulimic. At the moment she's being tutored at home by the Manchester Hospital Schools Service. They're doing a good job, but it's going to be a long haul, and my guess is that she may never get over it.'

'And the father?'

'He was as depressed as she was. Started drinking; but it's a measure of the man that he managed to pull himself back from the brink for her sake. He's still bitter, and solitary, but he seems to be holding it together.'

Caton found himself drawn beyond his professional boundaries. 'My guess is that he'd have a pretty good case under Human Rights legislation,' he suggested. 'Failure to protect, denial of education, that sort of thing?'

Sheila Naylor smiled. 'I believe you're right,' she said. 'And don't think we haven't thought about that.

Unfortunately, it's not our job to suggest such things, in fact it's positively frowned upon, because there are a hell of a lot more schools inside the Local Authority system than outside it, and I don't think our political masters, or the other heads, would thank us for starting that particular ball rolling.' She looked closely at him, and raised her eyebrows suggestively. 'But of course, if someone like you were to mention it to him in passing…?'

He shook his head. 'Sorry but I can't do that. You think *you'd* have problems.' He pointed to the list. 'Tell me about the others.'

She looked down at the names, hiding her disappointment well. 'Let's see. Denny Dooley. Quite a bright lad really. Mother Mary, single parent, doing a good job until four years ago when he got sucked into the local youth mafia. He was stealing mobile phones from other kids at the school to prove he was one of the lads. He got caught and was permanently excluded by Roger Standing himself. From that point it was all down hill. He refused to go anywhere else, to the point that we had no option but to send his mother a letter threatening prosecution – as if she could do anything to force a fifteen year old boy to turn up every day. She was in here in tears; at her wits end. Between us we managed to get him to agree to go to a really good school, on the border with Bury. Unfortunately, the day before he was due to start, the head rang up, and said he no longer had a place for him. It turned out that Standing had warned him that Denny was nothing but trouble, and not to touch him with a barge pole. Somehow Denny found out …' she looked at him to make sure that he could see she was telling the truth. '..and it wasn't me that told him. He made up a couple of Molotov cocktails, and lobbed them over the school wall. There was only minor damage to the bike sheds, but he got caught, and that was the point at which he became criminalised. After that, he was on a helter-skelter to self-destruction. He's in prison now. Taking a vehicle without the owner's consent, using it to ram raid a hifi shop, and setting light to it on a children's playground to destroy the evidence. One very bitter young man.'

'How long has he been in prison? Do you know?'

'He's five months into a two year sentence. His mother, Mary, keeps in touch. Though sadly there's nothing we can do anymore.'

Caton made a note to check that Dooley hadn't been out on compassionate leave, or had his sentence reduced, or some other unlikely explanation for how he could have been involved with Standing's murder, but he knew he was clutching at straws.

'And that just leaves Mickey Barton,' she beamed a really big smile. 'Now there's a success story! He was just starting his third year at Harmony. In the bottom sets for everything, underachieving big time. Wagged off more days than he attended. He was permanently excluded for carrying a knife to school. It was a three inch penknife. He claimed he had it for his own protection.' She nodded her head vigorously, 'And that much was true. There were older boys beating up and threatening younger ones for their dinner money and lunch vouchers; in school, and on the way to and from school. Standing kicked him out. He took, a hard line on knives. Its one of the ways he got rid of a lot of undesirables in the early days.'

And who could blame him, Caton mused, knives caused more deaths and serious injuries than any other weapon.

'He got into St Marks in Blackley, and he's never looked back. Heading for all A-C grades in his GCSE. Plays for the soccer team; different boy entirely.'

'But I thought he'd threatened to kill the Principal, and the Chair of Governors at Harmony High?' Caton said, checking his notes.

'Ah, no, that was his step-brother Dwain, a different kettle of fish entirely,' Taylor told him. 'When Mickey was excluded Dwain stormed up there mouthing off. Since he had a record for violence they took it seriously and applied for an injunction against him.' Suddenly she stopped, and a dawn of enlightenment broke across her face. 'I get the connection! You're wondering if any of these had anything to do with the murder of Roger Standing. But I thought you already had someone in custody?''

'We have to consider all possible avenues; leave no stone unturned,' Caton said, embarrassed to find himself speaking like a stereotypic 1950s detective. 'So what do you think? Could any of these three have gone that far?'

She pushed her chair back from the desk. 'Do you have children Mr Caton?' He shook his head. 'Are you familiar with the work of Benjamin Zander?' she tried.

Caton nodded. 'Which?' he asked. 'The Boston Philharmonic, or his books?'

'The books.'

'I've read *The Art of Possibility*,' he said. 'One of the few self-improvement books I've ever finished, and genuinely enjoyed.'

She reappraised him for a moment; a well read policeman.

'Then you'll understand.' she said. 'Every time a child is born its parents have shining eyes. They stand in the presence of possibility. Every dream its parents ever had, and never realised, is reborn with that child,' she waved at the pile of paper on the table behind her. 'Each of these reports is a story of heartbreak, disappointment, opportunities missed, personal failure, injustice of one kind or another. Of dreams dashed. Most handle it with a stoicism borne of bitter experience. But every now and again a parent or a child will feel it like a dam bursting, and then, who knows what they might do – to themselves or to others. Do I think any of these three, or their family, capable of such an extreme response? I don't know. I very much doubt it. But I really don't know.'

Caton had been doing some reappraising of his own. He had allowed her homely, scatty, appearance to affect his judgement. She was not only dedicated, passionate and bright, he decided, but very wise. And she was right. There were no short cuts to eliminate any of these, or any of the others on the list. But at least he had a better understanding of what they were dealing with, and a better understanding of how Standing had created Harmony High.

14

One phone call was enough to confirm that Denny Dooley had been securely locked away on the night of Standing's murder. There was always the possibility that some of his fellow gang members could have done it, but Caton doubted it. It was almost four year years since Dooley had been excluded. Far too long. But they would have to check it out. He dug out the second list, and found the address for Gemma Watts. It was less than two miles away, on the other side of Rochdale Road.

Number thirty seven, stood at the end of a row of Victorian terraced houses facing Boggart Hole Clough. He had been here before. Eight years ago, when he'd joined what was now the Force Major Incident Team, the first case on which he had worked had brought them here. A young woman had gone missing. Her body was found in the Clough by a worker from the local brewery, and it became a murder hunt. It took only two days to get a confession from her former boyfriend. One of the easiest cases he had ever been involved with.

A far cry from his new brief; cases that had gone off the boil, but not so old as to belong to the cold case team. With the latest advances in DNA, especially single cell matching, that team was snowed under with hundreds of rape and murder cases stretching back decades. So he had been handed the really sticky ones; recent, exhausted, and time consuming. Except, he reflected, that it looked as though there had been a subtle change in policy. He was now expected to keep that work going while filling gaps whenever it suited Hadfield. Gaps that increasingly seemed to be full of politically hot potatoes. First Bojangles, now Roger Standing. What next?

A net curtain twitched in one of the upstairs windows of the house immediately opposite the Watts'. It was a slight movement, that could easily have been missed. But Caton had a reason for being alert to it. The house had steel shutters on the downstairs windows, bars across the remainder, two separate alarm boxes, and a heavy steel door. Caton knew that there were two locks and three bolts on that door. When he'd worked with the Tactical Aid Unit they had tried, and failed, to batter it down. Probably as well given the two bull mastiffs waiting on the other side. It was the home of Charlie Mason. Local fixer, fence, arms dealer, and all round scum bag. When they'd finally gained entry, through Mason himself, they found a stash of weapons that he claimed were for his own protection. Caton could well believe that, but the judge still sent him down for a six stretch. He would be out by now, reclaiming his territory…if he had ever lost it. Was it possible, he wondered, that Mason had done his neighbour a favour? He had the resources, and the mind set. It would be like swatting a fly to Mason, only much more satisfying. Anything was possible. He locked his briefcase in the boot, alarmed the car, and approached number thirty seven.

The windows were grimy, the paintwork peeling, and the small front garden neglected and overgrown. The garden gate dropped off one of its hinges as he pushed it open, and hung awkwardly. In this row of neat and sturdy houses where the other owners had made a real effort – including reddening their steps, and hanging baskets full of bizzie lizzies – it looked sad, like an outcast. He rang the bell, and waited. No one came. The cast iron knocker was ready to fall off, and it occurred to him that the bell was broken. Instead of chancing it, he rapped on the glass panel with his knuckles. He heard a muffled curse. Moments later a figure shuffled down the hall towards him. The door creaked open.

'What?'

The man standing in the doorway barred it aggressively, menace in his voice, white knuckles gripping the door jam. He was a head shorter than Caton. Naked from the waist up, he wore a pair of grubby track suit bottoms. His feet were bare, his hair unwashed; with a two day beard on his face, and his eyes heavy and red, he looked a good ten years older than the forty years Caton guessed he must be. His stomach hung obscenely over the top of his trousers.

'Mr Watts?'

'Who wants to know?'

Caton held up his warrant card, and sensed the curtains twitching in the fortress across the road.

'Detective Chief Inspector Tom Caton. I'd like to talk to you about what happened to Gemma at Harmony High School, Mr Watts. Can I come in?'

The look of hostility morphed into one of anticipation. His careful introduction may have ensured entry into the house, but there was a good chance it was going to rebound with a vengeance if Jack Watts felt that he'd been tricked. Watts opened the door wide, and stepped aside.

'It's about time someone did something about that place. Come on in'

Stairs climbed to the right of a small entrance hall that opened up into the front living room. A three-seater mock leather sofa took up the whole of the wall beneath the front window. A leather arm chair that had seen better days faced an excessively large television screen. Between them was a glass topped coffee table. A crumpled can of lager lay on the floor between the chair and the gas fireplace. On the arm of the chair sat a plate with the remains of a meat and potato pie swimming in a sea of brown sauce. Through an open door Caton could see a table in the kitchen with a pile of school books on it, and a glass of water. Caton waited for Watts to sit down in his chair before sitting on the sofa.

'I thought you might have been out at work Mr Watts.' he said. The man's expression hardened.

'I had to give it up. I couldn't leave Gemma. I'm scared she might do something to herself.' His voice was a cocktail of anger, despair and self-pity.

'Doesn't she have someone who comes in to help her with her school work?'

He scratched nervously at the stubble on his chin, in a manner reminiscent of Gordon Holmes.

'A teacher comes by, but it's only three half days a week, and it's not always the same days. I try to help her with the work she leaves her, but I don't understand the half of it myself. I'm trying to save up to get her a computer, but it's not easy on family credit and they're even threatening to take my dole off me because I gave up work.'

'Can't you apply for a carer's allowance instead?' Caton asked him, dropping into social work mode for the second time that day.'

'Have you any idea how hard that is? For a start they reckon that Gemma's illness is psychosomatic, and I just need to get her to snap herself out of it. Secondly, they don't believe I have to stay with her when the teacher's not here. This is all down to that bloody bastard Standing. He got what was coming to him.'

'Mr Watts,' Caton said, as calmly as possible. 'Please understand that I have no option at this point but to read you your rights. It doesn't mean I think you've committed an offence, but in view of your outburst I have to do this to protect us both.'

Watts looked at him with his mouth open, his jaw slack, eyes uncomprehending.

'Jack Watts, I must caution you that you do not have to say anything, but if you fail to say something that you later rely on in court, it may harm your defence. Do you understand?'

Watts remained sitting. He appeared stunned.

'Do you understand Mr Watts?'

Suddenly he pushed himself out of his chair and towered over Caton. Nothing but the coffee table between them. His face contorted. Spittle foaming on his lips, spraying in Caton's direction.

'I understand all right. You think I did Standing. Well I wish I fucking had! And I'm glad somebody did. He got what he deserved, the bastard! I'm only sorry the rest of them didn't too. What they've done to my Gemma, it's criminal. When she was at Churchtown Primary she was a little star. Happy as the day is long, bright as a button. And if there was any justice, you'd be dancing on his grave not worming your way in here, accusing an innocent man. We've suffered enough.'

Caton stayed seated. He sensed that Watts was using the coffee table as a barrier between them, creating a safe distance from which to vent the rage that boiled inside him; not just at this moment, but day after day. Had he intended harm the table would have become a weapon. He waited for the onslaught to subside.

'I'm not accusing you of anything Mr Watts,' he said, more calmly than he felt. 'Now, sit down please.'

He stared down at Caton, hands clenched, eyes glazed, seeming not to have heard.

'Sit down Mr Watts.'

From upstairs came the sound of someone retching. A hollow sound, with a slight echo; suggestive of a toilet, or a tiled bathroom. The mist cleared from Watts' eyes. He looked down at his hands, and then at the policeman on the sofa. 'Now look what you've done,' he said. 'I'm going up to Gemma. When I come down you can arrest me, or piss off.' He turned, and headed for the stairs.

Ten minutes passed, during which the retching ceased, a toilet flushed, water ran in a basin. Then there was silence. Caton wrote briefly in his notebook, and settled back on the sofa, to wait.

'Are you still here?'

Watts had calmed down. His voice subdued, his manner resigned, his breathing laboured. He sat down, and began to pick with his fingers at the stitching on the arms of his chair.

'I'm sorry,' Caton told him. 'I can't begin to understand what you must be going through. But I have to ask one more question. And then I'll go away.'

Watts nodded; too exhausted to protest.

'Where were you last Saturday evening?'

The fingers stopped working as he thought about it. He looked up at Caton.

'I was fishing.' His voice was flat, matter of fact.

'Fishing? Where exactly?'

'Up at Debdale. Debdale reservoir.'

'From when, until when?'

'I got up there about six o'clock, and went through till just after five thirty the next morning.'

'Fishing, on Debdale, all night?' Caton tried to envisage it. East Gorton. About three miles as the crow flies, further by road. But there was no sign of a car outside. It was feasible. But overnight? And he would never have left his daughter.

'I know what you're thinking,' Watts said. 'I never get out, not since…I had to give up work. My sister comes round now and again to give me a break. Respite, she calls it. Fishing is all I've got left. There's some massive pike up there. Put up a real fight they do. Makes me feel alive again.'

'Did you get one?'

Watts shook his head. 'No. But I got a thirty pound perch. I've got a photo of it on my mobile.'

Caton made a note of it. It should be possible to determine when the photo was taken. That would be a start. And it was a warm evening. There would have been people walking around the reservoir.

'Did anyone see you?' he asked.

'There were people out walking, early on, when I was setting up. And there was another bloke on the other side. He had a windbreak tent like mine. Didn't have a purpose-built pike rod like me, but he had a light sea rod, and a big spinner, so I reckon he was after them too.'

'Did you speak to him?'

'No. Neither of us wanted to leave our tackle. Can't afford to with pike. But we exchanged a wave.' He looked down at his feet, tiring of the conversation.

'How did you get there Mr Watts.'

He looked up sharply; signs of agitation returning. 'I've got an old van. It's parked down the side. Look, I've told you I had nothing to do with it.' His hands gripped the arms of the chair as he levered himself to the edge of the seat. He thrust his hands out in front of him. 'You can have my fingerprints...my DNA. D'you want to swab me? Go ahead. Let's get it sorted, then you can leave us in peace.'

'I may take you up on that,' said Caton. 'But I think you should speak to a solicitor first.'

'I don't need a bloody solicitor. I keep telling you. I didn't do it.'

There was a cough upstairs. They instinctively cocked their heads to listen. Caton decided that he had more than enough. It was time to leave before he intruded further on this man's anguish. He closed his notebook, and stood up.

'Thank you for your time Mr Watts. If you could just show me your mobile phone, and let me have your sister's address, I'll be on my way.'

The photograph appeared to confirm Jack Watts story, and as did his sister Janice's account. She lived just four streets away, and since she didn't have a mobile phone – or so she claimed – and her land line had been cut off weeks ago, it seemed unlikely that Watts had been able to forewarn her. Caton was ninety percent certain this was a blind alley. Nevertheless, he determined to get Jack Benson to send someone out to get those fingerprints, and a swab. Up until now there was beggar all to match them with, but you never knew. It wasn't inconceivable that the knife would turn up; stranger things had happened. Then it occurred to him - the way connections often seemed to do between random thoughts – that anglers used knives for cutting lines, and gutting fish. He kicked himself for not thinking about it when he had the chance. Now he would have to get a warrant to search. The threats that Jack Watts had made would be sufficient cause, providing Caton also argued that the alibi was less than secure. He'd make sure Joanne Stuart and Nick Carter served it together, and get them to use a bit of sensitivity. He just hoped that all this didn't push Gemma Watts even further towards the edge.

Mickey Barton was out at school, but his mother was in. 'You've just caught me,' she said, flustered, waving the front door key in her right hand. 'I just popped in for a minute, and now I'm off out.' She wore a green three quarter length dress with a badge on the left breast pocket he couldn't quite make out. Her hair was permed in tight curls where beads of moisture glistened in the afternoon sun. She smelt of sweat, honestly earned.

'What is it you do Mrs Barton?' Caton asked her.

'I'm a Care Worker for Social Services,' she told him. Making beds, cleaning up, emptying jerries, and generally making sure they're alright. I see twenty in a day. They're lucky if they get more than twenty minutes of my time, and my feet never touch the ground.' She hovered in the doorway, reluctant to turn back and go inside.

'Look, I'm sorry to catch you like this,' Caton said. 'But it's really important, and it shouldn't take more than a minute. Can we go inside?'

She thought about it for a moment, glancing up and down the street to see if anyone was about. 'Go on then, but you'll have to be quick. Some of them keep a note of when we come, and when we leave, and there others who are so lonely I'm the only human being they see in a day.' She retreated a few strides into the hallway, and stopped. She searched his face, her eyes pleading. 'Please don't tell me it's Mickey, he's been doing so well.'

Caton had seen that look so often. Mothers who worked every hour God sent them to raise a son who paid them back with disappointment and hurt.

'Where was Mickey between six thirty, and ten thirty, on Saturday evening Mrs Barton?

She racked her brain for a moment. Relief flooded her face. 'He was with me. We were visiting my son Dwain, his stepbrother, at Thorn Cross. You know, the

Young Offenders Prison out Warrington way. When we came out we had a meal at the pub over the road – the Thorn Inn. We didn't get back till gone eight thirty. Then Mickey went down the Youth Club. My husband picked him up about ten.'

'Is your husband in Mrs Barton?'

She shook her head. 'No, he's at work. He works for the council. The housing department.'

Caton thanked her, and left. The alibi would be easy to check out. As he walked down the drive she pulled the door shut behind her, and called after him.

'He's a good lad you know. Never been a spot of bother since he went to St Marks's. Best thing that ever happened to him leaving that place.'

Ged was waiting for him as he entered the incident room.

'I'm sorry Sir,' she said. 'Superintendent Gates has been on twice. She needs to speak with you as a matter of urgency.'

Caton needed to speak with DS Gates like he needed a hole in the head. 'I'll take it in my office Ged.' He said.

It was one of the few major incident rooms where the senior investigating officer's room was both physically separate, and not divided by a glass partition. It suited Caton well. He could do without members of the team reading his body language when he was on the phone, especially when it was one of his superiors. Helen Gates was fine, but she had to play the political game like everyone else at Chester House, and sometimes it made for uncomfortable conversations. Caton had a feeling this was going to be one of them.

'Tom? What the hell's going on?'

He held the receiver away from his ear; never one to mince words this time she must really be under pressure. He forced himself to smile. 'Good afternoon Helen. What can I do for you?'

'Don't mess me around Tom. I'm getting loads of flack here. Why are you still pursuing enquiries at the school when you've already got Quinn in custody?'

He took a deep breath, and exhaled slowly. When he spoke, he measured his words carefully.

'Because Quinn didn't do it Ma'am. And even if he had, we wouldn't have enough evidence to hold him. It's not his form, and he's no motive to kill Standing, and even if it was robbery gone wrong, there's no way he would have had the presence of mind to come prepared to wrap him his victim up like that, and lock him in the trunk.'

Her silence was leaden. Caton guessed she was working out how she would tell Hadfield, and the Chief Constable.

'But I thought his fingerprints were all over the car?' She said at last.

'They were on the passenger door handle, and the briefcase, but nowhere else. The forensic evidence indicates that the window was smashed after Standing was knifed. Whoever knifed him had to be inside the car. Why would someone get out, drag him into the boot, bind and leave him, and leave the briefcase locked inside the car? And then go back for it, breaking the window to gain entry? Whoever killed him already had the key. It wouldn't make sense.'

'What if the perpetrator threw the key away, and then couldn't find it when he went back?' She persisted.

'Standing was killed by someone sitting in the passenger seat. The briefcase would have been between their legs all that time. You don't forget something like that. And it was all planned meticulously. Why else was Standing parked up in that particular spot? It's way off his route home. And then there's the duct tape; that was brought for a purpose. Anyway, the Tactical Aid Unit scoured the whole area. They used metal detectors to try and find the knife and the keys. If they were chucked, it must have been some way from the scene. Too far to risk going back.'

'Unless it was all about the briefcase in the first place?'

'In which case, he would never have forgotten it.'

The reasoning had run its course. He could hear her mind ticking over.

'You're not going to release him?'

He knew she was thinking about the egg on Hadfield's face. In the end that was his problem.

'I don't have an option,' Caton told her. 'I'm going to let him go on bail. All we've got him for is theft of the briefcase, and he's admitted to that. It's not enough to hold him.'

'When?' she asked.

'As soon as the rest of the forensics come through. If there's nothing there to link him with the murder, he's out.'

Long enough for Hadfield to find a way to save face. The spin doctors would be working overtime tonight.

'So where are you going with this?' she asked.

'We've got some leads. People who'd made threats

against Standing. It has to have been someone he knew, and had arranged to meet, or he wouldn't have let them into the car.'

'Unless he was forced into it at knife point?'

'Not by someone who then went round to the passenger side to get into the car.'

She thought about that for a moment. 'Perhaps there were two of them?'

'We have him on CCTV leaving the school in his car. On his own. The doors on that car lock as soon as the engine starts. No. He let whoever killed him into that car.'

He thought he heard her sigh. 'This is going to get messy isn't it Tom?'

'I'm afraid it already is Ma'am. Perhaps you can try and find out why Special Branch and MI5 are involved. Then I wouldn't be wandering around with one hand tied behind my back,'

'MI5?' She sounded genuinely surprised. 'Are you sure?'

Caton took a deep breath. 'Well, according to Crispin, Chief Superintendent Hadfield knows all about it. I left him a message but he never came back.'

He could imagine the look on her face. Hadfield was in real trouble. Getting Gates to do his dirty work, while leaving her out of the loop, was a big mistake. She was going to go ballistic, and of the two of them he put his shirt on her. She was going to make Chief Constable long before Hadfield got out of the blocks. The last thing she needed was her boss painting her into a corner.

'Thanks for that Tom,' she said quietly. 'I'll find out what I can. And Tom... take care.'

Caton put down the phone and looked at message on his computer screen. *You have mail*. He clicked his mouse and checked the mail box. There were thirty seven new messages. He looked at his watch. The rest of the team were still busy chasing up people who had been out to work the previous day, and whose children had been at school. It would be exactly eight days since Standing was murdered, and seven days since the investigation began. They would touch base, and carry out some further visits while they still had a good chance of finding people in. If they'd cleared the majority by mid afternoon, he'd call it a day, and they could all catch whatever was left of the weekend.

It turned out exactly as he had predicted. The search of Watt's house had been uneventful, and fruitless. They found two knives, neither of which fitted the details of the post mortem. Benson had brought them in anyway, because identifying blades from injuries was notoriously unreliable. Watts had allowed his fingerprints to be taken, together with a swab for DNA; hardly the actions of a guilty man. DS Stuart had met the daughter, and confirmed that she was fragile; physically and emotionally. It was one of those unavoidable aspects of the job that Caton hated. Putting innocent vulnerable people like Watts and his daughter under even more pressure.

None of the persons visited had provided a fresh lead. Most had watertight alibis, and the few that had not were those least likely to hold that kind of grudge. They would have to make further checks in due course, but right now it was important to get through the rest of them.

By two forty five there were only five unaccounted for. One was somewhere in the Trafford Centre; probably in one of the cinemas since there had been no response to the announcement Holmes got them to put out over the public address. The other four were all on holiday. Tackling those would have to wait till they got back. By three forty five the incident room was empty. Caton locked the door, went to his room, and rang Kate.

'We're done here,' he said. 'I'll pick you up in twenty minutes.'

'Is that going to be long enough Tom? You'll need a shower.'

'That's what I've got a wet room for. I'll be straight in and out. I packed last night.'

'I love you Tom.'

It still had the same effect as the first time he'd heard her say it.

'I love you too.'

He replaced the handset, switched off the computer, and left.

15

They had planned it weeks ago. It was sod's law, that the heat wave should choose to end this weekend, Caton reflected as they drove past the Tickled Trout up the long motorway incline out of the Ribble valley. On the other hand, the coolness had come as a relief, and as far as he was concerned sunny spells and showers were what the Lake District was all about. It felt good to be getting away with Kate beside him, her head tilted back as she drank from a bottle of spring water.

'How come you've never been to the Lakes before?' he asked, lowering the volume on the radio.

She turned to look at him, spluttering as some of the liquid went down the wrong way.

'You shouldn't try to drink and speak at the same time. It's not an endearing habit,' he said, grinning.

She screwed the top back on the bottle, replaced it in the holder behind the handbrake, and punched him playfully on his shoulder.

'That doesn't answer the question,' Caton told her.

'Mum and dad thought the world ended north of the Watford gap, and I never had cause to come up here. All roads pointed south. When we were young, it was always Devon or Cornwall for holidays – in B&Bs or chalets - and then when I was older, and independent, it was as easy to hop across the channel.

That's how I got interested in France, and Italy.'

'But why not when you came up to Uni?'

'I don't know. There was just so much else to do in Manchester. And I always went back to Teddington to visit my parents at Christmas, and I worked for most of the other vacations. It's not as though I was ever a rambler or a mountain climber.'

Caton smiled. 'You don't know what you've been missing, you soft Southern jessie.'

By the time they'd reached Tebay Services Kate already had more than an inkling of what he meant. The first glimpse of the mountain ranges standing proud on the far side of Morecambe Bay had made their mark, and then the Howgill Fells reared like a herd of elephants above the motorway as it threaded its way through the Lune valley,.

'You were right,' she said, 'It's lovely up here.'

'You've not seen anything yet,' he told her as they stretched their legs in the car park. 'This was voted the best motorway service area in the country. And I dare you not to buy something from the farm shop.'

They sat by the long window, looking out across the rolling fells towards the peaks, making the most of the late afternoon sun as it dodged in and out of the thickening patchwork of clouds.

'Remind me; why did you say you brought me this way?' she asked him.

'Because this is about the worst possible time to visit the Lake District. The southern lakes will be teeming with day trippers, clogging the car parks and creating endless tailbacks as their coaches attempt to negotiate impossible bends. Coming at it from the north you'll get a chance to see much more, and we'll be hitting the central fells just as everyone else is heading the other way.'

She frowned. 'So why did we come now, if it's so busy?'

'Because you kept on hinting that you wanted to; because I needed to clear my head; and because I thought if your first introduction to the fells was when the sun was shining, I might stand a better chance of getting you up here in proper climbing weather; in the autumn and spring.'

She pointed towards the bank of clouds. 'The best made plans of mice and men.'

As they reached the outskirts of Keswick he surprised her by pulling off onto a side road, signposted *Castlerigg*.

'Nearly there,' was all he said.

They stopped at the top of a rise in the road. Caton parked the car close up on the verge, and led her through a gap in the hedge. They were on a plateau of grass pasture surrounded on all sides by fells and distant mountain peaks; ahead of them, a large ring of standing stones, around which, grazed a flock of sheep. Apart from the sheep, and a solitary crow picking at carrion, they were alone.

'It's beautiful,' she said. 'Wild, peaceful…timeless.'

'I know,' he said. 'That's why I brought you here. Its one of my favourite places. As far from the city as the moon from the sun.'

He led her to the centre of the circle. The circumference had been formed using stones between three and five feet high. At one point there appeared to be a small enclosure. A little further on two massive stones stood sentinel over the entrance. Caton held her shoulders lightly, and turned her towards the south. In the distance, a series of rugged purple hills masked the horizon.

'The Lake District was formed over five hundred million years. The slate came from sediments in the ocean that covered this region. Then the Earth's crust lifted in folds, like corrugated paper, and volcanoes erupted. The limestone on these fells is the remains of billions of dead crustaceans. The sandstone formed when it was a desert. The mountains and the lakes are the remains of a ring of volcanoes rounded off and gouged out by Ice Age glaziers, and the melt waters that followed. Right now you're looking at volcanic crags; Hill Rigg, and the Helvellyn range.'

He turned her through a hundred and eighty degrees until she was facing north, towards a pair of large, smooth, and rounded slopes, suggestive of a woman's breasts.

'Skiddaw and Blencathra. Not much to choose between Skiddaw and Helvellyn in height, but totally different beasts to climb. Thousands of years ago man came here, when many of these hills were dense with native woods and forest. They came to hunt, to make and trade flint axes and arrow heads, and then to farm. If they stood here today, they would tell us that little has changed, except for the trees. When I sense that I'm getting out of kilter, that work is controlling me, and not vice versa, I come up here. Breathe in the air, drink in the view, walk off the sludge in my veins, muscles, and mind, and go back refreshed. And with a sense of perspective.

She stood there for a moment taking it in. 'I can see what you mean,' she said. 'It makes you feel small, and insignificant, yet strangely strong and centred.'

'You wait until you get up on the tops,' he said. 'You can multiply that feeling by a factor of ten.' He took her hand, and started back towards the car. 'Providing you remember to switch your mobile off.'

Neither of them spoke during the latter part of the journey. They drove the length of Thirlmere, beneath the looming presence of Helvellyn, through Grasmere, and up into the enchanting Langdale valley. It was seven thirty when they pulled up at the New Dungeon Ghyll. The hotel nestled in six acres of Lakeland valley, beneath the steep slopes of the Langdale Pikes and Pavey Ark. The reflection of the setting sun fired the windows against the blue slate building like so many golden eyes.

'God, this is beautiful,' she said as she leaned against the car.

'You're beginning to repeat yourself,' Caton said, opening the boot and taking out their bags.

'OK then. It's really romantic.'

'It's even better in the winter, half buried in snow, with a roaring fire in the lounge bar.' He led the way through the gate and up to the ivy wreathed front door.

'I'll settle for this,' she replied.

'Wait till you see the bedroom.' He said.

She laughed. 'Now *you're* beginning to repeat yourself.'

They made love in the king sized four poster. Later, in the dining room, they settled for the smoked salmon and followed it with the venison and a bottle of Cairanne 2001. To round it off they went for the Cartmel sticky toffee pudding. Then they went through to the lounge sat by the open fire, and sipped their brandy.

'That was fantastic,' she said.

'Thank you,' he said. 'I do my best.'

She poked him playfully in the chest. 'It's not always about you, you know. I meant the sticky toffee pudding.'

He made pretence of being hurt. 'It's not often I come second best to a pudding.'

'No seriously, I've never tasted anything like that.'

He sipped his brandy. 'It's a good job I made you buy a couple at the farm shop then. Perhaps we could have one every time you ravish me. What an incentive. Only we'll need a van load.'

'Tom! Stop it.' She blushed, hoping that no one had overheard.

'Actually, we can order them on the web,' he said. 'No need to ration ourselves.

That made her laugh, but it didn't stop her kicking him.

'How's it going with the good Professor Stewart-Baker?' he asked, rubbing his shin.

Kate's eyes came alive in a different way; animated by the reminder of her latest intellectual challenge. Caton promised himself that one day he would drop unannounced into one of her lectures. He could imagine her students' rapt attention. She'd have them eating out of her hands.

'Not bad actually,' she began. 'First of all we're suggesting a common protocol for the use of offender profiles. Setting it out clearly for the senior investigating officer that profiles should not be used in evidence. That the courts would almost certainly throw them out as falling under 'evidence of propensity', and certainly not amounting to 'reasonable suspicion' for an arrest, let alone a conviction. Just because someone has a tendency, a weakness towards certain forms of behaviour, that doesn't mean they've actually done anything about it, let alone committed a particular offence.'

Caton nodded. Kate's own profile had been spot on about Bojangles, but it would never have stood up in court. It was just a pity that they had got there too late to spare her the ordeal he'd put her through.

'It might be permissible in the States,' she was saying. 'But not over here. Not yet. And if it ever is, I can see more innocent people being put away, like poor Stefan Kiszko.'

'That wasn't on the basis of a profile though.' Caton reminded her. The twenty six year old tax clerk had served sixteen years in prison for the murder of eleven year old Lesley Molseed. He'd died a year after his release on appeal in 1992. 'That was about false statements given to the police, and, allegedly, the suppression of other evidence.'

'Yes. But the statements by those girls were taken at face value, and fitted the kind of profile the policemen had in their minds. And there's always the danger that detectives might ignore, or give less weight to, evidence that doesn't quite fit the profile.'

It was a danger Caton worked hard to avoid, and to

warn the team about, but it was always a temptation.

'We're also suggesting that profilers should work in pairs,' she continued. 'And that statistical profiling should go hand in hand with academic profiling; though why they call it *academic* is beyond me. Behavioural and psychological would be more accurate.'

'Yes, but that's two words; hard for mere policemen to cope with,'

She grinned, realising that he was teasing her, that she had begun to get carried away. 'All right then tell me about the Head Case. How's it going?'

It was Caton's turn to be surprised. 'How did you know the team are calling it that?'

'Where have you been? Everyone's calling it that. The newspapers, the radio. It's obvious really; they can't keep calling it the Standing investigation. It doesn't work somehow.'

'Fair enough,' he said. 'But I've got a rule, I never bring work away with me.'

She bristled slightly. 'Then why did you ask me at about mine? That's not fair.'

'You're right,' he said. 'I shouldn't have. I'm sorry.'

She put her hand on his. 'Apology accepted; on condition you tell me some more about you. I don't even know where you were born.'

Whether it was the brandy or something else Caton would never know. But he found himself reminiscing about a happy childhood and, without realising that he was going there, he had begun to tell her about the crash. How two idyllic weeks in the Pelyponnese ended when the tanker rounded the bend on the wrong side of the road. How he had woken in a hospital in Athens to learn from his father's sister that his parents had both died in the crash. His aunt had found comfort in the fact that their deaths had been instantaneous, but there had been no refuge there for Tom. He explained how he'd been saved by the sleeping bags piled on either side of him in the back seat, acting as a cushion as the car tumbled down the sheer hillside before coming to a halt, sandwiched between an ancient olive tree and a stone wall.

'And is that what you remember when you have the nightmares?'

He nodded. 'Not exactly that, and I don't know if it's a memory, or a reconstruction that my mind attempts from its imaginings, but it feels real.'

He swirled the remaining brandy in his glass, tipped his head back, and finished it off. He put the glass down on its side to let the spirit condense. The light from the candle reflected images of the glass into the iris of Kate's eyes; diamonds set in an emerald sea. He saw the sadness in them, and placed his hands over hers.

'But it's fine now, really. I haven't had one in months. Not since…' he tailed off and she prompted him.

'Not since?'

His grip tightened over her hands.

'Not since I met you.'

When the waitress came to clear, the brandy glasses lay on their sides, each nestling a golden tear drop.

'But it's only seven thirty! And we're on holiday.' Said

Kate as she followed him reluctantly down the stairs.

'We've a proper breakfast to get through,' Caton told her. 'And if we're not up on the fells by nine it'll be like Blackpool in wakes week.'

The allusion was lost on her. The breakfast was not. Fruit juice, Cumberland sausage, four rashers of dry cure middle back bacon, two eggs, grilled mushrooms and tomatoes, Cumberland oat cakes, and a pot of coffee.

'I can't eat all this,' she told him.

Caton had already started to tuck in. 'Just do your best,' he said. 'You've a long day ahead of you.

It was exactly nine o'clock as they crossed Rydal Bridge opposite the Glen Rothay Hotel, and headed up through the woods above Elterwater, leaving the river, bright with clumps of yellow flag crowding its margins. Intermittently, the sun attempted to find its way through a heavy mist, and light drizzle.

'I can see where the Lakes come from,' Kate complained, wiping away the drops of water that had dripped from her hood onto the end of her nose. 'Is it always like this?'

'Wait and see,'

Caton showed her how to tighten the strap of the rucksack around her waist, and slacken off those across her shoulders. Then they set off up the clear path, soon to emerge from the woods at the entrance to the disused Loughrigg quarries. 'Surprise number one,' he told her. 'Now close your eyes, take my arm, and trust me.' He led her confidently over the stones, and onto the grass apron. 'Open your eyes.'

They were standing at the entrance to a large cave,

carved from the surrounding slate. The steel blue walls were shot with streaks of red ochre, reflected in an emerald and turquoise pool that filled the floor of the cave. Lime green ferns sprouted from cracks in the banks, struggling for a hold together with blue scrub juniper, and golden lichen. The colours reflected perfectly in the crystal clear water. A series of large white limestone slabs had been placed as stepping stones that stretched invitingly towards the furthest reaches of the cave.

'It's...' she checked herself. 'Fantastic!'

'And beautiful,' he teased. 'Would you believe there are fish in there, and it's large enough to hold the entire population of Ambleside?'

'I'd believe anything, except that you can better this.'

He took her arm and led her towards a path branching away towards the South. 'I'll let you be the judge of that.'

For the next half hour they climbed steadily through bracken that gradually gave way to purple heather. They rested for a few minutes on the boggy flat section known as the amphitheatre, where the soft white heads of cotton grass were almost lost beside the towering stems of valerian following the course of Troughton Gill, crowned with masses of pink buds, and creamy white flowers. A succession of small tarns shone like a string of pearls where the sun's rays caught them each time a gap appeared in the clouds. The rain overnight had brought the bog to life, and it was soggy under foot. The heather here was pink rather than the purple of the drier slopes.

Soon they were on the well worn track that ran north along the ridge. The drizzle stopped, the mist cleared and the clouds showed signs of thinning, but it was still impossible to see anything for more than fifty yards on either side. They ascended three summits, each topped with a cairn of stones. Kate was disappointed that the view from the highest point was limited by the cloud base, and wanted to stop for a rest and a coffee on the carpet of green velvet turf. Caton insisted they press on. Just as they reached the slightly lower east summit, the clouds lifted, and the sun burst through from an azure sky. Kate's breath caught in her throat.

'Surprise two.' he said quietly.

She sat on the flat top of the cairn, where tens of thousands must have sat before, and stared in silence. Grasmere lake stretched out ahead of them; a cobalt mirror reflecting white puffs of cotton wool clouds. A sliver of beach gleamed silver beneath them. Emerald trees crowded the banks. The town was a series of small white dots in the distance. Towering above it all, a semicircle of mountain peaks from Scafell to Seat Sandal stood majestic in the morning sunlight.

Kate turned to find Caton looking out over the hills to the West, towards the fierce Langdale Peaks. There was something in his stance that moved her to ask. 'Did you come up here with your parents?'

There was no reaction. She sensed that she was intruding on a private grief, and regretted having spoken.

He nodded slowly, and answered her without turning. 'This was the first walk we ever did together. I was seven. They later told me that this was where they would want their ashes scattered. Little did they think that a few years down the line I would be reading that in their will.'

He paused, and she watched as strands of his hair fluttered in the breeze.

'Three months after I came out of hospital my uncle and I came up here with two urns.'

A wave of compassion for this man-boy moved her to stand up and step beside him. She slipped her arm through his.

'When you get up here,' he said at last. 'You realise that life is a game that you play the best you can, and then move on. It doesn't do to take it too seriously.'

16

It is a truism, that whilst the rain in Spain falls mainly on the plain, in Manchester it brings the traffic to a grinding halt. Caton could never understand why people didn't have the sense to set off earlier. If anything, they left it that bit later to begin their journey in the vain hope that it would clear just for them. That combined with the usual Monday morning mayhem, and it was no surprise that the briefing started thirty minutes late.

'Now that we're all here,' he said, pointedly. 'Let's get on. Duggie's got something for us.'

Wallace stepped up to the media console. 'That's right Sir. We've finally managed to get hold of the CCTV from the factory car park, and clean it up a bit. This is it.'

They leaned forward as he pressed play. Although they must have expected it, it still came as a disappointment that the camera showed only the car park and the stretch of Collyhurst Road that led up past the paint factory. The spot where Standing's car had been found was hidden behind the hedge and wall that formed the boundary of Fitzgeorge Street. The time on the screen was eight ten pm.

There were just two cars on the car park. A white van drove past heading north. A woman appeared in shot coming down the road from the right. She had a dog that looked like a short haired terrier on a lead.

She passed the factory, and turned left into Fitzgeorge Street, heading up towards the railway viaduct. Three minutes later, a boy in his early teens, bouncing a football, appeared from the direction of Sandhills. As he reached the road he dropped the ball and began dribbling it in the direction of the factory, stopping every few yards to play keep-ball. They watched until he was out of shot.

'Sign him up,' Holmes said to break the tension.

Wallace advanced the tape. 'There's nothing for the next fifteen minutes,' he explained. When he pressed play again two men emerged from the factory gates and crossed the road towards the car park. They stopped to chat briefly, unlocked their cars, and drove off in opposite directions. The car park was now empty.

'Here comes Roger Standing,' Wallace told them. The unmistakeable bonnet and headlights of the Maybach came into view. They craned forward as one, to see if they could make out who was in the car. There appeared to be just the driver. The indicator blinked, and the car turned left and disappeared up Fitzgeorge Street. It was eight twenty eight and forty seconds.

'This next bit is really interesting,' he said, allowing the tape to run. The tension was becoming unbearable. At eight thirty one precisely, a silver Mondeo pulled into the car park, and parked up.

'It's not you is it Gordon? Nick Carter quipped.

Seconds later a black Nissan Micra turned into the car park, and pulled up alongside the Mondeo. A middle aged woman climbed out and got into the passenger side of the Mondeo.

'I hope not.' DS Stuart said. Holmes refused to rise to the bait.

Suddenly the camera began to zoom in on the car, and move to left and right, as though trying to get a close up of the couple.

'Are you doing that Duggie?' Caton asked.

'No Boss. The camera is obviously linked to a network control room. The operator must have taken over manual control.'

'The dirty beggar!' DC Woods ventured.

Almost as though they knew they were being watched, the couple got out of the car, linked arms, and set off towards the exit.

'Go right,' Holmes encouraged them. Adding 'Bingo,' as they turned into Fitzgeorge Street heading directly for the Maybach, and the wild parkland beyond.

Wallace fast forwarded the tape again. When he stopped, the clock said it was nine twenty nine. It was beginning to get dark, especially here where the Viaduct cast its shadow, and the picture was less distinct in the absence of street lights. A small white Escort van emerged from the factory gates and drove towards the car park, slowed as it passed Fitzgeorge Street, stopped momentarily opposite the spot where the Mondeo was parked, and then accelerated away towards the city centre.

'That will be Simes, the security guard,' Caton reminded them.

Again the tape was forwarded, this time covering just under five minutes. A youth in a dark hoodie top, dark trousers that looked like jeans, and a pair of baseball boots, came jogging down Collyhurst Road and turned in to Fitzgeorge Street.

'Well hello, Danny Quinn.' Holmes muttered.

The youth stopped on the corner, looked across towards the Mondeo, and then up the street in the direction of the Maybach. They watched as he pulled his hood over his head, looked over his shoulder at the factory, and then glanced to his right at the CCTV camera. He walked slowly in the direction of the railway arch, and disappeared from view. Two long minutes passed while they stared at a blank screen. A man and a woman emerged from the shadows of Fitzgeorge street. They each had an arm around the other's back. The woman had her free arm wrapped around the man's chest, and her head buried into his shoulder.

'The lovers return,' Carter announced unnecessarily.

They stood facing each other, and kissed, long and hard, before getting into their respective cars, and driving away. It was nine forty three precisely.

'That was some nookie,' DC Woods whispered to Nick Carter. 'Fifty nine minutes. Good job it was a warm night, but I bet they got bitten to buggery.'

Wallace stopped the tape. 'That's it,' he said, 'Until five fifty two in the morning when we see the security guard turn into the street with his dog, and then all hell breaks loose.' He returned to his seat.

'Thank you Duggie,' Caton said, picking up the notes he'd been making. He stepped up to one of the white boards, picked up a pen, and drew a timeline from left to right, with the times of each incident across the top, and a brief description below. He stepped back to check it, and turned to the rest of the team.

'So, what does this give us?'

Joanne Stuart was the first to speak. 'Six new potential witnesses who might have seen the murderer shortly before, or after, he killed Standing.'

'That's three actually,' Holmes told her. 'I'm pretty sure the two blokes who came from the factory, and the woman with the dog, were among those who already came forward. At least the statements match what we've just seen.'

'Let's get the interviewing officers to verify that from the CCTV, just to be on the safe side.' Caton decided. 'That leaves the boy and the courting couple.'

'I don't suppose the couple are going to be in a hurry to come forward,' said Carter.

'We've already checked the car registrations.' Wallace told them. 'The man, assuming he's the owner and registered keeper, lives in Cheadle, the woman in Prestwich. They probably work together.'

'I want you to arrange to have these two picked up at exactly the same time,' Caton told him. 'So there's no chance of them tipping each other off. Let's do it discreetly. Preferably not at the home address. Then you can use as a lever the suggestion that they could lose their anonymity unless they co-operate fully.'

'They must know that we'll get round to them eventually, Boss,' Holmes pointed out. 'They clearly knew the camera was there.'

'There's always that possibility,' Caton agreed. 'But they could be hoping that it wasn't recording – that it's a dummy. You know how people tend to go ostrich in these situations; put their heads in the sand.'

'They don't actually do that Boss,' said DC Woods.

They turned to look at him.

'Ostriches. Contrary to popular belief, they don't bury their heads in the sand. What the hen does - when she's sat on the nest hatching her eggs, and gets spooked - is press her neck flat along the ground so she looks like a bush.'

The silence was deafening. Woods waited for someone to say something. When no one did he began to colour up. 'It was on one of them nature programmes on tele,' he said as though that was some kind of excuse. The rest of the team turned back towards Caton.

'You know the routine Gordon,' he said, 'If they've got a story together you'll soon pick it up from the language they use, the identical detail, the lack of distinguishing embellishments. Then you can put the squeeze on.'

'The lad with the ball is bound to live locally. I'll get Inspector Saifi from Collyhurst to track him down for us.' Holmes suggested.

Nick Carter put his hand up. 'Standing was obviously there to meet someone,' he said. 'There's no way he would drive in, and park up there, otherwise. Which means his killer was either already in the car, out of sight, or he must have come down through Sandhills, and gone back the same way.'

'So we're looking for someone he knew, or agreed to meet.' Dave Woods ventured, attempting to redeem himself.

'I think we can safely say that's likely DC Woods,' Caton said. 'But it doesn't entirely rule out a mugging, or a car theft gone wrong. He could have gone there to meet someone, and fallen foul of a third party, although I accept it's unlikely.' He noticed Inspector Weston deep in thought. 'What are you thinking Sarah?' he invited.

'These timings fit with the estimated time of death

from the post mortem.' She said. 'The report said somewhere between ten pm and two am, but that he could have taken up to four hours to die. That means he was stabbed somewhere between six pm and midnight. If Quinn was telling the truth, Standing had already been put in the boot by twenty to ten. We know from the video that there wouldn't have been time for someone to kill him, drag him to the boot, and tape him up, in the time between Standing arriving, and that courting couple walking past. That means the stabbing must have taken place between eight thirty one and nine forty,' she paused for a moment. 'And it also means that Standing may still have been alive when Quinn saw the briefcase for the first time. It's even conceivable that he was still alive when he came back and stole it.'

Silence descended while each of them played out the scene of those final hours in their mind's eye. Nick Carter winced. 'Doesn't bear thinking about,' he said.

'What should we do about Quinn, Boss?' Holmes wondered.

Caton looked at Sarah Weston. 'What do the forensics tell us?'

'Well, there's no evidence to connect him with the death. We know from the prints he left on the door handle that he wasn't wearing gloves so it's safe to assume that he would have left prints on the outside and inside of the boot, on the tape, and on the body. Also, there was no trace of any blood on his clothes, and we've just seen from the tape that they were the same ones he was wearing that night.'

'In that case,' said Caton. 'I think we should release him on bail.'

There was general assent around the room. Joanne Carter raised her hand.

'He's not going to like that is he Sir? I thought he wanted to be locked up for his own safety.'

'Now that we know it was Special Branch and their Friends who were following him, and that it was all about the briefcase, *and* that they know that the contents were burned, I don't think he's got anything to worry about.' Caton replied. 'But before we let him go, I think we'd better see if he can remember anything more about anyone being in the parkland when he crossed it that first time, on his way to the Mayflower.'

Sarah Weston had a question. 'The samples of pollen and spores our forensics team took from the crime scene; they want to know if they should send them to a palynologist for analysis, or wait until we have samples from a suspect to compare them with?'

Caton thought about it. With the lack of other forensic evidence it could turn out to be really important, but there was a cost involved. On the other hand, he was aware that it had turned out to be really useful in other cases nationally, including the Soham murders, and that it took quite some time to do the matching.

'Tell them to go ahead,' he said finally. 'Let's get them logged now, and then they'll be able to turn the results round that much faster when we do get something to match them against. Speaking of which, where does this leave us in terms of lines of enquiry?' He picked up a marker pen and lobbed it to Joanne Stuart, who stood up, and took it over to the flip chart. 'Let's start with the least likely,' he suggested.

'A car theft gone wrong,' DC Woods called out

'A mugging,' Nick Carter suggested.

DS Stuart began a vertical list, writing them down and drawing a separate triangle around each of them. The suggestions dried up.

'OK then, what about ones that could be more feasible?' Caton asked.

'Domestic, Boss,' said Holmes. Stuart placed it inside a circle.

'Has to be there,' Caton agreed. 'There's nothing pointing that way but we certainly can't exclude it at this stage.'

'Work related; something to do with the school or the Trust.' DI Weston put forward. Another circle.

'Any more?' Caton asked them.

DS Stuart stood back from the chart to let them see. She was the first to respond. 'What about the interest from Special Branch and MI5? We haven't the faintest idea what that's all about, but it must be something more than just because he was an unpaid advisor to the Government?'

Caton nodded. 'Good point Jo, they may have stopped running interference, but there is something they're not sharing with us. They must have a good reason for not wanting us to dig further into his affairs. And it's unlikely that they've passed on everything they found at the school, and his apartment.'

'And what was in the briefcase that was so important?' Holmes ventured.

They stared at the flipchart in silence; like a herd of ruminants chewing the cud.

'So what about possible motives?' Caton asked them.

Joanne Stuart picked up a different pen – a red one – and held it poised, ready for action. Their response came like a burst of hail.

'Money…Greed!'

'Jealousy!'

'Envy!'

'Sexual Obsession!'

'Revenge!'

'Psychosis!'

There was a lull in the onslaught, and then, very quietly, Sarah Weston added another.

'Betrayal.'

Caton waited until DS Stuart had finished writing. 'Thanks, Jo,' he said. 'Nick, I'd like you to do the connections.'

Stuart and Carter changed places and the young detective sergeant took a blue pen and began to draw lines connecting the possible motives to the potential lines of enquiry. When he'd finished the first two lines of enquiry – mugging and car theft – had been linked to *Greed*. The next two, *Domestic, and Work Related*, had been linked to all of the other motives. Only the government related line of enquiry lacked a connection. Caton rose from the edge of the desk on which he had been sitting, and picked up the red marker pen. Under *Betrayal* he added the phrase *Self-Protection* to the list, then picked up the blue pen and linked them both to *Government-Related.* He stepped back and took a long hard look. There were many in FMIT who would regard it as just an academic exercise, but Caton knew that the visual image would make a stronger impression on the team than the words alone. It would stay up there for them to see every time they came into the room. Their brains would automatically refer back to it every time they took a statement, or looked at a piece of data, and sooner or later the penny would drop. It was just a matter of time. Something Chester House was reminding him daily that he didn't have.

'What about the press cuttings on Standing,' he asked. Is there anything there that might link with any of this?'

'I've got them here Boss,' Wallace hurried over to his desk and returned with a folder of print outs. 'Basically, he comes across as Mr Perfect. The earliest go back about ten years, but I'm waiting for some to be sent up from Kent. About a third are to do with his work on China – his articles and books basically, nothing to do with his school-based work. The rest more or less chart his rise to fame as an outspoken headteacher. There are some statements about quality of teacher training, the curriculum, greater freedom for schools to experiment, more testing, and parents taking responsibility for their children's behaviour and attendance. The more recent, and most detailed, deal with his links to BUCS, the formation of the Trust, the design and launch of the Academy, and his CBE. There are some short pieces from the Guardian, and a long article in the Times Educational Supplement about him being part of the education circle closest to the Prime Minister. The last piece before he was killed is a pretty strong article about Local Education Authorities being a complete waste of time and money.'

'I bet that went down well locally,' said Holmes.

'I'll be finding out this afternoon.' Caton told him.

I've got an appointment with the City's Chief Education Officer.'

'I've got a separate file,' Wallace continued. 'For the obituaries, and the articles spawned by his death. Most of them are either sycophantic, or scare mongering.'

'Thanks Duggie.' Caton said. 'I'd like to see those as soon as.' He looked at the chart again, and then at his team. 'Unless there's anything else, that's it for now. I know that with Quinn out of the running it feels like it's going to be a long hard slog. But you also know that as long as we keep the momentum going something's going to turn up just when we least expect it. But it has to come out of data you're gathering. It's got to be hidden somewhere in the detail. So let's find it.'

He took the folder from Wallace and headed back to his room. The Lakes felt a million miles away. And there were other mountains to climb.

17

Caton stood at the furthest window of the seminar room, high up in Overseas House. He had a perfect view of the traffic streaming up from Quay Street on his left, straight across Deansgate, onwards along Peter Street, past the Great Northern Square; a perfect example of the architectural and historical fusion that was Manchester.

The Grade 2 listed Great Northern Warehouse, built in 1885, had been transformed following fifty years of derelict neglect, and a hundred million pounds of investment. At the height of Manchester's reign as *Cottonopolis*, three hundred and fifty men were employed at the goods station. Eighty horses were stabled beneath the viaduct alongside the tunnels that linked road, canal, and station. He knew that the boast had been that any package received before four pm would be delivered to a named station, anywhere in country, by eight am the following day. He doubted that would hold true today.

The five storey sandblasted red brick building still proudly bore, in the original large white lettering, the proclamation *Great Northern Railway Warehouse*. It now contained a sixteen screen Megaplex Cinema and shopping development that bustled with cafes, bars, and restaurants. A sunken, lawn filled, stone stepped amphitheatre, and an elegant landscaped public square, separated the front entrance of the warehouse, and the elegant all glass Bar 38. Beyond the square, clouds moved slowly across the mirrored face of the twenty six storey Great Northern Tower apartments; a turquoise slash across the dramatic city skyline.

'Impressive isn't it?'

A tall slim man, in his late fifties, with strong features, and a good head of curly black hair stood in the doorway. There were dark rings beneath his eyes, and worry lines etched into his face. He advanced into the room, and held out his hand.

'Duncan Chilver,' he said. 'Chief Education Officer. You must be Detective Chief Inspector Caton.'

Caton grasped his hand. 'Tom, please,' he said.

'Tom, it is, and call me Duncan. Come on through to my office.'

They passed through the office of the personal assistant who had already gone to get a coffee for her boss, and a mug of hot water for Caton. Glass fronted wooden bookshelves stood along one wall of Chilver's office. Bright and skilful works of art by Manchester pupils, that Caton would gladly have had in his own apartment, hung on two walls, above shelves that held mementos of exchanges and projects with St Petersburg, Wuhan, Clermont Ferrand, and Bologna. The fourth wall consisted entirely of windows that looked out over Deansgate towards the Great Northern. Chilver placed his suit jacket over the back of the chair behind his desk, and invited Caton to take one of the comfortable chairs surrounding the coffee table, where he joined him as the drinks arrived.

'Thank you Jan,' he said. 'And please hold all messages. I don't want to be disturbed until I've finished my meeting with the Mr Caton.'

She smiled, and left the room. Caton sensed that she'd been curious as to the purpose of the meeting, and that Chilver must have had a good reason not to have revealed it. The Chief Education Officer picked up his cup and saucer, took a sip, and said.

'So Tom, you wanted to ask me about Roger Standing?'

Yet again Standing's title had slipped away almost as quickly as had its owner.

'That's right,' Caton said. 'The more that we know about Mr Standing the closer we're likely to come to understanding why someone would want to kill him.'

Chilver put his cup and saucer on the table, and sat back in his chair. 'So you don't think that this was a random killing – a thief or a mugger?'

'We can't be sure one way or the other,' Caton replied. 'But I'm sure you understand that we have to cover all of the angles?'

Chilver nodded, shrewd enough to know that this was an evasion. 'Of course. So what do you want to know?'

'What you thought of him. How he was regarded in the city. His relationships with colleagues. That sort of thing.'

The education officer took a deep breath, held it for a moment, and let it out like a sigh. 'If you don't mind Tom, I'd like to leave my opinion of him till the end.'

Caton didn't see that it would make much difference since whatever he was holding back for later would inevitably colour how he answered the other questions.

'You have to understand,' Chilver continued. 'That he and I arrived in Manchester at more or less the same point. I think he was about ten months ahead of me. The Education Department was in a bit of a mess. They'd just had an Ofsted Inspection of the Authority that, frankly, had papered over the cracks. Although there had been some real improvements since the previous inspection, some of the heads – mostly led by Standing – had more or less coerced the previous CEO into giving them more control over resources, and re-organising some of the services, including ones that had been making good progress. Blackmailed, would probably have been a more accurate description, but it's hardly politically correct. Standing led the charge. Either you give us more money and control over services, or we give a bad report on you and your department to Ofsted.'

His mouth began to dry up. He picked up his cup, and had a drink.

'You see, a significant part of the inspection is a questionnaire that the heads complete individually, although we know that some of them get together and co-ordinate their responses. The Local Authority only gets to see the overall analysis. It carries a lot of weight.'

Caton could see how that would be a perfect lever to get what they wanted..

'The net result was,' Chilver continued. 'They got the money and the influence, and I picked up a massive deficit, a list of recommendations as long as my arm, and less staff to implement them. Add to that the fact that Children's Services are now run from the Town Hall, so that I have to report to the former Head of Social Services, and it's a very different world to how it used to be. In the intervening period between then and now, the chickens have come home to roost. The rest of the heads had sussed out Standing, and sent him to Coventry, although he'd got what he wanted and didn't give a damn.'

Caton was confused. 'If he helped the heads to get more money, resources and influence, why did they turn against him?'

The CEO shook his head wearily. 'When he came to Manchester he came to a city where the heads had historically had a good relationship with the Education Department. When Ofsted inspections began, school league tables were introduced, and schools were given devolved budgets, in common with most local authorities its resources and influence was inevitably eaten away. But the schools still believed in co-operation with each other, and with the Department. Then a new breed of heads came along. Standing foremost among them. The difference was that he teamed up with some of the reactionary old guard, and spawned a dog eat dog mentality. The winners were Standing and his Trust schools. The losers, were the rest of the schools, and the Department. I'm dreading the next inspection.' He passed a hand over his face as though washing away the thought.

'So, apart from the Trust schools, most of the heads would have had a pretty poor opinion of him?'

'Hate him, is probably the word you're looking for, although despise would probably be more accurate.'

'As strong as that?'

'Oh yes. When Standing put his Trust together he cherry picked the best supported schools in middle class areas. He used back door selection to start his own Academy. He excluded at the drop of a hat any pupils that didn't fit his mould, or caused any trouble. The rest of the schools had no option but to pick them up. Because of the way the trust works, it was a one way street. He never took any of their troublemakers. When it became intolerable for some of the local schools we ended up having to take those excluded pupils into our pupil referral units, most of the money for which had been transferred to the schools. Add to that the fact that the rest of the schools are forever having their results compared unfairly with Harmony's, and with the Trust as a whole, and it's become a living nightmare for the rest of the city.'

'I don't understand. Why did the City let him do it?'

'Because on paper it looked like a good deal. All that extra money; a state of the art building; all those primary schools improved. The Government for its part was pushing it. And in the hands of someone else, it might just have worked for the city as a whole. But not with Roger *Competition* Standing at the helm.'

There was a vitriol in Chilver's voice that Caton had heard before when Standing's name came up; first from Jack Millington, and then from Gemma Watt's father. He remembered some research that suggested that when people in America and the UK were asked to pray for certain patients, they recovered at a noticeably quicker rate, and remained in remission longer, than those in the control group. Some who were considered terminal had even recovered completely. He wondered if the reverse applied. If so, perhaps Standing's nemesis had been a corporate curse.

'And that wasn't the worst of it,' Chilver continued. 'We've had to pick up the pieces of most of the staff he either dismissed or *persuaded* to leave. He paused to drink his coffee which must by now have been lukewarm.

'And the tragedy,' he continued. 'Is that it didn't have to be like that. Take Pankhurst High in the South of the city.'

Caton knew of its reputation. A brand new, state of the art school, built on Local Authority land adjacent to the previous school, that had been demolished to make way for a multiplex cinema and leisure park. The sale of the land for the new development had gone a long way to finance the new school. Examination results had climbed steadily, and with it the house prices in already fashionable Didsbury, as parents with resources and high aspirations fought to buy in the immediate catchment area.

'Now there you had a Head,' said the CEO. 'Known for his integrity, and blue sky thinking, who earned his knighthood. His standards and his expectations were just as high as Standing's, and his methods used no less rigorous but at least they'd been professionally, ethically, and morally sound. He also remained firmly within the local authority system and worked to involve the rest of our schools, and share some of his resources and his experience, while achieving Leading Edge status for his own school and recording the highest results in its history.

'So how did Standing get a CBE, and why was he being tipped for a knighthood?' Caton wondered, not for the first time.

Chilver smiled wearily. 'God knows. I certainly don't. Do you know what they say about the Order of the British Empire Tom?'

Caton shook his head, although he had a feeling he had heard it before.

'It stands for *Other Buggers Efforts*. And do you know what our heads reckon Standing's motto would have been if he'd been knighted, and made it to the House of Lords?'

He shook his head again

'*Bugger All the Others*! He did exactly that. Anyone who wasn't part of his precious set up; heads, teachers, staff, pupils, parents, the Department, the City; he buggered us all. I doubt if that would have been a big enough motive for anyone to kill him. But you won't find many tears shed in this city for Roger Standing.'

They shook hands on the steps of the building, just as the first coaches began to pull up further down the street beside the Opera House. Chilver seemed to Caton to have perked up. It was almost as though it had been a catharsis for him. But he still looked a very worried man.

Caton joined the stream of office workers heading for the Great Northern Car Park. He realised that it had been more than two hours since he'd had a drink, and stopped off at the History Bar for a sinful coffee and a piece of carrot cake; but mainly to process what he'd just heard. He sat at one of the aluminium tables outside in the square.

The showers had long since ceased, and people were sitting outside the bars and on the steps of the amphitheatre taking advantage of an early *happy hour*.

Everything seemed so normal. That was the thing about the job he found hardest to come to terms with. Strangely, it wasn't the deaths, the abuse, and the cruelty as such, but the fact that it all seemed to take place in a parallel universe. Over the years he had developed the ability to separate out the world in which he worked, from the one in which he could be himself. Just occasionally, he found himself caught between the two. Too often in the early days that had been the case. He had no doubt it had cost him his marriage. And now, for the first time in a long time, there was someone else in the equation; Kate.

18

Caton was up at six the following morning. It was almost a fortnight since he'd managed a session at the Y Club. An hour or so would set him up for the string of interviews Ged had pencilled in.

Tuesday mornings were always popular with the office workers who got in early to beat the rush. With the advantage of living nearby, he was at the front of the queue.

Thirty minutes of aerobics, twenty on the weights machines, and fifteen lengths of the pool, gave him the perfect excuse to linger in the steam room. As he luxuriated in the moist heat he knew exactly why he kept renewing his membership, and why his membership card clung to the fridge door as a constant reminder.

It was surprising what people revealed to complete strangers in the false security of a steam filled box. He had a vision of interviews at the station conducted in just such a room, equipped with a moisture free, steam penetrating, video camera. Officers in wet suits, suspects and counsel in trunks and bikinis. A real Monty Python moment. He shook his head at the thought, spraying globules of sweat over his hidden companions.

A violent hacking cough cut through the air, rippling the steam. Caton got up to leave, two women a heartbeat ahead of him.

Saskia, the ever present Polish receptionist, with a huge crush on Caton matched only by her personality, took delight in calling after him as he headed for the Café exit.

'You're going to need your umbrella Tom!'

Rain fell like stair rods from an overcast sky. It drummed on the roofs of the green and red narrowboats moored in the twin channels of Potato Wharf; thundered on the taut canvas canopy above the terraces of Castlefield arena; peppered the surface of the canal, and poured in rivulets down the steps from Liverpool Street. Sweeping in across the Cheshire plain it paused to inundate the city, before rising to meet the granite flanks and wild moorland of the Pennine hills. It was not true that rain fell incessantly in Manchester. But when it did, it made a proper job of it. Caton had no option but to put his head down, and run for it, leaving on the broad Yorkshire flags perfect footprints that disappeared as quickly as they formed.

On the other side of the city, Gordon Holmes had a new lead to follow. Duggie's search of the Manchester Evening News archives had thrown up a story about Standing and the North Manchester drugs gangs. It transpired that Standing had decided to take a stand against the dealers who hung around outside the school in the mornings, and when school broke up. He had been successful enough to get a mention on *Look North*. This looked like as good a motive as any. There was no telling what some of those scum would do to protect their turf. The only downside was that it meant crawling to DI Lounds as the lead for the Force Drugs

Unit in the North. He doubted that Lounds had forgiven Caton's team for letting Bojangles spike his drugs operation, never mind that it had dealt a massive blow to gangs across the city. Still, it was an excuse to get out of the station, and take the Mondeo for a spin; even if it was pissing down.

Detective Inspector Dicky Lounds sat with his feet up on the desk, hands behind his head, a supercilious grin on his face.

'Well, well, well. Fancy you showing up here Sherlock. Up against the proverbial brick wall are we?'

There was a time when Gordon would have swept his feet off the desk, and wiped away the grin. This was not such a time. Instead, he pulled up a chair and sat down. No point in pleasantries though; he got straight to it.'

'Roger Standing, Dicky. I hear he did your lot a bit of a favour.'

'As I recall, hearing was never one of your stronger points Sherlock. So, where did you get it from then?'

'The Manchester Evening News as it happens. Not that it's relevant where I heard it. The point is, I need to find out if it has a bearing on Standing's death.'

Lounds moved one of his hands to his crotch, and began scratching. 'No,' he said with an air of finality. 'It doesn't.'

Holmes leaned forward. 'I'd like to be the judge of that.'

'No need to trouble yourself. I'm telling you. They're not connected.'

'I'd like to be the judge of that.'

Lounds stopped scratching, took his legs off the

desk, and sat up in his chair. He put his elbows on the desk and brought his hands together in a steeple. He stared at Holmes for a moment, as he might a cockroach. How was he going to rid himself of this irritant? He made up his mind. Short and sharp, just get it over with; like stamping on a roach, only less pleasurable.

'The Cheetham Hill mob,' he began. 'Had a strangle hold on the drugs scene long before Standing arrived to amalgamate those two schools. They had dealers at the gates, and dealers inside. Every now and then we'd bust a couple, and they'd be replaced the same day. It was like that Dutch kid with his finger in the dyke,' his smirk at the double entendre turned to a scowl when Holmes refused to take him on. 'Within weeks of his arrival Standing started to make it uncomfortable for them. He refused to allow pupils to leave the grounds during the day. He had security guards patrolling the streets outside, before school, and when pupils came out. He introduced drugs tests for pupils with dilated pupils,' he smirked again. 'Or who gave any sign of being spaced out. If their parents objected the kids got kicked out. He had CCTV installed, and set up an anonymous reporting system where kids could put the names of bullies, drug dealers, and the like, on a piece of paper, in a locked box. He caught two inside dealers that way, expelled them, and reported them to the police.'

'I don't suppose that went down too well?' Holmes said.

'He was threatened. Had a bottle full of acid thrown at his car. Then - and I've only got third party reports of this - the security firm that works for the

Trust paid the gang leader and two of his lieutenants a visit. They turned up carrying automatic pistols, and baseball bats. Scared the shit out of them they did. Standing had no more trouble after that. In the end it simply shifted the problem to other schools, and over the border into Salford where they ran up against the Broughton gangs.'

Holmes was trying to process two things simultaneously. This was the first they'd heard of a connection to the gangs. And as for Standing, he'd really put the cat among the pigeons with the drug barons.

'Sounds like a pretty strong motive to me, Dicky.'

'Motive yes. Opportunity, no. Thanks to that debacle you called Operation Bojangles, the gang leader, and the lieutenant in question, have been banged up for the last eight months with no prospect of release this side of my retirement. The other one, who's now el supremo, was conveniently under surveillance by us on the night of Standing's murder. It's over three years since he chased them off. They'd have done him long before now, with a burst of gunfire. In any case, I think they'd just be too plain scared. That security firm is full of real mean bastards.'

Holmes knew he was right. Still, they should have been told. Not had to work it out for themselves and come cap in hand for Lounds to ration it out.

'Just one more question, Dicky,' he said. 'How did a foul mouth like you make inspector?'

Lounds put his feet back up on the desk, resumed his indolent pose and grinned. 'That's simple Sherlock. Simple…just like you. Where I work it's not about sounding good, it's about the number of villains you take off the street.'

Holmes stood up. 'That's the problem with you Lounds, you still haven't grasped that it's not about the villains at all, it's about the drugs. And year on year there are more of them, each more venomous than the last. Not to mention all the crimes committed to feed the habit. And you're not making the slightest difference. Simple, or what?!'

19

Caton joined the M60 circular motorway and headed north; or was it clockwise? It didn't really matter unless the traffic information was about to tell him of an impending bottle neck. Two hours either side of rush hour it would be more like the M25 but, given the time of day, and the brand new stretch past the Sale Water Park, he was confident he'd make it to Bolton by eleven thirty.

The Area 2 Regional Office for the National Union of Teachers had arranged for him to meet three ex-members of staff from Harmony High, all of whom were on his list. In one sense, it was going to save him a lot of time

It was exactly eleven twenty two as he pulled up outside the row of Georgian terraced houses. The last time he'd been here it was to attend the victim of a fatal stabbing, dead on arrival at the Royal Infirmary tucked away behind this terrace. The hospital had long since moved to Plodder Lane; far more accessible from the spaghetti junction of the North.

Mary Jenkins responded to the bell. She was a tall, slim, smart, friendly woman, with smiling eyes and sensible spectacles. Not at all what Caton had expected. Scruffy rottweiler was the vision he had of union activists; except within the force, where his experience was less attack dog, more poodle.

'Come in Detective Chief Inspector. We're ready

for you.' There was a confidence and toughness to her voice that confirmed one part of his stereotype. There *was* a rottweiler here; a smart one, with a touch of emotional intelligence. A new breed for a new century. She led him past a small office, and up the stairs. Five chairs had been crammed in a tight circle inside the room. A man and a woman rose with unexpected civility as he entered the room

'This is Detective Chief Inspector Caton,' she announced. They introduced themselves in turn.

'Harriet Blaine.'

'Peter Watts,' said the man in the grey suit. I'm actually with the NASUWT.'

'Which is?' Caton asked him.

'The National Association of Schoolmasters and Women Teachers,'

'We have a common interest in this so I offered to host the meeting,' Mary Jenkins explained. 'Peter's rep had to leave on urgent business, but he's left you a written statement,' she handed him a foolscap envelope.

As they took their seats Caton made a quick assessment. Blaine was what his aunt would have called comely. In her mid thirties, five foot four, with a full figure and slightly overweight. Her black hair was cut and blown into a loose bob framing a pleasant rounded face. She wore a thin denim jacket over a white tee shirt and jeans. Peter Watts wore a plain white shirt and red tie. His short hair, already beginning to thin, showed touches of grey the colour of his suit at the temples. Caton searched for signs of similarity between them; save for their ordinariness, there were none.

Their stories were almost as uniform as their appearance. Both of them had contributed to the undercurrents of concern in the staffroom about excessive monitoring, and over preparation – especially in advance of the Ofsted Inspection. They suspected that some of Standing's favourites had informed on them, because simultaneously they had begun to attract his attention.

'He'd walk into my Design and Technology room,' said Derek Morris. 'And pontificate about CAD/CAM machines, and how they were waste of resources if I wasn't going to use them more often. He knew bugger all about it. But the kids didn't know that. It just undermined my authority with my classes.'

'In my case,' Harriet Blaine said, leaning forward in her seat. 'He did all those things, but he wasn't just unprofessional, he was downright rude, in a personal way. Not content with savaging my lessons, he told me that my trousers were too tight, and my tee shirts and blouses were provocative,' she opened her jacket wide revealing a full bosom firmly upholstered, demurely hidden beneath a round neck tee shirt. 'I ask you; provocative? He even went so far as to tell me that I needed to lose weight because I was a bad role model in a school committed to healthy eating.'

'If I can just interpose,' Said Mary Jenkins, 'What is exceptional about Harriet's case is that the rest of the complaints we picked up from women were very much the reverse. They were about sexual harassment of a predatory nature. You'll hear more about that shortly.'

It was apparent to Caton that however interesting these stories, they were unlikely to bring him nearer to identifying likely suspects. Both of them had resigned, and won industrial tribunals. He had a strong hunch that at least one of them had probably been a weak teacher, but that still didn't justify Standing's brutal underhand approach.

There was a knock at the door. In burst a breathless young woman. Water dripped from long blonde hair onto the sodden shoulders of a jet black anorak.

'Thank God! I thought I'd blown it.'

She slipped off the anorak and draped it over the back of a chair, revealing an hourglass figure in a red and white cotton print dress with shoe string straps. As she fought to get her breath back it was all that Caton could do to tear his eyes away from her heaving breasts. Conscious of Mary Jenkins watching him, he felt himself begin to colour. The union officer stepped forward.

'This is Sylvia Jack, Detective Chief Inspector,' Jenkins said. 'Sylvia, this is Mr Caton.'

The young woman wiped her wet hand on her dress, and held it out. It felt soft, warm, and innocent in Caton's grasp. She sat down, crossing her legs demurely, angling them away to protect her modesty.

'Sylvia was only able to come during her lunch hour. Fortunately she teaches at a nearby school,' the union rep explained. 'Her case is fairly typical.'

'I haven't got long I'm afraid, I've got a food technology GCSE class to set up for first period after break.' Sylvia Jack told him.

'I don't expect it'll take very long, and I certainly don't want you to miss your lunch,' Caton reassured her. 'Just tell me in your own time.'

She composed herself, smiled nervously, and began.

'I was really chuffed when I got the job. I'd only been teaching two years and it was a promotion. A brand new school, brilliant facilities, nice kids. I was really up for it. Then Mr Standing started wandering into my lessons. At first he'd smile, and nod, and talk to a few of the pupils, and then leave. Soon he was sitting right through the lesson, claiming he was really impressed, and learning so much. I could tell he was looking at me, you know, like men do; but I was used to that.'

She was looking straight at Caton, and said it with such honesty and lack of affectation that he felt himself beginning to blush again. She didn't seem to notice.

'Then he said he was interested in cooking; that because of work he was spending more time on his own, and perhaps I could give him some tips. I was flattered,' she grimaced. 'Bloody stupid more like. I took him through some basics after school, just two or three sessions. We'd cook together, then he'd come and sit with me to eat it. Just like I did with the pupils. On the third occasion he turned up with a bottle of wine. At the end of the meal, he placed a hand on my leg. He said that on a future occasion we could do the same thing at his apartment. The penny dropped with a clunk. I moved his hand, and got up to start washing up. He came up behind me at the sink, stood really close,' she looked away embarrassed. 'I could feel him, hard up against me. I squirmed away. He treated it like a joke. I was really frightened. I told him not to be silly, that it was the wine. He could see I was upset, and backed off. He said I was right, it was the wine; but that he was attracted to me as any man would be. That he hoped I would forgive him.

After that I started making excuses as to why I couldn't manage to keep up the sessions after school. He began pestering me big time. He'd suddenly appear just as lessons were ending so that I couldn't get out of the room. He'd suggest alternatives, like weekends, or during the half-term break. Eventually I told him straight, to leave me alone. That's when he turned nasty. He called in my lesson plans and savaged them. He said he had reports from cleaners that my room was left in a mess; that food was left out, and it was a magnet for rats. I'd start crying for no reason at all. My nerves were shredded. I was close to going off sick. Then one of my friends I was at college with told me to contact the union,' she looked across at Mary Jenkins and smiled awkwardly. 'It was like a miracle. I wished I'd done it as soon as he started to come on to me. Mary helped me to gather evidence, and then I resigned, citing his harassment. I've got a new job, a fresh start, I've paid off my student loan, and got most of what I need for a deposit on a flat.'

'Harriet's was our most recent case,' Jenkins told him. 'They made an offer rather than get dragged through another industrial tribunal. It makes me sick that he gets off so lightly. The worst of it is, that he just moved on to the next victim.'

'What did your boy friend think about all this Miss Jack?' Caton asked. It was the only way he could think of finding out if there had been a man in her life angry enough to confront Standing.

She brushed wisps of hair away from her forehead where it they had begun to stick, and fixed him with innocent blue eyes.

'I was between men at the time. Looking back, I suppose that was why I was a bit more vulnerable than I might have been.' He saw her glance surreptitiously at her watch.

'You'll need to leave,' he said. 'I'm sorry to have troubled you, and grateful that you were able to spare the time to talk with me.'

Anxious to get back, she stood up. She smiled again as she shrugged on her anorak. Caton could see why any man would be drawn to her. Nor was it the first time he'd known a married man, twice the age of the object of his obsession, risk career and reputation for someone so beautiful and innocent

'No, thank *you*,' she was saying. 'It helps to talk about it.' She made towards the door, then paused, half turning. 'It was terrible what happened to Mr Standing. I wouldn't have wished it on anyone, but at least no one else will go through what I did.' A blush began at her throat, and began to spread. 'Oh dear, that doesn't sound quite right.'

Caton got up, and held the door open for her. 'On the contrary,' he said, 'It sounded exactly right to me.'

20

Thursday August the fourth promised sunshine and showers; exactly how Caton's day was panning out. None of the interviews that any of the team had been conducting had thrown up the slightest lead. He was beginning to wonder, in another Pythonesque moment, if they would have to offer a reward to any student coming forward with information about a sordid affair between Standing, and one of his pupils. He didn't know which would cause him the most problems; the reaction from the establishment, his superiors, and Standing's family, or the number of hoax responses they could expect. Just as well it was only a thought. DI Carter stood up. It was his turn to report.

'It's obvious from what we've heard so far, that Roger Standing was a serial womaniser. Well I can tell you,' he said, getting into his stride. 'That this was neither a recent phenomenon, nor one that he confined to his immediate school.'

Holmes sat up straight. DC Woods stopped doodling, his pencil suspended in mid-air. Carter waved a sheaf of papers in his hand.

'With Duggie's help, I've come up with quite a list of Standing's infidelities. Left a trail across the country did our Roger.' He held up the first sheet. 'Thirty years ago, there was a sixth form student in the grammar school he worked at, in Kent. He was four years older than her. Seems he gave her some private French lessons, and she gave him some French kisses.'

Woods couldn't resist it. 'French letters, more like.'

Nervous laughter bounced around the room, eyes sliding in Caton's direction. Impatient to see where it might lead, he let it ride.

'That would be just before he got married?' said Joanne Stuart who had been doing the maths again.

'That's right, Jo. And according to our source, he kept it going for at least another three years, which was *after* he'd got married. She was at university in London, and he'd find excuses to go to town to do some research.'

'Is that what they called it in those days?' Dave Woods called out.

Holmes turned on him. 'Enough already, DC Woods'

'Who was this source exactly Sergeant?' Caton asked.

'An ex-colleague of his; someone who worked at the school at the time. He's retired now, but he's in the same Masonic lodge as the divisional superintendent, who just happens to have done a course at Bramshill with our very own Superintendent Gates. Small world isn't it?'

'Does Superintendent Gates know about this?'

'Bound to Boss. Apparently they still keep in contact from time to time, so he'll have emailed her at the very least.'

Which meant that Gates would be on to Caton any time soon. 'Where is this girl now?' he asked.

Carter looked at the sheet. 'She's fifty three, married, with three grown up kids. Lives in Rochester, and is a well respected editor of non fiction books.'

Holmes asked the obvious question. 'Any chance that they were still at it when he died?'

'Our source says not. Apparently it was her that dumped him, not the other way round. Got a model marriage, dotes on her husband, and lives for her grandchildren and her work. No room for a chancer like Standing, or so our source says.'

'And the next one?' Caton wanted to know.

Carter transferred the sheet to the back, and scanned the next two to refresh his memory. 'Nothing more, until he moves to Cheshire. According to the local schools, and the community officer on that patch, as soon as his death was reported the rumours bubbled up to the surface. Seems he tried it on with a probationary teacher, and with the school secretary. Had them both going at the same time by all accounts.'

Dave Woods was about to say something when he caught Gordon Holmes eye, and thought better of it.

'The probationer left at the end of her first year, and moved to a school in Cornwall; to get away from Standing is the general consensus. His affair with the secretary rumbled on until the year before he moved up here.'

'What happened Nick?' Sarah Weston asked.

'Apparently, although it was common knowledge in the town, his wife put up with it until he made the mistake of rubbing her face in it. She'd gone with a party of kids from her school to the theatre, and there was her husband with his mistress,' he grinned, and allowed himself an observation. 'Bad planning or what? Anyway, she gave him an ultimatum, and he gave the secretary the old heave ho.'

'That was a long affair. Any chance the mistress could have been bent on revenge?' Sarah Weston wondered.

Carter shook his head. 'If she did, she did it long distance. She emigrated two years ago to join her son and his family in Melbourne, Australia.' He looked at the final sheet. 'And then Standing moved up to Manchester. This is a really interesting one we got from one of our police graduate entrants in Wigan. Seems there was a rumour that Standing had got one of the foreign students on her course pregnant. He thought we might be interested.'

'Too right,' said Holmes.

Do we know where she is now?' Caton asked.

'There's a bit of problem there. She left the course halfway through, and just disappeared.'

'Could be someone in her family set out to take revenge on Standing.' Woods suggested.

'When was this exactly?' Gordon Holmes asked.

'Two years ago,' Carter said. She hasn't been seen or heard from since.

'How did the two of them meet?' Caton asked.

'She was on a mentoring scheme Standing got going between the University and his students. It's supposed to be a way of encouraging inner city kids whose parents have never been to university to consider it as a serious option.'

Caton remembered what Kate had told him about visiting one of her students on the scheme. 'Well the university are bound to have followed it up when she dropped out.' He said. 'And they'll have a contact address. Get onto the International Division Team. Get them to give you her home and overseas addresses and contacts, the name of her tutor, and the name of her Counsellor if she had one. Also the names of any other students on her course, and any particular friend or friends she may have had. And check with Immigration. They'll have a record, and they may even have a file. And well done by the way.

'What about Mrs Standing Sir,' DS Stuart asked. 'She must have known what was going on; she certainly did about the ones in Nantwich. Maybe she finally came to the end of her tether?'

'I doubt she had the strength to get him into the boot, and why would he have agreed to meet her in a god forsaken spot like that?' Gordon Holmes pointed out.

Joanne Stuart came back at him. 'She might have got a boy friend of her own at last. He could have done it, or even her son.'

'That's not impossible Jo, and you can help me check it out this afternoon,' said Caton.

'This afternoon Sir?'

'It's the funeral.'

'I didn't know we'd agreed to release the body.' Holmes said, bristling slightly, feeling left out of the loop.

'The cause of death is well documented and incontestable.' Sarah Weston explained. 'The forensics examination was thorough, and double checked. There wasn't any point in hanging on to this one. In any case it seems The Chief Constable was anxious that we didn't.'

'In any case, she's gone for burial,' Caton added. 'So if we ever need to take another look we can. I'd like you to come too Gordon. I need someone to watch the rest of the mourners, while DS Stuart and I concentrate on the family. We'll have to take both of our cars. We leave at half past twelve. So you'd better grab whatever you want to eat before then'.

By the time they reached Coppenhall, slanting showers were falling from a leaden sky, soaking the small party of mourners as they hurried into the tiny church. Beyond the beech trees lining the path the tops of ancient tombstones hung suspended above a sea of mist that rose from graves and grass, warmed by the morning's sun. Caton paused to read a sign on the wall just inside the porch.

Among the graves in this cemetery lie those of twin brothers, who were responsible for changing the course of naval policy. Both brothers joined the Royal Navy during the 1st World War and were assigned to the same ship. Unfortunately the ship sank, killing the twins together with many other young men from Crewe and the surrounding area: The death of the two brothers led to the Royal Navy prohibiting relatives of immediate family from serving on the same vessel.

'I wonder if Standing will get a plaque.' Gordon Holmes whispered.

'Not if his wife has anything to do with it.' Joanne Stuart whispered back.

Margaret Standing had been true to her word. Caton counted only thirteen people in the church apart from themselves. It struck him as odd that they were all seated on the left hand side of the church. On the front row sat Mrs Standing, her son, and another woman who from her profile he took to be Margaret Standing's sister. Behind them, on the next two rows, sat an assortment of three men and seven women, all aged between forty and seventy. Caton recognised none of them from the school. On the fourth row, a woman in her thirties sat alone. DS Stuart leaned over and whispered again.

'That's the Cheshire police family liaison and victim support officer,' she whispered. 'None of his immediate family are here. Parents deceased, and him an only child.'

The service was brief. It began with Psalm 23, *The Lord is My Shepherd,* and ended with *Oh Lord My God.* In between, a simple committal was punctuated, briefly, by a eulogy given by the son. Caton made a point of switching on his voice recorder, thankful that the church was so small, and they were so close and they were using a microphone. John Standing placed a single sheet of paper on the lectern, which he gripped with both hands. He cleared his throat and began to read.

'On behalf of my mother, and myself, I would like to begin by thanking you all for being with us today. You will know that the school of which my father was headteacher, and the Trust which he established, are arranging for a memorial service in his honour in Manchester at some time in the future. I am sure that will be a significant occasion at which much will be said about my father, and by many people. You will all of course be welcome to attend. Today, at my mother's request, those of us who perhaps knew him best, and friends of my mother's, have gathered to commit his body to the ground, and his soul to the mercy of God. The fact that we also have with us members of Her Majesty's Constabulary is a reminder that we live in times as troubled now as any that the generations interred in this cemetery might have known.'

A woman four rows from the front half turned her head at the mention of the police, and, thinking better of it, turned back. The rest hung on his every word.

'They are also a reminder that my father, my dear mother's husband, was torn cruelly from this life. None of us are perfect; my father was certainly not. But who is to say that any of us deserve to die in such a way?'

He picked up the sheet of paper, and held it at his side, delivering his concluding comments unaided.

'Please remember my mother in your prayers, and in your kind attention over the months to come. We very much hope that you will be able to join us later at the house where we can thank you in person.'

And that was it. The strangest eulogy that Caton could recall. No sense of emotion of any kind – other than his obvious affection towards his mother – and not a word of praise for his father. There had been a strong sense of collusion between him and the rest of the mourners, as though there was a sub text that they shared, and from which Caton and his team were excluded.

The rain carved gullies in the mound of earth piled up at the foot of the grave. Tiny streams had formed that came together at its base, and snaked their way towards the deep trench; the sound of the tiny waterfall at its edge, drowned out by the patter of rain on the raised umbrellas.

The vicar stood at the head of the grave with Margaret Standing and her son. The remainder of the mourners took up positions on either side of the grave. The coffin was lowered, prayers intoned, and the time came to throw the symbolic handfuls of earth into the grave. The mourners followed each other in silent file past the pile of earth, where each of them stooped to take a handful, before returning to their places. Margaret Standing let the first handful drop into the chasm, followed by each of the mourners in turn. It seemed to Caton as though the vehemence with which the earth was thrown gained momentum as the action moved around the group. For a short moment the sound of the rain was superseded by the drumming of soil on the coffin lid. Finally came John Standing's turn. He lifted his arm high above the grave, letting the earth fall through his fingers like so much chaff in the wind. In reminded Caton of an act of immolation he had seen as a child in a film about the Apache nation. It occurred to him that John Standing was of an age where he might just have seen it too.

'What do you want me to do Boss?' Gordon Holmes asked as they made their way to their cars. 'No one else has turned up except this lot, and they'll probably all be going back to the house.'

'Have you managed to video them all?' Caton asked him quietly.

Holmes nodded. 'It won't be brilliant with all this rain, but I've got enough to identify them if we have to.'

'In which case, why don't you come on back to the house with us. You can mingle with the guests and see what you can pick up. At the very least you can find out who they all are.

They parked behind the string of cars on the gravel circle, and made their way to the front door. The family liaison officer had gone back to work, leaving just the three of them. As Stuart pointed out, they still represented a quarter of the people there.

'Maybe this is what they mean when they talk about the heavy mob?' Holmes quipped.

'It isn't funny Gordon,' Caton told him. 'We're going to have to tread lightly. I've got enough complaints from Chester House as it is.'

As it happened, Margaret Standing was not the slightest bit phased by the size of the police presence, had her son take their coats, and insisted they have a drink and help themselves to the buffet. There were canapés, vol-au-vent, a whole salmon, slices of chicken, ham and turkey, whist pies, and a selection of side salads. There was cheese and biscuits, and gateaux, to follow. Two waitresses offered sherry, bucks fizz or champagne. An assortment of lager stood in a large ice bucket.

'This is more like a wedding breakfast than a wake,' Holmes observed as he piled up his plate.

Rather than insinuate himself into conversations, Caton took a seat on the periphery, waiting to see if anyone would draw him into one of the tight knit circles that always evolve on such occasions. He was content to sip his orange juice, and bide his time, leaving Holmes and Stuart to practice their insertion technique. Eventually John Standing came over.

'I appreciate that you felt you had to be here Chief Inspector,' he said. 'But don't you think you may have overstayed your welcome?'

Caton rose to face him. 'I understand that it must

be difficult for you Mr Standing, but we are investigating your father's murder, and I'm afraid I don't believe that you or your mother have been totally frank about relationships between the three of you. If you think you can clear that up now, then perhaps we can leave you both in peace. How about it?'

John Standing checked that his mother was busy talking with a group of mourners. 'Not here,' he said. 'We'll use the study.'

21

'My father was domineering,' he began. 'He set high standards that it wasn't always possible to live up to. I can't remember exactly when it began, but I know it was before we started primary school. I was the confident one, into sport, the first to volunteer for anything. Bruce was quiet, and introspective.'

'Bruce?'

'I had a twin brother Chief Inspector. That's the only thing we've been keeping from you. If you let me explain, I'm sure you will understand why.'

'Please do.' Caton said. It was always best to let them tell the story their way.

'Our father had no patience with him. He would accuse him of being a mummy's boy. In a way, that became a self-fulfilling prophecy, because our mother and I became protective of him.'

He played with a glass crystal paperweight, turning it slowly on the surface of the table, looking deep into its centre, fathoming its depths.

'It was a kind of emotional abuse. He was much the same with our mother. He insisted that she stop teaching in order to look after us, and then he'd accuse her of being shallow, of turning into a typical housewife. *"Housefrau"*, was the term he used to denigrate her. Scorn and derision were his weapons of preference; until we reached our teens.'

He looked up at Caton. 'My father was also a serial adulterer,' He waited for a response.

'We know,' Caton replied quietly.

Standing looked at the other officers, and then back at Caton. 'Of course you do. Once you started digging it was only a matter of time. I don't suppose it took very long?'

When no one responded he began to fiddle with the paperweight again. Behind him, through bay windows, the sky was turning black.

'Our mother finally reached the end of the road. We were living in a large house in Kent. Bruce and I were in our games room up in the roof space. There was a table tennis table, a record player, a mini pool table, and a couple of divans. We were fourteen. I was playing pool, and Bruce was sitting on a divan reading. We heard this almighty argument. A shouting match really. They were two floors below us, but the sound travelled up through the chimney breast. She threatened to leave him, and take us with him. She said that if he tried to stop us she would expose him. Bruce stopped reading, and suddenly went white. Then we heard her screaming. We both raced downstairs. I still had the cue in my hand. They were in the master bedroom. Our mother was lying across the bed. He held her by both arms and was shaking her like a rag doll. She was still screaming. Bruce snatched the cue, grabbed one of our father's arms, and began to hit him across his back with the cue. Our father let go of her, and turned on us. For a moment I thought he was going to kill us. His face was red, his eyes were wild, his mouth drawn back over his teeth. He raised one arm, and instinctively we flinched. Mother struggled up, grasped his other arm, and hung onto it. 'Don't hurt them John,' she pleaded. The colour drained from his face. He shrugged her off, and walked past us, and out of the room without another word.' He stopped speaking and stared again at the paperweight.

Caton gave him a moment or two, and then said 'What happened next?'

Standing looked up and around the room, as though disturbed from a dream. He pushed the paperweight away. 'After that he ceased to criticise and belittle her. On the contrary, he even tried to be pleasant. Every Friday he would bring home a bunch of flowers. We knew it was an act, but the rows stopped. His attitude towards Bruce however, worsened if anything. By the time we left for university neither of them were speaking to each other. If the truth be told, Bruce hadn't had a civil conversation with our father in years. I think that he suspected that a lot of the rows were about our mother sticking up for him. And he was right; she'd given up letting his peccadilloes get to her years before. The Christmas of our second year at university Bruce came home one evening and discovered that our father had been hitting our mother. He found her curled up by the fire clutching her stomach. She had a red mark on her face, and was crying. It turned out he'd been hitting her for years; whenever she annoyed or criticised him, always where the marks would never show. Bruce challenged him when he came back from the club. He told him exactly what he thought of him, and what he'd do if he ever touched our mother again. Then he got his things, and stormed out of the house.'

'What exactly did your brother say?' Caton asked.

'I know what you're implying Chief Inspector. But I wasn't there, and I was never told. I just know that Bruce never returned to the house from that night on.'

'How did your father react?'

'He cut him out of his life completely. He shredded all of the photographs he could find of him, and forbade us to mention his name in his company. He didn't even acknowledge his existence when he sent in his entry for Who's Who. He would fly into a rage if anyone brought him up in conversation. As far as he was concerned it was as though he had never existed.'

'What happened to Bruce?'

'He went back to university. He was living in a house with a group of fellow students; they got him through it. He did the exchange year of his degree in Lille at the same time that I did mine in Clermond Ferrand. We actually met up a couple of times.'

'How did he seem?'

'Much the same as ever. A little more distant perhaps. He asked after mother but never mentioned our father, and I certainly wasn't going to bring him up.'

'And then?'

'He disappeared as soon as his course was over. Without as much as a goodbye. Every year up until December 2003 I'd receive a card on our birthday, and mother on hers. They were always postmarked Paris. But it turns out that they were posted for him.'

He got up from the desk, walked over to the bay window, and stared out into the gathering gloom.

'Then we had a phone call from the British Consulate in Marseille. The police in Perpignan had contacted them about the disappearance of a French citizen who turned out to have dual British citizenship. The man's name was Jean Macquart, but the name in his British passport was Bruce Standing.'

'How is that possible,' Caton asked. He wouldn't have been resident long enough to qualify?'

Standing turned slowly, and faced him. 'It seems that he joined the French Foreign Legion,' he paused to let it sink in. 'They can change your name, or you can ask for it to be changed. After three years service you can ask to be considered for French nationality.' He took up the thread again. 'He was based in Calvi, the 2nd Regiment Parachutistes. Apparently he served with distinction in Bosnia, Somalia, and Rwanda.' He looked down at the desk, and then back at Caton. 'It's ironic really. Our father would probably have been proud of him.' He sat back down on the chair as though weary. 'He left after seven years and settled in the south west. He taught scuba diving for a while in Colliure, where his regiment had done a course in underwater warfare. Then he moved twenty kilometres or so inland, to Corsavy, a village on the lower slopes of the Eastern Pyrenees, to work as a mountain guide. He set off late one evening and never returned. It was over a week before he was reported missing. A search party found his rucksack in a crevasse on Mount Canigou. The investigating magistrates decided that suicide was the most likely outcome, but in the absence of a body, declared him missing presumed dead. Under French law the file was kept open and no death certificate was issued. There was only the house and its contents for someone to inherit, and no one to mourn him. The lawyer given the responsibility of tracing relatives found his British Passport, and tracked us down. My mother and I flew out there. We spent a month, and several thousand pounds, on guides and a private detective; to no avail.'

'What did your father have to say about all this?' Caton asked him.

'He didn't know. We told him that we were going on holiday. In any case, he was away himself most of that time.'

'How did your mother take it?'

'She was distraught. When we came back my father thought she was having a breakdown. We didn't tell him any different.'

'He had a right to know, surely?'

'He'd surrendered whatever rights he had years ago.' Standing began pushing the paperweight slowly around the table top, staring into it as though there was something he could see there. 'And then, eight months later, came the news. A pair of climbers had discovered Bruce's remains at the bottom of a gully.'

Caton picked up a chair that stood in the alcove between the bookcase and the window, and drew it up to the desk. He sat facing Standing. The downlight from halogen spots in the ceiling, cast shadows over Standing's face, highlighting his brows and cheekbones, making his eyes seem dark and sunken. Caton reached across the desk and switched on the desk lamp.

'Why did you keep this from us Mr Standing?' he said.

'Because it had no relevance. Bruce is dead.'

'But you must realise that the events you've just shared with us, and the obvious impact that they had on you and on your mother, provide a motive for either, or both of you, to have been involved in your father's murder? I'm afraid that I am going to have to ask you for details of your movements on the day prior to your father's death, and the day following it.'

There was a change in Standing's demeanour. He sat upright, pressing so hard against the back of the chair that it creaked under the strain. His voice was instantly firmer, his eyes alert.

'I was in Paris for a meeting. I stayed overnight, and was still there when my mother phoned with the news.'

'And what time was that exactly?'

'Ten past twelve. We'd just broken off our meeting for a coffee, and a comfort break.'

Allowing for the time difference Caton put that at over three hours after Margaret Standing had been told of her husband's death.

'Was it a message delivered to the hotel, or direct to your phone?'

'Direct to my phone. Why?'

'And was your phone on during the meeting?'

'I always have it on silent vibrate during meetings, so that I can check if any incoming messages are urgent without interrupting the meeting.'

'And is that what happened on this occasion?'

'Yes, it began to vibrate just as I was pouring my coffee.'

'And what time did your meeting begin?'

'At ten thirty.'

Caton's brain was whirring. If Roger Standing had been killed between eight thirty and nine forty in the evening, there would have been plenty of time for his son to make it back to Paris for a ten thirty start the following day; albeit that their clocks were an hour ahead. Would the mother really wait three hours to ring her son, unless it was to give him time to establish his alibi? If it had been him, there was no way he could have avoided leaving a trail. Likewise, if it was the other brother, he would have had to enter, and leave the country somehow, always assuming that he was still alive.

'Can you prove any of this Mr Standing?' Caton asked.

He appeared surprised. Either that or he was feigning it; Caton couldn't tell which.

'Do I have to?' he said.

'I'm afraid so.'

'Are you saying I'm a suspect?'

'Until we've verified the account you've given me it's hard for me know.'

He turned it over in his mind. 'You really think I may have killed my father?'

'I don't know. What I do know is that you've held back information that could be vital to this investigation.'

Standing wrestled with it, then turned both palms upwards on the desk. 'In that case I'd better put your mind at rest as soon as possible. He reached down to his belt, slipped a slim black mobile phone from its pouch, and handed it to Caton. 'Here's my mobile phone. I'm sure that between this, and my phone records, you should be able to establish that I never left France, or Paris for that matter. I can also let you have a credit card receipt for the hotel I stayed at, and for the return train ticket I booked from Lyon to Paris.

I also went to the Louvre on the afternoon of the first day. I paid for that by credit card. I think I may even still have my copy of the guide for the exhibition that was on. Of course, I can also let you have details of the people present at my meeting. If there's anything else you need, please just ask.

'That's very helpful of you Mr Standing,' Caton said. 'Do you have a car you use where you're over here? Or do you hire one?'

'I have my own car. It's a bit of a banger really, a seven year old Peugeot 307. It's kept in one of the garages for when I'm over here.'

'In that case, unless you have any objections - in which case I shall wait here until we get a warrant – I'm going to ask my scene of crime officers to come and take samples from the clothes you have here, and from your car, and from your mother's car. For purposes of elimination you understand.'

Standing observed him coolly. 'I understand that it'll probably be the quickest way to help this household return to something approximating normality. But I hope they're going to respect the fact that my mother has just buried her husband?'

As if on cue Caton heard DS Stuart's muffled curse and the door burst open. He turned to find Margaret Standing and her sister framed in the doorway, and his sergeant rubbing her back where the handle of the door had struck her.

'John,' said his mother said sharply. 'This is where you are. What's going on here?'

'I'm sorry Sir,' Joanne Stuart began, wondering if she should try to usher them out.

'It's alright Detective Sergeant. Caton said.

'They know about Bruce, mother,' the son said rising from his chair. Her hand flew to her face, and the colour left it. For a moment it seemed that her legs might buckle. Her sister put her arms around her shoulders to support her. Caton got up and walked towards them.

'That's true, Mrs Standing, and although this isn't the best time, I'm afraid I need to speak with you about that. But not with your son present.'

'This is going too far! I won't allow it.' John Standing came from behind the desk, and crossed the room to his mother.

'No John, it's alright,' she said. 'Best to get it over with. Helen can stay with me. That's alright is it Mr Caton?'

'Of course.'

She straightened up, gently prising her sister's arms from each shoulder in turn

'Perhaps we could talk in here Mrs Standing,' Caton said. 'It shouldn't take too long. You son was about to show Inspector Holmes his car.'

Holmes moved on cue to John Standing's side. For a moment it looked as though the son would object. He settled for placing one hand on his mother's arm.

'You'll be alright mother?'

The look that passed between them proved impossible for Caton to fathom.

'Don't worry John. I'll be fine,' she said.

'I'm sure you can appreciate that it does seem strange that neither of you mentioned Bruce to us,' Caton said, as soon as they were settled.

She looked tired but composed. 'I don't think you

realise how hard it was… still is, for me Mr Caton. For the past twelve years one of my sons had been cut off from me. To not even be able to talk about him openly in my own home; to have to keep photographs of him hidden, taking furtive bitter sweet pleasure in looking at them only when my husband was away, and then to discover that he had gone missing. And finally to have to spend the last three of those years hoping against hope that he might still be alive.'

She clasped one hand within the other, squeezing and turning it as she spoke. Reminding Caton of the term *wringing one's hands*. He had been with parents whose children had been missing for some time, some of whom were never found. The hoping and the grieving never ceased. 'Not knowing must have been the hardest thing of all.' He said.

She looked up at him, holding back the tears in her eyes. 'I'll tell you what *is* hardest Mr Caton,' she said. 'That in all that time my husband would not allow his name to be mentioned in this house, nor any photographs to be displayed; that my son was so bitter that he asked in his will that he be buried in Colliure, rather than back here in England. She dabbed her eyes with the handkerchief her sister had handed her.

Outside, on the driveway, the rain had picked up again, resounding on the lead roof above the bay, running like tears down the window panes.

22

The rain had stopped, and the clouds hovering above the city had cleared to a thin layer, tinged pink by the lowering sun.

Carter had some news for them. 'We've had a reporter from the Sun sniffing around. Wanted to know if we thought Standing's death had anything to do with his connections with the Government. I gave her the usual line - no comment, enquiries are proceeding - and packed her off in the direction of Chester House. But I got Duggie to dig a bit deeper; the internet, Education Guardian, Times Educational Supplement, his credit records. It turns out he had a flat in Kensington. Used it in preference to hotels when he was up in the Smoke.'

Caton had never understood why people still referred to London as *The Smoke*. It was over fifty years since the last great smog resulted in the phasing out of solid fuel fires in the capital. And why did people from the North go *up* to London, when it was self-evidently *down*?'

'And, according to his credit card,' Carter continued. 'He had a favourite restaurant just off Sloane Square. And from the size of the bills I'd say there were always two people eating. Even more interesting is the number of purchases from the following,' he consulted his notes.

'Lingerie-Confidential; Designer Lingerie; Figleaves; Heavenly Bodice; and Bond Street Jewellers Limited. Now who do you think they were for? The now grieving widow?' He closed his notebook with a flourish. 'I doubt it.'

'You lucky devil,' Kate told Tom later that evening. 'A couple of days in London. I wouldn't mind coming with you. I am free you know.'

'Firstly, I'll be working,' he said. 'Secondly, that really would go down well with the accountants at Chester House. *Officer takes lover on spree to West End.*'

Her face lit up. 'Lover. I like the sound of that. So much nicer than mistress. Anyway, I was only teasing. As it happens I'm seeing one of your FMIT colleagues come Monday.'

'Who's that?'

'Rob Lancaster.'

'The arson case?'

'That's right.'

'And they want the help of a profiler?'

'Right again. They think it may be a repeat; part of a pattern, rather than a random one off.'

'Has Rob told you on what basis?'

'The MO. It's the same kind of entry, accelerant, container, and point of origin. Apparently all of this has been common to two previous fatal arson attacks. And there's something else he wants me to see for myself.'

'Please tell me they're not racist attacks?'

'No, they're not.'

'Thank God for that.'

'In some ways it would be easier if they were.

There would be obvious suspects, and not much need of a profile.'

'And the seeds of the biggest civil unrest this side of poll tax riots.'

'Much worse than that,' she said.

They took a moment to think about it.

'It'll be an opportunity to try out our proposals for multi-level integrated profiling,' she said. 'I'll let you know how it goes.'

Caton checked his watch, and handed her her glass. 'Drink up. We've got a film to catch.'

She drained her gin and tonics, and picked up her clutch bag. 'James Bond. I can't wait. From what I've seen of the promo's – him coming out of the sea, rippling muscles glistening with water and oil - there's a real man.'

'Pity you won't be taking him home tonight.' He said, taking her arm.

She fixed him with her deep green eyes, the grin widening. 'I wouldn't be so sure of that. Once a girl's closed her eyes, you'd be surprised who turns up.'

Caton tightened the grip on her arm. 'In that case, you'd better keep those eyes wide open.'

'What the hell are you doing Tom?'

It sounded like Superintendent Helen Gates was having a bad day. He checked the time on his mobile. 8.35am. She'd been quick off the mark.

'I'm on a Pendelino, just approaching Stoke, Ma'am,' he said.

'Cut it out Tom, I'm serious. I rang Longsight because you haven't given me the courtesy of an update, and your office manager tells me you're going to London. Why?'

'I'm sorry about the update Ma'am,' he said, realising too late that if he had called her he could have avoided this particular unpleasantness. It was a bad mistake. Gates was the only buffer he had between himself and the politics of Chester House. 'It's been a bit hectic.' It was all he could think to say.

'Skip that, Detective Chief Inspector, just tell me why you're going to London.'

'It's a bit difficult Ma'am,' he said lowering his voice to a whisper. 'I'm in the quiet compartment.' Actually, he wasn't, but how would she know?

'Then get yourself out of there. Go to the toilet or something.' She was becoming increasingly irritated.

'And risk losing the signal? It's bad enough on here anyway Ma'am. Don't worry, I'll just be careful.'

'Get on with it then.'

'The deceased had a flat in the West End; in Kensington,' he whispered into the phone.

'So?'

'I need to see if there's anything there that can help us.'

There was a long pause. 'That's not it is it?' she said.

'It?'

'Don't play the innocent with me Tom, I'm a detective, remember? You're pursuing a lead. Or what you think is a lead. Something to do with the Government. Why didn't you tell me?'

Caton was certain that no one in the team would have told her. So how did she know? There was no point in trying to explain why he'd kept it from her. To be honest, he wasn't even sure himself. It was just a gut feeling that Hadfield would have blocked it, or insisted on going himself instead.

'Well it was just a hunch,' he said. 'Nothing concrete. Just something to eliminate really.'

'Well Martin's gone ballistic, so you'd better walk on egg shells, or you can kiss goodbye to the SDU. It was only a pilot scheme, remember?'

So, it was *Martin* now. Not Chief Superintendent Hadfield. Was that a slip up in the heat of the moment, Caton wondered, or something more? And now they were threatening to pull the plug from under his team. What the hell were they so worried about?

'Don't worry, Ma'am,' he said more calmly than he felt. 'I can handle it.'

'Well just make sure you do. Don't you go anywhere near MI5 or…' The phone went dead, and the lights dimmed in the compartment. They had entered a tunnel. The second they emerged into the light Caton tried to redial. There was no signal. He looked out of the window. A narrowboat was moving slowly along the canal that ran alongside the railway. Beyond the canal, a river snaked across the flat meadowlands at its margin. Sparsely wooded hills rose towards the horizon. He knew from experience that this was the beginning of a dead zone for his mobile phone. It would be Milton Keynes before he could get a decent signal again. He just hoped that Helen Gates would accept he hadn't cut her off on purpose. He switched his phone off, and got back to the Great British Breakfast congealing on the plate.

The first thing Caton noticed at Euston was the number of policemen. Not just British Transport

Police, but Met as well. As he passed the barrier, two specialist firearms officers, a man and a woman, walked slowly past, Heckler and Koch MP5 sub machine guns cradled at forty five degrees across their chests. It was getting more like Manchester Airport. Perhaps Hadfield's sent them to bring me in, he joked to himself. He made his way across the concourse and started down the steps to the taxi rank. While he waited in line he made the call.

By the time they reached Foulis Terrace, just off the Fulham Road, the taxi driver had explained how the congestion charges, road calming measures, and cameras at box junctions, were part of a conspiracy to put him out of business; sought three times to find out what it was that Caton did and what had brought him to London; and had provided a unique solution to the Middle East crisis. Caton climbed out close to brain dead. He stood with his overnight bag, searching the street for the key holder.

A young man, in his early twenties, got out of a silver BMW parked ten metres down the street, and came towards him.

'Mr Caton? I'm Andrew. From Godber and Godber. I'm sorry, but if you don't mind, I need to see some identification.'

Caton showed him his warrant card. 'Don't be sorry,' he said, 'If more people did, it would make our lives a lot easier.'

The young man grinned. 'It's just that you can't be too careful, especially around here.' He led the way past the railings, and up the stone steps of the Georgian four storied terrace. The flat was on the second floor.

'Some of your colleagues were here not so long since,' the estate agent said, as he opened the door. Caton's heart sank.

The flat was small, but perfectly formed. A kitchen diner, and the one double bedroom with a king sized bed, looked out onto well kept communal gardens. A modern wet room provided for all of the ablutions in a single space. The lounge looked as though it had been furnished with a sofa, chairs, mirror, paintings, and a glass chandelier, direct from a department store. The phone had been disconnected. All of the cupboards were bare. He wiped his fingers across the surface of the mantelpiece. Not a trace of dust. The young man moved to the sash windows and looked out.

'It's amazing who lives around here. That big row of terraces next door belongs to the Royal Brompton Hospital. Some rich old dear left them in trust for the exclusive use of doctors and nurses. Right opposite them, that house there…' he pointed to a substantial Georgian mansion. '…Madonna lived there before she moved up to Notting Hill. And Robbie Williams had it after that. Cool, or what!'

Caton stared at the glass on the inside of the window. Not a smear, not a single mark. All that Caton could see was the absence of anything remotely resembling evidence that Standing, or anyone else for that matter, had ever lived here. He had not the slightest doubt that this was yet another place that had been sanitised.

'My colleagues. Did you let them in?'

The young man turned from the window. 'Oh yes. And I checked their ID. Very polite they were, but they insisted that I leave them alone in the flat until they'd finished.'

'And how long was that?'

'An hour and a half I'd say. They rang me on my mobile.'

'I don't suppose you recall the name of the officer who showed you his warrant card?'

The young man grinned. 'It was hardly a name you'd forget. Like, it didn't really fit him, if you know what I mean. A regular bruiser...with a name like Miles? I ask you. Miles Crispin.'

Caton left his bags at the hotel and decided to risk walking the mile to the restaurant. His route took him past the faded grandeur of Eaton Square, and the private gardens on either side, into Sloane Square. Realising that he'd overshot the entrance to Doyley Street, he turned back on himself around the Church of the Holy Trinity. It occurred to him that to anyone following, this would look like a deliberate attempt to shake them off. He turned left into Wilbraham Place, and stepped back into the second doorway. A minute passed. No one rounded the corner. He chided himself for allowing paranoia to creep up on him, and crossed the street. The entrance was not immediately evident; a modest nameplate beside a simple door.

If the entrance was all but anonymous, the interior was astonishing. Caton was led to a raised bar area from which he could see down into the dining area. The room was stylish in an understated way. The chic wooden tables, with matching chairs, were empty but for crystal glasses. White curtains, floor to ceiling, created floating screens dividing the deceptively large room into a series of smaller, more intimate, spaces. It was empty; too late for lunch, unfashionably early for dinner. Caton picked up a shiny instructional menu. This was the first French restaurant that he had come across exclusively serving tapas sized portions. Not a nine and ten course gourmet menu as such, but genuinely individual servings to mix and match. He would love to bring Kate here.

'How can I help you sir?'

Caton stood to face the duty manager. Landis Dupont; a tall, lean man, as elegant as his restaurant. 'I'm Detective Chief Inspector Caton,' he said. 'I'm sorry to disturb you this close to your lunch sitting. But this is important, and it shouldn't take long.'

Dupont appeared unruffled. 'Please sit down Chief Inspector. May I get you a drink?'

'No thank you. As I said, it shouldn't take long.'

They sat facing each other.

'Mr Roger Standing. I understand he was a frequent diner here?' At the mention of the name, he saw the blinds come down.

'I'm sorry,' the manager tried to keep his voice steady, but there was the faintest tremor. Caton had heard it a thousand times before. 'Roger....?'

'Roger *Standing*. Not an easy name to forget. After all, a Commander of The British Empire must be a coup, even for a restaurant such as this?' Caton took out his notebook. He took his time finding the page. 'According to his credit card he dined here once in April, twice in May, three times in June, just once last month. It probably would have been more,' he stared at the manager, leaving him no place to hide. 'But he was murdered.' The poor man looked around for support. It was obvious to Caton that Dupont had been got at. 'You do remember him don't you?'

'Now you remind me, yes I do,' his voice faltered. 'It was shocking… the way he died.'

Caton sensed that he wanted to help. He only needed an excuse to do so.

'Yes it *was*, Mr Dupont. And I am investigating a murder. I don't care who's spoken to you, or what you've been told. If you refuse to answer my questions, I shall arrest you for obstructing the police. Do you understand?'

He saw the man wrestle with himself, and lose. His eyes cleared, his shoulders drooped; as much in relief as in defeat. 'What is it you want to know?'

'Mr Standing was accompanied when he came here?'

'Always.'

'Always the same person?'

'Yes. A woman,' he pointed to the far side of the restaurant, where a raised booth was curtained off for extra privacy. 'That was their table. After the first few times he no longer needed to request it. It was automatically reserved for him.'

'Can you describe this woman?'

Dupont rose to his feet, conscious that the first lunchtime diners were due. 'Better than that, Detective Chief Inspector, she came here several times herself for lunch with a female companion. If you give me a minute, I can get you her name and contact number.'

Caton stood on the pavement. He looked at the name again. Miranda Horne. It tugged at his memory. He had heard the name, and seen it before. He took out his mobile phone.

The man who answered repeated the number. No name, no hello, just the number. A classic cautionary move. One that Caton used himself as a matter of course.

'I would like to speak to Miranda Horne,' he said.

'And you are?'

'My name is Detective Chief Inspector Tom Caton. Greater Manchester Police.'

There was a dense silence. Like a chasm between them.

'I see Sir. Well I am afraid that Miss Horne is not available at the moment, but if you would like to leave your number, I'm sure that she will ring you back.'

Caton weighed it up. Should he declare that he was already in London, and try to get her to agree to meet him this evening, or find out where she lived, and surprise her in the morning. He decided to let her sweat overnight, give himself time to do his homework, and turn up when she least expected it. He gave his mobile number.

'Thank you Sir. I'll see she gets it as soon as possible. Good evening Sir.'

Whoever the hell she was Caton decided, she had a very well trained butler.

Outside the restaurant the heavens opened. There were plenty of taxis. They sped past, mocking him with orange *busy* lights, the occupants peering through the windows, counting their blessings, pitying the drowned rat as he jogged through Bloomsbury. He was drenched by the time he got back to his hotel.

Dried off, and changed, he sat in front of the television monitor and connected with the internet. It took one just one Google hit. Miranda Horne, Senior Policy Adviser to the Prime Minister. A Double First at Oxford in Politics, Philosophy and Economics; an MA in Media, Politics and Power. From Pembroke College to Parliament.

Twenty minutes of net surfing later he had learned everything he needed to know. Three weeks prior to Standing's death it had been announced that she was to stand for a safe seat at the next election. Rumours immediately surfaced that she was about to be jetted into a ministerial post. There were predictions that she was being groomed to be the next female Prime Minister. Since Standing's death, there had been niente; da nada; a big silent nothing.

He ordered room service, and spent the next two hours going through his notebook, identifying dead ends, teasing out connections. Finally, he set it aside and logged on again. He found himself wandering aimlessly through the web like a butterfly. Alighting for a moment, and taking off again. The next time he looked at his watch it was twenty to midnight. He logged off, and climbed into bed; to sleep, perchance to dream. Some hope. He lay awake staring at the ceiling, his mind buzzing with permutations.

23

Thursday the tenth of August was cool, with the smell of rain in the air. Caton made himself a breakfast tea from the complimentary tray, and switched on the television. The newsreader was talking over a live feed from Heathrow Airport. Armoured cars patrolled the perimeter. The booking halls and waiting areas were packed with frustrated passengers and their luggage, many of whom had been there since the small hours. Armed police were everywhere.

'The Department for Transport has issued the following advice to air passengers: Following this morning's police action, security at all UK airports has been increased and additional security measures have been put in place for all flights. With immediate effect, the following arrangements apply to all passengers starting their journey from, and transferring between flights at, a UK airport. All cabin baggage must be processed as hold baggage and carried in the hold of all passenger aircraft that are departing UK airports. Passengers may take small items through the airport security search point, in a single (ideally transparent) plastic carrier bag. Nothing may be carried in pockets.'

The film skipped to footage, filmed in the early hours of the morning. Big burly policemen in riot gear, accompanied by armed officers, bludgeoned their way into suburban homes, accompanied by a voice over.

'Arrests were made earlier in London, Birmingham, and in the Thames Valley. We understand that today's action

has been the culmination of a long standing covert anti-terrorist operation.'

Like millions of others, Caton sat transfixed on the end of his bed. He was about to go down for breakfast when his mobile rang. It was Martin Hadfield.

'Caton, what the hell are you doing?'

His voice was on a slow burn, ready to erupt at any moment. Caton knew there was no point it trying to be evasive.

'I'm going down to breakfast Sir, and then I'm hoping to interview someone.'

'Who?'

'Miranda Horne.'

Hadfield took a deep intake of breath. 'You lay off her,' he hissed. 'Do you understand?'

'Well actually, no Sir, I don't. I believe that she may have something to tell me that could have a bearing on the investigation.'

'Nonsense Caton. She has no bearing on the case.'

And how would he know that? Caton wondered. Come to that, how did Hadfield know he was planning to see her today? He had only told Gates about the meeting with Cole. He had planned to tell her about Horne after breakfast.

Hadfield wasn't waiting for a reply. 'You know the rule,' he said. 'Follow the evidence, not the suspect. You're on a fishing expedition man. Get back up here,'

At that moment there was a knock on the door. The heavy rap of officialdom, not the whimper of room service.

'Hang on a second Sir, there's someone at the door.' Caton held the phone away from his ear, walked over to the door, and looked through the fish eye. Even distorted in this way they were unmistakeable. It was Crispin and Warhurst. He spoke into the phone.

'Sorry Sir, it's Special Branch. I don't know if you've seen the news, but all hell has broken out down here. I'll have to call you back.' He didn't wait for the spluttered reply, he just switched off.

'Now then, Tom, whose being a naughty boy?' Not the most original greeting, but Crispin made it sound more objectionable than most.

'You've got five minutes,' Caton told them. 'I'm on my way to breakfast.'

'And then straight on the next train home. That's right isn't it?' Warhurst sneered.

'No it isn't as a matter of fact. I'm waiting for a phone call, and then I shall be going to a meeting.'

They looked at each other. It was the old double act again.

'I don't think so,' Crispin said. 'You see there isn't going to be a phone call, unless it's from your boss, telling you to bugger off back to Manchester. And there isn't going to be a meeting, other than the one we're having right now.'

Caton put his phone in his pocket, picked up his wrist watch from the bedside table, and put it on his wrist.

'In that case, good morning gentlemen,' he said, heading for the door.

Warhurst stepped into his path.

'Let's stop pissing around shall we Tom?' Crispin said, sitting down on the bed. 'Just hear us out.'

Caton turned to face him. He looked at his watch.

'You've got three minutes left.'

'She's not going to call you back.' Crispin told him. 'That's the message we've been asked to give you. *We* can tell you everything you need to know.'

'That's not how it works Crispin. You know that.'

'It's how the Prime Minister wants it,' Warhurst said, earning a fierce look from his companion.

'Are you telling me that the Prime Minister is obstructing a murder enquiry?'

'That's not what he meant, and you know it.' Crispin spat out. 'We're police too, in case you've forgotten, and we can tell you what you need to know.'

Caton shook his head. 'I'd rather hear it from the horse's mouth, than the donkey's arse.'

Crispin stood, smoothed out his jacket, and straightened his tie. 'I wonder what your Chief Constable would have to say if he found out that your girl friend, *Ms* Webb, has been seen regularly in the company of a Sadiq bin Ali, who the SIS and Anti-Terrorist Squad tell us has a connection with Basheer bin Qurban-Aziz, a known member of an al-Qaeda network, and someone who worked closely with Osama Bin Laden in Afghanistan when the Taliban were battling with the Russians? What would her University say if they knew? What about her role as a Home Office Profiler? It would bugger that up good and proper, don't you think?'

Caton fought back the temptation to floor him. 'I don't know what kind of crap you're peddling here,' he said. But I'll tell you one thing. You leave Kate Webb out of this, or both of you will have cause to regret it, however long it takes. And as for Ms Horne, whose name you can't even bring yourself to mention, this is a murder enquiry. *My* murder enquiry. I don't have an option but to speak with her. And what's more if I don't get an interview, I'll get a subpoena. If that gets blocked, I'll have no option but to find out what the tabloids have on the relationship between her and Standing, and work up from there.'

A new tension showed on Crispin's face; somewhere between a botox injection, and a face lift. He got up, pushed past Caton, and opened the door. 'Inspector Warhurst and I have a call to make,' he said. 'I suggest you wait here.'

They were back in three minutes. Crispin was curt, and to the point. 'You're to be at the gates to Downing Street at one fifty this afternoon,' he said. 'And if I don't see you again, enjoy your retirement. I hear there are vacancies at B&Q.' He closed the door quietly as he left. It seemed to make the point more eloquently than a slam.

As Caton approached the famous wrought iron gates, his phone beeped. It was a text from Kate. Her usual text speak. He wondered if she knew that mobile phone text was based on something called the Rebus principle. Come to that, he wondered if Ian Rankin did.

'carnt wait 2 see U 2nite. No xcuse this tym. Pic U up from train. Let me no wich 1 Ure on.'

He rang her straight back. It was engaged. He left a voice message, switched off his mobile, and showed his warrant card to the duty officer.

Number 10 Downing Street turned out to be a warren. They passed through two halls, two corridors, and three doors. Finally he was shown into a small wood panelled room.

Miranda Horne was a surprise. At only five foot one or so, she radiated the authority of a pocket battle ship. Her jet black hair, shot with streaks of purple, created a wild yet perfect frame for her pale face which was a perfect oval. Pencil thin eyebrows arched above dark brown eyes. Her snub nose, turning up slightly at the tip, was softened by pale pink glossy lips. Her charcoal grey pinstripe business suit, cut to flatter, exposed three inches of white silk blouse. From her place at the head of the table she eyed Caton with open curiosity. To her left sat a tall figure familiar to Caton; Sir Michael George, the Attorney General. To her right sat a slim, dark haired, serious looking man in his mid fifties, in dark pinstripe and purple tie. He spoke first.

'Detective Chief Inspector. My name is Peter Lockridge. I am Secretary to the Cabinet. May I introduce Ms Miranda Horne, and Sir Michael George, the Attorney General.'

If this turnout was meant to impress it succeeded. Sir Peter Lockridge, no less; responsible for the Cabinet office, and the whole of the Home Civil Service. As for the Attorney General, nothing could have underlined the seriousness of Crispin's threat than his presence here. On a day like today, when the balloon had gone up, it was little short of miraculous that these two had found time to squeeze him in.

'Ms Horne is here voluntarily, to assist you in connection with the tragic death of Roger Standing.' Lockridge continued. 'It has been a difficult time for her, and I am sure that you will appreciate that both she, and the Government, would prefer that, as far as possible, what had been an intimate and intensely private relationship, should not now be brought, needlessly, into the media spotlight.'

That just about covers all the bases, Caton decided. It sounded like a carefully prepared speech, somewhat unnatural, spoken for the record. None of them, he noticed, were taking notes. It was a given that anything said in this room would be digitally recorded. He decided a simple nod would suffice for now.

Miranda Horne began to speak. Her voice was firm and clear, yet personal. It was soft and easy on the ear. She was a born communicator. He listened intently as she told the story of their relationship. How they had met at one of the Prime Minister's education focus groups here in Number Ten. How they began to socialise when he was up in London. How he assured her that his marriage was over, and pledged eternal love. She stopped at that point. The background had been sketched. It was an invitation for him to find the right questions. Caton decided to get the obvious one out of the way first.

'Do you mind telling me where you were on Saturday the twenty third of July Ms Horne?'

Both men looked ready to protest. She raised her hand imperiously, stopping them in their tracks. It was a question she had expected, and prepared for.

'I was working at Number Ten until eight pm that evening with two speech writers, whose names I can provide. Our heads were spinning by then, so we went for drink, and some food, to The Phoenix, on the corner of Palace Street and Stag Place. I paid with my credit card.' She raised her eyebrows, to underline the point. 'I was back in my flat by eleven. I had to be at work by six thirty in the morning for a breakfast meeting. It was a busy time. We were working on some speeches for the Party Conference, trying to get as much done as possible before the summer recess.'

'Parliament was about to close down for the summer?'

'Yes. The following week.'

'Were you planning to go on leave?'

'Yes.'

'With Mr Standing?'

Peter Lockridge was becoming impatient. 'I don't see what possible relevance…'

She leant across him, one hand on his arm; an intimacy that spoke volumes for her standing within this building.

'It's alright Sir Peter,' she said. 'Yes, we had been hoping to spend some time away together, but…'

She looked across at the Attorney General who nodded almost imperceptibly.

'Our relationship had begun to cool.'

'Why was that?'

'I had been given evidence of his – track record shall we say.'

'His previous infidelities?' Caton saw her flinch. It was almost as though she'd been slapped across the face. He had reminded her that she was not just a lover, but an adulteress. Just another of Standing's mistresses. She gathered herself.

'Yes. He had been promising to leave his wife. To get a divorce so that we could marry. It was a risk I was no longer willing to take.'

'You told him this?'

'Yes.'

'When?'

'The last time we met here in London.'

'Which was?' Suddenly it was like pulling teeth.

'The Saturday before; exactly a week before he was killed.'

'How did he take it?'

She looked straight ahead, speaking into the middle distance. 'We rowed. At first he was angry, really angry. He said that I must have been spying on him. Then he calmed down, and made a lot of promises. He swore he would tell his wife, and move out straight away, and permanently, to prove he was serious. I told him not to bother; that it was over. He refused to accept it. In the end I asked the restaurant manager to call a taxi, and left.'

'This was at Le Cercle?'

She looked at him, startled for a moment.

'Yes.'

'Did he try to contact you after that?

'Yes, he bombarded me with emails, text messages; he rang my mobile so often I had to change the Sim card. You've no idea how inconvenient that was.'

Caton had a pretty good idea. She would thrive on networking. She must have had hundreds of people to contact. He wondered if it could be done by a single message to everyone in her address book. Everyone that is, but Standing.

'He sent me flowers everyday. It became highly embarrassing. I even received a bouquet on the day after his body was found,' her voice dropped. 'He must have arranged it on the day he died.'

'Have you ever had any contact with, or from, Mr Standing's family? His wife for example, or his sons?'

The surprise in her eyes was genuine. The Attorney

General and the Secretary to the Cabinet exchanged glances. Whoever had done the digging had missed that.

'Sons?' she said, watching him intently. 'He only had one son, John.'

'Another secret I'm afraid. John had a twin brother, Bruce. He went missing some years ago. I take it he never mentioned him to you?'

She shook her head. 'No never.'

Caton closed his notebook. 'In that case, I have no more questions for you Ms Horne. I would like to thank you for being so helpful. I realise it must have been difficult for you, and I hope you appreciate why it was necessary?'

She nodded. 'In a way it's been a relief. I knew it would have to happen, it was only a matter of when. Best that it came sooner rather than later.' There was an implied criticism in her voice. He sensed that she had been overruled in her desire to get it over with, among others, by those present.

The Cabinet Secretary leaned forward. 'None of this need enter the public domain.'

Caton addressed himself to Miranda Horne. 'I am afraid I can't give that assurance Ms Horne. The Attorney General will tell you that I have no option but to check your alibis. Regardless of whether or not what you have told me has any bearing on the case, it will have to go into the file. If we reach the point of preparing a prosecution against the perpetrator, defence counsel will see it. If it has no relevance, there would be no reason for them to use it. But if they were to suspect that I, and my team, had not checked this particular avenue thoroughly in order to rule it out, they could try to use it to place reasonable doubt in the mind of the jury. What I can promise is that I and my team will respect the confidentiality of what you've told me, within the confines of this investigation.' How's that for the record, he thought.

The Cabinet Secretary looked ready to object but Miranda Horne stayed him with her hand, pushed back her chair, and stood up. The two men followed her lead.

'Thank you for your honesty Detective Chief Inspector,' she said. 'And the professional manner in which you've conducted yourself. I only wish I'd come forward at the outset. It might have saved you a lot of trouble, and me a great deal of soul searching.'

She turned and left the room, followed by the Parliamentary Secretary. The Attorney General paused in the doorway. He stared at Caton, as though committing his face to memory. Then he gave a curt nod, and left. .

Quite what that meant Caton could only guess. He picked up his notebook, and put it safely away. So presumably their concern to recover the briefcase, and the search of Standing's office and penthouse, were only about recovering any embarrassing material – diaries, appointments, whatever - that might identify Ms Horne, or that might contain embarrassing revelations shared in the intimate afterglow that always seemed to accompany illicit sex. Would Miranda Horne recover from this? From what he'd seen he sincerely hoped so. Careers had been halted mid stream over far less. If the restaurant knew, there would be others. The tabloids would be only a step behind. Sooner or later she would have to deal with it. Another future blighted at worst, interrupted at best, by association with Roger Standing.

It was evening rush hour. The only seat he could find was a window seat on a table for four. Caton stretched his long legs out, claiming the space between the table leg, and the wall. By the time they reached Milton Keynes he had finished the London Evening Standard, the small plate of chicken and sun blushed tomato pie, and the complimentary glass of wine. From the coverage of this morning's events, it was clear that the suspected bombers had been under observation for some months, and the security operation planned well in advance, with the Government's response prepared beforehand. Which explained how the three of them had been able to squeeze him in. He put his head back on the seat, felt the Pendolino sway gently back and forth as it negotiated the notorious bends of the West Coast line, and fell asleep.

The sky was dark, full of brooding clouds; the landscape unfamiliar. Huge, steaming, cone shaped mounds of black spoil, filled the middle ground. Weary figures, in silhouette, bent to till unyielding earth. From time to time they called out to each other in French. Caton walked towards them. Two figures advanced on an unsuspecting third. She turned. They seized her, and threw her to the ground. One of them, a woman, pinned her down while the other threw himself on top. He knew then what was happening, and how it would end.

Caton woke with a shudder. Two of his companions

were asleep; the third busy reading his book. His legs were beginning to cramp. He stretched them gingerly, and sat up. Emile Zola. *Germinal*...no...*La Terre*. That was it. The scene where the greedy couple rape and kill Francois. Why had his sub conscious chosen to dreg this up? He racked his brain for a clue. And then it hit him. Jean Macquart! Jean Macquart was the central character in the novel. Next, the couple kill the old man. In the case of the daughter, that made it patricide. And Bruce Standing had chosen the name Jean Macquart when he'd joined the French Foreign Legion. It seemed too much of a coincidence. Had he intended to revenge himself upon his father? But wasn't he supposed to be dead? Or had his brother John taken up the mantle? Stranger things had happened.

24

He saw her waiting at the end of the platform. She stood out, even among the jostling throng rushing to head the queue at the parking pay station. It wasn't just the stunning auburn hair, loose on her shoulders, aflame in the glow of the light beneath which she stood. There was an aura that set Kate apart. He felt sure the others must see it too, as they hurried home to their lovers, partners, children, their lonely apartments. She spotted him, and came forward, arms out to envelop him. They hugged and kissed, oblivious to the grumbling tide of humanity forced to divide as it reached them.

'Come on,' she said, hooking his free arm. 'I've got a Mediterranean fish casserole in the oven, and a bottle of Chablis on chill.'

They studiously avoided talk of work until they were in the car, and out of the car park. As they turned into Store Street, Caton was reminded that this was where Bojangles had picked up his second victim. He glanced across at Kate. It was amazing how she'd taken all that in her stride. They had to wait a minute or two beneath the railway arch while a tram did a ninety degree turn into the station. He used it as an opportunity to broach the subject he knew he had to raise; to get out of the way as quickly as possible. He tried to make it sound casual, not accusative.

'Do you know a Sadiq bin Ali, at the University Kate?'

She looked across at him, surprised, then quizzical.

'Sadiq? He's a senior lecturer in the Politics and Philosophy faculty. I work with him from time to time on the Manchester Leadership Programme.

'What does that entail?'

'It's a new programme for undergraduate students promoting social justice and developing students' skills. It's a way of involving them in the university's engagement with the local community. They do a short module called Leadership in Action, which Sadiq co-ordinates. There are a series of lectures from external speakers, and then they do some service in the community.' The lights changed, and she shifted into gear. 'Why are you asking?'

He told her then what Crispin had said about the supposed connection. She said nothing as they negotiated the rush hour traffic. He was unable to decide if she was concentrating on her driving, or deeply hurt. As soon as the traffic began to move freely she burst into laughter, that subsided into uncontrollable giggles.

'Six degrees of separation Tom.' She managed to get out 'They're winding you up. Six degrees of separation. You must have heard of it?' Then she was off again.

He had. The hypothesis that anyone can be connected to any other person on the planet through a chain of acquaintances with no more than five intermediaries.

'Someone tested it out didn't they?' he said.

She struggled to regain her composure. 'Several people have. The American Milgram was the first in the 1960's. He sent almost three hundred people selected at random, packages intended for a stockbroker in Boston. They were told a number of details about the person, and then asked to send the package to a person they knew who they thought might be most likely to know the stockbroker, or to know someone who might be able to deliver it by hand. Eighty percent of all the successfully delivered packages made it in four or fewer steps. Almost all of them got there within six or less. Since then, the same results have been achieved using thousands of senders in over a hundred and fifty countries, and with just under twenty targets. Pretty conclusive don't you think?'

'Your point being,' he said.

'Got a calculator in your organiser?' she asked.

Intrigued, Caton got his BlackBerry out, and switched it on.

'Let's assume you've 40 contacts in your address book, and each of them has 40 contacts, and so on,' she glanced across at him. 'Are you following this?'

He grimaced. 'Give me credit.'

'OK. Let's assume five steps. Do the multiplication Tom, and tell me what you get at each stage.'

'Step one,' he said 'One thousand six hundred; step two, sixty four thousand; step three, two hundred and fity six thousand; step four, one point two four million; step five, forty billion, nine hundred and sixty million.' He stared at the screen. 'That can't be right.'

'Oh it will be,' she said. And the world's population as of right now is only about six and a half billion. Even allowing for all those intermediaries having some contacts in common, it still means that you, Tom Caton, are only five steps away from contact with Osama Bi Laden.'

He switched his organiser off, and put it in his pocket. 'Makes you wonder,' he said. 'Why it's taking them so long to catch him.'

'Is there any more of that casserole left?' he asked before draining the wine in his glass.

'No,' Kate replied. 'And you've already eaten two thirds of it. Do I take that as a compliment, or are you just indiscriminately ravenous?'

He stood up, and walked behind her, bending over to cup her breasts, and kiss her on the side of her mouth.

'Yes, it's a compliment. And yes, I'm ravenous. If it's alright with you, I'll skip cheese, and move straight on to the dessert. I'd like to take it in the bedroom.'

She twisted in her chair, pulled his head closer, and kissed him full on the lips.

Breaking away for a moment, she murmured. 'We don't do desserts in this establishment. You must mean pudding.'

Bending lower he placed one arm around her back, the other under her knees, and scooped her up.

They lay in the afterglow, locked in each other's arms, her head on his chest. He listened to her steady breathing and wondered if she was asleep.

'What do you know about patricide Kate?'

She stirred, snuggling closer. 'God, you say the sexiest things, Tom. You really know how to turn a girl on.'

He shook her gently. 'No seriously, how common is it for a son to kill his father?'

She lay still for a moment, before easing herself free. She reached down, took hold of the edge of the sheet where it lay crumpled at the foot of the bed, pulled it towards her, and wrapped herself in it. She plumped a pillow up, propped it behind her, and sat up.

'Is this what turned your wife off Tom?' she asked. 'Bringing your work into bed?' It could easily have been cruel, and portentous, but the tone in her voice was more curious. Caton sat up beside her.

'Not so much to bed,' he said. 'We passed like ships in the night most of the time. But I wanted to talk about my job with her and she didn't want to hear it; I'd ask her about hers but she wanted to leave hers behind. In the end there was nothing for us to talk about at all.'

She put her hand in his. 'It's not going to happen with us. For a start, neither of us works shifts, and secondly, my work is closer to yours. I share your fascination with it.'

'I wouldn't call it fascination. Absorption, obsession even, not fascination.'

'Alright. Intellectual curiosity,' she squeezed his hand. 'Just try to pick your moments a little more carefully, OK?'

'OK.'

'So, patricide,' she said. 'I can tell you what the text books say. It's a lot more common than people think. There are no class stereotypes. The largest category are white males; adolescents in the main. The majority are those who have been neglected or abused. Children who have reached the end of their emotional tether, and who believe there is no other way out. Then there are those who are mentally ill, often paranoid, or with an anti-social serious personality disorder.'

'What about adults who kill their fathers?'

'Much the same, although there's been a little less research on that aspect. If you ask me, most them are adolescents who, by virtue of their experience in the family home, never really grew up.'

'If you were putting a profile together, what would it look like?'

She had to think about it. 'There's Dr Kathleen M Heide, Professor of Criminology at South Florida.' she said at last. 'She wrote a seminal paper on the characteristics of those who commit parricide; basically children who kill a close relative, their parents in particular. In this instance it includes children who killed in adulthood – some not until their late fifties. Her list of characteristics is probably the most comprehensive and best documented. She didn't just cover the offenders, but also the social and environmental factors that they tend to have had in common.'

'Which are?'

She began to tick them off on her fingers. 'There is usually evidence of violence in the family; there is a strong likelihood of alcoholism, or drug abuse, on the part of one, or both, of the parents; there may well have been attempts by the child to run away, or to commit suicide; they are likely to experience, or choose, isolation from their peers; the family situation will have become increasingly intolerable; the child feels helpless to change the home situation; and will also be acutely aware of their inability to cope with what is happening to them,' she paused at that point, clearly stuck part the way through the list.

'What are the most common methods employed,' Caton prompted.

She nodded, back into her flow. 'In every case involving patricide that Heide followed up a gun was used, but don't forget, this was America, and guns were freely available in the home; none of them had a prior criminal record; a high proportion claimed amnesia after the event.' She looked across at him to check that he was following. 'It may have been an understandable attempt to blank it out. And finally, the victim's death was viewed as a relief by everyone involved.'

She looked to Caton for his reaction. He was staring at the window, deep in thought.

'A penny for them,' she said poking him gently on the shoulder.

'I was thinking of Bojangles,' he said, turning back to face her. 'There's a lot there that would have fitted him. But he never killed his father.'

'You're right,' she said. 'Heide says that whilst the majority of abused children don't go ahead and murder their parents, some of them do go on to kill others instead. And nearly fifty percent of the women she interviewed who had been abused in childhood, had at least harboured thoughts of killing the offending parent or relative. And that was just the women. What might be the percentage of testosterone charged males do you think?'

Caton's mind had already shifted to Bruce Standing. It didn't fit exactly, but then, as Kate was always at pains to remind him, that wasn't the purpose of offender profiling. There he was, the younger brother, isolated, increasingly made to feel a failure, unable to protect his mother, running off to the Legion; the possible attempted suicide; the change of name. And if anyone had the capability to do it, surely it was him.'

'Was that helpful?' she asked, nudging him again.

'More than you know.'

'In that case,' she said, cuddling closer. 'Work over. It's payback time.'

'Just give me a second,' he said, sitting up. 'There's one phone call I have to make. I won't be any use to you until I've sorted this.'

'That's beginning to sound like a mantra.' She called after him. It sounded like a warning

Caton was first in the Incident Room. He made himself a drink, sat on a desk, and perused the display boards.

Half an hour later, every perch in the Room was taken. The word had gone round. Gordon Holmes had pulled rank on the others, and was first to bring them up to date, but only when Caton had filled them in on his trip to the capital.

'It doesn't mean someone else didn't kill Standing to protect Miranda Horne's reputation, does it Boss?' Carter asked when Caton had finished.

'How do you work that out?' Holmes got in first. 'It's had the opposite effect hasn't it? There was no need to kill him. With his track record, after a couple of weeks he'd have got tired of chasing her, and found other fish to fry.'

'Inspector Holmes has a point Sergeant,' Caton agreed, reverting to rank because of the size and nature of the audience. 'And since when has an unmarried political adviser having an affair with a married man – been a cause for resignation?'

'Yes, but surely she'd have known that if it all came out, she'd look pretty foolish, hooking up with an ageing Casanova?' Carter insisted.

'In that case, she'd be likely to get a sizeable sympathy vote from most of the women in this country,' Joanne Stuart pointed out.

'It could have been about cash for honours.' DC Woods had surprised them yet again. They waited for him to spell it out. 'All that money from BUCS, for the Academy, and the Trust. It's one of the Government's pet schemes isn't it? What if Standing brokered it in return for his CBE and a promise of a knighthood? Knowing him, he'd have probably taken a kick back from BUCS as well. If that came out, and she had anything to do with it,' he tailed off. 'Well…'

He had a point, Caton conceded; a good one at that. It wasn't something they'd even considered, and from DC Dave Woods; just when you least expected it.

'Hardly worth killing for though is it?' Holmes said dismissively.

Caton came in quickly. 'Still, it's a thought DC Woods. And I *am* always saying we have to consider every possibility however remote. We can at least find out who proposed him for the CBE. Well done. Now, what have you lot been doing while I've been away?''

'We've been busy Boss!' said Gordon Holmes.

'Busy, busy, or busy productive?' Caton wanted to know.

'Busy both. DS Stuart, why don't you go first.'

She stepped up to the whiteboards. A new one had been added while Caton was away. The lines connecting names, events, evidence and hypotheses had multiplied, and threatened to snake out of control.

'We managed,' she said, 'to track down that university student Standing was alleged to have got pregnant. She was called Katerina Klein. She kept herself to herself when she was at Uni. Studied hard, and rejected any suitors other than Standing. She had an abortion over here, and went back to Düsseldorf to complete her studies. She's working as a software designer, and is in a longstanding relationship with a solicitor. He doesn't know anything about her affair, or the abortion. That's how she wants it to stay. She was a complete loner in Manchester by all accounts, so there's no boy friend or lover over here likely to want to get even.

'Alibi?' he asked.

'On holiday in Capetown with the boy friend. Sent me a fax with dates, reservation, booking confirmation. It all checks out.'

Holmes nodded to DS Carter, who went to stand beside the original whiteboard.

'We've looked into the alibis for everyone we interviewed who might have had a motive. They all check out Boss,' he pointed to the list of names; some of them accompanied by photos. 'I can go through them in turn if you want me to.'

Caton shook his head. 'No thanks,' he said. 'So long as you're sure.'

'Yes Boss, we're as positive as we can be,' DS Carter replied. 'We even tracked the guy who was fishing up at Debdale the night that Watts claimed he was there. Swears Watts was there when he arrived at half past six, didn't leave his pitch till the sun came up in the morning.'

'How about you DI Holmes,' Caton said. 'Did you get anwyhere with the French police?'

'Soon as you called I got on to them. Got transferrred a couple of times, and ended up with the guy who organised the recovery of the body. A Lieutenant in the Gendarmerie,' he consulted his note. 'A Gerard Ceret. His English was about as pathetic as my French so I asked Inspector Weston to take over.'

Sarah Weston stood up. 'Apparently Ceret was stationed in Arles Sur Tech, the town nearest to Corsavy where Bruce Standing lived. He knew him by sight, and to talk to. He was the first to positively identify him. Not only that, but they had his full medical records from his time in the French Foreign Legion. Ceret says there's no doubt about it. Bruce Standing died on that mountain four years ago.'

Caton opened his office door and was confronted by a mountain of paper that teetered unsteadily on his in-tray. He sat down on his swivel chair, placed his elbows on his desk, cupped his chin in his hands, and thought it through. There was still no shortage of suspects. Sandra Given had a motive of sorts. Then there were those staff that had been harried, or sexually harassed. The pupils and their parents forced out, or let down. The politically threatened. The wife cheated on and humiliated. The son that had lost his twin and watched his mother humiliated. What was it Hadfield had said? *Follow the evidence, not the suspects.* Right now there was not a shred of evidence connecting any of them directly to Standing's death.

He shook off the torpor that was threatening to engulf him, and took the first piece of paper from the stack. Accounts were questioning his latest stationery request. Apparently it was in excess of the monthly departmental target towards the paperless office. He shook his head in disbelief, screwed it into a ball, and tossed it into the waste paper recycling box. Now there was a target he could meet without any difficulty. Just so long as they kept sending these memos.

25

The weekend had been a damp squid on several counts. Nothing new had turned up, but then he hadn't expected it to. The labs shut up shop midday on Saturday. Kate had been working on the serial arsonist case, and then breezed off on a planned trip to Cheshire Oaks Retail Outlet with her best mate Trish. To cap it all, another wet front had swept in from the Atlantic, topping up the reservoirs, imprisoning Caton in Castlefield. It was Sunday morning. Caton was an hour into a session at the Y Club, sweating profusely, when Saskia came to tell him he was wanted on the phone. It was Helen Gates.

'I'm sorry Tom,' she said. 'But this won't wait till tomorrow. It's Given. She's dead.'

Flashes of sheet lightening punctuated a sky the colour of jet. Caton could hear the rumbles of thunder above the clack of the windscreen blades. He slowed to twenty passing Ordsall Old Hall. The grade one listed Tudor mansion was barely visible in the murkiness. The last thing he needed was a kid stumbling into his path; especially not here. On this estate it took bugger all to start a riot. At the junction with the A5063 the lights were on red. He pulled up, and stared across the dual carriageway towards the Quays.

Within weeks of its opening in 1894 Manchester Ship Canal had broken the strangle hold of the exorbitant docks and harbour fees at the port of Liverpool, and made possible the development of Trafford Park – the first and largest industrial estate in the world, from which textile manufacturing machinery was sold across the globe. Ironically, it was the success of those very exports that was to bring about the decline of the Ship Canal itself, and the Manchester docks that it served. Cheap imports of cotton goods made on the machines that had originated here all but destroyed the Lancashire cotton trade. By the late 1970's these docks were derelict. Over the past two decades Caton had watched them rise like a phoenix from the ashes.

Now Salford Quays was a vibrant centre of business, enterprise, culture, and sport. The canal basins, and the waterway itself - only a decade before a stagnant mire - now held perch, roach, and pike, so DS Carter assured him. The canal itself - one of the most successful venues of the Commonwealth Games – was the home of the annual World Triatholon Cup. And, miracle of miracles, the BBC was moving some of its major departments from London to Salford's Media City in the centre of this complex. Over one and a half thousand people currently lived here. As of this morning, he reflected grimly, there was one fewer.

When the lights changed, he crossed over, turned right, then first left onto Merchants' Quay. He was brought up short by a patrol car blocking the road. He let the window down and held up his warrant card. Water dripped from the peak of the constable's cap onto Caton's hand.

'I'm sorry Sir. I'm afraid you'll have to park up, and walk from here.'

'I'm the Senior Investigating Officer.'

The officer shook his head, spraying water indiscriminately. 'It's up to you Sir, but the SOCO said no one. Even the pathologist has had to walk.'

'Who is it?'

'The SOCO or the Pathologist?'

'The Pathologist,'

'Mr Douglas.'

Caton smiled to himself. 'I bet he wasn't happy about that.'

The constable grinned. 'No Sir. And he didn't have a coat or an umbrella. He's going to get soaked.'

Caton pulled into a residents' parking space. It was a struggle getting into his Tyvek suit, but at least it provided another layer of protection from the rain. He put on the pair of waterproof boots he always carried for occasions such as this, slipped on a pair of overshoes, and his anorak, took his murder bag from the boot, and set off. Anyone, he decided, who had been on a bender on Saturday night, pulling back their curtains and seeing him trudging down the street, would get the fright of their lives.

The body was barely visible. It was not just the overcast sky and beating rain. High winds had driven a mass of detritus into this corner of the St Louis Basin. Sandra Given, her matted hair, once blonde now filthy brown, floated face up, among the coke cans, plastic bottles, and sodden food wrappers. It was beyond Caton why they hadn't taken her out of the water.

'She's snagged on something. Either that, or someone tried to weight her down.' Jack Benson said, as though reading his thoughts. He paused for a moment to direct the photographer to take some shots from further down the quayside. 'We're waiting for the underwater team to get here. Shouldn't be long now.'

Caton brushed the drips from the end of his nose. 'How did you know it was Given?'

Benson pointed to one of the houses behind them. A huddle of women stood just inside the doorway at the end of the garden, behind a line of sorbus trees, and a low white picket fence. 'The guy who found her knocked on that door to get them to ring for help. The owner recognised her. Apparently Given lived just round the corner on South Bay.'

'Where is he?'

'The guy who found her? He's inside the house having a brew with Mr Douglas. There was no way Douglas was going to hang around out here until we got her out.'

'I'll go in and have a word then. Give me a shout when you're ready. And Jack, if any of the team arrives, send them in.'

Caton stood for a moment committing the scene to memory. It would all be captured by the photographs and the video footage. But nothing would adequately reflect the mood of this place at this moment; dark, dank, and depressing. But there was something else. He couldn't quite put his finger on it. Normally he would have a sense of foreboding. That this was the beginning, or continuation of something evil. Not this time. It wasn't that. What the hell was it?

To his credit, the pathologist waited until Caton had been given his mug of tea, and the women had made their way back to the front door, before he let rip.

'What the hell were they doing calling me out in this before they'd fished her out?'

Caton could see his point. His hair was matted to his head, and steam was rising from his clothes. He smelt like a wet Labrador. 'Why didn't you bring a raincoat?' he asked gently, hoping to divert some of the anger away from Benson. 'You usually do?

'Because I was just coming out of a church service, and surprisingly enough coming down here and standing about in the rain had not been on my itinerary when I set off from home this morning!'

'Well I'm sure Mr Benson had no idea the body was going to be so difficult to retrieve. And he did tell me how bad he felt about you getting wet.' Before Douglas could reply Caton turned to the man at the table with them. 'So what time did you find the body Mr Percy?'

In his early fifties; average height, overweight, going bald. Mr Percy had at least come prepared for the weather. He wore a full length oil skin coat of the kind favoured by drovers in the Outback; a matching hat lay on the table beside him. His face was ghostly white, and not just from the cold. His hands shook as he put down the mug.

'About an hour ago. Just gone nine.'

He had a strong Salford accent. Probably walked it down from Ordsall Caton decided. 'What were you doing there?' he asked. Stupid question really. The man had his tackle box on the floor beside him, and his rod was propped up in the corner of the room. But he always started with an open question, because you never knew where it might lead.

'Looking for a spot to fish.'

'Wouldn't you have been better on a stretch of open water?' Caton actually had no idea himself, but it seemed like a reasonable question.

'It depends. Sometimes when it's like this they seem to take refuge in the basins rather than out in the main channel.'

'So where were you when you saw the body?'

'I was about ten yards from the end of the basin. I'd already decided to cross over between this one and the St Francis Basin, to try my luck off Waterfront Quay, when I saw a bird fly up from one of the floating islands out there in the middle. I thought there might be a nest there. It flew low, directly over where the body was. I thought it was a load of old rags at first. As I got nearer, I thought maybe a dummy someone had chucked in after a stag do. Floating upside down it was. Then it slowly rolled over, and that's when I saw her face.' His hands began to shake uncontrollably, and the mug drummed a frantic beat on the table top.

It was over an hour before the body was lifted onto the quayside. By then the press and television crews had set up camp on the far side of the basin, and a small crowd had begun to gather behind them. Caton was glad for once that the rain had continued unabated. This way there was a limit to what the zoom lenses might pick up. Everyone, he reasoned, was entitled to their privacy; even in death. A piece of wire, the other end caught around the anchor chain of one of the floating islands, had snagged her clothing. There were two dark brown gashes low on the left side of her once cream tee shirt; just above, and to the side, of her navel. Douglas lifted the tee shirt carefully, and exposed matching entry wounds, less than two centimetres apart, just below the ribs. The water had removed all traces of blood save for that on the tee shirt, and on the band of her pale blue knickers visible above the top of her boot cut jeans.

As the photographer moved in to take some shots Douglas looked up at Caton and Benton standing beside him.

'Does this look familiar to you?' he said.

'Standing.' Caton replied, beating Benson to it by a hairsbreadth. 'Only two stabs rather than one.'

'Exactly so.' He palpated the stomach with his fingers, and then slid his hand around her back. 'No exit wounds. From the shape of the tears I'd say these were thrust up beneath the ribs, and if they prove to be as long as those in the case of Roger Standing, either one or both of them are likely to have punctured her heart. In which case death would have been swift to say the least. I expect that that was what killed her, rather than immersion in the water. Unlikely to have been drowned, and certainly not hypothermia. But all of that is supposition. As to time of death, I can't tell you, except that it wasn't within the last eight hours. And before you ask, I'll bring her to the top of my schedule tomorrow morning. So if you'll leave me in peace for the next few minutes, I'll finish up here, and get home to a nice hot shower, and the bosom of my family. I think it's roast beef for lunch today, and I'm the only one who knows how to carve.'

They had found the key to her house in the pocket of her jeans. The front door had been locked, and all of the windows closed. All of the downstairs ones were secured with integral locks. The alarm had not been on.

'So either she wasn't expecting to be out for long, or she never bothered to set the alarm.' Joanne Stuart surmised.

'That seems about right, unless she was taken from here at knife point and forced to lock the door behind her.'

'Why not just kill her here, and be done with it? She probably wouldn't have been found as quickly'

'Fair point. Anyway, remind me to add that to the list of questions for the door to door. Someone may know if she made a habit of setting the alarm.'

Caton and Stuart were searching the last of the rooms. Caton pulled out the final drawer, got down on his hands and knees and felt behind it. He pushed it back in, stood up, and stared around the room. 'That's it then. Nothing unusual, nothing hidden, everything in its place. That's not normal.'

DS Stuart sat down on the bed. 'You only think that because you're a man. Me? I think it's normal.'

She was probably right. 'The one thing that we have established,' he said. 'Is that she didn't sleep in her bed last night. And if Mr Douglas is right she was murdered before the time she would normally have gone to bed.'

'In which case, why was her body not found sooner?'

'Because of that damn wire,' he said. 'Or because it was raining so hard no one was out and about, and even if they had been they'd have had their hoods up, and their heads down. The last thing they'd have been doing was sauntering along the quayside looking for ducks to feed.'

'What was she like Sir? Sandra Given.'

He had to think about it. 'She came across as tough, arrogant, superior, self confident, sarcastic, outwardly professional, and completely committed to her job. Obsessed with it more like. But to tell you the truth, I've no idea what she was really like.'

'Doesn't sound a good enough reason to murder her.'

Caton headed for the door. 'No Jo, it doesn't, but you and I know people that have been killed for a lot less.'

Outside the rain had stopped and the storm clouds were replaced by thin patches of white in an otherwise clear blue sky. The sun shone brightly. The body was on its way the mortuary. The mobile operations van had been set up, and Holmes had arrived, late enough, and feeling guilty enough, to offer to co-ordinate the actions with Jack Benson. The tactical aid team was still crawling over the area. The Underwater Team was searching the Basin quadrant by quadrant, in the hope of finding the weapon and the victim's mobile phone, neither of which had been found on her person, in the house, or in her car outside. House to house enquiries were underway. All the angles were being covered. Caton decided to get back to Longsight, and go over the case files. There had to be something they'd missed; something that involved both Standing and Given. Something important enough to explain two murders. If it was only two murders.

He walked to the end of the promenade and looked out across the stretch of open water to where the sun glinted on the sharp edged stainless steel cladding of the Imperial War Museum North. A flight of swans swooped in, and landed elegantly just yards from where he stood. Suddenly it struck him that this had been neither the beginning of a new evil, nor the continuation of an old one. In some strange way it felt more like an ending. But of what, he had not the faintest idea.

26

For the past four hours Caton had worked his way through the files, tried a dozen search permutations on the main case file on his computer, and revisited the boards in the incident room until his head was spinning. Jack Benson had given him a call to say that things were not looking good on the forensic front. What there was, pointed towards the attack having taken place at the side of the basin, close to where the body had been found. They had found blood on the trunk of one of the Sorbus trees, but the rain had destroyed the rest of the trace evidence. No foot prints on the flags. Apart from finding one of her shoes in the sediment at the bottom of the basin, the search teams had drawn a blank. The Underwater Team were already depressed by the size of the task facing them. They would now have to widen the search to cover the other two basins, and then work out into the tributary canals, and then the main waterway itself. Their best hope was the metal detectors, but there would be so many false readings along the way it could take forever.

According to Gordon Holmes, the door to door had been as much of a washout as the weather. The rain had kept most people indoors. Those few who had gone out the night before had seen nothing, and nobody, out of the ordinary. Nor had anyone heard anything. No raised voices, no screams. But the wind and the rain had been that heavy there was not much chance that they would have done anyway. They would have to see what CCTV footage might turn up in the morning.

To cap it all, there was an email Caton had been waiting for from Europol. John Standing's alibi's checked out. He had been at the meeting in Paris just as he said, and he was a regular at the hotel he stayed at. Not only was the receipt genuine, but hotel staff remembered that he had been there that evening. He had even ordered room service. Whatever else, he was out of the frame for his father's murder. Was it too fanciful to imagine that he might have hired someone to carry out the murder? Probably. Both murders had been up front, face to face, personal. Brutal, yet controlled. In any case it looked as though both Standing and Given had known their attacker. He had driven to a fairly remote spot. She was around the corner from her house, but not where she might have simply bumped into someone as she left or returned to her flat. Nor had she been dressed for the weather. Just slipped out. Perhaps not wanting whoever she was meeting to know exactly where she lived. That triggered a thought. Caton picked up a marker pen and wrote on the flipchart he'd set up that morning. "Umbrella?" Something else for the teams to look out for.

He checked his watch. It was three thirty five in the afternoon. He was expected at Chester House at 4pm for a press conference. This was going to be big news. Not just national either. First the principal, then his successor. Barry Underhill was flying back from Monaco in his own private jet. The leader of Salford

Council was going to be there with the Chief Constable, keen to point out how safe the Quays really were, and how this was really a Manchester problem. This time he'd bet his shirt on Hadfield staying well out of it. He'd know full well that Caton would be coming empty handed. Not a time to be taking the limelight. He would let his Chief Inspector mouth the platitudes for a change.

Caton took a last look around the incident room, locked up, and set out for the car park. He'd call at the Quays first, to make sure he was really up to date. At least, he reflected, this afternoon hadn't been a complete waste of time. He had double checked that neither Given nor Standing had a relationship outside of work, at least not while they had been at Harmony High. But they had one thing in common. They had both worked at the same school in Nantwich. She had been his Deputy there, and he had brought her with him. Just like a Premiership manager asset stripping his old club when he moved to a better one. If they had made enemies in Manchester, then why not there? That, he decided, was where he would be going in the morning; to Nantwich.

The Head of Beam Heath High School, had met neither Standing nor Given, and knew of them only by reputation. He had arranged for him to see the Chair and Vice Chair of Governors. The two of them had been involved in the appointment of both Standing and Given, and had served on the Governing Body throughout their tenure. They were waiting in the head's office.

Marion Wilkinson, the Chair of Governors, turned out to be the manager of a local Bank. In her late fifties, Caton surmised from the lines on her neck and the liver spots on the back of her hands. Other than those few clues he would never have guessed that she was approaching retirement age. She wore a tailored nip waisted black trouser suit, over a crisp white open neck shirt. Her platinum blond hair, cut in a one length bob, swayed gently as she shook his hand. Her grip was firm, her grey eyes clear, intelligent, and probing.

'Chief Inspector.' She said rising to meet him. 'A dreadful business. First Roger, and now poor Sandra Given. I don't how we'll be able to help, but we'll do our best.' Her voice was as confident as her grip. 'This is Canon Jacobs. Martin is our Vice Chair of Governors.'

At five foot five and close to eighteen stone it was an effort for him to get out of his chair, and almost as hard to get back into it. The niceties concluded, Caton had to endure from the Chair of Governors several minutes of plaudits for each of the deceased that would have graced any obituary. As soon as she'd finished he wasted no time in getting to the point

'I appreciate all that,' he said. 'But, distasteful though it maybe, I am afraid that I'm really more interested in anything which they may have done, or been involved in, that might have caused someone to want to harm them.'

He waited for their reaction. The Canon stared at the floor. Marion Wilkinson appeared genuinely puzzled.

'I'm sorry Chief Inspector,' she said. 'I don't follow you?'

'It's quite simple,' he said. 'Someone – we believe that it was the same person – had a reason to want both Roger Standing and Sandra Given dead. If we can discover what might have motivated that person it takes us that much closer to catching them. I'm sure you understand that?'

She nodded her head, confirming the reason her hairstyle was called a bob. 'Yes of course,' she said. 'But what does that have to do with this school?'

'At Harmony High, I'm afraid that both Mr Standing and Miss Given appeared to have made quite a few enemies – if that's not too strong a word – among staff, pupils, and parents. There were claims of unfair treatment, harassment, and excessive use of exclusions. That sort of thing. I need to know if that was the case during their time at Beam Heath High.'

The two of them exchanged a swift glance that told of an unspoken understanding. For Caton it was more like an acknowledgement. Marion Wilkinson crossed her legs at the ankle, and eased back into her chair.

'Well every school has its difficult pupils…and parents and staff for that matter,' she began. 'I can see that a brand new school such as Harmony High would bring its own challenges, especially in an inner city area. Headteachers setting out to establish an ethos for the school often feel the need to lay down the rules, draw a line in the sand. When Mr Standing arrived here this school already had a good ethos, and a good reputation. There was less pressure to raise standards, of attainment or behaviour.'

'Even so…' The Canon said quietly, his eyes still on the floor.

'Even so,' she repeated acknowledging his cue. 'There were times when the Canon and I were a little concerned that *perhaps* Mr Standing had gone over the top. In fact on several occasions we had to have a word with him about it. Pupils that had never been in trouble being excluded for something minor. We even had to overturn some of the exclusions on appeal.'

'Did any of these involve Sandra Given?' Caton asked.

'Oh yes, I'm sure they would have done,' she replied. ' She was very much his guardian of standards. In fact, I think he actually referred to her as such on one occasion.'

'What about staff grievances?' Caton wanted to know. 'Did any of them claim harassment? Were any forced to leave?'

Now they both looked uncomfortable.

'Not as such,' the Chair replied, 'There were no industrial tribunals, nothing formal, but two or three of the staff did come to one or the other of us with complaints.'

'What about?'

'Undue pressure, having their work monitored too closely, that sort of thing.'

'Were any of them female?' he asked.

She hesitated a little too long. The Canon answered for her. 'All of them,' he said, looking up for the first time. Every one of them.' Caton detected a mixture of bitterness and resignation in his voice. 'We had no option but to ask them to make a formal complaint, which none of them did. Two subsequently left to get jobs elsewhere.'

'I'll need you give me their names and recorded contact details.' Caton told them. 'As far as you know, were any threats made as result of any of these incidents?'

They looked at each other and shook their heads. There was an uneasy silence. Caton let it grow. Finally Canon Jacobs looked across at his colleague. 'What about Mercer?' He said.

'I don't think that's relevant Martin,' she replied. 'It had nothing to do with Roger or Sandra.'

'Perhaps I should be judge of that,' Caton told her.

Suddenly she seemed reluctant to do the talking. She folded her hands in her lap and looked across at her colleague. The message was clear. You started this, you can damn well finish it.

'Well,' he began, hesitantly. 'We had a member of staff – appointed by Roger Standing shortly after he joined us. John Mercer – Head of the Art Department. He had only been with us a matter of months when parents began to make complaints of a rather delicate nature. They alleged that he was…' He struggled to find the words. Marion Wilkinson was unable to help herself.

'*Touching them up* is the expression I think you're groping for Martin; their daughters that is.'

His face flushed red, and he wriggled uncomfortably in his chair. 'Yes…exactly. They said he would place his arm around their shoulders, touching their…'

'Breasts!' She prompted.

'Chests,' he said. 'It was also claimed that he would ask them to sit on a stool on one of the tables for life drawing classes.'

'Nothing unusual about that, surely?' said Caton.

'Providing that you're not also looking up their skirts.' The Chair of Governors responded.

How did Mr Standing react to the allegations? Caton asked.

'At first he said it was all a misunderstanding and he would deal with it. Some of the parents were unhappy and came to the Governing Body. We asked him to undertake a full investigation and report to the disciplinary sub-committee, chaired by Martin here.'

The Canon picked up the story. 'The allegations were explained away as perfectly normal but ill advised attempts to help them with their drawing technique. Any…brushing against their chests, entirely accidental. The accusations about him, shall we say, positioning them in certain ways, were difficult to substantiate, and put down by Standing to fanciful female imaginations.

Mercer claimed it was all a misunderstanding, nothing smutty intended. He apologised if he had given any offence. Standing recommended that he receive a written warning about his future behaviour.'

'And that was all?' Caton had difficulty containing his surprise.

'You have to remember Chief Inspector that this was before child protection came in. I'm afraid that there were no clear guidelines about what burden of proof their should be, the weight of a child's evidence, anything like that.' The words lacked conviction, and sounded hollow.

'So he carried on teaching here, just like that?' Caton said.

'Yes. One of the girls – allegedly a particular target of his - was removed by her parents, and sent to another school. Mr Mercer lasted another two years, but his position became untenable. Whispers, cat calling, graffiti on the chalk boards, that sort of thing. There were subsequent allegations about approaches he had made to several girls; even more difficult to prove one way or the other. He got another job somewhere up North. A Girls School in Yorkshire if I remember rightly.'

'We should have got rid of him straight away. You know it and I know it.' Marion Wilkinson said.

Martin Jacobs nodded despondently. 'You're right of course,' he said. 'Particularly in the light of subsequent events. Vaticinium ex eventu.'

The Chair of Governors raised her eyebrows quizzically.

'Prophecy after the event,' Caton said without thinking. 'Hindsight is a cheap commodity.' He was surprised how easily it had come back to him. All down to the Manchester Grammar Oxbridge candidates Latin booster classes. .

'Exactly so,' Martin Jacobs said, staring at him with a mixture of surprise and respect.

'So what was it in this case that might have been forseen, but was not?' Caton asked him.

'I don't know that any of us could have forseen it Chief Inspector,' Marion Wilkinson replied. 'It seems he got himself into some sort of trouble up North, was arrested, and committed suicide whilst on remand.' She sat up straight, and placed her hands back on the arms of her chair. 'But to be honest, I don't see what possible relevance this could have to the murders of Roger Standing and Sandra Given.'

27

Caton sat back in his chair and scratched the back of his head; as though it might, somehow aid the thought process. It was creeping up on him he realised, like Holmes' habitual rubbing of his chin.

In front of him was a stack of five manilla files the Headteacher's secretary had brought him. The pattern of behaviour that had become endemic at Harmony High had already been evident here in Nantwich. Marion Wilkinson was right. It was neither on the same scale, nor of the same degree. Certainly nothing likely to trigger a cold and calculated killing spree. He judged them all to be red herrings, with the exception of the one that lay open on the top. They'd all have to be followed up of course, just to be on the safe side. This last one, he had decided to reserve for himself.

Jessica Walker had been fourteen years of age at the time. She was the one at the centre of the allegations against Mercer. The one whose parents had removed her from the school. Not before they'd kicked up an almighty stink. Involved the police. Hired a solicitor. Caton had experienced all too often the strength of a father's love for a daughter harmed; victims of sudden death; of assault. You never knew which way it might tip; into all consuming grief, or manic rage. Not that this one really warranted either. But in his experience, you could never tell.

There was a knock on the door, and secretary came in clutching two sheets of A4 paper.

'Chief Inspector,' she said. 'Here is the reference that you were asking for. I have attached a copy of the job description. I thought you might be interested.'

He thanked her for them, and for the tea, told her that he would be leaving shortly, and asked her to pass on his thanks to the Head for his co-operation. He'd already started reading before the door closed behind her.

His eyes widened involuntarily. John Mercer had had the gall to apply for the post of Head of Art and Head of House at an independent all girls school in Yorkshire. The Elms School, in a town called Birkenshaw, between Leeds and Bradford.

According to the job description, he would be line manager for a small team of House Tutors responsible for the pastoral care of a hundred and fifty girls aged between eleven and eighteen. Presumably he would be privy to quite sensitive and personal information about these girls, and have privileged access to them. Caton read with even greater incredulity the reference that Standing had provided. Apparently, Mercer was a first rate teacher, a warm and compassionate human being, and a consumate professional. He provided a clear sense of direction for his department, and had a good eye for talent. That last phrase, Caton decided, was just about the only element of truth in the entire letter. If the Chair and Deputy, and the files he'd just finished reading, were anything to go by this was the most outrageous piece of fiction he'd read in a reference. And that was saying something. No wonder Mercer had got himself into a spot of bother up there. Just a shame the school hadn't dug a little deeper; sought another reference or two. Perhaps they had.

Euromart was just a mile and a half from Beam Heath High. According to the sign, it was open twenty four seven, three hundred and sixty four days of the year. Harry Walker turned out to be the Manager. In his mid forties, he wore a grey suit, white shirt, and red and blue striped tie. His face looked open and honest, and the smile with which he greeted Caton genuine; until Mercer's name was mentioned. Then it clouded over, his mouth pursed, and his pupils narrowed.

'Mercer! That bastard. What's he gone and done now?'

'To be honest,' Caton told him, 'I'm not completely sure. But I can tell you that he's dead.'

'Dead? How did he die?'

His surprise seemed genuine to Caton. 'It seems he took his own life.' He said.

Walker motioned the detective to take a seat just inside the office, closed the door, and sat down beside his desk. 'Well I'll not pretend that I'm sorry,' he said. 'I won't say that he had that coming, but he was certainly self-destructive, as well as destructive of others.'

It struck Caton as a strange thing to say. 'Self-destructive?'

Walker shuffled a couple of printouts on his desk. 'Well, you know what I mean. Taking risks like that in front of so many witnesses. How the hell did he think he could get away with? It was only a matter of time.'

He did though, didn't he? Get away with it?'

'Only because of Standing, and that witch Given?'

Caton straightened up. 'Witch? It what way?'

Walker's attention was suddenly caught by something happening down on the shop floor. He reached for a small microphone on a flexible stand, and pressed the button. 'Supervisor to checkout seventeen please. Checkout seventeen.' He waited until a flustered woman in a navy blue uniform, clipboard in hand, headphone waggling precariously on the top of her head, arrived in a flurry at the penultimate check out. Then he turned back to Caton. 'She's devious, scheming, ambitious, hard as nails, and a right bitch. On top which she's a liar.' He almost spat out the words.

'*Was* a liar,' Caton said quietly. 'She's dead too.'

This time Walker's pupils dilated, and his mouth fell open. 'Bloody hell,' he said. 'Not another one. I heard about Standing, but Mercer, and now Given. Don't tell me she committed suicide.'

'No. She was murdered.'

The supermarket manager nodded sagely. 'Thought not. Not her style. When did it happen?'

'Her body was found yesterday,' Caton replied, careful not to commit himself.

'That it explains it then. I worked a double shift. Haven't had a chance to watch the tele, let alone read a newspaper.'

'You said she was a liar. What did you mean by that?'

'Roger Standing bent over backwards to get Mercer off the hook, but it was Given that really saved him. She was the one who Standing got to carry out the internal investigation. She rubbished our daughter's evidence, and made up evidence of her own, making out that Jessica was a liar, and a fantasist. Given even claimed that she'd made a complaint against another teacher, even though she never had. That was what really got me mad. Making Jessica out to be a liar. Causing us to doubt our own daughter.'

'That was why you took her away from the school?'

'There was no way she could stay there. They'd made a laughing stock of her. Anyway, Mercer was still there.'

His head was down, recalling how it had been. His hands on the desk. In tight balls.

'How did that make you feel?' Caton asked him.

He looked up. 'How the hell do you think it made me feel?' Realisation dawned slowly. His eyes widened, and a thin smile appeared. 'You're wondering if I did them in? Standing and Given?' He shook his head. 'No, if I'd gone after anyone it would have been Mercer. Stop him from pestering some other poor girl. Anyway, however angry I was at the time, it wasn't as though he'd had sex with her was it? Now that would have been another matter entirely.'

Precisely what Caton had been thinking. 'Has your daughter got over it?' he asked.

Walker's eyes lit up. 'Completely. To be honest it took us by surprise how fast. She made a new set of friends. Did brilliantly at her new school. She's in her second year at Uni. In Bristol. Loving it.'

Walker had a cast iron alibi for both nights. He had been on a long weekend residential training session in

Sussex when Standing had been murdered, and working all evening right here, from mid afternoon on Saturday, until 6am on the Sunday. He had only just come back on duty. Caton had seen the time sheets, and two of the manager's colleagues had confirmed it. Although he was still waiting to hear from DI Weston, Caton knew those timings would rule him out. He'd suspected as much as soon as he saw Walker's reaction to the news of Given's death. Caton could always tell when they tried to fake it. Well, almost always.

Detective Inspector Gatley, at the Specialist Investigation Unit based in Crewe, was surprised to hear that Caton wanted to dig up the paperwork on the original complaint about John Mercer, intrigued to find it being linked to two high profile murders, and at a loss to make a connection.

'Happy to do it though,' he said as he searched through the files. Give me a break from this.'

On his desk was a series of photos of a traffic accident, and the beginnings of a written report.

'Ever since they scrapped CID,' he said. 'Called us Strategic Investigations Unit, took away murder investigations, and landed us with fatal and serious road accidents along with everything else, I've been struggling to come to terms with it. The rest of it I can handle, but this traffic stuff can take forever. Not what I became a detective for.'

Caton could sympathise with that. Most days he thanked his lucky stars he was part of the Major Incident Team.

'Do you remember the case?' he asked.

'Like it was yesterday. I was a DS then. Handled it from start to finish. Not that there was a finish.' He handed over the thin file; just a couple of forms, and three or four statements. 'Mercer was guilty as hell of course, but the school covered it up. I wasn't surprise to hear he came a cropper up North. Never would have guessed he had the balls to top himself though.'

'How did Walker take it when you closed the case?'

'Not a happy bunny. You can imagine. But his wife had had enough of it. Just wanted to let the daughter put it all behind her. These days Mercer would never have got away with it. He'd have been on the Sex Offenders Register like a shot. No chance of working with children ever again. Not since the Soham Case. You know how it is. Another world entirely.

Gatley found Caton an empty desk in the squad room, and logged him on to the system. Within minutes he was looking at Mercer's record. He had been charged in Leeds with indecent assault, rape, and sex with a minor; a fifteen year old called Chloe Norton. It had all come to light when the girl committed suicide. Her diary led them straight to Mercer. The night he was charged he was held on remand at HM Armley Prison Leeds. The jail had fifty per cent more inmates than it was supposed to accommodate, and the normal units in Block A, where vulnerable prisoners were held, were already full. There had been no reason to place him on suicide watch. Nevertheless, he was checked on hourly. At 4 am he was found hanging in his cell. Paramedics attended, and he was pronounced dead on arrival at hospital.

Caton pushed his chair back from the desk, and stretched out his legs. For the first time since the investigation into Standing's murder began he had the scent of a plausible motive. This time Mercer's victim had killed herself. Another father, brother, uncle, with an even better reason to wish him dead. But that was the rub. Mercer was already dead. The last few hours, however, had given him a connection to Standing and Given. What if Chloe Norton's family had found out why he had left his previous school? Had got their hands on Standing's reference? Had found out about Given's whitewash of Mercer? It was stretching it a bit, surely. He switched to the internet and carried out a search on Mercer. There were a number of reports of his death. Two about his arrest. Each of them short and to the point. Five minutes later he was looking at a short article about the victim, and her grieving family. He printed a copy, put it in his pocket, and logged off. A phone call to West Yorkshire Major Crime team provided him with a contact in the Child Protection Unit, and a meeting arranged for the following morning. He thanked DI Gately for his help, and left. Surprising the difference a couple of hours away from the office could make, he reflected as he climbed into the driver's seat. Just like the old days.

The normal torture of rush hour on the M6 motorway was bad enough even without the ubiquitous roadworks. The onboard computer told him that the outside temperature was still 26 degrees at five thirty in the evening. Here in the air conditioned cabin it was a steady 19 degrees. That, and Albinoni's Adagio in G Minor, made the journey cooler in every sense, and just that bit more bearable. Nevertheless, it was gone seven when Caton finally arrived back at Longsight. Everyone had gone home, except for Gordon Holmes, who had his feet up on the desk, a mug of coffee in his hand, and a file open on the computer screen.

'What are you doing still here?' Caton asked him.

Holmes took his feet off the desk, and swivelled his chair round.

'I thought I'd wait for you Boss. Marilyn's visiting her mother, so there's no pressure there. I've been going over what we've got on Given.'

Caton pulled a chair up, and sat down. 'And?'

'Not a thing. Jo's been up at the school interviewing everyone again. Doesn't look like Given made any real enemies. Some resentment over her appointment, and her heavy handed approach, but that's nothing new. As for relationships, she didn't seem to have any. Not with either sex. Bit of a loner really. Lived alone. Died alone. Bloody sad when you think about it.'

'She wasn't exactly alone when she died.' Caton reminded him.

'Holmes rubbed his chin. 'You know what I mean.'

'So what have we got?'

'No leads, beggar all from the scene of crime – just like Jack Benson predicted. Just a lot of men in wet suits getting colder and colder, and more and more hacked off by the hour. The post mortem report's on your desk. Confirms the cause of death. Given's heart was punctured by two stabs with a knife at least eighteen centimetres long. Same as Standing, except that in his case the blow had been angled less steeply, and had ruptured the spleen. Which is why it took him longer to die. The time of death is estimated at somewhere between nine thirty and eleven thirty. Nothing so far from the CCTV. A couple of groups of youths in hoodies, making their way to the basins. Nothing unusual about that. They come down from Ordsall with their cans to sit on the benches, have a smoke, a drink, and generally lark about. There were less than normal because of the rain, and they didn't stay long. A few individuals were shown entering the South side, but they either had an umbrella, or an anoraka or parka with a hood. What with the rain, the clothing, and that fact it was dark, we won't get anything we can use from that. As for Given, like I say, we haven't found anything remotely interesting. She was a lonely woman, wedded to her work.' He finished his drink, and put the mug down. 'What about you Boss? Was the trip worth it?'

Caton gave him chapter and verse. Holmes was understandably sceptical.

'It's not a lot to go on though is it? Lots of ifs and buts. Worth a try I suppose. Ged's left a note on your desk. She's made a tentative reservation for you tomorrow night at the Old Swan in Harrogate, just in case you have to stay overnight.'

'I know, she sent me a text message confirming it .'

'The Old Swan. Isn't that where Agatha Christie turned up after she'd done a runner?'

Caton nodded. 'In 1926. It was the biggest police search of the decade. Over a thousand officers involved. The first time an aeroplane was ever used for a search if I remember rightly. One of the staff recognised her from the photo on one of her old book jackets.'

'Why did she do it? Disappear like that?'

'They never found out. There were lots of theories. She claimed she had amnesia. Now it seems more likely that it was because her husband had just told her that he'd been having a long term affair, and wanted a divorce. She just wanted to get away for a bit. She did Old Swan a favour though. They host Murder Mystery weekends, and the annual Theakston's Harrogate Crime Writing Festival starts there this weekend.'

Gordon Holmes smiled thinly, took hold of the mouse, and exited the file. 'You might want to stay over then,' he said. 'Run this lot by them. We could do with all the help we can get.'

'Am I making too much of this Kate?' Caton asked as he sprinkled some parmesan on the bowl of pasta, and placed it on the table between them.

'The pasta, or this motive you're proposing for the deaths of Standing and Given?'

He sat down opposite her, and began toying with his fork. 'The motive. It just seems a bit excessive. Why kill Standing and Given? It was Mercer who was really responsible.'

'Not at all,' she told him. 'It's called transference of rage. The perpetrator is dead. The anger isn't going to go away, and there is no one to focus it on. They haven't even had the satisfaction of their day in court. If they can't find someone else to blame, then they're going to turn it in upon themselves, or worse, each other.' She poured him a glass of Amarone. 'No, if someone in the family found out about the part that Standing and Given had played in saving Mercer's neck, and getting him the job in Yorkshire…well, suddenly there's a target for all that rage. Two in fact. So yes. It's feasible. All it takes is someone with an underlying personality disorder. Now, can we eat?'

He drizzled some olive oil and balsamic vinegar over the pasta, and plunged his fork into the centre. Suddenly his appetite had returned.

28

It was twenty past nine in the morning as Caton turned out of Station Avenue into North Park Road. He'd made good time despite the light drizzle that had started on the outskirts of Skipton, and obscured some of the best of the scenery as he dropped down into the dales. Almost immediately, he found himself facing the imposing gates of the Harrogate Police Support Facility. DS Maggie McEwan was waiting for him. She was tall, sturdy, with a friendly face, and smiling eyes that softened the otherwise masculine impression. Her handshake confirmed the steel behind those eyes.

'Detective Sergeant Maggie McEwan,' she said. 'Victim Support. And to save you the trouble of asking, my great grandfather was a Glaswegian iron bridge builder. He worked on the Forth Road Bridge, and the Sydney Harbour Bridge, as it happens. But my grandfather moved down to Leeds, which is where I was born. Hence the accent. As for the Maggie bit, it's a family tradition.'

'Tom Caton,' he responded. 'The Caton bit is Irish, from Listowel in County Kerry. The Tom is apparently because my mother had a thing about Tom Paxton, the singer. The accent you can blame on her, and on Manchester Grammar. Public schools tend to discourage regional accents.'

'There you go,' she said, leading him down a broad

corridor. 'That saved us looking each other up on *My Space.'*

She paused to get them both a coffee from the machine, and then took him to her office. It was a shared one, with three desks, each sporting a computer screen. She paused there to pick up a file, and then led him through to a smaller room, tastefully decorated in muted pastel colours, with four easy chairs set around a low coffee table.

'We do our best to work with our clients in their own homes, but when they do come here this is a better environment in which to work with them. Puts them at their ease.'

He could see that. It reminded him of the family rooms adjacent to Accident and Emergency Units where he'd too often had to break bad news to anxious friends and relatives.

She put her coffee on the table, and flipped open the file. "September 2004. Chloe Norton. Fifteen years of age. I'd just joined the Unit. It was referred to us by the investigating team. Not difficult to see why. Parents, Mandy and Ronald. He worked on the oil rigs in the North Sea, out of Aberdeen. They were both really broken up as you can imagine, but he was the one who found her diary. If we hadn't got to Mercer first, I think he would have killed him. He went ballistic when Mercer committed suicide. Wouldn't leave it alone. Wanted us to prosecute the Head, the Governors, someone, anyone. He became that obsessed, his wife left him. It didn't help that he blamed her for insisting they send their daughter to that school. She moved out, and two years later they were divorced. From what I remember, their marriage was already heading for the rocks; what with him being away on the rigs, and having a jealous streak.'

'He had a jealous streak?'

'We actually had a domestic call out about five years back. He took some leave without telling her, claimed he wanted it to be a surprise. Only she wasn't in. She'd signed on for a course at the local Tech. Conversational Spanish, something like that. He drove up to the car park and waited for her to come out. She was chatting, as you do, with some of the others on the course; men and women. It was completely innocent by all accounts. He followed her home. Next thing, the neighbours call us out. Voices raised, mother and daughter screaming, things being smashed. You know the sort of thing. No actually bodily harm. No charges made. Just a friendly warning.'

'When was this?'

'March 2004. About six months before we were pulled into the investigation following Chloe's suicide.'

'What happened to the mother?'

'I think she moved away after the divorce.' She consulted the file. 'That's right. She moved to Norfolk eighteen months ago. Last we heard she was trying to move on with her life. We offered them both trauma counselling at the time. It seemed to help her, but he never took us up on it.'

'Is he still on the rigs?'

'No. He packed that in almost immediately after his daughter died. They offered him up to two months compassionate leave, but he never went back.' She consulted the file. 'He started working as a parcels courier.' She turned the file around and slid it across the table so that he could make a note of the details.

She grinned. 'Not very original is it? The Harrogate Same Day Courier Service.'

Caton pocketed his notebook, and finished his coffee. 'No,' he said. 'But just like us, it does what it says on the tin. Have you still got her diary?'

'No. After Mercer died there was no case to pursue. The coroner's inquest was done and dusted. The family wanted it back. I handed it over personally. You wouldn't have wanted to read it, believe me. Very sad. The bastard had been grooming her for over a year. He might even have got away with it. But she thought she was pregnant. She was terrified that her father might find out.'

'Was she?'

'As it happens, she wasn't. Just made it all the worse, if that was possible.'

'Who did you give the diary to?'

'The father. The mother didn't turn up.'

'You said you thought he might have murdered Mercer if he'd got to him first. I take it that wasn't figurative? You actually meant it?'

'Oh yes. The state he was in I think anything would have been possible.'

'But what about later, much later, when the initial shock and rage had died down? Could he have done it in cold blood?'

She thought about that for a moment, then nodded her head. 'I don't think the rage ever died down,' she said. 'If anything, Mercer's suicide just set it off again. He may have managed to bury it, but I doubt it'll be far below the surface. Put it this way. I wouldn't want to accidentally run into the back of his car. D'you know what I mean?'

The Harrogate Same Day Courier Service occupied a small suite of offices in a smart block close to the International Conference Centre. Apart from the office manager there were just five other staff, all but one of them women. The lack of allocated parking space, and the absence of any vehicles with the brand logo, was soon explained away.

'We have five large vans used for moving unusually heavy or bulky deliveries,' John Smart, the owner and office manager explained. 'Those are kept in a secure compound about a mile from here. The remainder of our vehicles are leased and maintained by us, and kept by our couriers. They claim the business mileage from us, and have personal use of the vehicle up to an agreed mileage level. We take out a new lease every two years. A small number of our couriers are self-employed. They all have their own cars or motorcycles which they insure for business and personal use. We use them for small jobs, or when demand exceeds our own capacity. That way it cuts down on our overheads, and it suits the drivers.'

'And Ronald Norton? Does he have the use of a company van?'

'Ron?' He wrinkled his eyebrows, evidently surprised that this enquiry had anything do with Norton. 'Yes, of course. He's been with us for just over two years. He's one of our most conscientious employees.'

'What sort of runs does he do?'

'Well there are a number of regular ones, including the bank run.'

'Bank run?'

'That's right. We picked up the contract last year.

Very lucrative. I put Ron on it because he's never let us down, not once.'

'And what exactly does that involve?'

'Well, he has the keys, and short term access alarm codes, to all of the branches of two of the major banks within a ten mile radius. Twice a week, after they've closed, he lets himself in, picks up the sealed bags of cheques, and delivers them to the Head Office clearing house. It's very sensitive work.'

'So you carried out a police record check before you gave him the job?'

A pained expression appeared on Smart's face. 'We get a police check on all of our couriers, Chief Inspector, including those who are self-employed.'

'And apart from the regular runs?'

'Well, anything that might come in. Anywhere from John O'Groats to Lands End. With Ron being single, and...' he paused searching Caton's face for clues. 'You know about his daughter I suppose?'

'Yes sir, I do.'

'Yes, well, very tragic. He told me when he applied for the job. Well, he had to really. I knew of course, from all the publicity. To be honest I wondered if he'd be up to it. What with his wife leaving him as well. But fair play, he'll take on anything I throw at him. Day or night. He particularly likes to work weekends, which is a Godsend because no one else wants to. Sometimes I have to remember that he's entitled to some time of his own. Though God knows what he does with it. If it was up to him he'd work 24 hours a day.'

'So that would include trips to Manchester for example?'

'Oh yes. We get plenty of those. And pick ups from Manchester to anywhere in Yorkshire'

Caton gave him a sheet of paper on which were written two sets of dates and times. They covered the twenty four hour period either side of the estimated times of death of Standing and Given.

'Could you check your records for me Mr Smart, and tell me what runs Mr Norton was given during each of these periods?'

Smart set to work on his computer, and printed off a copy of Ronald Norton's log for each of the days in question. He handed it to Caton.

On the morning of Standing's death Norton had a slow start but set off at eleven thirty to take a package to Birmingham. Arriving there at mid-day, he had a two hour break before picking up a set of art designs to take to York. No sooner had he arrived there than he was given an urgent run that involved coming back to Harrogate to pick up some twelve boxes of conference materials that had been misdirected to the Conference Centre, and taking them down to The Alexandra Palace in London where they should have gone in the first place.

'We get that all the time.' Smart observed, looking over Caton's shoulder. 'Some of these organisations that manage conferences and exhibitions take on far too many at once. They end up sending all sorts of stuff to the wrong venues. Not just leaflets, handouts and delegate packs, but posters and audio visual equipment too.'

Caton worked it out. Norton had only set off from Harrogate at six in the evening. He arrived at Alexandra Park at nine twenty seven, and left at nine forty. Even assuming he'd driven flat out on the way back there was no way that he could have been there in time to meet, let alone kill, Roger Standing. He shifted his attention to the second printout. Another Saturday. That was an itch he had been scratching ever since Given's body had turned up. They had both been killed on a Saturday. He still didn't believe in co-incidences.

This time Norton had been allocated only one run. It was to take a set of papers, marked highly confidential, from a private residential address in Ilkley to another in Highgate, in London. The pick up was timed at six forty five in the evening, and the drop off at ten fifteen. That sounded about right; a Saturday night, not too much traffic on the road. There was no way he could have made it to Salford Quays in time to kill Given. Not unless the pathologist's estimates were way out. He folded the print outs and laid them on the desk in front of him.

'Just how reliable are these times?' he asked.

Smart smiled. 'Rock solid,' he replied. 'The business depends on them. The clients have to sign the packages out, and in.'

'And how do you know that they've done that?'

'We have a record of their signatures, and as a matter of course we ring every client within twenty four hours to check that the delivery met their expectations. It's not just good practice, its good for repeat business.'

'OK. But how do you know that the time of delivery is accurate?'

'The courier has to phone in straight away, with the name of the signatory, the delivery number, and the time of delivery. They have to do it within thirty minutes of making that delivery. Most do it straight away. We only allow that lee way in case of bad connection.'

'But how do you know which courier has made the delivery? Surely anyone could do it who was told the system?'

Smart shook his head. 'You've been reading too many detective stories Chief Inspector. The industry wised up to that years ago. It's not a risk we can afford to take. Every courier is issued with an individual and uniquely identifiable phone. In any case, I'm on cover most weekends. I have a phone, and a networked terminal at home. You can see from the logs that I issued both of those jobs, and registered the deliveries. Ron Norton made those runs. Take my word for it.'

Caton left with a copy of Norton's log history for the previous six months, a copy of his photo, and his address. John Smart had accepted Caton's story that these were only preliminary enquiries designed to eliminate his employee, and had given a promise not to mention any of it to Norton himself until Caton had had a chance to talk with him. He doubted, however, that the man would be able to keep it to himself for more than a day or two.

He dined alone in the Red Lounge on one of the few singles tables in the room. The hotel was bursting at the seams with tourists, businessmen and women, and people staying over for the County Show. He thought about ringing down for room service, but wanted to clear his head, and knew that people-watching would be far more effective than moping in his room, or watching television. The food was fine. Warm goat's cheese and black olive tart; saddle of rabbit stuffed with chicken and spinach farci, served with buttered carrots and minted potatoes; a selection of fine English and Yorkshire cheese - he loved the implication that Yorkshire was somehow other than part of England - and a half a bottle of house red. He returned to his room replete, but far from satisfied. His mind was racing. He searched through the address book on his BlackBerry and found the number for Harry Walker at the supermarket. He rang on the off chance, and was pleasantly surprised to find that Wallace was working the late shift.

'I'm sorry to bother you again Mr Walker,' he said, but I was wondering. Did anyone ever contact you asking about Mercer? After his death perhaps?'

'Well, I'm not sure about that,' he said hesitantly. 'I mean I didn't know he was dead till you told me. When was it he died exactly?'

'Three and a half years ago. September 2004.'

'Well I suppose it would be about that time. Nearer to Christmas I think. This reporter came to see me. Said he was writing a piece about paedophiles in Education, and the response of the authorities. Said I'd get a fee if the story was printed. He promised me anonymity if that's what I wanted. '

'What did you say?'

'That I'd think about it. He never told me that Mercer had committed suicide. Anyway, I answered a few of his questions then I got a bit scared. I was bothered about being sued for libel. I mean, you never know. Told him to bugger off. He never got back to me, and as far as I know the story never appeared.'

'I don't suppose you remember his name?'

'He must have told me, but I can't say I remember it,' he paused while he racked his brains. 'Hang on. I might still have the card he gave me. Give me a second.'

A minute later he came back on the line. 'United Press Associates. A Roger Connolly. There's a phone number if you want it?'

As soon as heard the number Caton knew it was false. Only half of the area code, and one digit missing from the rest of the number.

'Mr Walker,' he said, more calmly than he felt. 'I'm going to get one of my team to come to see you tomorrow morning, and show you a series of photos. I want you to see if you recognise any of them as this Roger Connolly. Can you do that for me?'

'No problem,' he replied. 'I'll be in about ten thirty. Can't vouch for my memory though.'

'That's alright Mr Walker,' Caton said, his heart beginning to race. Whether it was the food, the wine, or a rising sense of anticipation he had not the faintest idea. 'Just do the best you can.'

An hour later he'd managed to sweet talk his way past Marilyn Holmes, and had explained to Gordon what he wanted set up for the following day. The final call of the evening was to Kate.

'I'm sorry,' he said. 'I tried to get you earlier. Did you get my voice message?'

She sounded a lot happier than he'd anticipated.

'Yes Tom. You're staying over at the Old Swan

Hotel. Good for you. You can bring me some of those famous pastries back from Betty's."

'I will if can fit it in,' he said. 'But this is a murder I'm investigating, in case you've forgotten.' He heard her chuckle down the line.

'And there was me thinking you were just *Swan*ning around."

29

Caton was mopping up the vestiges of egg and bacon with a piece of bread when Gordon Holmes arrived.

'It's all right for some!' He said as he slumped down in the chair opposite.

'Help yourself,' Caton told him, gesturing towards the buffet counter. 'They'll just charge it to my room.'

'How you going to explain that away then Boss?' Gordon said, grinning as he stood up. 'Mistress, partner, or sharing your bed with a junior officer?' He ducked as Caton threw his serviette, caught it deftly with his left hand, and tucked it into the breast pocket of his jacket. 'Just what I needed,' he said, patting it fondly as he set off in search of sustenance.

'So…' breadcrumbs fell like confetti as Holmes bit into a roll crammed with sausage, bacon, black pudding, and scrambled egg. '…Jo's on her way down to Nantwich, and Nick Carter's busy emailing copies of Norton's photo to the signatories on all those drops he's supposed to have done.' He brushed a smear of egg from the side of his mouth, and reached for his cup of coffee. 'What have you got lined up for us today?'

'That rather depends on what Nick and Jo turn up,' Caton told him. 'But something was bothering me all night. Then I remembered. When you get a parcel delivered at home, or say they come to read your electric meter, how do they record your signature?'

'Gordon's brow furrowed. Not because it was a hard question, more because it was a bizarre one. 'You sign on a screen,' he said. 'With one of those stylo thingys. Like a biro, but without any ink.'

'And where is the screen exactly?'

'One of those hand held computers. Like a big mobile phone.'

'But not a phone?'

He paused, the last piece of roll suspended in mid air. 'Well, I suppose it could be, but it looks more like a computer to me. Like your BlackBerry, but twice the size.' He put the roll in his mouth, chomped slowly, trying to make it last, then washed it down with a mouthful of coffee. 'Why, what's that got to do with anything?'

'Norton's boss kept talking about him having to phone in the signature, delivery number, and time of delivery. That sounded like it put him in the clear. But what if it wasn't really a phone call? What if it was an electronic message? An email, or a text message? No voice contact at all?'

'Then anyone could have done it. Provided they had the handset.'

'Precisely.'

'Which is why you wanted Carter to try his photograph out on the signatories?'

Caton eased his chair away from the table. 'And why we start by paying Mr Smart another visit.'

John Smart was clearly put out. He had assumed it was all done and dusted. Now there were two of them here asking questions.

'I told you Chief Inspector,' he said. 'They are phoned in.'

'Yes, but how exactly?'

'Well, the delivery code and details are all ready programmed in when we allocate the job. All the courier has to do is get the recipient to sign on the computer screen and phone it in.'

'Computer?'

'That's right. It's like a big PDA. A palm top computer, hand held.'

'But you talked about phoning it in?'

'Well it's just a turn of phrase isn't it? Up until two years ago everyone did literally phone in; talked to someone in the office. But this is much easier. And saves on office costs as well.'

'So how exactly does it come in?' Caton asked, barely keeping his cool.

'By mobile phone line, or WiFi, whichever has the best connection.'

'So electronically, straight to your computers?'

'That's right. But one of my staff is always on duty, so we see the messages as they come in, and check them off on the central log.'

'But you don't get to speak to the courier?'

'Not anymore. No.' Caton saw his pupils dilate. Smart by name and smart by nature. Finally, he could see where this was leading.

Caton's BlackBerry began to ring. He excused himself, withdrew to the corridor, and took the call. It was Carter.

'Mixed news, Boss,' he said. 'On the day that Standing was murdered Norton definitely did the

Birmingham and York runs. He also picked up the stuff from Harrogate. The premises manager there remembers because Norton's done a lot of pick ups and deliveries there, and he complained about how much stuff there was. But the bloke at Alexandra Palace is less sure. To be honest, it sounds like he barely remembers it. He's not prepared to swear to it one way or the other.'

'What about Given? That's less than a week ago?'

'That's the better news. I haven't been able to reach the guy in Ilkley. He's on his way back from hospital apparently. But the woman who signed for the package in Highgate – she's the housekeeper – is certain it wasn't Norton. Norton's got a large head, and short hair. This man had black hair. Lots of it.'

Caton joined Holmes and Smart back in the office. Smart now looked distinctly nervous. Caton's nerves were jangling too.

'I understand that Mr Norton is something of a loner,' he said. 'But there must be someone in the organisation he gets on with. Someone he might work with from time to time?'

They stared at the photo stapled to the personnel file. Eric Buckley stared back at them. In his mid fifties, with large eyes set in a face much too small to contain them convincingly. His face was surrounded by hair; long black hair, flecked with grey, that sat uneasily on narrow shoulders.

'Where is our Mr Buckley right now?' Caton asked.

Smart leant over his computer keyboard, and checked the relevant log. 'He's about twenty minutes away from a delivery in Liverpool, then he's clear.'

'When he reports in, can you get him to come straight back here?' Caton said. 'Don't tell him why, let him assume it's for another job.'

Smart nodded his understanding.

'And what about Mr Norton? What's his schedule for today?' Said Gordon Holmes.

Smart checked again. 'He's on his way to Newcastle with a delivery. He's got an hour's wait, then he's got a pick up there to take to Leeds. He'll need to get a move on because he's got a bank run to do this evening.'

'You may just need to make other arrangements for that bank run Mr Smart,' Caton told him. 'Just in case.'

While they were waiting for Buckley to arrive, Gordon Holmes received a call from Joanne Stuart. She had taken her lap top, loaded with a set of different digital photographs, down to Nantwich. Even identity parades were becoming a thing of the past. It was much easier, and less nerve racking for the witnesses, to present them with a set of images of people closely matching the descriptions given, or the suspects detained. In this case, Walker had no doubt. Even after all this time. The Roger Connolly who claimed to be a reporter was actually Ronald Norton. They had barely got over the excitement when Nick Carter rang Caton back.

'Whoever it was made that pick up in Ilkley, it wasn't Norton,' he said. 'It sounds like it was our friend again with the long black hair.'

'Are you still there Nick?' Caton asked him.

'Yes Boss. I'm in the drive. Big drive it is too.'

'Right, I'm going to email you a photo. Take it

inside, and show it to him. See if he recognises it.' He sensed Carter hesitating at the other end.

'That isn't going to prejudice any subsequent identification is it Sir?' he asked tentatively.

'Don't worry,' Caton told him. 'I'm more interested in who it wasn't than who it was. Don't bother to ring me the answer, I may be tied up. Just send me a text.'

The text came through just as their man entered the building.

'Bingo Boss, Buckley!'

Caton forgave him the alliteration. The message was everything. The timing perfect.

Eric Buckley turned out to be a wannabe Hells Angel. He had the leathers, and the long hair, and when he wasn't driving the van, he rode around on a treasured 1967 Triumph Bonneville. In reality, he was so far removed from the real thing, in personality and appearance, that he had always hovered on the fringes. His wife had never understood his passion for biking. Ronald Norton was the only person who seemed to understand. It was clear that Buckley had no idea why they wanted to speak with him.

'Humour us sir,' said Gordon Holmes. 'It will all become clear shortly, believe you me.'

'Friends help each other out, Mr Buckley, isn't that true?' Caton said, watching him closely.

Buckley looked from one to the other of them trying to work it out. He nodded. 'I suppose.'

'So, you and Ron Norton; how do you help each other out?'

He looked genuinely puzzled. 'I don't know what you mean.'

'Maybe you help each other out with your deliveries? Like last Saturday for example?'

Buckley's face was a picture. Dawn breaking over the Pennines; storm clouds on the horizon.

'There you are Sir. I told you it would all become clear.' Said Holmes, leaning closer.

Buckley shifted in his seat, and stared nervously past them, through the glass partition to where John Smart was watching from the far side of the main office. Caton followed his gaze.

That's the least of your worries Mr Buckley,' he said. 'You may or may not lose your job. The question is, are you willing to lose your freedom?'

As soon as they cautioned him he started to talk.

'It all started when my son had an accident.' He said. 'He was knocked off his bike outside the house. Nothing too serious, but the wife wanted me to take them to the hospital. I'd only just started as a courier. I didn't want to mess it up by ringing in and asking if someone else could take my run over. So I rang Ron Norton. After that we'd help each other out on the odd occasion. Swapping our PDAs when one or the other had a problem. But never the bank jobs. The banks all had CCTV cameras. Only recently, it was Ron wanting all of the favours. To tell the truth, it was beginning to worry me. I had no idea why Norton wanted me to do his runs for him, but frankly I hadn't been too bothered. The extra money came in handy.'

Buckley confirmed that he had covered for Norton on both of the relevant dates, signed his statement, and was asked to wait in the staff rest room with his office manager. His mobile phone and PDA remained behind on the table.

'We've got the motive and the opportunity,' Holmes observed, 'But that's not enough is it Boss? Not for the CPS, and maybe not even to get a search warrant.'

Caton shook his head. 'Certainly not for the Crown Prosecution Service, but enough for a search warrant I would have thought. But let's just make sure we strengthen our position shall we; not weaken it?'

'How do you want to play it Boss? Frontal assault or sneak attack?'

Caton smiled. He didn't approve of Gordon's military terminology but couldn't fault its relevance. 'He doesn't know we've spoken with Buckley. Let's tell him we're following up something in his past. We're sorry to have to bring it all up again, but we'd be really grateful if he could just answer a few questions. If he goes along with that, fine. If not, then I'll have to caution him, and we take him in. Let's hope he's confident enough to dig his own grave.'

They needn't have worried. Norton was desperate to give the impression that he had nothing to hide. That was how Caton read it anyway. Not overconfidence, just a compulsion to keep the charade going. In his shoes Caton would have done the same; gambling that the police had nothing concrete to go on. Between them, they'd led him on gently; focusing on his daughter's suicide, and the role that Mercer had played.

'So you admit that you would have killed Mercer if you could have got your hands on him?' Holmes was saying.

'Norton nodded. In the artificial light his skull shone like a bronze helmet through the close cropped hair. 'Any father would have felt like that,' he said pressing his hands down on the table top. The definition of his upper arms and shoulders were discernible through the tight denim shirt. His neck formed a perfect triangle between his head and shoulders. His eyes were fierce with anger and remembered pain. Anyone less like Buckley, Caton could not imagine. 'Anyway,' he continued. 'I never got the chance did I? So we'll never know if I could have gone through with it or not. Will we?'

'That must have made you feel pretty frustrated, angry even. Mercer topping himself like that. Depriving you of your day in court?' Holmes said casually.

He shrugged. 'What do you think?'

'How did that make you feel about Roger Standing then?' Caton asked.

Norton looked him straight between the eyes. Focusing on the spot over the bridge of the nose. Almost as though he'd been trained to do it. 'Roger who?' he said.

'Roger Standing. Mercer's former headteacher.'

Norton still hadn't blinked. That alone was a giveaway. Hardly admissible in court, but as good as a confession. 'Never heard of him,' he replied.

'So you you've never met him? Never been to the Sandhills district of Manchester on a delivery, or a pick up, for example?'

'No.'

'To Marcel Guest Paints perhaps?'

'Never heard of them.'

'So you've never been anywhere near the railway arches off Collyhurst Road?'

'Never heard of them either.' The stare was unwavering. Their eyes locked.

'Alright,' Caton said. 'Just a couple more questions. Perhaps you can tell us where you were last Saturday evening?'

'That's easy,' he replied, smiling confidently. 'I had a pick up in Ilkley with the drop off in Highgate. Big posh place. Electronic gates, wide drive. Foreign Housekeeper. East European, something like that. I grabbed myself a kebab, and can of coke. Didn't get back till twenty to two in the morning. Why don't you check my log sheets. It's all on there.'

It was well rehearsed. But something subtle and indefinable changed in his expression as Caton unfolded the copies of the log sheets, and slid them towards him.

'Don't worry, we have,' he said. 'What about this one?' He pointed to the Saturday evening trip to Alexandra Palace, circled in blue. 'Did you make this delivery too?'

'Yes.' He replied without hesitation, looking straight at Caton; daring him to contradict it. But it was obvious that his mind was working overtime.

'OK,' Caton said retrieving the printouts. 'Tell me about Sandra Given?'

'Whose she when she's at home?'

'She led an investigation into allegations against Mercer at his previous school. But you'd know that of course.'

'And how could I possibly know that?'

'From your visit to Mr Walker.' Said Caton. For the

first time Norton's eyes wavered, and his pupils contracted.

'I don't know what you're talking about.'

'I think you do Mr Norton,' Caton told him. 'Have you any idea how long that supermarket keeps its CCTV tapes? You'd be surprised.'

Norton clenched his fists, leaned back in his chair, and folded his arms. 'I've nothing more to say to you.'

Caton stood up. 'Ronald Norton, I am arresting you on suspicion of the murders of Roger Standing, and Sandra Given. You do not have to say anything. But it may harm your defence if you do not mention something which you later rely on in court. Anything you do say may be given in evidence. Do you understand?'

Norton stared mutely at the desk in front of him.

'We'll take that as a yes then shall we Mr Norton? Holmes said, moving in and grasping him by the arm.

30

'Tens of thousands of anti war protesters are gathering in front of Manchester town hall this afternoon for a massive peace march through the city. They are coming from all around the country to make their feelings known ahead of the Labour Party conference, which will start a few hundred yards away tomorrow at the Manchester Conference Centre. The organisers are predicting up to eighty thousand will take part in the march which is due to set off at around two pm. All police leave has been cancelled. At the same time, Tony Blair, and his wife Cherie, are expected at the Radisson Hotel, where they can expect enthusiastic applause from party activists.'

Caton switched off the radio, and headed for the front door. They could not have chosen a worse day for Standing's memorial service. Apart from the fact that the city was a no go area to traffic, and an exclusion zone had been thrown around the Conference venues, it was the hottest day in weeks. And here he was, in black suit, shirt, and sombre tie. The only plus side was that Hadfield, as one of the Force's official representatives, would have to sweat it out in his ceremonial uniform. Caton set the alarm, and had just stepped out, when his mobile rang. It was Holmes.

'I'm at the Cathedral Boss. I thought I'd better warn you what's going on out here. There's a Military Families Peace Camp in Peace Park, and there are tens of thousands in the city centre already. They're all milling around Lincoln Square, St. Ann's Square, and Albert Square. It isn't supposed to kick off for another couple of hours. God knows what it'll be like by then. I suggest you forget the car, and leg it here. If you nip through St Mary's Parsonage you should be alright. Where do you want to meet me? The Mitre, The Crown and Anchor, The Old Wellington, or Sinclair's Oyster Bar?'

Caton had to smile. 'It's a Memorial Service, Gordon, not a pub crawl. So we're on duty, remember?'

He heard his DI chuckle. 'It's not as though it's a funeral though, is it?'

'Wait for me in the Hanging Bridge,' Caton said. Get yourself a coffee. I'll be about ten minutes.'

Holmes was sitting at a table for two, in the basement of the Cathedral Shop in Cateaton Street, looking down on the exposed section of the original medieval stone bridge from which the café drew its name. The bridge used to link this part of the city with the Cathedral, across the ditch in which the rivers Irwell and Irk met. Whether people were ever hung here, Caton's Local History studies at MGS had never revealed. Holmes finished his drink, and together they climbed back up to the shop, turned right outside, and started the short journey to the Cathedral entrance.

'This is going to be an uncomfortable do isn't it Boss?' Gordon mused. 'None of that ...*we come to bury Caesar, not to praise him,* malarkey.' It's not as though everyone here doesn't know what he was really like.'

'That still doesn't justify what happened.' Caton reminded him. 'If every manipulative, controlling, sexist, adulterer, was fair game for vigilante retribution think what a slippery slope that would be.'

'One without a hell of a lot of captains of industry, not to mention the upper echelons of the forces, the Establishment, and half the nation's police forces.'

'And he did do some good, even if his methods were worse than dubious.' Caton pointed out, deftly ignoring his inspector's analysis.

'Norton's not going to plead, is he Boss?'

'We don't need him to. We can prove motive and opportunity. There are the stack of lies he told about the deliveries, and the total lack of an alternative alibi. The visit to question Wallace he denied having made shows that he knew about their role in putting his daughter in harm's way. But it's the palynology results that convinced the CPS. Not just the purple buddleia, and the red poppies, but the pattern of spores and seed from grasses and lichen specific to that site. It's as good as a fingerprint according to the scientists. His van was there. If not on the day he killed Standing, then shortly before; probably when he sussed it out for the meeting.'

'It was neat the way you got him to say he'd never been anywhere near Sandhills, Boss. Up until then he thought he could talk his way out of it. Might have done too.'

'You know what *Thought*, thought?' Caton said, pausing to let a hushed group of Harmony High pupils file through the gated entrance.

Holmes grinned. 'He followed a dust cart, and thought it was wedding.'

The Cathedral was filling rapidly. Only the front section of this, the widest nave in England, had been set out with chairs in order to achieve the illusion of large numbers. Nevertheless, the turnout was impressive. Caton and Holmes chose seats at the back, in the north aisle, with a clear view of the flame red window of the military chapel. The cathedral was as imposing as Caton remembered from the first time he had come here as a member of the school choir. The graceful gothic arches soared skyward, above the magnificent mediaeval quire screen, towards the intrically carved roof of the nave, punctuated by golden sunburst bosses. He had always thought that the carvings on the misericord of Reynold the Fox, and the woman scolding her husband for breaking a pot, were a testimony to the fact that Mancunian humour had its roots in history.

Most of the seats had been taken up by pupils from Harmony High, and the other Trust schools. The school choir sat with choristers from the Cathedral, ready to perform their tribute. At the front, on the left, he could make out Juliette Postlethwaite, Ronnie Payne, and Roisin Murphy who already had her handkerchief to her face. Behind them sat a row of solemn faced men and women whom he took to be headteachers and governors from the Trust. Of Underhill, the Chair of the Board and BUCS' senior representative, there was no sign.

Hadfield sat two rows back on the right hand side, beside the Chief Constable, the Chief Education Officer, and one of the lesser known Manchester MP's. None of them looked comfortable at being there.

'No really big guns then.' Holmes whispered.

Caton nodded. The minute that Norton's arrest had hit the streets, the press had had a field day. The speculation far exceeded the reality. Miranda Horne had kept a low profile, and had so far avoided the inevitable flack. Almost all of Standing's former acolytes had either expressed surprise, or claimed that they had suspected it all along. Everyone of note, who might have had their own reputation besmirched by association, had rapidly distanced themselves. When it came down to it, almost everybody here had come out of a sense of duty rather than respect, and certainly not out of affection.

Margaret Standing was on the right, at the front, her son beside her. They sat ramrod straight, with a quiet dignity far surpassing anything that Roger Standing might have attempted. Beside them, a seat had been left empty. The organ began to play, and the congregation rose as one.

They stepped out into blazing sunshine. Eighty metres away the front of the March for Peace was swinging right to head up towards the Triangle and Exchange Square. A mass of red and black posters held high on poles, jostled with each other, dancing in the air. Hooters, whistles, and drums, gave it the appearance of a summer carnival; a Mancunian Mardi Gras. Crude effigies of Bush and Blair on stilts, bobbing above wide trade union banners, gave the lie to that. A coffin appeared, held high, surrounded by black balloons. And in the centre of the seething mass, rode a ten foot high figure of death; black hooded, scythe in hand.

Caton glanced back towards the main Cathedral entrance, hoping that they had the foresight to lead the mother and son out through the side door.

All those weeks ago when he had suggested that she accept a family liaison officer, she had replied *'I don't really want to have to feel like a victim.'* And then she had paused. Caton now knew that she had been going to add: *'I've been one for far too long.'* He thought about the empty seat, and the missing twin. About Chloe Norton; and about what he had just read back there in the Cathedral, on the memorial tablet to the Lever children.

> *Here d'yd their Parents' hopes and feares'.*
> *Once all their joy, now all their teares',*
> *They'r now past hope, past feare, or paine,*
> *It were a Sinne to wish them here againe.*

'Come on Gordon,' he said, removing his tie and slipping it into his jacket pocket. 'Just this once. Let's make it the Crown and Anchor.'

'How does a pub get a name like that? Holmes' pondered as they set off in the opposite direction to the crowd of protesters.

'From a game of dice with a crown on one face and an anchor on another,' Caton replied.

'That figures,' his DI responded, rubbing at his chin. 'It's what life is after all...a game of chance. Except that some people have to play with the dice loaded against them.'

'You're so right Gordon.' Caton told him, stopping to watch as John Standing led his mother down the steps ahead of them to the car waiting to whisk them away. Mary Standing ducked into the rear seat and disappeared from sight as her son climbed in beside her. The chauffeur closed the rear door, climbed into the driving seat, and drove off heading south down Deansgate. 'But then again,' he added. 'Perhaps it's just the choices that we make.'

'In that case,' said Holmes setting off again. 'Make mine a pint of Humdinger. You can't go wrong with that.'

If only it were that simple Caton reflected. He was thinking of Kate. He wondered if she was prepared to risk it all on him. And if he was really honest, he wasn't sure that he was ready to roll the dice. To try again. To hazard both their futures on his ability to change.

'Come on Boss, you haven't got all day!' Said Gordon Holmes, now a good ten yards ahead of him.

'Don't I know it.' Caton muttered to himself, as he hurried to catch up.

The Author

Formerly Principal Inspector of Schools for the City Of Manchester, Head of the Manchester School Improvement Service, and Lead Network Facilitator at the National College of School Leadership, Bill Rogers has numerous publications to his name in the field of education. For four years he was also a programme consultant and panellist on the popular live Granada Television programme *Which Way*, presented by the iconic, and much missed, Tony Wilson. He has written six crime thriller novels to date – all of them based in and around the City of Manchester. His first novel *The Cleansing* was short listed for the Long Barn Books Debut Novel competition. His Fourth novel *A Trace of Blood* reached the semi-final of the Amazon Breakthrough Novel Award in 2009.

Also By Bill Rogers

The Cleansing
The Tiger's Cave
A Fatal Intervention
A Trace of Blood
Bluebell Hollow

www.billrogers.co.uk   www.catonbooks.com

If you've enjoyed

THE HEAD CASE

You will certainly enjoy the novel that first
introduced Detective Chief Inspector Caton

THE CLEANSING

Christmas approaches. A killer dressed as a clown
haunts the streets of Manchester. For him the City's
miraculous regeneration had unacceptable
consequences. This is the reckoning. DCI Tom Caton
enlists the help of forensic profiler Kate Webb, placing
her in mortal danger. The trail leads from the site of
the old mass cholera graves, through Moss Side, the
Gay Village, the penthouse opulence of canalside
apartment blocks, and the bustling Christmas Market,
to the Victorian Gothic grandeur of the Town Hall.

Time is running out: For Tom, for Kate…and for
the City.

Short listed for the Long Barn Books
Debut Novel Award
Available in paperback
ISBN: 978 1 906645 61 8

www.Amazon.com
www.catonbooks.com
www.billrogers.co.uk

Also Available in EBook format

Lightning Source UK Ltd.
Milton Keynes UK
UKHW010137140919
349738UK00001B/18/P